Gunga Din Highway

A NOVEL BY FRANK CHIN

COFFEE HOUSE PRESS :: MINNEAPOLIS

Excerpt of "Gunga Din" by Rudyard Kipling, from *Gunga Din* © 1987 by Gulliver Books, a division of Harcourt Brace & Company. Used by permission of the publisher.

The publishers would like to thank the following sponsors for assistance that helped in the publication of this book: The National Endowment for the Arts; Dayton Hudson Foundation on behalf of Dayton's and Target Stores; General Mills; Honeywell; The Lannan Foundation; The Andrew W. Mellon Foundation; the Minnesota State Arts Board; Star Tribune/Cowles Media Company; and The McKnight Foundation. Major new marketing initiatives have been made possible by the Lila Wallace–Reader's Digest Literary Publishers Marketing Development Program, funded through a grant to the Council of Literary Magazines and Presses.

Coffee House Press books are available to the trade through our primary distributor, Consortium Book Sales & Distribution, 1045 Westgate Drive, St. Paul, MN 55114. Our books are also available through all major library distributors and jobbers and through most small press distributors, including Bookpeople, Inland, and Small Press Distribution. For personal orders, catalogs, or other information, write to: Coffee House Press, 27 North Fourth Street, Suite 400, Minneapolis, MN 55401

Library of Congress CIP Data

Chin, Frank, 1940–
    Gunga Din highway : a novel / by Frank Chin.
        p.   cm.
    ISBN 1-56689-024-1 (hardcover)
    I Title.
PS3553.H4897G86   1994
813'.54—dc20   94-12597
                          CIP

10   9   8   7   6   5   4   3   2   1

Printed in Canada

For
Wardess Taylor

Tonight forty-six of your friends rumble up Telegraph
leathered on our loyal Hondas, Harleys, and BMWs
for a double bill of Marlon Brando and Toshiro Mifune,
One Eyed Jacks and *Chushingura,*
one cap and a latté.

Much to their credit, the Chinese view prejudice with a very healthy attitude. They were never overly bitter. They have gone into occupations which command respect and which lessen conflict from competition. The Chinese are not concentrated entirely in one section of the country. More dispersion away from the vortexes of San Francisco and New York should be encouraged. This ought to be a long-range goal of the Chinese because distribution reduces the degree of visibility.

—Betty Lee Sung, *Mountain of Gold*

The only great government I am acquinted with is singularly masculine. It makes up its mind, and once having reached a decision, adheres to it!

Henry Stephanson as Sir Charles Macefield in
The Charge of the Light Brigade

'E carried me away
To where a dooli lay,
An' a bullet come an' drilled the beggar clean.
'E put me safe inside,
An' just before 'e died,
"I 'ope you liked your drink," sez Gunga Din.
So I'll meet 'im later on
At the place where 'e is gone—
Where it's always double drill and no canteen.
'E'll be squattin' on the coals
Givin' drink to poor damned souls,
An' I'll get a swig in hell from Gunga Din!
       Yes, Din! Din! Din!
  You Lazarushian-leather Gunga Din!
      Though I've belted you and flayed you,
      By the livin' Gawd that made you,
  You're a better man than I am, Gunga Din!

        —Rudyard Kipling, "Gunga Din"

Author's Note

The world of Chinese myth begins with the twin stories of "Poon Goo, the Creator of Heaven and Earth" and "Nur Waw, the Mother of Humanity."

After 18,000 years, the giant Poon Goo wakes up, with his axe, inside an egg. He breaks out and for the next 18,000 years separates the indies of the egg into heaven and earth.

When the sky stays up and the earth stays down, he dies and his breath becomes the atmosphere, one eye becomes the sun, the other, the moon; his blood runs clear and becomes the waters. Other parts of his body become different minerals and geographical features covering the stuff of the egg with soil, mountains, rivers, forests, and plains.

His sister, Nur Waw, comes down to a world that is a garden but has no animal life. She creates animals for six days, and on the seventh day, she creates human beings. She saves the world from a disaster falling through a flaw in the sky. She saves the world from a disaster gushing up through a flaw in the earth. She invents music and retires to the wilderness.

The world, the giant, and the Mother of Humanity create a world where every hero is an orphan, a failed scholar, an outlaw, an outcast, an exile on the road of life through danger, ignorance, deception, and enlightenment.

This book is therefore divided into four parts: *The Creation, The World, The Underworld,* and *Home.*

—Frank Chin

Part One: The Creation

Longman Kwan: "Gee, Pop!"

It's a long long flight from Hollywood to China on Pan American Airways' China Clipper. I never made it, never went back to China to fight the Japanese before they bombed Pearl Harbor. My publicist's Hollywood myth about me says I was about to catch the Clipper back to China and make my way to the Chinese air force to fight for China against the invading Japanese. No such thing. But people enjoy thinking of me as a hero of my people. Everyone agrees, my people need a hero.

The flight from Hollywood to Honolulu via United Air Lines is long enough for me, though I have another flight to another island to catch yet to make exteriors for *Hawaii Five-O*. There's word of a new Charlie Chan movie in the air. NBC Vice-President David Tebet is on a much-publicized round-the-world search for a Chinese actor who speaks English well enough to be understood by American audiences to become the first Chinese to play Charlie Chan, the Chinese detective. The sons of Charlie Chan, Keye Luke, Benson Fong, Victor Sen Yung, and me, all feel the magic of the movies we made, setting us aglow. We strike casual poses by the phone, waiting for the thing to ring, just in case God happens to walk from one room to another with a camera.

I've come to meet my movie father, Anlauf Lorane, the Charlie Chan to my Number Four Son. We are old men when we are the money stars in the Bs of twenty years ago, though I always look and photograph younger, much younger than my actual age. And we are older old men now. He's too old to play the new Charlie Chan, and probably looks it, and doesn't want to. I don't understand.

I don't look too old, of all the sons of Chan I look the youngest still, and want to be the first Chinese to play Charlie Chan on the screen. Keye looks and acts too old, and the older he gets, the more foreign he seems. Not Chinese foreign. Some kind of European foreign with a pseudo-British accent. Benson is just too rickety. And Victor looks awful and has lost it. Of the four sons who've lived to take over the part of Pop in a Hollywood movie, I'm the only one. My time is near. Big screen or little screen: I want to be the first.

I land in Honolulu in one of those island rains with drops of falling water as big as eggs breaking on everything. The air is so thick with water it seems United Air Lines has landed me under the sea and I'm breathing watery goo and can't tell if the mud is falling on me or splashing up at me. All I hear is water and squawking muck. Through the water washing sweat and hair in my eyes I can see only blobs of grays and blues and vague greens and bluish reds. I can't see what is airplane and what is airport, what is slipping rainwater and what is glass and steel. Five blobs distinguish themselves from the mass by calling my name, and vague aloha shirts come into view.

A very wet toasty brown-skinned hula girl in a plastic hula skirt and toothpaste smile drops a wet orchid lei around my neck that immediately makes my nose run, and presses her wet gooey lips against my wet gooey cheek. The hula girl disappears and the five vague aloha shirts pat me on the back and laugh.

There is no difference between air and water, land and sea until I am in the dry quiet insides of the limousine the brothers from the tong hired to meet me. Old-time Honolulu brothers of the good-time Boom Boom tong are more good-time Charlie American than my Boom Boom brothers on the mainland. Not that they don't own and run honky-tonks, bottle clubs, and see girls run through their business and take their share during the war, but there is law in Seattle, and San Francisco and Los Angeles. In Hawaii the war is the law and boys of the Boom Boom tong are happy soldiers, judges, juries, and executioners of the law.

The brothers from the good-time Boom Boom tong tell me sometimes late at night when they get home from their business and turn on the TV and flip the channels through the old movies, looking for one to watch a while, not often, but sometimes, around four or five times a year, a movie I die in is broadcast from every station in Hawaii. The brothers think of me as a bigshot star of opera and movies still. Though I am here as a Guest Star on a two-part episode of *Hawaii Five-O* and expected McGarrett would send a limo for me, the brothers were only too pleased to meet me at the airport and escort me to my Waikiki hotel, and too happy to let *Hawaii Five-O* publicists take pictures and write stories about the old tongs of Honolulu looking on Chang Apana, the detective sergeant in the Honolulu police and the fat Charlie Chan the detective as the creators of the happiest memories of childhood and wartime businesses in their Honolulu Hotel Street Chinatown, on the piece of island real estate that suddenly is the bleeding end all be all of American honor. And in the movies of the time, I was, I am Charlie Chan's Number Four and most American-born and Americanized son. In real life, whatever that is, I was born in China. The South. Tang People. Cantonese. It all blends into a nice story about me that the newspapers and publicists blurbing me want to believe. I love it.

"The part I've come to Honolulu to play is nothing special," I tell the brothers. "But it is paying my way to party with my brothers in Hawaii and visit the last white man to play Charlie Chan still alive."

"You mean he's on the islands?" the brothers ask. "We had no idea!"

"I seem to be the only one he trusts with his address. He craves anonymity," I say. "He wants his privacy. I have several offers from advertising companies for him to put on the white duck and Panama straw hat of Charlie Chan again and sell a few products for them. I'm going to try to talk him into coming out of hiding and making a little money."

They're impressed at my humility and loyalty and still want to know about my part in *Hawaii Five-O*. Do I live? Do I die? Am I Chinese? Am I Japanese? Am I southern artist? Am I northern bureaucrat? Does it make any difference? Am I squinty? Am I swishy? Am I bald? Do I have big eyebrows? We laugh a lot, stirring up old laughs, old short-sleeved Hawaiian shirts, old memories of old movies and happy days in the war. This ceremony over, the brothers grin at me, open-mouthed as catfish, their old bottomfeeder's eyes shine as if they'd swallowed strong drink. In the eye of their swirling wait, they're ready to know about my part on *Hawaii Five-O*.

I tell them, "I'm another cultured slimy warlord smuggling drugs into the United States through Hawaii who runs afoul of McGarrett, Chin-ho, Danno, Zulu, and the whole Five-O show, and, of course, I die in the shadow of Diamond Head."

They love it. *Hawaii Five-O* has really perfected the Charlie Chan formula, they say. They love the villains from World War II movies finding new life on the show. It's a breath of the old days.

"And it gives me work," I say, and we all laugh.

On the way to the hotel I see that *Tora! Tora! Tora!* is still playing in a big first-run Honolulu movie palace. "Ah, yes," I say, "A peace movie."

"A peace movie?" a brother asks.

"A war movie made in peacetime. I remember playing in war movies made during the war, with John Wayne, Van Johnson, Cary Grant."

Yes, the Hawaiian brothers remember the names and the stars who partied here after Pearl Harbor. The brothers ran restaurants or bars, or honky-tonks during the war and remember me flying over from Frisco or L.A. to play an ugly Japanese spy or sadistic Japanese officer who screams "Aiiieeeee!" when I die then head down to Chinatown for dinner and rice before painting Honolulu red, with the other sons of Chan and Willy and Kam chasing the tails of our fame and all the Chinese and Japanese women we can find from club to club from Chinatown to Waikiki. And the soldiers and sailors on the town and off-limits recognized us, grinned and laughed, put their arms around us, and we put our arms around them. They patted us on the head and we patted them on the head and watched them totter away to the whores or back to their bases.

Aiiieeeee! Aloha! Gung ho! Goong hay fot choy! The movies and Chinatown were exciting then. They had a future waiting for them after we won the war. There was an electric light night life. There was a Chinatown class and style. Padded shoulders. Wide lapels.

Double-breasted suits. Straw hats. They were happy days for me too.

"There are people in Hawaii who object to the Charlie Chan movies and John Wayne war movies, and World War II movies on the late-night TV," the brothers tell me. "No sense of history."

"The younger generations don't remember when Americans thought all Chinese were sex perverts, opium smugglers, and torturers of women," I say.

"That's right, you and Keye, and Benson, and Victor were a more positive and real lifelike image of the Chinese," a brother says.

"As was our father, Charlie Chan," I say.

Yes, turn on your TV late at night to any old Charlie Chan the Detective or World War II in China movie and you are reading my life story. Every night from some tower over Honolulu or New York, or Chicago, one bit of my life or another unspools like smoke. I still like turning on the TV in another town to get away from it all, and being pleasantly surprised with the best days of my life.

For nearly fifty years, half a century, I am the most famous Chinese in America: an actor. I am Charlie Chan's Number Four Son; the Chinese nicknamed Die Say or Say Die. Yes, I am the rhythmic Christian of Charlie Chan's movie sons, the martyr, the one famous for saying nothing but "Gee, Pop!" and "Gosh, Pop!" I am The Chinaman Who Dies.

Fifty years of acting in movies and TV has washed out a better me, a bigger name, a set of brighter memories from the mundane, ordinary facts of my life. I am no longer born in a village in south China and apprenticed to a floating opera company on the Pearl River. I am born and last seen being carried off by Hollywood alley cats into a dark soundstage. I cry bald and naked in a bombed out railroad station in a Shanghai air raid scene. William Bendix finds me in the rubble of a Chinese village during another Japanese air raid in my next movie. At my dead momma's withered tit, I wail hoarse, high, long long wails that end in sputtering lungs. The movie is China.

I am the symbol of helpless, struggling China in the arms of

William Bendix. He says I'm a "cute little fella." He names me "Donald Duck."

Alan Ladd and William Bendix leave me in the arms of a Chinese convert to Christianity played by a white woman who looks me in the face and coos, "Who but monsters would want to kill one such as this?" and from this shot on, I am known forever to people who go to the movies as The Chinaman Who Dies.

I take a breath. Then another wail from my endless lungs goes from movie to movie, Jap air raid somewhere in China scene to singing "America the Beautiful" with Kate Smith on the radio into the homes of Americans who cherish the memory of me dying when they buy one more War Bond.

Kate Smith smelled as sugary as she looked, and a little spicy, like a hot pan of huge friendly cinnamon rolls fresh from the oven.

I am adopted by Gary Cooper and his girlfriend, the Red Cross nurse, in a missionary movie. A Japanese officer with slime on his teeth slicks the long straight blade of his samurai sword into me, jolting me to scream, "Maaaaaaamaaaaaaaaaa!" as it slides on through my body into my mother's heaving body and out of her back, as the camera turns to see my face just behind the blinding gleam of moving the long sword slurping, out of us, against the sucking lips of our long wound, I scream the one word the poet from the Office of War Information says crosses all languages, all ages, all time, "Maaaaaaaaaaa!" until the sword is all the way out of my little body and, unpinned from my mother China, I thump to the ground at the officer's feet like a large roach. And there we are, the triplet, the poetic form of the war movie as emotional weapon: A, the bloody dead Chinese mother; B, the bloody dead Chinese son; C, the leering Jap wiping his blade clean of blood.

The Japs torture me into giving up John Wayne's secret position, throw me into a truck and bounce the little life left in my little battered body over bumpy roads. Out to get the jump on John Wayne, leading my missionary teacher from Indiana and all of my Filipino guerrilla friends through the jungle. I grab the wheel of the truck. The Jap soldiers scream. I wail in the key of tears and pull the truck off the edge of the world and down we go into the darkness.

My body rolls out of the burning truck to the feet of John Wayne and all my surprised friends working their stealthy way through the jungle with Anthony Quinn. America sees my face by the flame light of the burning truck full of burning Japs. They see me trying hard not to cry out in pain. Tears stream down my cheeks.

"Don't try to talk," John Wayne says softly. Anthony Quinn turns away, sniffles, and loads his Tommy gun. And John Wayne and the missionary teacher who failed to teach me how to properly spell "America" A-M-E-R-I-C-A instead of A-M-E-L-L-I-C-A exchange looks and shake their heads. All the soldiers and all my friends are getting down on their knees around me. The music also rises.

"I failed," I gasp. "I guess I'll never be promoted to sergeant now," and my eyes roll back into my skull and my breath shrieks like tearing sheets in a windstorm. My lungs sound like a man filing a steel girder on a steel bridge with a long file. I cough. A half pint of blood rosebuds out of my mouth. By the light of burning Jap bodies sizzling, sputtering, and bursting like sausages in the background, women in the shopper matinées with their paper sacks and red meat tokens see tears in John Wayne's eyes. He removes the bird colonel bird insignia off his collar and pins it on me.

"You didn't fail," John Wayne says, and has to lower his eyes and gulp down a sob before he can say, "He-yeck! You get that promotion!" He adjusts the little bird on my bloody shirt and says, very low, very soft, "I got orders from the President himself to promote you all the way to colonel!"

My eyes open. I struggle for breath. The music rises just so.

"Teacher?" a tiny voice climbs up out of me. "I can't see!" And I can't see.

And the missionary teacher from Indiana has to put her ear to my mouth to hear me agonize my last words out.

"Ayee!" I say, "Emmm!" My eyes come open and shine gleaming silver like something crazy. The missionary teacher wipes blood from my lips, from my eyes, and arranges my hair, a bit at a time, avoiding the patches of matted blood and open wounds, as I continue. "Eee!"

"Easy, champ," John Wayne soothes. He shrugs violently and looks back into the flames of the burning truck.

"Ell! Ell!" I scream from out of my croak. My chest heaves like the back of a mating dog. "Eye! See! Ayyyy!" I cry triumphantly and struggle up to my elbows. "AMELLICA!"

The missionary teacher screams.

John Wayne says, "At ease, colonel," and I fall back into a shot of John Wayne sighing and furrowing his brow and I am dead dead dead in his arms.

John Wayne turns to the missionary teacher from Indiana and says, "I oughta shoot ya for not teaching him how to spell America with an 'R.'"

"Cut!" the director shouts and directs me to spell "America" properly with an "R." I think of wishing him a joyeux Noel too, but contain myself.

The brothers of the Hawaiian branch of the tong like my stories of making the movies they see me in.

They want to know if I ever played the part of a pilot. Did I ever fly in the movies?

I tell the brothers about the time they think it will be funny to play me against my type, and I am a fanatic treacherous Jap pilot.

The old men want to hear about that. Stories of Chinese who fly in Hollywood movies are rare.

One day flying my Zero low across the water in a fog, I see Cary Grant's American submarine, the USS *Copperfin,* sailing toward Destination Tokyo. I drop a bomb on the sub but it doesn't go off. I turn around and rake the sub with my machine guns, sew a line of bullets across the conning tower, and knock down Alan Hale Jr.

John Garfield shoots me down with the deck gun. As I trail smoke and sing a nasal swan song into an out-of-sight crash, the Yanks in close-up cheer with wonder. They blink in the light of an explosion that washes me over to the side of Cary Grant's submarine. A sailor jumps off the deck into the water to pull me in. I flash my eyes, show my teeth, and knife the American sailor in the back.

The skinny full-lipped pharmacist's mate who will disarm the bomb I dropped and then will perform an appendectomy on a very nervous Elisha Cook Jr. on a mess table with a boning knife and a potato peeler during a depth charge attack is fresh from the bacon-and-eggs sunrise-to-sunset three-squares-a-day Iowa where he has obviously never come across anything so rude, impolite, and ungrateful as someone like me stabbing my rescuer in the back. "Welcome to World War Two, kid," I say at the kid's stupid look, and scream *"Aiiieeeee!"* as the kid's first bullets crash into my body. The same William Bendix who found me as a baby in the rubble of my village watches the skinny kid machine gun me into goo floating on the sea. My ad lib becomes guttural nasal gibberish in the release print, and the kid's good Christian Thou Shalt Not Kill upbringing is sick with Freudian shadows from having tasted real hate and enjoyed killing a man.

Captain Cary Grant pats the kid on the back, lights his pipe, and says, "Son, you killed a Jap, not a man."

The kid's too young to shave, never been kissed, never been laid. He doesn't quite know the difference between boys and girls. He has Lana Turner's voluptuous lower lip. He doesn't understand. The machinery hums inside the tight little submarine. The steel walls sweat. Cary Grant gleams and shines but does not sweat.

Cary Grant puffs his pipe and thinks, then takes his pipe from his mouth and says, "This is not just a war of one nation against another nation. We are in a war that will decide whether or not decency will survive in the world. This is a war of good against evil." The captain muses and puffs his pipe.

The kid's Adam's apple bobs as he swallows hard and blinks. Alan Hale leans in to listen, wiping his hands on his apron.

"I identify with that kid," Benson says in the office of one of his Polynesian fantasy restaurants around L.A., watching *Destination Tokyo*, a black and white on TV. "I wish I were that kid when I was a kid," he says hesitantly but without his usual stutter that slows his emotion and makes him seem less than spontaneous. "I could have joined a fraternity. Gone to frat parties, danced with sorority girls."

An officer puts his hands on the table and bends closer to Cary Grant. It looks a little like Da Vinci's "The Last Supper" humming underwater toward Tokyo. Cary Grant lets out a deep breath and says, "It makes one wonder about these Japanese who sell their daughters off at thirteen to be married—or worse." He shakes his head and hardens his voice, "The Japs know nothing of the love we hold for our women."

The smart pert bright-eyed Hyacinth teaches me that even before there is Pearl Harbor to make the difference between Japs and Chinks there is Pearl Buck sorting out the good Christian "Chinese-Americans" from the evil Chinese "Chinamen."

I was young. I converted, and the other opera men stranded here by the tide of war did not. I was too young, a mere apprentice. I shouldn't have come over. I wasn't a real star of the Cantonese opera. My sister born of a mother in America is an American citizen and helps me. The real opera stars, Wong the Handsome, the Great Kwan Lee, the voice, wait out the war going from Chinatown to Chinatown performing Cantonese opera, getting cheated and robbed, and shooting Chinese movies in the Sacramento Delta. Now, it's as if no one had ever heard of them and I was the greatest and the only star of Cantonese opera to land in America before the war.

Unlike the other sons of Chan, I have lived the part of Charlie Chan. I have crossed from Cantonese opera and Chinese movies to Hollywood. I have converted to Christianity. I have become Americanized. I have used the ear and voice trained by Cantonese opera to sound looser and more at home with jive talk than stiff stuffy old Keye Luke trying to make his voice sound deep. I could play anything, any age, from a one-year-old baby in diapers to a hundred-year-old leper, unlike the pouting, stuttering, choking Benson Fong. For that shot of me wailing in the bombed-out rubble of Shanghai railway station, they padded me in a flesh-colored suit and built an oversize set so I would look like a barebellied baby. I am more American than the very American-born Victor Sen Yung.

Being married to The Chinaman Who Dies is not good enough

for my wife, Hyacinth. She's an American-born girl, fourth-generation American born, but more old-country Cantonese and serious about opera than I ever was. Her American-born mother has spoken nothing but Chinese all her life, a Kwangtung dialect so old I've never before heard it spoken. The old woman agrees with Hyacinth. She is not happy with the idea of her grandsons growing up watching me die in the movies. "What kind of example is that to set for your sons?" she asks.

"That's just what I ask him, Ma," Hyacinth says.

"For our sons," I tell her, "I promise to be the first Chinese to play Charlie Chan in the movies."

"Charlie Chan?" Hyacinth and her mother ask.

"You are not Christian, but as you see, I do love you anyway. As Charlie Chan I shall lead you to your great salvation. For, it is written: As God the Father gave up a son in the image of the perfect white man, to lead whites to walk the path of righteousness toward salvation, and praise God, so the White Man gave up a son in the image of the perfect Chinese American to lead the yellows to build the road to acceptance toward assimilation. Ah, sweet assimilation. Charlie Chan was his name."

"Of course Charlie Chan. Where would any of us be without Charlie Chan?" the brothers say and we laugh like the dreams and hallucinations of a star alone in his limousine. The privacy, the intimacy me and the five brothers feel inside the unreal quiet and cushiness of the limo turn us into laughing fools. And it's nice to feel like a movie star again. At last.

"You were in that movie *China* where Victor Sen Yung's pompadour steals the scenes from Alan Ladd," a brother remembers.

"Number Three was Victor Sen Yung, the greatest Chinese-American actor the screen has ever known," I say. "He was the first of us Sons of Chan to make Hollywood acting his whole life. I still seek out his old movies for the little bits of him in William Wyler's *The Letter,* starring Bette Davis, and riding in the truck with Alan Ladd and Loretta Young as a luminous missionary in China, to catch the seconds he and his greasy pompadour steals the screen from the stars."

The brothers of the tong give me a fine banquet and invite the stars, staff, and crew of *Hawaii Five-O*. All very straight for McGarrett. A good, straightshooting Christian man. No drinking in sight. No smoking. No cussing. No dirty jokes. A round of speeches. The brothers are effusive. McGarrett in the same blue suit as he always wears on *Hawaii Five-O*, is serious, gracious, charming, and skeptical, and very low-key and cool. They call for me. They want Number Four Son. I give him to them.

"Gee, Pop! to you all, brothers, friends, *sum, moh, jiyeh, mooey,* and *Hawaii Five-O.* I say, Gosh, Pop! In the name of Charlie Chan, The Father, Keye Luke, the Son, and Earl Derr Biggers, The Holy Ghost. It's great to be an American and chew the fat with fellas who speak the same lingo."

A suckling pig for every table. A tea-smoked goose. Fish flesh of all colors and textures, and because we are Cantonese who must have our rice, a perfumed rice is one of the nine courses.

"I feel good tonight. My horoscope is just swell. Great biorhythm graphed in the paper. I feel good about today. I'm going to be okay. Say, this must be the Spirit of Aloha!" Even McGarrett smiles and applauds. The brothers laugh and nudge each other with their elbows.

"Let me say it right here and now. To us Charlie Chan is the Chinese Gospel of the New Testament. And Warner Oland, Sidney Toler, Roland Winters, and Anlauf Lorane are the prophets of Charlie Chan.

"I am the one lucky son of Chan who has had the privilege of meeting Earl Derr Biggers, our Holy Ghost, our creator, right here in Honolulu, in the bar of the Royal Hawaiian. He was working on his new Charlie Chan novel, *Charlie Chan in Winnemucca,* and I was over from the mainland with Benson about to die in a Gary Cooper missionary movie. Benson wasn't about to die. I was. I was having a laugh with Mr. Biggers about teaching the local Chinese children to sing 'My Old Kentucky Home' in Cantonese, to play Chinese mission school children greeting Gary Cooper to his mission in China.

"Mr. Biggers didn't laugh it up with me. Instead he became very serious. He said of all the sons of Chan I had a tragic dimension. For this certainly I was the most American of all the sons, he said, and at that moment he thought me the most likely to be the first Chinese to play Charlie Chan on the screen. I was surprised at how well he knew my acting. He said the roles that I played created a new character: the Chinese American as a casualty of the Fall, the Chinese American as victim, the Chinese American identity crisis as disease.

"The author Earl Derr Biggers saw all that in me. This was the Chinese American that sold, he told me. And he studies me for his next book *Charlie Chan in Winnemucca.* In the book and the movie, you will remember Charlie Chan has a chance meeting with a dishwasher named Chan from Pop's tong, in the kitchen of a Reno casino," I say, and people around the tables nod and smile in recognition.

"*Charlie Chan in Winnemucca* was Anlauf Lorane's first assay of the role of Charlie Chan. I was, once again, Honorable Son Number Four. Anlauf Lorane was a six-foot-four Belgian, five years my junior, and the fourth white man to play Charlie Chan. The role that almost brought him Hollywood stardom was General Yen, the seducer of Barbara Stanwyck, a young Barbara Stanwyck in Frank Capra's *The Bitter Tea of General Yen.*

"Anlauf told me Capra had him cut his eyelashes short, as he was convinced short eyelashes were the secret to making Caucasian eyes look Oriental. Until his eyelashes grew back he had to wear visored hats and dark glasses, he tells me.

"I tell him the word for the number four is *say* in Cantonese. And the word for dead is *say* in Cantonese. And *say yeah!* such a joyful exultant affirmative blast in English, is 'dead thing!' a curse, in Cantonese. And we have a good laugh together.

"In the book and the movie, but especially in the movie, Pop pities Chan the dishwasher for being as Chinese as the day he was born, a bigshot in the tong in San Francisco and Winnemucca's little Chinatown, but just a dishwasher in the real world, and in that real world, the dishwasher still looks on Charlie Chan, the detective sergeant of the Honolulu Police in immaculate white duck, with contempt, and Pop sighs and asks Why? Why is he contemptible in the eyes of the Chinese dishwasher? Because humble detective trod path away from the barbaric ways of old China, and toward the path of progress and became a Christian, became Americanized, Pop says."

The mood is down. The sounds of eating in the banquet aren't to be heard. They are moved. They're listening to me.

I say, "My second son, who Hyacinth insisted we name Ulysses after the banned novel, lived to be ten years old without once seeing me die in a World War II movie. The first movies he saw were in grammar school, on rainy days. When the kids weren't allowed out to run around the yard at lunch without getting soaked miserable, they showed movies in the auditorium. He was ten when I bought the family a television set and he saw *Charlie Chan in Winnemucca* late at night when no one thought of him watching television alone."

They applaud as if that is the end of that story. I leave it at that, and grin while I'm ahead. No point in telling them Ulysses hates Charlie Chan and hates me.

"Wanting to be the first Chinese American to play Charlie Chan is not too much to want. Keye, Benson, Victor, and I have all paid our dues. We all deserve a chance. Charlie Chan's sons numbers One, Two, Three, and Four have studied Charlie Chan as life and art and prophecy at least once a year at one of Benson's high-concept plastic tropical islands and have watched one Pop or the other come onto the color TV over the bar.

"And we listen to the old dialogue for clues, genuine mysteries of our lives, cosmic epiphanies with every utterance of Pop's passive objective innuendo.

"We don't talk about it, I don't know why, because I would love for us all to talk about the World War II bomber movie we made together. The four of us were the crew of the Consolidated B-47 Liberator with a shapely Chinese babe in a Dragon Lady hairdo winking over her shoulder on a couch of pudgy letters spelling out her name and the name of our bomber, *Anna May Wong* with quotation marks."

They applaud and whistle at the name Anna May Wong. This is probably the first time they've heard it in years.

"Keye was the pilot, Victor the co-pilot, Benson the bombardier, and I was the turret gunner. It was only shown in China and only during World War II, but it was a real movie. We flew in a real Liberator. Benson had taken flying lessons, but he was never a real pilot.

"I flew in Chiang Kai Shek's antique air force briefly. I flew an open cockpit P-26A, although I knew it was no match for the new Japanese Zero fighter. They rejected me finally. Ulysses found the certificate of my commission to fly in the Chinese Nationalist Air Force. He liked the little engravings of a formation of P-26s over the clouds. He remembers the certificate. He reads the Chinese he could not read when he saw the paper of my commission. No. It's as if he photographed it, and later when he learned to read a little Chinese in Chinese school, he looked at the photograph and read my commission. He called me a deserter." As love and sadness from everyone in the crowd fills the air I explain, "I was sixteen when I came to this country with the opera. How can I be a deserter at sixteen? How do you argue with your smart-aleck kid? I have lived the part of Charlie Chan with my own sons."

I see tears in their eyes, smiles on their faces. They have stopped eating long enough. I say, "We all deserve the part. But none of the other sons of Chan has died the way I have died, or as often, thanks in great part to my friends of *Hawaii Five-O.*"

The banquet is fit for the wedding of a prince and princess. McGarrett and Five-O give me face with my tong brothers, and vice versa. And they all give me face with the Honolulu papers.

Pictures in the morning paper with a story. "Charlie Chan and his Number Four Son gave me strength," Pandora Toy says in the *Honolulu Star-Bulletin.* "Neither his Hollywood brothers nor his own American sons see the great step Longman Kwan has made for

Chinese America, for a new generation of actors, as Charlie Chan's Number Four Son and as The Chinaman Who Dies." She's a writing fellow at the Writers' Workshop at Iowa City.

She's doing some kind of internship at the Honolulu paper while her husband teaches high school. I shouldn't like her. She chatters about writing and being a writer too much like my son Ulysses. And try as I might, I finally accept the fact I just don't like him. But I like Pandora Toy. She looks a little like my mother when my mother was young. Hyacinth looked a little like my mother to me too, when I was attracted to her. Pandora, young, soft, unearthly, is like every moment of sex with every woman I've ever had. I see their faces all over her skin, their bodies in her every motion.

What Pandora Toy writes about me makes me want her. She breathes new life into this old dead man. I hope they're reading what she writes about me in Hollywood, in New York, in NBC.

With a little fib, she writes, "Though the sentimentalist in me is tempted I will not betray the whereabouts of the last white man to play Charlie Chan in the movies." But it was *I* who would not betray the last Charlie Chan's whereabouts to *her*. I expect Pop to read today's *Honolulu Star-Bulletin*, recognize my picture, recognize his own name, and be more inclined to listen to me and accept the offers I bring. He should like the article. What Pandora Toy says about *Charlie Chan in Winnemucca* brings tears to my eyes:

"And it is the look on Longman's face, the tears in his eyes, the quaver in his voice that makes Charlie Chan, the venerable Pop, at this instant a hero, a martyr, a real Chinese-hyphen-American and the Chinese/ slash/ American Identity Crisis. It is because of Number Four Son that the Chinese American Identity Crisis was born in a B movie. And that Chan never dies, never. That Pop waits in the darkness of every theater, in every TV, ever ready to come to light again at the flick of a switch.

"To every Chinese American poised on the cultural edge of American assimilation, the world won't be right until Longman Kwan, Charlie Chan's Number Four Son and the quintessential

Chinaman Who Dies, takes over the role of Charlie Chan and lives until The End. Sooner or later, in one Chan movie or the next, the Chinese are sure, Number Four Son, the son *die say* will die and be reborn as Charlie Chan, the Chinese detective. I look forward to that day when Longman Kwan's name appears over the title of a new Charlie Chan movie. At last, I will sigh. There is justice in Hollywood. He will have nothing to worry about, for Charlie Chan never dies. He lives beyond—way beyond—The End."

I'm stunned. I'm glad I'm alone when I read the paper, for I must be blushing. I'm glad she didn't read her piece to me over the phone or show it to me before the Honolulu paper ran it. *Parade* magazine calls saying they want to include the banquet and my speech in a story about the search for the new Charlie Chan, timed to come out the same week as the episode of *Hawaii Five-O* I'm currently filming in Hawaii.

The shoot and my two weeks' work is done in ten days. Since I have four days to myself, I look up the Tiki Adult Bookshoppe and Arcade in the Yellow Pages.

Anlauf Lorane is the last prophet of Charlie Chan alive and I am the only son he trusts to keep his current identity, Henly Hornbrook, Honolulu pornographer, secret.

He's fat. He is very fat. Fatter than Charlie Chan. More bald than Charlie Chan. He turns and holds his bald head in one hand like a basketball. Fat, sleazy, notorious, convicted of obscenity. Oh, no, convicted of obscenity. Charlie Chan cannot be convicted of obscenity. I see dollars for Anlauf Lorane flying away into aloha— "Goodbye."

"If I did not care about being recognized as the last white man to play Charlie Chan alive, I might have made my little small business in rubber cunts and dicks, some made with human hair, a First Amendment case, gone to the Supreme Court," he says and laughs. I'm not prepared for the inside of this place, the smell of all this pink rubber in the dim, vulvalike interior of a Quonset hut. He lives in the Quonset hut next door.

His fantasy Tahitian bamboo and rattan porn parlor—adult

books, adult toys, sex aids, adult films and 25-cent movies in private booths—has the look and unstated substance of Benson's tropical fantasy Chinese restaurants down cold. Plastic plants and inflatable rubber women. Yes, this is what's missing from Benson's. Rubber dicks and five-fingered French ticklers. And the tropical damp smell from the private movie booths, like the smell from dark stuff under the trees after a rain, I don't ask about and don't take for granted as natural.

His Charlie Chan moustache and goatee have grown wild and self-indulgent to Shakespearean pretensions. He looks like thousands of fat, goateed men with artificially inflated vocabularies I have seen in places like this, all on the edge of Chinatowns, all fat, watching a little TV set on a counter full of flesh-colored rubber genitals and faces with open mouths. His face is without worry and age lines, like an overinflated balloon. Pop is lost inside his own wilderness of fat globules, playing Henly Hornbrook, Honolulu pornographer, in his Tiki Adult Book Shoppe and Arcade, between the highway and Chinatown, looking out onto the street, not watching his little Japanese television set pouring the gray light of *The Hatchetman* all over his hairy right arm, that looks like a fat baby seal on a rock.

To the southwest is Chinatown and the prostitutes. Just around the corner is a street of men crouched over pinball machines and men in dark booths like the ones here, where they drop dimes and quarters into movie machines and stare into a slot to see a minute of sucky fucky with, hopefully, the woman with the face and body of their dreams. Every time he moves, bulbs and drooping bags of fat wobble all over and seem to ooze out from under his sleeves.

"Gee, Pop! You chose a hell of a place to hide!" I say, still hoping this is all a joke of some kind.

"I have to be where all those old movies are haunting the atmosphere for everybody to see. I wandered the Hawaiian islands for a year or so, so scared my asshole's afraid to open, sure the Chinese will assassinate me as soon as I try to take a shit and reveal my whereabouts, and there are Chinese everywhere, baby! Everywhere!

Then Charlie Chan told me to *become* my hiding place. Hide Charlie Chan in a blob of shapeless fat."

"You're not hiding in the porn shop, you're hiding in your fat?" I ask.

But then another bald-on-top, fat white man with a moustache and goatee and a mouth full of vocabulary shows up, and Pop climbs down off his stool and ignores me as he makes pornographer's small talk with his look-alike. Then he walks me through sudden rain around a couple of tall skinny palm trees to the Quonset hut he calls home and introduces me to his fat blobular fifth wife.

To celebrate our reunion, our renascence, I hope, Pop announces he will make another five gallons of his world-famous chili con carne. While it simmers for five hours, he says, "We'll smoke, drink, and shoot the shit." Does he mean he's shooting drugs? I don't ask. No. He smokes Maui Wowie, the local super-duper *pakololo.* It's better than what we had in alleys behind the clubs with the bands during the war. One puff for the peace pipe effect and social cool, then that's it for me. He doesn't do cocaine. "Fat people shouldn't do cocaine," he says. "Otherwise I love being fat."

His wife helps him tie on a huge bibbed apron with "The World's Greatest Cook!" Day-Gloed from the right hip to left shoulder. He puts a large stainless steel pot on the stove and begins filling it. "I have good chili. I have good meat for the carne—sirloin. But the secret of good chili con carne is neither the chili nor the carne," he says, browning onions and garlic, a bay leaf and various kinds of fresh and dried chili peppers, "but the con, my son. The good con."

Longman Kwan: "Gosh, Pop!"

His bare feet disappear in the obscene lawn of wall-to-wall long Day-Glo pink and orange synthetic fiber. "Yeah, it looks like I bought all the wigs in Frederick's of Hollywood and laid them on my floor, doesn't it," the fat bald-headed man says.

"It was fate. Destiny. Charlie Chan—oh, excuse me, rather: The last white man to play Charlie Chan arrested for obscenity," he laughs, then suddenly leans toward me, rippling the muscles in his forehead. "You know what will happen if they ever give you the part of Charlie Chan? I mean, if they ever give the part of Charlie Chan to an Oriental actor, you know what will happen, don't you? Your son, or grandson, whatever they make him, will be some young semi-hot bitch boy or male starlet, as Sterling Hayden called himself before he became an actor, a Caucasian boy, and he will be the star, and you will be second banana again. Like Keye Luke playing a blind Buddhist priest teaching David Carradine how to dive in *Kung Fu* on TV. How embarrassing! You ever watch that? Sure, you've been in it, I've seen you."

I laugh and it's my turn to furrow my brow. I ask, "You were arrested for obscenity?"

"They raided me on December seventh—Pearl Harbor Day. Thank God it was Maui and not Honolulu and no one did any digging or asked too many questions. If they had known I was Charlie Chan, the irony of me being arrested for obscenity would have been irresistible." He stops and blinks and looks like Charlie Chan hatching an idea, then shakes his head. "No, it's too late."

"Too late for what, Pop?" I ask without thinking. "Oh, yes! Way too late to let the world know Charlie Chan was arrested for obscenity! But, you know, some of the people behind some of these offers might dig it, man."

"Dig it, man!" Pop says after me. "Oh, son, you are too much!"

"Gee, Pop, thanks!" I grin.

He smiles, raises his eyebrows, and sighs instead of laughing. The hollows in his skull and bags of fat make his face a natural passive resonating woofer. The deeper tones of the gurgling pot of chili on the stove honk and boom out of his face like the sound of laughter. His wife Milagro offers me a plate of chocolate chip cookies. I take one. She lays the plate on the little table next to me.

"They confiscated thirty-six reels of obscene pornographic films, my obscene stereo and amplifier, and a stack of my pornographic LPS. I think we were playing obscene Dave Brubeck at the time." He chuckles. Milagro sits and settles into the tidal motion of his fat with two movie hero coloring books and a big box of crayons. She opens the coloring book of cowboy stars. She colors between the lines of John Wayne in *Hondo* with all the blues in her crayon box and sinks into Pop's fat as he smokes his marijuana cigarette without offering it to me, Bogarts it (I understand that expression now), and speaks in a murmur meant to be seen in close-up, as his voice fades. "Once I was a bandy-legged candy butcher in the burlesque, thirteen years old, living by my wits. And in the world of right now, I am your porn entrepreneur lost in the crowd of pornographers, pimps, whores, the rubber-eyed low-down horny come-to-suckscum in Honolulu. I am, I was *and* I am more like the real Charlie Chan than the pornographic cartoon I was before the cameras."

I look over to the TV through the steam of hot chili beans from the kitchen and don't understand a word of what he says. Contact high? Oh, no! I must be stoned! Why do they call it stoned? The smoke of incense that smells like burning Juicy Fruit chewing gum, all a-shimmer and a-glitter to the tinkles and twangs of Ravi Shankar playing a schizo cat stretched on a rack on the stereo tuned to sound like a huge car radio.

This place is not House Beautiful or *Sunset*. The round walls and ceiling from one end of the Quonset hut to the other are lined with a huge pastel-on-black-velvet mural. An imaginary landscape of otherworldly plants, flowers, and creatures on the north side. On the south wall, it looks as if Rousseau, doubling as a tattoo artist, has created a jungle on Mars at night. Stars and planets rise up to the Milky Way flowing overhead, while below fantastic fish and sea life swim in an undersea landscape on the ocean floor of Toys 'R'

Us. An aquarium with flickering black light purples the water, and a gurgling pump barely rises above the pile of beanbags and big pillows all over the place. The lamps jutting out of the walls, the pillowy bulbous furniture, piece by piece, color next to color, have all been put together with a purpose, I see. They call this bughouse home. They relax and cook and wash and eat and sleep here.

The Quonset hut is a huge backseat of a huge car at a drive-in on Venus, and I'm in it with Pop and Milagro, and up on the screen I see Spencer Tracy after all these years. Spencer Tracy. I used to confide in Spencer Tracy, when, in order to wear away my accent and study American acting, I watched endless American movies. I didn't confide directly to the man. I never actually met him. Even in the movies in which we appear together, I never meet him. But I go to see the man's movies. I confide to the man on the screen. I sit in the front row and talk to him when he comes on in close-up. The people in the audience at the Bijou I go to when I want to talk to Spencer Tracy usually sleep through the movies, which run all night.

Sometimes, and I swear it is not my imagination, Spencer Tracy talks back. "Sorry the place is such a mess," he says to me in Malaya. He wears white duck and a Panama straw hat, with the brim snapped the way I wear my Panama as the jivetalking slangy Japanese-American Jap spy that Bogart kills in *Across the Pacific*. "But my Chinese boy's been drafted and my Jap boy's interned." James Stewart usually has those lines in Malaya, but for me and my family, the movies are living beings, they grow, they change.

"Animals like my second Chinese boy, Ulysses," I tell Spencer Tracy. Both Spencer Tracy and James Stewart are dressed like Pop and me in *Charlie Chan in Winnemucca* and *The Black Castle*, all in white duck and Panama straw hats. They stop and listen. Everyone in the whole movie dresses like us. Wait till the boys hear about this. Ulysses is not surprised. He tells me Hyacinth takes him to the movies to show Spencer Tracy his report cards and encourage him to do better in math.

Anlauf stirs and says, "Mmmmm. Smells good," then rolls another joint.

"For a star, fat is the difference between playing leading men or character parts. Fat is the difference between romantic leads and comic second leads. Fat is the difference between getting a job in the almighty Industry and pornography. I'm too fat to be seen. Too fat for the screen. Fat is my shield, my fortress. I'm too fat to be cute and cuddly. Too fat to be funny. My fatness is physically repulsive, smelly, unloved, rejected, sweaty. An affront in the sight of civilized eyes. Nobody takes a good look at an old white man traveling this world of woe inside a fat meteoroid of marshmallow. I swim and clamber inside my three dimensions, my jostling, grunting, and gasping bellies, as through the bodies of generations of my family. The Chan family, of course," he says, and adds homemade beef stock from a crock he keeps in the fridge. "I'm fat, sweaty, and smelly, and I love it. At last, I am away from, far away from ever having been Charlie Chan. And you want to bring it all back. No."

Perhaps he *was* too far gone into his fat to be a star again.

"But animals and small children like me," he says.

"Animals like my second son, too," I say. "Dogs just walk up to him and wag their tails."

Pop stirs the pot with a wooden spoon, tastes, and continues smacking his lips and smiling. "I was talking about animals and small children liking me. We'll talk about your son's problems later. Oh, there's just so much of me to be me. I like the distance. The geography inside me. I tried to make that distance real distance. I escaped from Hollywood and thought I had escaped from Charlie Chan. I thought I was free. Free of Belgium. Free of Hollywood. Free of Charlie Chan. To atone for my sins of Chan and mix a little fun with pleasure—make that business with pleasure—I took to the road on a Harley, wore a German World War II black ss helmet, a black leather jacket, a clerical collar and a huge crucifix around my neck worn tight up under the collar, like an Iron Cross First Class, dig? I called myself Chaplain Charlie, Preacher of the Road, and learned to make this chili con carne, a big pot of it at a time like this, for my prayer meetings at bikers' rallies. And, though

I was a big man, six foot four and always was something of a gourmand, I was frequently beaten up by subdivisions of the Hell's Angels—the Jokers, the Losers, the Snake Eyes—who took exception to early versions of this recipe. And it was hard, a difficult row I hoed, bringing the Holy Gospel to the motorcycle heathens I had chosen as my flock."

"Really, honey?" Milagro says, looking up from her crayons and coloring books. "I never heard about this."

"One of the advantages of being my fifth—or is it sixth?—wife. You never had the misfortune of knowing Chaplain Charlie, preaching the Gospel, performing marriages and funerals, and praying to God for the sins of motorcycle gangsters. Upon entering one biker's saloon with my Bible, this bouncer obstructed my forward progress to the bar, pointed a .22 automatic between my eyes, and ordered me to pray," Pop says.

I don't know whether or not I should believe this story, but this is something my second son, Ulysses, would do. I wonder if, out on the road, he might have run into Ulysses, or perhaps seen my first son, Longman Jr., on one of his freight trains.

"He pulled the trigger and shot me between the eyes. The next thing, I woke up in a hospital. A nurse raised the shade and it was morning, whereas it had been night when the lights went out. And it's a week later. I didn't press charges. I told the police it was an accident. I returned to the biker saloon and the bouncer all but fell on his knees and kissed my hand. He loved me."

"It's hard to believe," I say.

"Yeah, I was a real by-the-book Christian.'

"I mean, you were shot between the eyes and lived?" I say, a little surprised at the question in my voice.

"Oh, yeah, that was God's work, all right. You can still see the scar, if you look closely. And man, when this place is lit with nothing but the black light, the scar shows up between my eyes like a splatted squid."

He snaps off the fluorescent lights. And as the black light makes the pastel fish and animals and imaginary beings of land, sea, and sky glow ghastly on the black velvet, it also raises the white scar of a wound between and just above his eyes.

"Did they get the bullet out through the same hole it went in?" I ask straight out, as if weary of talking lies. The whole Quonset hut is stuffy with marijuana smoke.

"They didn't take it out. They were worried about how many circuits they'd pull apart going in after it. It was steel jacketed. I seemed to be all there. So they left it alone. And there I was back in the biker saloon ready to punch him out."

I listen on but am not past wondering how much and what to believe of what I'm hearing and wish he'd snap the lights back on.

"He said he had been in a paranoid flash and was certain I was a narc," Pop says. "Ha. Ha. My first soul. I baptized him in the Sacramento River. It became something of a pattern, a ritual. Someone in the gang would beat the shit out of me, sometimes the whole gang would beat the shit out of me, or one of them would shoot me, or stab me, and I learned the hard way that you cannot just turn the other cheek and expect to impress the goodness of Christian charity on the brothers. No, you have to stand toe to toe and fight back, fight dirty, and just when the battering and bloodiness hits about equal, you grab the brother and kiss him on the mouth and say, 'I love you, brother. Hallelujah! It's almost sinful how much I do enjoy trading kicks and punches with you.' It's all a matter of timing, selecting the right moment to turn the other cheek, forgive them, preach to them, baptize them. Most of the time I got away without broken bones. There is nothing like a motorcycle gangster for knowing just how to treat people like animals when they have a hard-on against you. I think I was their friend. But having a motorcycle gang on your side is like being a puppydog running with a pack of wolves. Then one night—I think it was the first time they'd taken acid—they looked at me and no longer saw Chaplain Charlie, but Charlie Chan wearing a Nazi helmet. They said they had a contract on Charlie Chan from some unnamed Chinese in San Francisco. But for the good times, for the good trips, they gave me seven days' head start."

"You don't think they might have been joking?" I ask. "The fact is, I see money just fluttering away instead of into your pocket."

"Five wives?" Milagro asks out of nowhere.

"I went out on the road looking for myself, a preacher in a crisis of faith. It was hell. But I realized that I am not a good Christian. I *am* a good sinner. I can't get away from that. That is me. I love women. I love food. I love fun. And yes, darling, you are my fifth wife. That's me. I am meant to live a life of nothing but fun, naked women, and dirty jokes instead of mom and dad. Hotdogs and hamburgers instead of sons and daughters. Eating what I want. Doing what I want. The insides! That is what counts. Under the skin. In the flesh. Inside the body. That has become my life. My life is pornography. Pornography is my life. I am one with everything."

"It just bothers me to see you miss out on all this easy money. Think about it. Charlie Chan can sell anything, Pop! If he can sell himself as a Chinese on the screen, he can sell anything. Anything. Candy companies want him. Breakfast cereals. I could make a good living collecting ten percent as your agent. Look, here's a university film school that would like to see us together as part of their Charlie Chan film festival, Pop!"

"I almost neglected to mention the point of that whole story was I learned how to make chili con carne while I was Chaplain Charlie. You might say, this chili con carne has saved my life. The Lord only knows what would have happened had they not approved of my cooking."

"Pop! Look at these letters, will you look at them? Our movies are being studied in universities! No bombs. No threats. No boos. No pickets. Nothing. Here's an insurance company. They want to know if you'll pose for print ads and be the star spokesman in their TV commercials. National, Pop! Thousands and thousands of dollars for two or three days' soft work. Here's a breakfast cereal. Ginger-flavored oats with coconut and honey."

"Sugar, air, and bleached flour! Trash! I'll eat it, but I won't sell it."

"Oats, Pop! The stuff they make Cheerios out of," I say, and pick up a stack of letters. "A couple of candy companies want you to do quotations from a character they call Sweet Tooth. Here's a new flavored candied popcorn. Here's an offer to do a public service spot for Social Security, now that you're a senior citizen. Gee, Pop! You can sell anything. Even doing nothing, you can sell. I'm not soliciting these offers. I mean, these letters get to me after they have gone to a lot of trouble trying to reach you through the Screen Actors Guild, Pop. Just look at them. There's talk of a big budget, big director, big distributor, big big deal Charlie Chan movie. Charlie Chan is coming back, Pop! And who better to ride this wave, than you, brah! You're history, nostalgia, tradition, everything Hollywood loves!"

"They're counterfeit. Don't you understand? Those offers are a Chinese trick to flush me out."

"Anlauf, come on!" I say.

"Henly, if you please. Henly Hornbrook," Pop says. "They all ask me to appear in white duck, as Charlie Chan, am I correct?"

"Yeah, Pop."

"And a Panama straw hat with the brim turned up?"

"Of course!" I say.

"There you are!"

"But, Anlauf, you were never anybody else but Charlie Chan. Nobody knows you as anybody else," I say.

"And I told you Charlie Chan is pornography."

"Pornography!" I scoff. "Charlie Chan is not pornography. Forget all that phoney Oriental philosophy or European Existentialist crap! Charlie Chan is American progress, Pop. Charlie Chan made you a star! Charlie Chan can make me a star!"

He laughs, and my skin creeps. "A porn star."

"Pop, you're not making any sense. Forget porn."

"Forget porn?"

"Okay, do Charlie Chan for money and porn as a hobby."

"You're a San Francisco boy. You'd like to see some porn that caters to your personal salacious tastes and sex fantasies in your home town, wouldn't you? San Francisco porn featuring a Japanese

American alumnus of Richmond High sporting a fake Chinese name, sucking and fucking black and white cock of every size, shape, and description? But no matter how many quarters you drop, how many arcades you visit, or how many different Oriental girls you see sucking and fucking in Frisco, Hollywood, or even Honolulu, where old country Chinamen are the most frequent clientele, you will never see them suck or fuck a yellow man, not anywhere within a thousand miles of Pearl Harbor, San Diego, Los Angeles, San Francisco, Seattle, or bad memories of mythical proportions. And that is Charlie Chan, pornographer."

As if on cue, an ancient movie fizzes to light on the TV. An old color movie. And it's me, the year my second American-born son, Ulysses, graduated from high school. I like this movie. I am Frank Sinatra's gunbearer in the movie jungle south of the Chinese border in full color World War II. The Japs ambush us, wipe out our field hospital as we arrive late on the scene, fighting the retreating Japanese rear guard. Frank Sinatra sticks his gun, a fine blowback-operated full-automatic M-4 greasegun, out at me while sharpshooting his glower off after the runoff Japs.

And his arm stays out there until he gets the idea I have not taken the gun from him. He turns around to see I am not there. I am on the ground a few meters back, blinking sweat out of my eyes a long time now, on my back with a twenty-two-pound Browning automatic rifle with bipod, a nine-and-a-half-pound M-1 Garand rifle, a Thompson recoil-operated machine gun with drum magazine, a Schmeisser, a Sten, a sack of assorted attachments, a sack of hand grenades, extra ammo, and extra Zippo lighters slung every which way over my shoulders.

"I have failed you," I say, sounding like a fast leaking tire.

"Don't talk now," Frank Sinatra says. All of our little renegade detail are in the tent around my cot. The doctor and Frank Sinatra exchange looks and shake their heads. I'm shuddering, trying not to cry. Breath whinnies from my lungs like mustangs on the distance. Frank Sinatra draws his Colt .45 M-1911A1 automatic pistol and chambers a round.

I swallow the blood in my mouth, smile bloody teeth and croak and rattle, "I always liked the sound of a good gun's works," then shudder and nod. Frank Sinatra tells everyone to leave the tent.

"You can't do it!" someone says while my eyes are closed. "It's murder!"

"It's either this way, quick, or let him scream all night long," Frank Sinatra says. "You wouldn't let a dog suffer like that."

"Observe, please!" Pop says, pointing at the color TV, "Honorable Son Number Four never heard from again in this movie."

I laugh. "It's true," I say, "But there was talk of a nomination."

"It was just talk, wasn't it," Pop says, and wags his finger at me. "You watch these things for a year or so, over and over again, and it becomes clear what Charlie Chan has done to the Chinese."

"Pop, listen to yourself. Even if the Chinese were out to get you for being either Charlie Chan or obscene, that was what, forty, at least forty years ago. Even if they hired a motorcycle gang to hit you, that was forty years ago. They're probably all broke or all dead by now. Everything's different, changed. The old Charlie Chan is nostalgia, not terror. There are no seventy-year-old bikers out there trying to make a contract on the last white man to play Charlie Chan. Even if at one time they honored a contract for all time, drugs have changed all that." I say, "Charlie Chan means jobs for the Chinese!"

"It is the time-space continuum moving from burlesque to the perfection of Platonic pornographic form in Charlie Chan. From candy butcher to Charlie Chan."

Pop is at home flooding every sense with trash, smoking, eating, touching, feeling, everything stupid and soft, and is high now. Somewhere in his fat he is happily suffering on the cross of Charlie Chan, waiting for Chinese assassins with knives, now in a Quonset hut from World War II repainted inside and decorated by his fifth or sixth wife, Milagro, a caramel-skinned, blond-haired woman of indeterminate race and accent.

"Her name means miracle in Spanish," Pop the pornographer tells me, smiling like so many other fat goateed balding pornographers I have trusted to make change. The smile speaks of mystery, of unsaid violence, of unspoken jail time, of unspeakable fits of bad temper. She does not sound Spanish or Mexican. I wonder how long she has had the name Milagro. Not out loud, but inwardly, sweetly, I wonder, and wait in my ears. Pop never could keep a secret from me.

"She made those cookies you're munching," he says. He pokes his finger in my direction. It looks like a gob of dough. I'm munching?

"Munching?"

"You've got the munchies, man. That's cool. Be cool."

"The munchies."

"There's a kind of poetry, a kind of justice, a kind of poetic justice," Pop says, rocking back and forth, bobbing like a bathtub toy in the bath, "in Charlie Chan being assaulted and assassinated at a state fair by seventy-year-old bikers with their tattoos showing and all that, hired by some mysterious Chinese. I've had my fun. Perhaps I should let the Chinese take me home."

"Take you home?" I ask.

"It's a Christian way of saying 'dying.' " he says.

"Of course. And if you make a little money before they get you, that will be poetic justice too."

"You've seen burlesque, of course."

"Gee, Pop, of course I have," I say. "My mother-in-law's mother was the madam of one of the largest whorehouses in Chinatown, before the Great Earthquake." But he doesn't hear me. I'm a planet away. Too far outside his orbiting fat.

"The white duck. The moustache. The perverted eyes. Don't you know that Charlie Chan is a joke from the stages of burlesque, where working stiffs and wage slaves have seen Tempest Storm, Evelyn '$50,000 Treasure Chest' West, Blaze Starr, the great strippers who migrated across the country and around the world from burlesque house to burlesque house, to old theaters that got older as *they* got older, and were dying like diseased geese, a species on the brink of extinction?"

"Who's watching the chili, Pop?"

"She makes those cookies with Maui Wowie."

"Oh," I say. "Maui Wowie." I say it to say it but can't grasp it.

"You're too straight to play Charlie Chan. That's your problem," he says.

"If the powers that be give me the part, I will play Charlie Chan just like you, Pop."

"The Chinese won't be able to complain then, will they," he says on a fast fade.

He watches me die in an old war movie with Spencer Tracy telling a steel room full of American carrier pilots, "Remember! Jap planes can't bank left," as if I am not in the same room breathing his bubbling pot of beans with him. He yields to the gravity of his massive disguise and rides his fat, loses himself in his fat. As his talk erodes to a barely minded hum and the chili ripens in the Quonset hut, all the furniture and decorations and the last white man to play Charlie Chan and his wife Milagro look more and more like expensive replicas of stuff you win at carnivals. Everything looks like cotton candy, plaster Kewpie dolls, and saltwater taffy. Everything has been chosen with the caution, taste, precise balance of whim, and middle-class morals that any other middle-class couple would exercise in adopting a child. What does he mean telling me I'm too straight for Charlie Chan?

"We are both children of the Great Depression. The Depression came in off the streets to sit down in a nice burlesque house and laugh at the stars on stage."

"Laugh at the strippers?"

"No, the comics and straight men. Robert Alda was a straight man in burlesque. Jack Carson's passed away, he was from burlesque. A great many stars you see on The Late Show came out of burlesque. Bud Abbott and Lou Costello, Ed Wynn, a lot of 'em. A whole lot of 'em. Including me. Me, the real Charlie Chan, keeping the peace on Hotel Street with gun, bullwhip and baseball bat. And Charlie Chan, the perversion of Chang Apana and Charlie Chaplin. The short little tramp in the baggy black suit and the tall fat Charlie in tight white duck. I was doing Charlie Chan the Chinese detective on the burlesque stage when I was tapped to do Charlie Chan in the movies. My Chan was like Warner's and Sidney's faggot act on the burlesque stage, it was for the man who was pretty hungry and it was a little difficult to laugh at himself. Watching me made it easier."

He fades into his globular disguise. "For thirty-five cents he could sit up in the peanut gallery, or for fifty cents he could sit downstairs, or for seventy-five he could sit in the loges or a box seat. And during the day, he had to stand on a street corner and sell apples, or dig ditches, and he had to wear his older brother's cast-me-down clothes. And his pants were baggy, and he had to tie 'em with a rope for a belt. But at night he could go to a burlesque theater and see the guy who was dressed exactly like him, but lower down, more rejected by society, and the guy would win out over the few well-dressed individuals who were left in the world."

"Gee, Pop!" I say.

"Gosh!" Milagro says, holding one of her blue crayons like a dart.

"Burlesque was the greatest form of entertainment of its time," Pop says.

"It sounds positively wonderful," Milagro says.

"Burlesque was trash, Milagro. Trash!" Pop rolls his beetleblack eyes, glimmering the rainbow of oilslick, onto me, and says, "Milagro is the only woman I could possibly love openly and freely. And marry." Pop says, "Until three years ago, she was a Catholic nun. She was innocent. Forty-two years old and a virgin."

Everyone smiles. Pop's fat sags. He relaxes in his cave of corrugated steel, his glorified storm drain. The fat around his cheeks and chin billows like the sails of the galleons of the Spanish Armada, filling with wind, as he closes his mouth and breathes deeply of the steam growing out of a large pot of simmering chili, up his nose, and out his mouth, again and again. A joy on every breath. The Quonset hut feels more and more like a tin can on its side, and we are the con carne getting cooked in the can with chili. Chili con carne in the name of Charlie Chan.

Then Spencer Tracy looks into the camera and talks directly to me, calls my name, in a lingering close-up no one in the audience has seen before. His eyes have a soft glow about them. A light of love and affection warms out of his face in extreme close-up and his face from the top of his brows to the bottom of his lower lip fills the screen. "Now, Kwannie, me boy, tell me what's this I hear tell about you not finding the part of Number Four Son to your liking, lad?"

Spencer Tracy talking to me! Life doesn't get any better than this. "Oh, I . . ." I lose all English. I don't dare speak Chinese to Spencer Tracy. Then Hepburn might talk to me out of *her* old movies, and I couldn't stand that. I lose all language. "Stand up, stand up, Kwannie old man, stand up, let's have a look at you," Spencer Tracy says, and I stand up. "Now, tell me," he says, "Man to man."

Hollywood movies are not such monsters after all. I look up into Spencer Tracy's huge eyes and say, "It's my wife. She's American born, and says she does not want our sons to grow up seeing me as nothing more than The Chinaman Who Dies and Charlie Chan's honorable Number Four Son, *die say*. You see, the number four in Chinese is *say*, and sounds like *say* which is *dead* in Cantonese, see? Or *see* in Mandarin, which sounds like see in Cantonese and means shit. It doesn't really, but to her ears, you know. American born. She's afraid I'm setting them some kind of bad example and will give them a complex about death."

Pop grumbles and sniffs the air. "Do me a favor and stir the chili for me, will you, Number Four?"

"Gee, Pop!" I say, "Speaking of vaudeville, here's something called the Star River Rock and Old Timey Festival and Pot Luck Fair asking you and a numbered son to be the masters of ceremony," I read, and pass the letter to him.

"Hip," Pop mumbles. "I like the idea of Charlie Chan and his Number Four Son emceeing a rock 'n' roll festival."

Milagro likes it too. It's her idea for Charlie Chan to call himself Buddha in the Age of Aquarius. I like her. I tell her I have a son around her age, American born like her, who despises my movies and despises me.

"You look more like Buddha than Charlie Chan, right now, Pop. The Chinese happy Buddha with a big grin on his face, and kids crawling all over him. So call yourself Charlie Chan, the Buddha of Rock 'n' Roll," I say. "It's a great idea. It could reignite both of our careers."

Pop takes a deep breath of the simmering chili, looks wet and droopy eyes at droopy dozing Milagro, and looks like Shakespeare hearing a great play in his head and nothing to write with. "Yes," he says, "Buddha."

"Rock 'n' roll, Pop! Live on stage, ad lib and all that vaudeville stuff you're talking about. You can do it! 'Charlie Chan Comes Back to Rock 'n' Roll as the Buddha!' It'll be like the penis rising out of the ashes!"

"No, that's my line," Pop says. "I'm the pornographer. You mean, of course, like the phoenix rising out of the asshole."

The year of my first American-born son Longman Jr.'s glorious return from World War II, I was living a strange life outside Hollywood playing the evil Jap officer who dies a horrible death after killing an innocent Chinese baby and his or her innocent little mother, with my sword, which, because the war was over, was being shot as a historical western in the desert and re-titled *I Rode With Genghis Khan!* The evil Jap baby-killer I played was transformed by costume and horse, not dialogue, into the Mongol military genius, Genghis Khan. I became Genghis Khan. I was suddenly the lead, the star. A Chinese Hollywood first! My all-American Hyacinth would have to be happy for me, and admit she was wrong to laugh at me for "going Hollywood," as she called it. But the ridicule did not end. Instead of saying my years away from Oakland circulating in the Industry were worth it, right in front of our son Ulysses, she said, "A Chinese man will never star as a Chinese man in a Hollywood movie! Never! "

"How do you know?"

"They'll get a white woman to play the Chinese detective before they star a Chinese man. They'll star a Chinese woman before they star a Chinese man as a Chinese man! They'll star a Chinese queer boy before they star a Chinese man."

"Why aren't you happy when I make it?" I ask her. "What do you mean, 'They'll get a white women before the star me'? They *are* starring me! What're you talking about?"

Her words were prophetic. I was bumped for John Wayne, who played Genghis Khan. Only a white known for playing heroes—not a yellow known for comic relief—could play Genghis Khan. I was grateful for the part of his son, captain of a company of horsemen.

The year of Longman Jr.'s great race in the caboose of a hundred-car train against one hundred trucks, I was Steve McQueen's sidekick in *The Sand Pebbles*. Junior was a *real* hero in a *real* adventure, the kind that are bought to make real movies, but he didn't know it. In the movie, the Chinese capture me as the American ship and Steve McQueen are about to sail away down the big Yangtze back to the sea. I am stripped to the waist, tied to a post, and tortured. The death of a thousand cuts. My screams, always my screams, *Aiiieeeee! Aiiieeeee! Aiiieeeee!* bring Steve McQueen to the rail cocking his Springfield U.S. rifle M-1904, aiming for my head, catching my eye through his peepsight, and he lowers his rifle a blink, then sees Candice Bergen on the deck above, watching him with longing and shuddering lips. I call Steve McQueen, and scream when they cut me, *Aiiieeeee!* and as the ship pulls away from the rioting Chinese and churns up mud and bloody water into the big river's stream, *kapow!* one shot, and I am out of my misery, and win an Academy Award nomination for Best Supporting Actor. A nomination! I'm the only Son of Chan ever to get a nomination. I didn't expect to get the Oscar. I didn't get the Oscar. But a nomination! I was something of a celebrity among my people and my sons were not.

Hyacinth still blames me for Junior flunking out of every college he entered till his G.I. Bill and a few thousand of our dollars were used up. She accepted the fact he was most likely too stupid not to flunk any real college but still blamed me because he tried to sell vitamins door-to-door on the side and because he borrowed three thousand dollars to start a chinchilla farm. He was such a handsome young man, I was happy to ask Auntie Phoebe to agent him. And though he was called "Hollywood Jr." for many years, he went back to the railroad. Perhaps it's her way of taking it out on Charlie Chan's Number Four Son and Charlie Chan. Perhaps Pop's nightmare of Chinese stalking his trail all over the world to kill Charlie Chan has a little grain of truth about it. Hyacinth, in a year or two, might just *be* one of the Chinese mad enough to blame Charlie Chan for all her troubles and give poor Pop's suffering the significance he wants. And Ulysses, my second son, who she insisted on naming after a banned novel, never liked me, or any of my movies, or anything about me.

"Confucius said the six arts regulate . . ." Pop begins, out of nowhere, dreaming, stoned, or waking up, I don't know.

But I can't stand him telling me about China and Confucius, and say, ". . . is dead in China, Pop. Banned by the Cultural Revolution. Chinese socialist realism. Grinning tawny-skinned wonders of brawny health and dentistry in love with their commune. Communist folk ballets of women giving up all identity for the Party and wiping out the armies of the landlords. Yuck! Charlie Chan never never shot some poor Chink for the heinous crime of collecting rent or reading a fairy tale to kids. Come on, Pop. No one. No one, you know, not even the Chinese take Charlie Chan seriously at all. He's a B movie, Pop!"

"In somebody's eyes we all have sins to die for, ours or somebody else's, but we have them. Chinese revenge stalks us all. Listen, son, late-night TV is the local collective subconscious. Late-night TV is the brilliant zeitgeist, the crock of myth fermenting in the private places, the unspoken escape, the blessed divine stupidity without expectations, without ambitions, without hope, without anticipation or danger. Ah, sweet TV. You can tell the soul of a place by its late-night TV and its porn," he says. His dark eyes shine like the backs of beetles and click across the slits between his fleshy, barely open lids.

Anlauf Lorane and/or Henly Hornbrook drinks and moans, "How can an old-time radical such as I live down shaking hands with Franco at the premiere of *Charlie Chan in Madrid . . . ?* I was for the Republicans!"

"I'm Republican too, Pop! Nobody remembers that. And it was Charlie Chan who shook the Generalissimo's gloved hand, not you."

"I almost joined the Abraham Lincoln Brigade to fight on the Republican side. Oh, I was pissed when the Fascists bombed Guernica. Then to shoot *Charlie Chan in Madrid* in Madrid instead of the usual back lot and then to be invited to the palace to meet the Generalissimo!"

"He was a fan, Pop. Charlie Chan transcends politics, even in Spain."

"The bastard didn't grasp my hand at all. We posed barely touching palm to glove if you will. And you! You had to speak to him in Spanish!"

"That wasn't me, Pop. That was Number Four Son!"

"The Existentialists are overrated. The Absurdists were merely vaudeville's last gasp, the skit flaring to brilliance before extinction. Speak to me of real things, what puts food on my table, money in my pocket. What moves the changes in the fortunes of men and the history of mankind. So says the Buddha of Rock 'n' Roll."

I cheer. Not too loudly. Sound is strange here. I whisper, "Like the Lone Ranger and Batman, Charlie Chan can live forever, making his bows at rodeos, state fairs, university film series. See here! A frozen food company wants you to pitch their new Chinese line on TV, a Hawaiian airline wants you to pitch Hawaii and island hopping in a TV-and-print campaign tied in with a United Air Lines Hawaiian campaign. Everyone wants your Charlie Chan to come out of hiding and waddle around and glow again. You do not have to do the personal appearances at rodeos and state fairs if you don't want to. The commercials you are being offered are more than enough to keep you a recluse in fine style and comfort."

"No, I don't like it."

"You don't like what, Pop?"

"The Buddha of Rock 'n' Roll doesn't sound right. I don't like it," he says. "There was a real Charlie Chan, the detective, you know. Did you know that?" he asks. "Did you ever ask if there was a real Charlie Chan? Did Keye ever ask? No! Benson? No! Victor Sen Yung? No. They are believers! They doth not doubt!"

"Gee, Pop, I know about Chang Apana. He was in the same family alliance as me," I say.

"Did you see Orson Welles' little classic, *Touch of Evil,* on the Midnight Lanai Movie, the other night? Between long takes of Danny Kaleikini talking with other Waikiki lounge singers on the merits of one-finger poi over two-finger poi, there was Orson as Hank Quinlan, obscenely fat, fat as your happy Buddha. Fatter!" Pop laughs. "A fat, fat, fat slovenly, unshaven, corrupt but honest cop—honest, mind you!—who solves crimes in the border town of Calexico by arresting the felon, then sticking the evidence on him and using it to convict him. Sergeant Chang Apana was like that."

"Wong the handsome, my opera uncle, you might say, played such a character in Canton after the war. In his return performance he wore a black cowboy hat, and introduced the bullwhip and the six-gun to Cantonese opera. It was something," I say, but who knows who's listening and who's talking now?

Pop mumbles on, lost in the rhythm of his chant, "He bludgeoned and kicked confessions out of the perpetrators of most of the crimes he solved. And like Orson, his instincts were more often than not dead on target. That seems very Zen. Very Buddhist. The people the corrupt cop railroaded really were guilty. And remember Kurosawa's *Seven Samurai*? What a movie! A classic! Remind me to tell you about the time I got drunk with Griffith, sometime. You've heard of D.W. Griffith. We had both just seen *The Seven Samurai.*"

"*Seven Samurai,* Pop?" I say, "I thought Griffith died in 1940, maybe 1949? But I'm sure he died before *Seven Samurai* was made." Got him! I see it in his eyes, fire leaps out, and the doors close. But his voice slippers his words out in dreamy mumbles, as sleepy as before.

"That sequence where the first samurai shaves his head by a stream and dresses himself like a poor Buddhist priest with a shaved head, charges into the hut to kill the hysterical kidnapper and rescue the little baby?" he says. "Remember that? Swoop! Oof! It's all over and out comes the kidnapper in slow motion, gutted with his own sword. Chang Apana did that," Pop says. "The real Charlie Chan! He charged into a whorehouse and saved the working girls from a gang of loonies gone berserk with his bullwhip and six-gun. Four men shot dead. One with his own gun. Chang was shot in the belly, and that's why some say he stayed skinny all his life. Now there's a rootin', tootin' Chinese character who captures your attention."

"Gee, Pop! That's beautiful. I wish you'd say that on *Johnny Carson,*" I say.

"The Star River Buddha," Pop says poking his finger in the air the way he does in the movies to point up a clue.

"What's that, Pop?"

"It's the Star River Rock and whatchamacallit Festival, right? I can't call myself the Buddha of Rock 'n' Roll. But Star River Buddha? I like it."

"Gee, Pop!" I say in character out of an ancient habit. "Charlie Chan, the Star River Buddha. Gee, man, that's hip!"

"Do you know the story of how the Buddha left the world in a flash of light?" he murmurs.

I breathe the swim of marijuana smoke, incense, and simmering chili con carne, with a lot of Pop's secret con, and my mind seems to drift between stations and fizz ghosts of straying broadcasts while Pop's color TV stays crisp on the old black-and-white movie. It looks a little blue on the tube, like the fish in their aquarium.

With the last of his consciousness Pop fades, "But my boys, my Honorable Sons Numbers One, Two, and Three, never heard of Chang Apana." And Pop and Milagro doze off and simmer in their giant pillows and big bean bags and snore like the chili con carne on the stove, with their mouths open. The aquariums gurgle. Their snoring is everything. They look more like brother and sister than strangers who met by chance. I sit slowly down into a pile of big bean bags and giant pillows and sink until they're out of sight over mountains of cushions, and I'm alone with Spencer Tracy on their TV.

Watching this movie one night at one of Benson's Polynesian fantasy eateries, Victor, Number Three Son, asks, "Have you noticed, brother Kwannie, have you noticed the Americans really show what they think of you by who they let pilot planes in the movies?"

"Have I noticed what?"

"Look, you and me and the rest of us are not getting jobs because of the blacks. The blacks are getting all the movie roles and all the jobs because they're out in the streets rioting and looting and all that. But no matter how much the Industry gives the blacks, you don't see any black pilots of P-47 Thunderbolt fighters in the movies. There *was* an all-black fighter squadron in World War II, so it would be easy. But what is it you see? Woody Strode playing some noble slob in the all-black U.S. Cavalry group on trial for raping and murdering a white woman, while Jeffrey Hunter—playing an Army lawyer defending Strode—and a white prosecutor argue racism and civil rights like Tracy and Hepburn arguing over Sidney Poitier marrying their daughter in *Guess Who's Coming to Dinner.*"

"You haven't shown your kids the movie we made with the *Anna May Wong,* have you?" I say.

"I'm afraid to show to it to them. I'm afraid they won't understand how, well, how unusual, how extraordinary, that movie is. I watch it and I don't see us. I don't see Keye and Victor and Benson and Longman, and the others. I see an all Chinese-American crew of a B-24, a plane designed to be a high-altitude bomber, so naturally, they've sent us on *the* low-level bombing mission of all time. Operation Soapsuds renamed Operation Tidal Wave, over the target of oil refineries and cracking plants at Ploesti that supply one-third of all of Germany's oil. I mean, I believe I really flew on that mission, Kwannie, and I can't explain that to the kids. Watching the movie makes me sob like a baby when we hit the heavy flack.

How about coming over to the little house and watching it with me some night?"

"How about *we all* put on leather flying jackets and come over to *my* place and watch it?" I ask too loudly.

"No, I don't want to watch it with Benson. That prick knows I hocked my clubs three years ago. I don't own a set of clubs anymore. And I haven't been getting any jobs in the Industry. Auntie Phoebe doesn't even call me anymore. And Benson, who has always got to show me he buys a new Cadillac every two years and has new suits made in three different countries, calls me up to invite me to play golf so he can show off his new clubs. He knows I have to beg off. And when I beg off, he tells everyone 'Victor is a snob,' can you beat that?"

"You and Benson!" I say in disgust.

"Forget Benson. How about you and me? I think we'd both enjoy *Anna May Wong* more, watching it in each other's company. Bring your family, I'll bring mine. We'll do it at your place. Mine is too small," Victor says and continues on, saying, "No, forget it. You are a real Chinese. And I speak Chinese in the movie and don't want you to embarrass me," he laughs.

He's right. I watch *Anna May Wong* like a raw reel of old home movies. I steep in the flashes of old experienced moments the way an old soldier tries on an old uniform. Alone for the memories.

"So now, tell me what your little woman expects a Chinaman to play in an American movie, Kwannie. Christ walking a tightrope?" Spencer Tracy asks me. The Sons of Chan, Keye, Benson, Victor all doze or stare drunkenly into a sleep lurking in the dark on the other side of the room, just as Pop and Milagro are asleep over the horizon of cushions. Or perhaps they *are* the horizon of cushions.

"At least *Charlie Chan*," I say, "She never says it in just those words, but that's what she means."

The sleepers smile in their sleep and hum. I hear sobs break out in the dark as Spence focuses his close-up on me, sucks on a bit of his lower lip, shakes his head, and says, "How can I tell you how you helped to win the war and brought the future absorption and assimilation of your people closer and closer every time you lived and died? It's very important to the United States of America, Kwannie. The more fondly America cherishes the memory of you dying, the less visible the Chinese in America will be. And the more quickly you'll all be assimilated. You see, it's psychology," he tells me.

"Ahhhhh!" the sons of Chan say in their sleep.

"Psychology. I like it," I say, like Paul Muni in *Counter Attack,* a movie shot by James Wong Howe. The next thing I know, I die in a movie where Spencer Tracy tells the pilots, grim young men in new leather jackets, that "Jap planes can't bank left," and "Jap pilots laugh out loud when they bomb hospitals. The kamikaze pilots aim themselves at American aircraft carriers and battleships and go down screaming original seventeen-syllable poems known as haiku into their radios." What he says strikes me funny. I am a Jap pilot in that movie.

"The *Anna May Wong* was one of the brushed steel silver bombers of Baker's Traveling Circus, in our movie, right?" Victor asks me a few weeks before he dies. "Remember Operation Tidal Wave?"

"It's a movie nobody's ever seen, Victor. Forget it," I tell him. "Cheer up."

"Ploesti. I remember it clearly. We started engines and warmed them up before dawn. I was the copilot. Starting the engines was my job. Our group followed the twenty-nine sandy beige bombers of the 376th Liberandos into the air. I liked that. We were behind the Liberandos! I heard there was a Japanese boy in the crew of one of our group's bombers. A flight engineer and turret gunner, I think. I intended to meet up with him after we flew this Ploesti thing and apologize to him for playing all those Jap spies and pilots. But his plane didn't make it back. *The Red Ass,* I think it was."

"Victor, it was just a movie. We made it in Palm Springs, not North Africa," I say.

"Remember General Bereton giving us that pep talk before the mission? It was outdoors. Remember those funny lightweight

Frank Buck hats we wore? And the flies! I laughs when that freak wind came up and blew the General off the stage." Victor laughs, "Say, Kwannie, remember that plane we saw lose its port wing and drop out of the sky from the Liberandos? Do you know who that was?" Victor asks, and answers himself, "That was the *Wingo Wango,* the lead plane with the mission's lead navigator: plunk! into the Mediterranean Sea. The *Teggie Ann* took over the lead, and led us straight to Bucharest, not Ploesti. What a day!"

"What a day? What a movie, Victor! If only they showed it in America!" I say.

Victor looks up at the ceiling without lifting his head out of his hands and says, "To quote Charlie Chan, the ultimate 'Gee, Pop' in *Charlie Chan in Monte Carlo,* 'Questions are keys to the door of truth.' So, I ask the question: 'Why me, Pop?' What do we say to our kids, eh, kiddo?" Victor laughs, claps his arm around me, and grins.

"Have you shown *The Anna May Wong* to your kids?" Victor asks.

"No. Let 'em find it and watch it after I'm dead," I say. "It's like my ace in the hole. After a lifetime of despising me, they might see us all in that B-24 and think better of me. Maybe give me a posthumous Oscar or Emmy, know what I mean?"

"Come on!" Victor barks. "You're not close with your kids?"

"Are you?" I ask back.

"If you die before me, I'll see that your kids see that movie," Victor says. "If I die before you, will you do the same for me?"

Victor had cats. When he died with the doors and windows closed, the cats drank out of the toilet and ate bits off of Victor for maybe two weeks before they found him. I read about it in *The L.A. Times* before anyone called me. Pernell Roberts the star of the original *Bonanza* that featured Victor playing the ranch cook, recited Shakespeare to a few people over Victor's body.

I get up to stir the chili con carne for something to do while Anlauf Lorane and Milagro sleep, and I hear Spencer Tracy depart from his usual "Jap planes can't bank left" speech. "Yes, in this world there is a season for Charlie Chan to come. And yea a season for Charlie Chan to go. And when the last Charlie breathes his last, his breath shall become the winds and clouds of change over Chinese America. And his voice shall become the thunder," Spencer Tracy says straight into the camera. I step out of the kitchen for a cautious closer look.

"Charlie Chan's left eye shall become the sun of Chinese America, and his right shall become the moon," Spencer Tracy says as if talking to Katherine Hepburn in *Guess Who's Coming to Dinner.* The spoon dripping chili con carne keeps me from moving closer to the TV and I hesitate to return to the kitchen and the pot.

Spencer Tracy tells the pilots, who are about to climb into their B-25 Mitchell twin-engine bombers and hurl themselves full throttle off a carrier at sea and bomb Tokyo, "Charlie Chan's lower body shall become the five great Chinatowns, and 180,000 Chinese restaurants of all colors. His blood shall turn white, then transparent, and become the sweetwater of the rivers and streams of Chinese America. His tendons and veins become the railroads, the bridges and trestles, tunnels and roads between Chinatowns and the suburbs. His flesh becomes topsoil; his skin and the fine hair on his body become the wheat grass, and rice and bamboo, tea, pepper trees, teak, coconut palm, mahogany and camphor wood, larch and pine trees and *bok choy* and *gai lan, doong gwah,* bitter melon, ginger and garlic, sugar cane and taro root. Charlie Chan's teeth and bones shall become the minerals and metals and crystals of geology. Charlie Chan's semen shall become the pearls of Chinese America. His marrow shall become the jade. Each hair of Charlie Chan's head, eyebrows, and Charlie Chan's moustache and beard shall become a shining Oriental star in the Hollywood firmament and praise his name just by shining bright."

"Does this mean I'll get the part?" I ask. "Or are we old men with nothing but hope and nothing happening for the rest of our lives? Will our films disintegrate in the vaults and stop being shown on TV, and my accomplishment, my influence, my reality as Charlie

Chan's Honorable Number Four Son and The Chinaman Who Dies be a faint rumor for centuries, waiting hard proof like the Buddhist monk they say walked from the Grand Canyon across the desert to Central America, teaching Chinese art and science to the Indians of Mexico and to the Mayans? I heard scuba divers discovered two stone anchors in Mexican waters made of stone definitely quarried in China and definitely more than a thousand years old. What do you think of that, Spence?"

But Spence is back in the movie. Thumbs up! The first fully loaded B-25 revs up its engines, strains against the brakes, throws itself off the end of the USS *Hornet,* and scrambles to catch some air and climb.

Part Two: The World

Ulysses: American of Chinese Descent

I am six years old, taking in the way the sunlight falls, the feel of the air, the look of the gnarled, arthritic knobby jointed scrub oak trees alone on expanses of tall grass dried yellow. I am near the house and the trees and the creek and the coyotes of my first memories, the night of my first hail, the night of my first frogs, the night of my first lunar eclipse. I remember the darkness. I remember the child-less retired vaudeville acrobat and his retired silent-screen bit player wife from Florida taking turns calling my name out into the darkness over the gold country. No moon.

"Kwaaaaa-neeee!"

The sky is scary with stars. The frogs stop singing. The big white dog named Guess sticks close by me and pants and dribbles drool off his tongue.

Once a week we drive the road the old woman in the next house says should be paved, into Diamond Springs to buy feed for the chickens, ice for the ice box, and coal for the stove, and pick up the mail from the postal box. Auntie Bea is always behind the wheel. She was a bit player in the silent movies made in Florida. "Not a star like your daddy, my little Chinese Dolly," she says in a voice refined even before sound motion pictures. She gives me a picture of her sharing a dressing room with Beatrice Joyce, a star of the silent movies. What's a silent movie? She honks at every curve. Uncle Jackie never drives. I never ask why. I don't drive either. But I figure I have time to learn.

"What are you doing with a Jap kid?" the one-eyed soldier says in the dim bar by the feed, ice, and coal store. Light glances off the blue of his one eye and the blue of something on his uniform. Auntie Bea and Uncle Jackie are blue-eyed, white-haired, old white people who have had their day in vaudeville and the silent movies and have retired to the California Mother Lode country to live in the wrinkle of yellow foothills, to love each other and raise me. That's what they tell me. That's all I know.

To all who see us three together, it is obvious I am not their child. Their eyes get more blue and glow in the dim light.

"I'm not a Jap kid," I say, "I'm an American of Chinese descent."

The one-eyed soldier's mouth drops open with nothing to say and I see the stuff in his eye socket move the eye that isn't there. The old folks smile. I have no idea what an American of Chinese descent is; it's what Auntie Bea and Uncle Jackie teach me to say when people call me a Jap kid. His one good eye blinks and tears swell up in it and shine. I look for tears in his empty socket. He apologizes. "I'm sorry, kid," he says. World War II is over for him. He asks Uncle Jackie if he can buy me a Coke.

Mom and *Dad* and *Mommy* and *Daddy* are words I hear on the radio shows, but never use, and never ask about.

Ulysses: El Dorado, California, July 4, 1946

It's the Fourth of July. I'm just six years old. Redhaired Uncle Jackie, the retired vaudeville acrobat, says I am a good-looking little man. Auntie Bea, the retired silent-screen bit player, combs my hair carefully. They dress me in my best clothes. Aunt Mercedez reads my palm and tea leaves. Nothing but good luck, she says. Mommy and Daddy are coming to take me for a visit to Oakland. I want to look good. Now I wait outside, wondering where Mommy and Daddy have been. Inside, Aunt Mercedez is making lamb stew. I smell it coming out of the house through the window. When the boys in the back of the pickup truck reach up to pull acorns out of the tree and slingshot them at me, I do not mess my clothes with tears or drool or dirt. The acorns leave no stain. I am the good soldier, stand up straight and don't show them I hurt when the acorns hit me. I keep my clothes clean.

No one tells me I'm never coming back to Mother Lode. Not even the people who take me tell me they mean to keep me away from what I have always known as home, forever.

Ulysses: Kingdoms Rise and Fall, Nations Come and Go

Ma, her four sisters, and their three children, my cousins, two boys and a little girl, and Grandma, live in Grandma's house on Sixth Street, in Oakland. Grandma doesn't like me. The cousins don't let me play with their toys. They don't speak English. There is a large electric train set up on a track in the front room. I ask Ma if I can play with it when the cousins are out playing in the backyard. Ma and the aunts tell me I have to ask Grandma. I have to call her *"Ah-Paw-Paw"* and say *"Ngaw oy nay,"* "I love you," in Chinese. They try to teach me. I don't try to learn. I take a walk outside instead.

I dislike and distrust flattery. I don't try to look good. I get a bad taste in my mouth and want to tear my clothes when people tell me I look good.

I am in the hands of strangers whose language means nothing to me. The only people who speak English are the Negroes and poor white people. Ma doesn't like me talking to them. She doesn't want me to make friends with them. *Kidnapped. Treasure Island.* I'm living the Robert Louis Stevenson adventures I hear dramatized on the radio in the country.

Ulysses: Fool the Emperor and Cross the Sea

The war is over awhile before they bring me to the house on Sixth Street in Chinatown. The boys are coming home.

The aunts pile fresh fruit in front of the statue of Kwan Kung and light sticks of incense, blow the flames out and leave them smoldering in front of the great Kwan ancestor. Our great ancestor is the god of fighters and writers, small businessmen, great and small avengers, and my brother, the hero. They show me old snapshots of a Chinese boy and tell me I look just like him. People say he looks just like Pa. "Junior is more handsome than your handsome father." Ma wants me to like my brother. She wants me to like Pa. She shows me a snapshot of herself and Pa holding a baby she says is me.

What is a brother? My brother, Longman Kwan Jr., The Hero, is home. I don't know anything about brothers. They want me to call Grandma *Paw Paw* and talk Chinese to her. She is a giddily happening pinball off the walls when my brother arrives home from Europe. How come I have one? Ma can't explain. She blushes. She orders me to be nice to my brother because it means a lot to my father. So what's "father" besides a nickname? Just do what she tells me and she'll explain later. She promises. Do this for her. I miss the country. At night, when I hear the trains roll and sing like old wolves, I think of the country. In The Movie About Me, I ride those trains.

Ma stops the car. She clenches and gnashes her teeth and she shakes her head, then nods her head as if arguing with herself. She wants me to like my older brother. For her sake I open the door and step out of the car and say to the only soldier I see, "Hi Hero, I'm your little brother, Ulysses." Ma is right. He does look like Pa. He is more handsome. But I don't look anything like him.

A rickety old woman they call Big Aunt Willy arrives, sitting in a seat that faces backwards in a white limousine, mad to touch and clutch The Hero, Technical Sergeant Longman Kwan Jr. Her clothes don't wrinkle when she moves. All the aunts and Grandma make way for her to say hello.

Poppy, Ma's oldest sister, I call "Big Aunt," but Big Aunt Willy is the Big Aunt of this branch of the Kwan family, grandma's older sister, well married and well heeled. She looks like a cantaloupe with a wig, glasses that make her eyes look big, and big wax lips out of a gumball machine. She is the historian, the collected memory, the master of ceremonies and stage manager of births and deaths. She appears only at the big occasions.

The Chinatown famous pearly whites of Longman Kwan Jr.'s girl-stopping grin are back in Chinatown, and they are all the Kwan sisters and Grandma see for days.

Pa drives up from Hollywood with his agent, Phoebe Koo. Her face looks like a cocoon with eyes, lips, and hair painted on. Powder drifts off of her like the soot off a moth.

Pa hosts a ten-table banquet to show off his first son to the Chinatown bigshots. Pa pays for a busload of Hollywood Chinese to attend. They sit one or two or three stars at every table of ten. Pa calls his first son "Hollywood Junior" and dreams out loud over the food of my first Chinese banquet about the Kwan family becoming the "Chinese Barrymores" of Hollywood. The agent, Phoebe Koo, says The Hero has the youth, the looks, and the voice, and is just what the Industry wants. She is sure she can keep him in enough movie roles to make a very comfortable living right away. Junior isn't interested. Everything disappears but him. The big electric train set in the front room is his. He says it's mine if I want it because we're brothers. I look for it but never see that train set again.

Uncle Morton Chu, Aunt Poppy's husband, comes home in his own khaki uniform of the fearless U.S. Army Signal Corps, with his thumbs hooked in his pockets, his ribbons for signalling from the thick of battles in Alaska and China, and stripes marking him a sergeant first class. And Aunt Azalea's husband, Jim, comes home in his uniform, driving a truck he bought from the Army. He knows better than to say anything at all. Nobody talks about him the way they talk about Mort.

Grandma and the Aunts and Ma all say Uncle Morton is too smart for his pants. I am holding a loop of yarn spread open between my wrists and learning about family. Ma unwinds yarn from around my wrists and rolls it up into a ball. Grandma and the aunts knit and clean bean sprouts and listen to the late afternoon soap operas on the radio. *Mary Noble: Backstage Wife.* We all breathe the smell of two wild ducks being smoked with tea and brown sugar in a pot in the oven. The aunts say they don't want to talk about Poppy, the first sister, being the hostess at Little Lucky's. Poppy says she doesn't mind.

Ma says, "Poppy and the friendly Italian, Little Lucky, are good friends that's all. Poppy made Little Lucky's very popular with the soldiers during the war. Little Lucky was good to Poppy, but a gentleman, always. And Poppy and the family took good care of Christian. He got glasses. Nobody starved or went naked and dirty in the streets. Mort has *nothing to say.*"

My three-year-old nearsighted cousin, Christian, speaks only Chinese, like Henry, Aunt Lily's son, a year younger than me. So I don't talk to my cousins. The aunts say Morton is a weak man. All the sisters so far have married weak men. Only Longman Kwan, the Cantonese opera heartthrob-turned-Hollywood-star, is different. And they sigh as if they all love him and break up giggling and laughing. Ma blushes and they point at her and tell her she's blushing and laugh.

Ma says Pa's weakness is women. Other women. And her mother and sisters nod. Women on the other side of ordinary Chinamen's dreams. Aunt Lily, married to the fourth son of the electric Buddhist church Din Dung family (who was not back from the war yet), says, "Hollywood Kwan is famous in Chinatown as 'The first Chinaman to sleep with Mae West'! Can you believe that? I heard it myself!"

"The first!" Ma yelps, "How many Chinamen has she slept with?"

"Wasn't he discovered by Mae West?" Lily asks.

"Yeah? Doing what?" Aunt Azalea laughs. Her husband, Uncle Jim, is outside with Uncle Mort scraping and puttying Grandma's house for painting. I hear them in the breezeway between houses, muttering the same words over and over "Putt-teee putt-teee! Seeement mixah!" together.

Ma says, "Big sister Poppy's husband, Mort, would never dare dream of sleeping with Mae West. He'd wet the bed and wake up before he'd dream such a thing!" and the aunts laugh until tears come to their eyes and they push each other around.

Ulysses: The Sea and the Jungle

I'm standing in the street in front of Grandma's house with Uncle Morton Chu. He points to a building with a Japanese roof on blocks and wheels, inching down the street, and he slaps me across the face hard. "The Japanese are coming back to Oakland. That is their Buddhist temple," he says without telling me where the Japanese have been. I have never seen a building on wheels before.

"Why did you hit me?" I ask, and he says he read it in H.M. Thomlinson's *The Sea and the Jungle*. An old book by a British banker who goes to sea. His father slapped him when he was four or five and told him not to forget he saw the Queen in the year of Queen Victoria's silver jubilee, and H.M. Thomlinson never forgot.

Until now, nothing like the Queen passing by in her royal coach during her silver jubilee had happened when Uncle Mort was with his son Christian or any of the cousins. So he slaps *me*. And it works. I don't forget the Japanese coming back to Oakland, shoving their Buddhist temple down Sixth Street, or Uncle Morton Chu taking his reading too seriously.

I don't forget the name H.M. Thomlinson. I find the book on a shelf in a used bookstore on the borderland of pawnshops, amusement centers, tattoo parlors, all-night movies, hotdog stands, and Gypsy fortunetellers between Chinatown, the Mexicans, and uptown. I come back to the bookstore and read it a little at a time. A boy dreams of going to sea and exploring the jungle. He grows up to be a banker. His friend the sea captain bets him two men will not climb onto a trolley car before it passes under the banker's window. If the captain wins the bet, the banker has to go to sea as one of the ship's officers. One man gets on the trolley. Before the car passes under the window, the captain runs out of the banker's rooms, down the stairs, and jumps on. And the banker loses a bet and goes to sea and travels up the Amazon in a ship, his boyhood dream come true.

I am under the house, alone. Under the joists. Among the posts and piers that hold the old house up. A little sun reflecting off the house next door melts through the dusty glass of a little window on either side of the house. I get in through one of them, and I am surprised to find a mass of rotting, faded silk and bamboo. It is the remains of a huge lantern. A tower of balconies. Around each balcony, costumed puppets of opera characters stand and lean and fall out of the ruins of the lantern. The mayonnaise light through the little fake windows catches a ghost of fire in the skin of the lantern, and the faint glow seems to come from inside. The old redheaded acrobat taught me to tell the real from the fake in the dark, how to read the flags of the world, the maps of World War II, and plans for rocking horses and outhouses in *Popular Mechanics* magazine. Uncle Jackie taught me the theory of using a chisel, and how to hammer a nail, use a handsaw, and cut curves with a coping saw. The old man shuddered and pulled his lips back low from his lower teeth and woofed like a dog at the thought of me handling a chisel or a screwdriver at my age. I think he was worried about my eyes. When I find the faintly glowing lantern, I know I have found the most Chinese thing I have ever seen in my life. I see to the bamboo bones and have a sense of what it looked like whole and how it worked from looking it over.

The colors of the costumes are faded. I find fresh color in the folds. The yellowish skin of the lantern is translucent and thin and veined like the stuff of dragonfly wings. The puppets have simply painted faces, and the stroked and dotted eyes still have penetrating gazes. The red of the women's lips are paled pinkish shadows of distant soaring birds and look more real that way than they probably did bright red. Some of the women wear helmets with tinsel tassels and still-trembling tinsel springs. The bearded men have faces covered with different colors and designs. War paint, maybe. The puppets are all attached, standing on the bamboo arms of a huge pinwheel that used to turn when the heat from the lamps inside passed up the lantern and out the top. And the puppets used to parade round and round. Where did this thing come from? It's too big for any of the rooms of this house. I wonder if they threw it away. I wonder if I can take it. I have no place to put it.

Grandma packs me and Aunt Peony's boy Henry and Aunt Poppy's boy Christian who speak no English off to school with the two Negro girls from across the street. She gives us each a cookie. One of the girls is named Sylvia. I love Sylvia. She is the first girl to give me the eye, to smile up bright and look for me at the sound of my name. She is the first to come looking for me, determined to find me and hold my hand and talk to me and like me. The two girls take me and my cousins across the street for breakfast at their house, in their kitchen. They believe my family is so poor all we have for breakfast is a cookie. I am strange to the Chinese of my family, and strange to Sylvia's family, and am the stranger in town, the stranger in the family ever since.

Ulysses: *Charlie Chan Is Superman*

Pa is never home. Home for Ma is Grandma's house. Grandma's house is full of Ma and three of her four sisters, the four famous Kwan sisters of Oakland. Perhaps they're why Pa never comes home. We all have the family name of the god of war, Kwan Kung. Kwan Kung is a statue in the shrine on the mantle of the gas fireplace in Grandma's front room. They say Kwan Kung is the greatest Kwan in the Kwan family. Ma says Kwan Kung is more like the Chinese John Wayne. Her big sister, Big Aunt Poppy, says he looks more like the Chinese Clark Gable. When the sisters are together with Grandma and Uncle Mort and Uncle Jim, they call themselves the Eight Immortals and giggle. I don't know what they're talking about.

Ma says Pa used to play Lowe Bay, Kwan Kung's blood brother, in the Cantonese opera, because he was so handsome. She expects to impress me with this. If Pa is never home, I can still always see him. She takes me to the movies, a Charlie Chan double bill. She brings a framed photograph of the two of them walking across the

Golden Gate Bridge. Ma wants me to laugh when we see Number Four Son say, "Gee, Pop," and "Gosh, Pop."

Ma buys the restaurant concession at the Hotel Westlake Eclipse, a residence and transient hotel a couple of blocks away from Lake Merritt in Oakland. This is a nice clean hotel where old folks come to die while living for their children to come visit and join them for dinner in the dining room on holidays.

We move into rooms above the big hotel kitchen. A room for Ma and Pa, a room for me, a room Ma sets aside as a "sitting room," a room for the dishwasher, and a bathroom at the end of the hall. Pa visits and spends a few days at Chinese New Year's time, in May, during the round of tong New Year's spring banquets in San Francisco and Oakland. Longman Jr., The Hero, always has a train to work and never goes to Pa's Chinese banquets. When The Hero comes by with his family for the Chinese dinner that the dishwasher makes for us after the restaurant closes, Ma says Pa is proud to be invited to sit at a front table and to be asked to speak at the banquets of the most powerful tongs running San Francisco, Oakland, and Sacramento. "Your father would really be so proud to have us all there as a family to see how the bigshots treat him like a bigshot," Ma says.

The Hero always says he'll think about it but never goes. Pa doesn't care if I go. I don't know Chinese. I don't know China-town. I don't know tongs. I won't know how to act. I don't even look Chinese anymore. But I'm getting to understand every language I hear when people talk about me.

Ma dresses me up, combs my hair, makes Pa tie my tie. I watch his face and his eyes when they're close to me. He breathes through clenched teeth. Ma smiles a lot. She loves Chinese banquets, she says, when we arrive there.

Not once do I come close to saying, "Gosh, Pop!" or "Gee, Pop!" She promises to laugh if I do. Please say, "Gee, Pop!" just for her. She so badly wants to laugh, she says. I won't say it. I'm shaking my head no, no, no, when I bump into Manuel the busboy.

The gallon of boiling water from the coffee urn slips from his hands onto my left shoulder and I drop to the cement floor of the hotel kitchen and hop around on my hands and knees like a wind-up toy, hop hop round and round and bark like a dog at all the waitresses and the dishwasher and the cooks yelling at me or betting on me or reaching for me. I can't tell and can't talk.

Ma reaches for me, fights me, grabs me, runs me through the dining room, through the hotel lobby and down the street to the little gynecological hospital a few doors down Jackson Street. There's a long narrow path of flat cement blocks through a lawn to the archway made of round rocks the size of grapefruit. The hospital looks like a house in the woods. The letters of the neon sign on the roof are blue, with a foggy white neon border around them.

The doctor in the white coat tells Ma to hold me tight. He cuts my shirt off. My skin comes off with the shirt. Lots of my skin off my chest, from my left shoulder across and my right shoulder and part way down my back. What's left hurts. I don't cry. The doctor dips his hand into a large can labeled Unguentine and scoops out a yellow goo. It hurts. I pant like a dog again. I can't stand it. I growl at the doctor. He jumps back as if I'm about to bite him. Ma laughs and sniffles. She slaps my arm lightly. "That's for scaring the doctor," she says and gags back a laugh.

The doctor says, "That's all right, as long as he doesn't bite . . ."

"I knew you were going to say that," Ma trills and they chuckle. He finishes slathering ointment over the burn. He washes and dries his hands and bandages me with gauze and wide strips of white adhesive tape.

As we're walking out of the hospital Ma falls and breaks her ankle, so we turn around and I help her hop back in.

That night I have a bad dream that gets worse every time I have it. It's always the same dream. And it gets worse and worse.

I am Superman flying low and slow in the grit and simmering shadows of the low brick and wooden buildings of Chinatown, Oakland, California, on a rainy afternoon in 1949. Huge clouds move overhead like deep-fried mountains surfing on chicken-fried steaks. It's so cold the sky sizzles. The old ladies of the old Victorian houses, recently painted in grays and yellows, rush from shadowy doorways to open storefronts, shopping for the after five o'clock sale, before the men and women clacking their beads throw the remains into the steel cans of wet creamy garbage. The old women in their black coats, black shoes, and slippers, and similarly bunned hair and gold teeth, hop and flit like birds through the boxes of greens on display on the sidewalks.

I fly low with my eyes about as high off the ground as their knees. I see their knees. They have their nylon stockings stopped in little rolls just below their knees, under the long skirts of their black *cheongsams*. I can only fly very low and very slow. My red cape drags on the sidewalk. Old women trip on it and hurt themselves, hitting their shins on my ribs of steel. I strain for height. I stretch and clench my teeth for height. Oh, to be fast! To be high! My arms stick out straight in front of me. My toes point out back. I am shaped for flight!

Charlie Chan as Superman has seriously limited superpowers. Being shot from Chinatown to earth is not the same as being shot from Krypton. This is the wrong movie. I can't wake up. Very slow and very low, I fly on into uptown. Oakland. It's the last seven shopping days before Christmas. The stores are open late. Traffic stops for me. Cars honk their horns.

There is my uncle Morton Chu's shiny maroon 1949 one-eyed four-door Ford. All the Christmas shoppers laugh at it. No one notices him when he comes home from World War II after The Hero, the prince of the family, my older brother, Longman Kwan Jr. I give him a look as I fly slowly across the street against the light and bat my eyes in Morse code, telling him I'd like to fly over to his one-eyed '49 Ford, to get in and let him drive me home, but I can't.

A dog trots alongside my outstretched flight and pants in my face. I bump into the legs of Christmas shoppers. Some trip on my dragging cape. Some hurt themselves kicking me. I want Oakland to run out, fall away from under me, give me height by going downhill under my level flight. Let me fly!

If I had never been Charlie Chan, I would be fast now. I would be high. I should wake up wetting the bed here. This is where I wake up. This has to be a dream I have dreamed before. And clumps of dirt fall off my arms. I feel an icy wind wolfing on the dead flesh of my hands and arms. It hurts. My fingers move in the air, fingering the cold painful emptiness. Owoooo! Hear that wolf? I miss the coyotes Aunt Mercedez said were wolves when we slept outdoors under the oak tree by her house.

Ice seals the twigs, the branches and trunks of all the trees as if they're vacuum-sealed in cellophane. I do not breathe. No steam comes from my nose or mouth. I am the corpse of the last white man to play Charlie Chan, risen from the grave. I would rather have wet the bed. It hurts. I can't wake up. Wrong movie. I am dead and stand up—all rotten hurt inside, every bit of rotten marrow, bone and muscle, and I am so hungry. So hungry.

The sisters swat at Ma and joke about her ankle, telling each other about her transcendent heroism on the nights the family plays mah-jong or poker at Longman Jr.'s. Ma is such a tightwad when she doesn't have to be, they say. The Hero shakes his head at the thought of what Ma eats when she eats alone. The Hero and the sisters buy Ma a crutch built like a car out of steel and they call her "Iron Crutch."

Ulysses: Oakland, California, July 4, 1951

Under the big oak tree old Chinamen play Chinese chess, wearing hats and watching the border like thieves, for those who cross between Chinatown and the Oakland pawnshops, for the patrons of the cheap all-night movies and the café serving Chinese American chop suey, and for the Gypsy fortuneteller palm reader that comes and goes from one storefront to another. As I walk through the park, they perk up and shout at me.

"*Wuhay! Hey, ah-Kid! Hey!* Where you gone, kid?" one shouts and the others look up from their seats and grin their empty gums and occasional teeth at me.

"Movie! Fox Oakland!" I shout back.

"What movie!" the old man with the loudest voice shouts across the dying cut grass. The sun is blood red. The sky shines like the bottom of a new steel pot.

"*David and Bathsheba, ah-Bok.* Ah-Gregory Peckery and Susan Layward, *wahhh!* I hear she shows tit in this movie."

"They don't show no titty in any movie they let you see, kid!" the loud old man shouts. "You know why? You Charlie Chan's grandson!" They laugh from way back there.

Independence Day. The Fourth of July. Pa comes home every Fourth for the clan picnic on the closest Sunday to the holiday and is always nervous.

One year they argue. I'm eleven. We are living in the rooms above the kitchens of the Hotel Westlake Eclipse on the west side of Lake Merritt. Hollywood Junior is working a train, earning triple-time, and won't be coming to the picnic. Triple Time. Pa is impressed.

Junior hates the Fourth of July. He was born on the Tenth of October, the tenth day of the tenth month. Double Ten Day. Chinese Independence Day. The family loves it. Pa loves it. Junior hates Double Ten Day with Pa, the tongs, and the Chinese Nationalist Party. He hates the Fourth of July with the family and Pa's Hollywood Chinese friends with funny eyes and funny smiles showing off at the tong picnics. Hollywood Junior hates Hollywood and the nickname "Hollywood Junior," but Pa loves it.

Junior hates the Chinese in Hollywood movies. He likes Hollywood *history* movies, movies with no Chinese, without even the *word* "China" in them. *Captain Horatio Hornblower,* starring Gregory Peck and Virginia Mayo, and *The World in His Arms,* starring Gregory Peck and Ann Blyth, movies on old sailing ships set in the distant past, those are his kind of movies. He wants to be a railroad *conductor*. He's taken the conductor's test. And passed. Now he stands in line waiting for a slot to open on the conductors Extra Board as he works boss brakeman on the "hot ice express" eastbound every morning from Oakland to Roseville and rolls back in on the westbound "auto parts special." Two trips a day. Plus Caboose rate. Pie money. Air rate. Radio rate. Thanks to the union he gets another dollar a trip—the radio rate—for being responsible for a piece of equipment not covered in the original contract: the two-way radio. Before the two-way radio, the caboose and locomotive would have had to signal each other with whistle signals as complex as Morse code. "Today's railroad," he says. "Easy job." He's home with the family every day. All the money and benefits of a bank teller, a school teacher, and college professor combined. He is home on the railroad.

He's married to a woman nobody in the family likes. He has daughters just seven and eight years younger than me. He lives in his own house, has his own life. He doesn't want to go to college anymore. He doesn't want to be the first Chinaman movie star in history to kiss Marilyn Monroe on the mouth in a close-up. He tells me that when I'm in high school, he'll help me get a summer job as a relief yard clerk, a mudhop. I can keep the job longer than the summer and move out of the house, make a transfer to road service if I feel like it, and live alone instead of running away from home all the time.

Ma encourages me to strip to my shorts and play in the water with the kids. I don't swim. I don't like the water since the day I spent trying to learn to swim in a cow pond bottomed with cow plop and full of red watersnakes. She wants me to learn Chinese, play with other kids, make friends, in the water. She sits with Pa, waves at me and takes his arm. They sit on the grass, in the sun. The wives of the tong men smile at him. I slip on the muddy edge of a drop off and go down, gulp water, hear water galloping cloppity cloppity wild horses on cobblestone streets, and my own voice blubbing nonsense. There's a whoosh in my ears as I break through the top of the water, open my eyes to glimpse my father, see him grin and laugh at me as I go down again. I kick. The brown sandy water gets darker as I sink. Streaks of sun melt into outlines of the water's musculature. I'm up again and see Chinese of every size swimming around me yelling at me. I glimpse my father laughing. His capped teeth flash. Ma doesn't see me yet, she's still in *her* movie about an American Fourth of July picnic.

Back in Oakland later that night for the fireworks over Lake Merritt. Ma and Pa aren't talking to each other again. It's about me. He doesn't see enough of me, she says. I only see him die in the movies. She wants him to love me. She wants me to have a father. "Go ahead, call him Pop, son," she says, touching my face. "You know, how he wants to be the first Chinese to play Charlie Chan. So how about calling him Pop, my Honorable Number Two Son?"

"Number One is piss. Number Two is shit," I say, and she flushes red in the face. She clenches and gnashes her teeth. "Please, don't get smart with me, young man."

He takes me out alone, down to Lake Merritt to watch the fireworks. We are on a huge lawn by the Oakland Auditorium. The spent bombs drift down over us, floating lower and lower on little blossoming white parachutes. Small patchy crowds look up and chase the parachutes as they silently descend, some still sparkling. One lands on a puddle of spilled gasoline at the gas station across the street and as flames unfold like raging butterfly wings, people jump from their cars and run. I look up to see one of the little parachutes low down, very close to me, as huge scrawls of flame wriggle from the gas station like colored flowers on lingerie. I can almost reach the parachute with a jump. "Come on, Pop!" I say, remembering to call him "Pop" like Ma made me promise. I run closer as it falls closer to the ground, but then I am run over. Feet all over my back. I look up. I get up and look back. Pa stands and watches. He hasn't moved. I want to go home. The visit with the Chinese is over. I want to go home.

"Wuhay! Ah-Kid-doy-ahhhhhh!" the loud old man shouts, "Hey! Kid! Where're you gone?"

"I go show! See a movie!"

"What movie, kid?"

"Samson and Delilah! Victor Mature! Heddy Lamar!"

"Wuhay! Where you learn talky de Ninglisses likee dat, kid? You Japanee boy? *Huh yut boon doy?"*

Benedict Han: Chinese School

Benedict Han, Ulysses S. Kwan, Diego Chang, early 1950s. In the afternoon, after American school, we went to Ninth Street in Oakland's Chinatown and attended Chinese school in the wooden Chinese Nationalist Party Headquarters building, and hated it. We said we hated it, but the truth is, we enjoyed it. Chinese school was where we became friends for life. Chinese school was where our friendship became famous.

Baldheaded Wong, the Chinese teacher, had what Ulysses said was a "military bearing." Ulysses had read that phrase in a Sherlock Holmes story and it seemed to fit the monstrous baldheaded Wong. The Chinese teacher wore tight three-piece suits with a gold watch and chain. He slapped our hands with a studded ruler and whipped our bottoms and legs with a bamboo feather duster.

I never got whipped. I did the lessons. But I was in the process of forgetting, losing Chinese, and did the lessons with less and less proficiency. Diego did the lessons with ease. He was a natural at Chinese. Wong whipped Ulysses often. Ulysses failed in reciting his lessons and failed to answer questions in Chinese, when called on. When he went to use the toilet in the back room, he left the toilet seat up and didn't wipe his dribbles from the floor. But Wong the Emperor never made him cry. The one phrase we understood in Chinese forever, because Wong the Emperor said it so often to

Ulysses at the end of every frequent beating, was "Don't look at me like that."

"He thinks I'm a camera taking his picture," Ulysses said, "I'm like a magic box catching his soul."

After school Diego took us to the back of a used bookstore and showed us a stack of nudist magazines with purple pictures of nude women. Ulysses looked around and found stacks of old Air Trails and *Model Airplane News* and *American Modeler* magazines full of plans and pictures of little rubber-band-powered model airplanes people made in the 1930s and '40s.

I didn't particularly mind being sent to Chinese school after our day at American public school was over. But in addition to the two dollars a month Wong received for each student, he also expected a carton of cigarettes from the lower grade students and a bottle of Scotch from the seniors at Christmas time. The Emperor Wong, we called him. Generations of American-born Chinese had hated him, Aunt Hyacinth said. Wong had also been her Chinese teacher when she went to Chinese school in the afternoons of *her* childhood.

Wong wore rimless glasses, and gave the lasting impression of having no hair at all. No eyebrows. No eyelashes. No hair in his nose. No lips. He had a beak. Ulysses said he had a beak, and I saw he had a beak instead of lips from then on. He walked like the sinister yellow military man Ulysses' father tried so hard to play in the movies.

"After 18,000 years, Poon Goo the creator of the earth, sun and moon, woke up inside an egg with his axe," recited the Emperor Wong.

"Where did he get the axe?" Ulysses interrupted in his horribly American-accented approximations of Cantonese.

"He had no memory of how he came to possess an axe," the Chinese teacher answered.

"How did he get in the egg?"

"Nor had he any memory of from whence he came."

Just like me, I thought. The giant in the egg with an axe, it struck me. He *was* just like me.

Wong the Emperor called Ulysses to step up on the platform, up to Wong's desk, and ordered Ulysses to hold out his hand. For some reason Ulysses held his hand out palm down. Wong picked up his studded ruler and whacked the back of Ulysses' hand. Instead of a meaty slap, the ruler hit with a hard crack that made everyone in class clench their teeth and close their eyes.

"Any more stupid questions?" the Chinese teacher asked.

"How did he know 18,000 years had passed?"

Wong gave Ulysses a hard cold stare. Ulysses grinned and said, "You asked for a stupid question. If you can't answer it, just say so. You're the teacher."

"I'm ordering you to stand right where you are until I am finished with the lesson," Wong said. This was a terrible punishment. Only the oldest boys avoided wetting their pants when standing next to the teacher's desk at the head of the class on the very spot Wong ordered Ulysses to stand. Wong always continued the lesson as they pissed. The sooner they lost control of their piss, the greater the contempt and scorn that chilled Wong's eyes and curled his lip. Only when they stopped and apologized for wetting his platform did he acknowledge them. First they went to the corner and picked up a bucket of sawdust and a broom, then they walked back to the front of the classroom and covered the puddle of urine with sawdust until the sawdust stopped turning dark with sopped up piss. And only then would Wong the Chinese teacher allow the offending boy to go to the back room and to clean himself up as best he could.

"When Poon Goo, the giant, broke out of his egg with his axe, he used his hands and feet and body to separate the wet stuff of the egg from the gooey stuff, creating the sky and the earth. And for the next 18,000 years, the giant struggled with his hands and feet and whole body to keep them separate, until they hardened and solidified."

Ulysses did not wet his pants. Wong paused and glanced at him.

"Then the giant died. One eye became the sun. The other eye became the moon. His hair became forests. His skin and other parts became mountains, continents, rivers, seas, oceans. The earth was a beautiful place to live now, but there were no living things."

The girls in class liked the fairy tales. They liked the rhyme and sing-song rhythm used in the telling of the story. When they recited, Wong seemed to be transported to paradise. He never slapped or whipped a girl. Ulysses tried to memorize the lessons at the last minute and mostly always failed, whether at reciting line-by-line solo, or in a round of students, each reciting a line in turn. And he got his hands slapped every time he missed.

Wong turned to see if Ulysses was making faces behind his back before continuing. When a girl sitting next to the door to the back room giggled, Wong turned suddenly and whipped Ulysses across his legs with the bamboo feather duster. Everyone knew the thin stalk of bamboo hurt. But he didn't cry. He didn't wet his pants.

"Nur Waw, the giant's beautiful sister, descended to earth. On her first day on earth, she created chickens. The second day she created dogs. The third day she created pigs. The fourth day she created sheep. The fifth day she created the horse. The sixth day she created oxen. The seventh day she was lonely for her own kind. She made a baby girl out of mud that came to life and called her 'Mama.' She wanted to make babies faster than one by one by hand. She cut a stalk of bamboo, dipped it into the mud, and whipped the bamboo switch this way and that. The mud splats that fell on leaves became babies with the family name 'Leaf.' The mud splats on limbs become babies with the family name 'Limb.' The mud splats on grass became babies with the family name 'Grass.'

"The earth was threatened by masses of water falling from a hole in the sky. Nur Waw melted together colored rocks from the bottoms of rivers and pressed the molten mass into the break in the sky with her bare hands. She killed a giant turtle, cut off its legs, and used them to prop up the sky. The sky has not fallen since," Wong said.

The girls who got good grades in Chinese school tittered.

Ulysses laughed. Baldheaded Wong turned. "The sky has not fallen since. Very funny, Wong Sin Sahng. I just had to laugh," Ulysses said. "This is America."

The girls laughed and Wong whipped Ulysses across the legs again and ordered him to turn around and face the blackboard.

"A black dragon stirred up floods that threatened the Yellow River Valley. Nur Waw killed the dragon and all the life-threatening beasts. To stop and turn the floodwaters, she burned the grass and reeds along the riverbank, mixed the ashes with water, and built a wall. She then invented a musical instrument, taught people to play it, and retired."

I came to the United States in an egg. I had no memory of China. The egg and the giant were one. He was his own food and water, his own air, his house. The egg was like our room over the kitchens of the Westlake Eclipse. Ulysses asked my mother's "opera man," Buck, who was always in front of the stove, to make us anything we wanted to eat, American food, Chinese food for Americans off the daily menu. After we carried our dinners to our room, we never had to leave, except to use the toilet at the end of the hall. Otherwise we had everything we needed for life and entertainment in our room. Radio. Ulysses had his loft workshop. I had my bed and desk and books.

Benedict Han: The Brothers of the Oath of the Peach Garden

Ah yeah mo die yee. Muklan mo jerng hing. Word by word, sound by sound, with the precision of military drill, the Emperor Wong marched the "Ballad of Muklan" in and marched it out of our mouths with his brass-studded wooden ruler. *Father has no grown sons. Muklan has no older brother.* He beat the poem into our memory. I recited it with the class in pairs, trading lines, and solo for a year before I knew what it meant.

Yurn wooey see ngawn mah. Choong chee tai yeah jing. Leave me buy a horse and saddle to ride in Father's place. He asked why we laughed when we recited the "Ballad of Muklan," and said, "Life is war. Everyone is born a soldier. Romantic love, pure love, is an alliance of fighters, back to back, fighting off the universe. Thus, after twelve years of war fighting back to back with her ally, Muklan goes home." Muklan takes off her armor of recent times and dresses her hair and puts on the gowns of old times. She steps out of the door dressed in finery, her hair in cloudy tresses. Her ally is agog!" he recited with a hint of tears in his eyes and a hoarseness in his throat. Shoulder to shoulder in twelve years of war, he never knew Muklan was a girl. Toong hung sup yee nien. But ji Muklan see nur long. It was a pure, classic expression of Chinese romantic love.

And the closing quatrain was innocence and pure sex, childish love hopping with rabbits. "Hoong toe gerk hawk sawk. Chee toe ngon muhi lay. Lerng toe bong day jow. Ngawn lung biin gaw see hoong chee. The he-rabbit tucks his feet in to sit. The she-rabbit dims her shiny eye. Two rabbits running side by side. Who can see which is the he and which is the she?"

Ulysses made vomiting noises and staggered off to the toilet. Wong whipped him, and his contempt seethed over the American-born scum's irreparable lack of Chinese couth, good sense, and honor. He loathed explaining the first chapter of the *Romance of the Three Kingdoms* to us because we were American born and incapable of understanding.

The Han dynasty had lost virtue and was collapsing. Cho Cho, a corrupt and ambitious soldier-bureaucrat, was prime minister. He betrayed the Han and tried to take over the throne for himself. Lowe Bay, the white faced, a member of the imperial family of the Han, read the imperial call posted in the square for men-at-arms to save Han China. He sighed a famous sigh. Chang Fay, a black-faced man of property and money, heard the sigh. While they got acquainted at the closest tavern, the bearded eight-foot-tall red-faced fugitive, Kwan Kung, blotted out the light in the doorway, demanding wine because he had to hurry on to town, join the army, and save China.

Chang invited Lowe and Kwan to his peach garden, where the

peaches were in bloom, to talk about saving China. In Chang's peach garden they swore an oath of blood brotherhood. "We three, Lowe Bay, Kwan Yu, and Chang Fay swear we are brothers, though we come from different families. We swear the cause of one is the cause of all. We will rescue each other from trouble and help each other in danger. We swear to serve China and save the people. We do not ask to be born on the same day but we look forward to dying on the same day. May all of heaven and earth turn against any one who breaks this oath."

Our announcement that we three were the three brothers in the Chinese book made the Chinese teacher spit pent-up anger. But we were the Brothers of the Oath of the Peach Garden, we were the Three Musketeers. "One for all, and all for one!" We swore the oath of the peach garden in perfect Cantonese to piss off the Chinese teacher, who sneered at us and called us stupid American-born punks.

I was Lowe Bay, the first brother, the pretender to the throne of the Han, because my mother was Orchid Han—the opera star who turned her company into a guerilla band to fight the Japanese in Kwangtung—and her current husband was Buck, an opera man known as "the Chinese Rudy Vallee" for being one of the most beloved of the opera stars. The Chinese Rudy Vallee was also famous in Cantonese opera gossip for killing my father under mysterious circumstances while in China. That fact was all I retained of the early years of my life in China. I don't remember China. Not one memory. Not one face. Not one fairy tale. Not even a lullaby.

From the beginning, I was Chinese royalty in America. Opera people, war heroes, refugees. I stood on the cement floor of the huge kitchen of the Hotel Westlake Eclipse, with Mother and her opera man. That's where it feels as if I was born. Recorded history begins with me standing there on the kitchen floor. My first permanent sensation of America was cement under my feet. The cement seemed to go down for miles. I lived here now. From that moment on, China was another lifetime, another life, somebody else, somebody dead. Ulysses' mother ran the restaurant concession at the hotel, lived in rooms on the floor above the kitchen, and shared a bathroom at the end of the hall. My mother was so special in the Chinese-speaking world, Ulysses' father, the Hollywood Chinese movie star Longman Kwan, trained up from Hollywood to welcome us. She was the star of opera I intended never to hear. She was a guerilla hero from a war that was over. I was a prince of a country that didn't exist.

The opera man, my mother's second husband (I refused to call him "stepfather"), worked at the hotel awhile as an apprentice chef. Ulysses' mother taught him how to cook American food and bake American pastries, pies, and cakes. Orchid Han, the opera heroine of World War II, waited on tables and learned the restaurant business from Aunt Hyacinth. We all lived together in the rooms above the kitchen until my family was ready to move on and start our own restaurant in New York.

Ulysses' father, Longman Kwan, was an opera man who had made a career of playing Chinese and Japanese of all kinds and all ages in Hollywood movies. He offered to introduce his opera brother and sister to his powerful Hollywood agent. After all, he said, there was no reason they should not become as famous as he had. But Buck, my mother's opera man, laughed and said he was too ugly to be in the movies. He wanted to make another batch of popovers to see if he had internalized them.

"Benedict Han has never been to an American movie," Auntie Hyacinth, Ulysses' mother, said. "Why don't you boys go to a movie?" and Ulysses called Diego Chang, and we went to see *Shane,* my first American movie, my first western. Not the panting, short-of-breath Palance huffing and puffing emotion, but the quiet Jack Palance who was so pissed and so sure, and so cool, he didn't bother breathing, didn't come all the way to life, didn't make a sound when he spoke, didn't care if you heard him or not. His eyes were dark stars. Elisha Cook Jr. looked into them too deeply and walleyed as Palance oozed his gun hand into a black glove. Ooh, Diego liked that. And the way Jack Palance oozed off on his horse, as smooth as if he was being shit from assholes in the sky.

"You know where I seen Jack Palance before?" Diego snapped all over with an insight.

"How could you see him before?" Ulysses challenged.

"He's Fu Manchu with balls. I mean, see Jack Palance acting more sissy. Presto! Fu Manchu! See?"

"Yeah, I see," Ulysses said.

I never forgot Diego's insight into Jack Palance and Fu Manchu.

Ulysses S. Kwan was the second brother of the oath of the peach garden because his name was Kwan, like Kwan Kung, and because he was always running away from home. Ulysses was raised by an old white couple and was out of place in Chinatown. When he walked around the neighborhood people yelled at him, *"Wuhay! Ah-Yut Boon Doy ahhh!* Hey, Japanese boy!"

Ulysses built things in his room. When I moved into Ulysses' room, Ulysses brought lumber upstairs and built a bed for me, an elevated platform that formed a second floor, a bed and a workbench on the platform and a ladder leading up to the platform. Ulysses spent most of his time home up there making model airplanes. He spoke English like an American. There was nothing Chinese in Ulysses' voice. When his Chinese sounded American, the Chinese teacher laughed at him. But Ulysses was American, all-American and unafraid. No one told him what to do. He did what he wanted. I didn't understand why he would run away. For a while the people at the restaurant always reassured each other— Ulysses had only run away to his older brother's house, after all, they were pals, they said. But I knew they were not pals. And when Ulysses ran away from home, he ran away from home. When they finally called Longman Jr.'s house, Longman Jr. was out being a brakeman on the railroad, and no one there had known Ulysses had run away from home again. Once I suggested Ulysses might have run to his father in Hollywood, and Auntie Hyacinth started laughing and couldn't stop. Sometimes Ulysses came home by himself. Sometimes the police brought him home.

Ulysses said he got to stay out late at night by himself by telling his mother he had gone to a Charlie Chan movie to show his American-school report card to his father. He said he hated his father's movies, but his mother dragged him along to see them, and my family and I were doomed to see them as long we stayed with the Kwan family.

But Ulysses didn't show his report cards to his father. Longman Kwan wasn't in any movies that Ulysses wanted to see. He showed his report cards to Spencer Tracy. Ulysses claimed his mother hated that because only she knew the right way to show his report cards to Spencer Tracy. When she did it, Spencer Tracy stopped and looked out of the movie into the theater at his mother, looked at his report card, and read it. Then he spoke to her, Ulysses said. I didn't believe him.

"It happened," Ulysses said. "It didn't always happen, but it happened." His father never stopped in his movies to talk back to him, but Ulysses told Aunt Hyacinth that he did, and Ulysses said that she believed him.

I liked Ulysses' father. He had a wonderful sense of humor. He was generous. I liked Charlie Chan's Number Four Son. I liked the Charlie Chan movies. They were so American. Number Four Son was so American.

I was surprised Ulysses admitted to me that he lied to his mother. "Why not?" he answered, since I had talked to him about my secret hatred of my mother's opera man. "Same thing," he said.

Diego Chang, who took the train over from San Francisco every day after his American school, was Chang Fay, the third brother of the oath. He knew where to find the best snack food in Chinatown before Chinese school and how to hustle it free or cheap.

Except for the other Brothers of the Oath, all of Diego's friends in San Francisco were Negroes. He lived above a Chinese restaurant on a Negro street, in a Negro neighborhood.

Diego talked like Negroes. He said he liked Negroes better than *lofan*. He said the Negroes were "really American." I didn't know what he meant by that and didn't want to. He confused and angered me, but no matter how frustrated I became with Diego, he never stopped liking me because he, and his father the restauranteur in the Fillmore, and his mother (who bragged about her husband, the tong bigshot from Boston, who had been sent to San Antonio, Texas to conclude sensitive tong business), loved the opera and knew all the stories of heroes the operas told. It didn't matter that I didn't recall the opera or that I did not go to the opera clubs on weekends with my mother and her opera man—Diego insisted I was his best friend. And Ulysses was his best friend too.

Diego always had secret stuff—rubber bands, bus tokens, valid bus transfers, slugs to plug the pay phones and make long-distance calls—and secret places he knew how to sneak into free, to share with us. Mostly we went to the movies together. Ulysses and Diego would sometimes go to the Chinatown movies together, but I never went. As I saw it, this was America. Besides, anything Chinese reminded me of my father's murder by my stepfather. Ulysses, Diego, and I would sometimes go to the horror movies together, but Ulysses would go to the scariest horror movies alone. When he wasn't making model airplanes or building things, Ulysses wrote scary science fiction horror stories and squeezed his zits. Then he would make me and Diego read his stories out loud. I liked them because there were no Chinese in them and no one could tell a Chinese had written them.

Ulysses: Daydream

A woman who looks just like my mother, in a white nurse's uniform and a waitress's or nurse's white rubber-soled shoes, sits and knits at the Lincoln School playground, and watches me and Diego play basketball for an hour before we walk down Ninth Street for two hours of Chinese school. She looks just like Ma . . . too much like Ma to be real. She is more perfectly Ma than Ma. No little mole near her hairline. No zit marks. Younger. No rings on her fingers.

No jade bracelet. As if she is an artistic creation inspired by Ma. I would rather see *her* naked than Ma. I always notice her when I have the ball and don't know what to do. She is too young to be Ma. Ma has just had her hair done, and it doesn't look like this. Still, the longer she says nothing, the more I come to wonder if she is Ma teasing me with a trick. I take a step to attract her attention, like bouncing the basketball off her book, to get close enough for a good look, to see if she *is* Ma, but instead I see that she has never seen *me* before in her life. In The Movie About Me, I never see this woman.

Benedict Han: The Chung Mei Minstrels

Diego always had money. Auntie Hyacinth told Ulysses not to let Diego spend so much money on us because his family didn't have any to spare. But Diego said he didn't get his money from his parents. He said he got it from telephone booths.

The three of us haunted Broadway and Tenth Street looking at guns from the Civil War and the old west for sale in the windows of pawnshops. We walked into old stamp stores and stores that sold police and military uniforms. Ulysses and Diego liked the used bookstores. One sold political memorabilia: old red white and blue ribbons and campaign badges, autographed pictures of old U.S. presidents, and letters they had signed before becoming President. Diego was amazed and fascinated. All the secrets of old dead U.S. presidents had become junk in dim, dusty, junky old bookstores in Oakland. I enjoyed sitting by the stacks of old *Life* and *Saturday Evening Post* magazines from the 1930s and World War II, and going through them one by one. I studied the *Post* covers by Norman Rockwell. I bought maps of the United States. At first, Diego focused on the presidential memorabilia, but then he found the magazines and books with pictures of nude women in the back of the store. Nudist magazines, photography magazines, how-to-draw-and-paint-nude-women magazines. I didn't want him to bother me with them. He was always so pleased with himself when he found a new one, but he had to stay quiet or he'd get us all kicked out.

Diego knew the story of the three brothers of the oath of the peach garden but didn't know how to tell it. Then Ulysses found an old translation from 1914 of *The Romance of the Three Kingdoms* by H. Brewitt-Taylor. Two volumes. The two volumes were always there when we came back. One day Ulysses said the three brothers of the oath of the peach garden did not die on the same day. They did not save China. They kept their word to each other and nearly saved China. Lowe Bay, the first brother, led his army to avenge the death of Kwan Kung, the second brother. Before they rode out, the third brother, Chang Fay, got drunk. His own men, who were afraid to fight, killed him in his sleep and ran away. Lowe Bay died an old man without putting Han China back together again.

"But they keep their word to each other, right?" Diego demanded. "Yeah, that's the Three Kingdoms I know."

One Saturday in the dry dusty warmth of the used bookstore, before we caught a double bill of *King Kong* and *Lost Island,* two monster movies, Ulysses found an old book, *The Story of Chung Mei,* by Charles Shepherd, for a dollar.

"Look at this," Ulysses said. He opened the book to the slick pages of pictures, pointed to the kid on the right end of the top row of kids in a group photo captioned "The Celebrated Chung Mei Minstrels." "Who does that look like?" Ulysses asked.

It was Uncle Mort, in a Chinese skullcap. He was a kid in the picture, but he still looked the same. He still stood the same. "It's Uncle Mort," I said. "The one who takes us to downtown Oakland and buys us confetti on New Year's Eve. What's he doing in this book?"

"I guess he was a Chung Mei Boy," Ulysses said.

"Wow," Diego said. Chung Mei Baptist Home for Chinese Boys was known as the place Chinese parents sent their bad boys when they gave up on them. *His* mother had wanted to send *him.* His father said they couldn't afford it, but Diego's mother really wanted to send him to the Chung Mei Home because nobody could handle him. Finally his father said Chung Mei Home was Christian. He would rather Diego be a bad boy than a Christian good boy. His mother thought that was spoken like a true China-man and never mentioned Chung Mei Home again.

The next picture showed the same boys in their shiny minstrel show tuxedos and blackface makeup. None of us could make out Mort's face in all the makeup and wigs, but there was no mistaking young Mort out of makeup, standing with the other boys.

The book included a big speech by Shepherd, persuading the boys to become the first Chinese blackfaced minstrel show in history in order to raise money to support the Chung Mei Home. After all, just one boy who learned to become honest might grow up to be a great captain of industry in China or maybe a great engineer who might build great bridges in China. And some day a boy who learned not to tell lies might even grow up to be president of China! Ulysses groaned and growled.

"So what's wrong with that?" Diego asked.

"None of the Chung Mei boys were born in China. They're Americans of Chinese descent," Ulysses said.

"So should he have told your Uncle Mort, 'One of you boys can grow up to be the President of the United States'?" Diego asked. "He couldn't have grown up to be President of the United States. And we can't!"

I didn't say so, but I knew Diego was wrong.

Benedict Han: "The Thing"

I couldn't build model planes. I had no talent with hand tools and wood. I didn't have Ulysses' patience and concentration. But I did enjoy the movies. I walked with Ulysses from the Hotel Westlake Eclipse to the Fox Oakland theater one Saturday afternoon to see *The Thing* and discovered the two of us were the only people in the theater. Ulysses insisted on sitting close to the screen. He liked the front row. No, I would not sit in the front row. Ulysses wasn't happy about keeping me company halfway up the aisle. Even there, the theater was too empty and the movie too scary for me. I said I had to go and walked out of the movie, expecting Ulysses to follow me out as the music shuddered discords and off notes. I didn't turn around till I was outside of the movie house. Ulysses was still inside. I waited. Ulysses didn't come out. I waited until I couldn't stand the music spilling out of the open door, then walked back home to the Westlake Eclipse, alone. I felt I had betrayed Ulysses, let him down, broken the oath of the peach garden. A week went by and Ulysses never said a word about it. I was sure Ulysses was getting angrier and angrier. No. He remembered only enjoying the movie. He had actually enjoyed being the only one in the whole theater. I wrote a story about going to see *The Thing* with no one in the theater, for class. The teacher liked it very much. Nobody noticed nobody in the story was Chinese. America! America!

Ulysses: July 4, 1953, in Oakland

This Fourth of July, Benedict Han is in my room with me. The hotel rooms are narrow and very tall. Ma gives me the money to buy the lumber to build myself a loft space more than high enough so that Ben can walk without bumping his head.

Manuel, the Mexican busboy, has invited me over to his house for the Fourth. I play with his brothers in their front yard, digging tunnels. We hollow out the yard, fill it with water. Michael, the brother on crutches, pisses in the water. Our plan is to cover the yard with the little skin of grass we saved and wait for someone to walk on it, cave in the tunnels, and get their ankles wet. To drop into water we have all pissed in seems the ultimate in humiliating traps. We all piss in the front yard. Only later do we realize what we have done to a perfectly good front yard, when the Mexican parents scream at the boys. But they're nice about it. I'm the son of Manuel's boss. They want to make a good impression.

We have made a pond of our communal piss inside a little network of tunnels that are covered with newspaper and a little dirt and grass. Their mother and father are right to scold us all, but still, what we did seems as fitting a way to celebrate the Fourth as anything else. Of course the yard is not fit for setting up the barbecue now.

Michael teaches me how to play chess as we watch the fireworks from the upstairs window in the boys' room. As I walk home to the hotel, Pa sputters and gags, he's so angry, yelling at me, how I missed the clan picnic and made him look stupid with his tong friends who brought their kids. His cold voice bounces off the cold wiped-down stainless steel ranges of the hotel kitchen. Uncle Buck, who cooks here with Ma, and Auntie Orchid beat Ma down the stairs and see Pa hit me. I punch him in the stomach, and he doubles up.

"Hit him!" he yells at Ma, and runs to the back, where the waitresses change into their uniforms. He emerges with his hands full of wooden coat hangers and hands them to Ma, "Hit him. You hit him."

She hits me and Pa stands where I can see him. "Hit him!" he says.

She hits me and gives way to crying, slopping her tears on me as she swings the coat hangers. "You don't go out without letting someone know first!" she says and hits me. She knows Manuel invited me over for the Fourth in front of her. He asked her first. She knows I won't blame her for doing what Pa tells her. She doesn't have to lie. When the coat hangers break, Pa hands her more. I don't cry. I stand and tell her I want to go home. I have been visiting them long enough. "What do you mean home, young man? You are home!"

"I mean home in the country with Uncle Jackie and Auntie Bea."

Ma whips a handful of coat hangers across my face, crying harder than before, and screams, "How dare you talk to me like that in front of our guests!"

"Whaddaya mean guests? They've been here for years! They live here! I'm the guest!" I say.

"Ah-Ben," Auntie Orchid harmonicas out of sight, "Go back upstairs, please."

"Hit him!" Pa urges, "What are you stopping for?" And she hits me.

Benedict Han: Sherlock Holmes

"'After eliminating all that is impossible, whatever remains, however improbable, must be the truth!'" Ulysses read out loud and snapped the book shut. "Boy, that's great!"

"Who's that, Davy Crockett?" Diego asked.

"Sherlock Holmes," Ulysses said.

"Wow, Sherlock Holmes," Diego said. "What he say again?"

"'After eliminating all that is impossible, whatever remains, however improbable, must be the truth!'" Ulysses said in a funny voice that sounded nothing like Basil Rathbone. We obviously were not reacting with the understanding and enthusiasm he expected.

Ulysses said, "It's better than 'Have you not studied our Japanese Judo wrestling, our philosophy? Do you not know we worship death, not life? Do you not know we always take the obvious and reverse it?'"

"But I have heard that before," Diego said seriously.

"Yeah, my father said it when he committed *hara kiri* in *Halls of Montezuma.*"

"Yeah, I knew I heard that before. So, what're you saying?" Diego said, descending into a deep thought.

"Sherlock Holmes is cool," Ulysses coolly exclaimed.

Yes, Sherlock Holmes was cool. Ulysses' father's dying words as a Japanese officer in *Halls of Montezuma* were cool, too. At least I thought so. I didn't say so out loud, but what Ulysses' father said made as much sense to me as Sherlock Holmes. Maybe more. And Diego thought so too.

Diego emerged from his introspective frown and said, "He was playing a Japanese officer, right?"

"Right," Ulysses put a period on this conversation with a nod.

"You boys aren't getting into any stacks of my nudist magazines, are you?" sneered the clerk by the cash register.

"Oh, no, sir," Diego trilled in a "teacher's pet" voice. "We're looking at the *Model Airplane News* and *Air Trails* magazines for plans to model planes you can build yourself."

"Fifty cents each," the voice came back.

We had to have our own copies of *The Complete Sherlock Holmes,* but Ulysses didn't want us to buy our copies in the same bookstore. Diego agreed, if the bookseller sensed Sherlock Holmes was a passion among Chinese boys, they might raise the price of the beat-up cheap copies with handwritten notes in the margins and underlined passages.

In "The Greek Interpreter," Sherlock Holmes and his older brother, Mycroft, looked out of an upstairs window of the Diogenes Club at a total stranger standing on a street corner, and, for fun, they looked the man over and deduced that he was recently discharged from the army, had been a sergeant major, had been stationed in India, and that he was traveling by train to visit his sister, who had a little girl.

"Quintessential Sherlock Holmes!" Ulysses said.

"We can do that!" Diego said.

We three brothers of the oath of the peach garden each bought our own copies of *The Complete Sherlock Holmes* in different used bookstores and religiously read the stories of crime and detection while appreciating the friendship between the world's first consulting detective, Sherlock Holmes, and his biographer, Dr. Watson. Although our stated reason for buying the books in different stores was to keep the price down, I liked to think Ulysses didn't want any one bookstore to know that all three of us were reading Sherlock Holmes. I thought that was very Sherlock Holmes of him.

Everywhere we went together, on the bus, on the electric train, around the lake, we looked men over for the calluses of cowboys and carpenters on their hands, more suntan on one side of the face than the other. We only studied men, because Sherlock Holmes only did it to men, and because we were barely in our teens and didn't know what to look for on a woman. And, with the possible exception of Diego Chang, we didn't know about sex. The nudist magazines didn't really help me. Pictures of families at play in the nude did nothing but confuse me. What was so great about magazines full of these pictures? Anyway, Diego said it wasn't cool for three Chinese boys to be staring at white women riding on the bus.

"But what if I see a woman more suntanned on one side of her face than the other? Does it means she shaves with the bathroom window open or she sits next to a window where she works?" asked Ulysses.

"Doing what?" I asked.

"On the pot! What else do you sit on in the bathroom?" Diego replied.

"He said 'sits where she works,'" I said.

"Oh, I thought what he said was where she did shit."

"I don't know what she's doing or where she sits. In an office. At a sewing machine. I don't know, I haven't seen her yet," Ulysses said.

"You could tell if a lady was a sewing lady, couldn't you?" the Sherlock Holmes in me discovered out loud.

"Especially if she's still wearing her thimbles," Ulysses said.

"And they carry these big bags with wooden handles," Diego said, taking me seriously. I liked it. "And the factories where they work have a starting time and quitting time, and so there are lots of sewing ladies and lots of sewing gentlemen in certain places at certain times, you know?" Diego continued.

"Don't the sewing gentlemen carry the big knit bags with flowers on the outside, and the wooden handles too?" countered Ulysses.

"Yeah, they do!" Diego shouted, discovering it was so as he said it.

On our way uptown and around the lake one Saturday for a kiddie matinée featuring a Basil Rathbone Sherlock Holmes movie and another episode in the Captain Midnight serial, Diego pointed at the bus driver and whispered, "I deduce the driver is Russian. His name is Borscht," and crumpled up with a case of the giggles and couldn't continue.

"Look at the man in the blue suit sitting alone just across the aisle," Ulysses said in his horrible Chinese.

"Yeah, what about him?" Diego laughed gasps and wheezes.

"He's a cook. He's not married. He lives alone in a hotel room or a rooming house, something like that. He does not own a car. He has the next couple of days off. He is going to visit somebody or to a funeral out of town. He's going to spend the night and come back in time for work. He's going to get off at Greyhound terminal."

I glanced at the man in the blue suit. A pudgy white man with brown hair. Bald on top. He had a dark zippered canvas bag next to him. "Really?" I asked.

"Ask him," Ulysses challenged, and Diego jumped across the aisle and sat down next to the man and said, "I see you're a cook, mister. Where're ya cookin'?"

Instead of being surprised and asking how Diego knew he was a cook, the man in the suit said, "I'm semiretired," as if he and Diego were old friends, no surprise in him at all. He hadn't so much as turned to see who was speaking to him on this bus that waddled so wearily and heavily up San Pablo.

"Oh," Diego said. He was surprised the man answered at all and didn't know what to say.

"I work three days a week at Providence Hospital," the man spoke in a desultory, mushy voice. "I get my meals there."

"Excuse me, but did someone you know die?" Diego asked.

"Well, yes," the man said with a sigh of resignation, "My sister's husband. My brother-in-law. I never really knew the man. I haven't visited my sister in years."

"And you have the next few days off, right?" Diego said, as if they'd been casually chatting for hours. The man nodded. He seemed very distant, a very sad man. He reached up and pulled the cord that rung the bell to signal he wanted off at the next stop. Diego moved back across the aisle and sat on an empty bench. The man got off the bus in front of the Greyhound terminal. "Good talking to ya," Diego said and waved. He had had a religious experience.

"Wow, man! How'd you do it?" Diego asked. "His hands were clean, right? Clean under the nails, right? I saw that. He had no wedding ring. No rings at all. So, most likely he's not married, right? Yeah, I got that right."

Ulysses said, "If he were married, he would have a car and be driving. His hands were soft and a little puffy as if they were in water a lot. His nails were trimmed and clean but not manicured. He had no suntan at all. It's summer, boys. So he has to be indoors a lot. More like all the time. Or he sleeps in the day and works at night. What kind of a guy is that? A bartender maybe?"

"Naw," Diego said, "He said he's a cook. He said he's a cook. Anyway bartenders look you in the eye and look at your hands when they talk to you."

"How'd you know he would get off at the Greyhound?" I asked.

"The suit. The fresh haircut. He got the haircut yesterday and washed his hair. No cut hair on his collar. He had planned it that way. He wanted to look neat and suited up for something special happening today but too far to walk. And too far to go and do his special event and come back, so he has plain clothes in his little bag.

He'll hang his suit up after the event, wear his plain clothes, and change his shirt and wear his suit back on the bus."

"That's pretty good," Diego frowned and nodded. "Pretty good."

"That suit was on a hanger a long time before he put it on," Ulysses said. "So putting it on had to be special. And the shoes were old but still weren't broken in. So most of the time he doesn't wear suits and nice shoes. I didn't figure he was a doctor. A doctor would be driving his own car. So would a dentist. He was a cook, and he was traveling."

"He *was* a cook! I heard him," I said. "Now, how about that woman who's just getting off the bus?"

The last rider on the bus was a Negro woman wearing a sweater, holding a large cakebox on her lap. We all looked her over for clues as she stepped down the steps of the front of the bus and got off.

"She bought that cake in Chinatown. You recognize that box, man. That bakery is a block away from Chinese school. She's wearing that sweater because it was cold early in the morning when she caught the bus to go to Chinatown to buy this cake. It's a special cake for a special occasion. It's so special, she won't take her sweater off and put it on top of the cake box. I'll bet it's a surprise party."

"Wow! You did it, man! That's just what I was thinking, but wasn't ready to say it till I had all the words for it, like you." I tried to glow like Diego.

"I want to shake your hand!" Diego said and grabbed Ulysses' hand. Diego and I both shook hands with Ulysses on the bus. We were cool because we were Sherlock Holmes.

"Yeah, the three brothers, man," Diego growled. "One for all. All for one!"

Benedict Han: The Horse

Big Wong the Emperor hadn't come downstairs and begun class yet. Everyone was seated. Everyone who rushed in late and expected to be called to the front and slapped was seated. Everyone looked too good. Something was wrong. No one left. We sat and waited. Diego passed Ulysses a rolled-up copy of *Sunshine and Health,* a nudist magazine, and put his head down in his arms and laughed hisses.

We heard the sound of the front door open to the street and close and several men walking somberly through the empty front classroom. The chiefs of the Oakland Chinese Nationalist Party walked up the center aisle and were a little flustered when they met the gas heater in the middle of the room. A tall, bony, baldheaded man in a dark blue suit stopped by the heater and stayed there. He turned to face the classroom and stood with his feet apart and his hands clasped behind his back. The three old men of the Chinese Nationalist Party stood up straight and frowned in formation on Wong the Emperor's platform. One stood in front of Wong's desk and said, "Your teacher and the principal of Wah Kue Chinese School for twenty-seven years of virtue, propriety, courage, loyalty, and discipline in the teaching of the Chinese language, and Chinese literature, and Chinese culture, and the vision of the founder of the Republic of China, Dr. Sun Yat Sen, died in his sleep last night. Standing in front of me is the new principal and teacher of Wah Kue School, Mr. Mah."

"Mah" was Horse, in Chinese. Written on the blackboard was the Chinese word, "Horse." From the beginning, he was "the Horse."

"The Horse!" Ulysses dry heaved and wagged his eyebrows at Diego and me.

The Horse heard him, and just as Ulysses unrolled *Sunshine and Health* to sneak a look under his desk, the Horse had his eyes on him and saw the nudist magazine. He pointed a bony finger at Ulysses and said, "I will take that, please!" in English.

Everyone, including the Nationalist Party boys, were surprised to hear an adult speak English out loud inside these walls. Ulysses rolled up the magazine and passed it to the Horse. The Horse unrolled the magazine and looked at the cover—women playing volleyball. The men of the Nationalist Party looked at the magazine. The boys gasped. The girls giggled. Everyone blushed, everyone except Ulysses.

The Party chief on the platform said the magazine was confiscated and Ulysses should be ashamed of himself. The next day's classes were canceled in memory of Master Wong. We were dismissed. It was Thursday. No Chinese school tomorrow. No Chinese school till Monday.

Benny Han: Lunch Wearing a Paper Bag

The Horse was a slightly horsefaced, high-browed, baldheaded, oily scalped, skinny man, who wore the same double-breasted blue suit he'd worn the day they announced Wong's death.

Ulysses said out loud that he looked like "lunch wearing a new paper bag" as the Horse passed his desk on his way up the aisle between rows of ancient schoolroom seat-and-desk combinations, toward his platform, his little stage, on which stood the armchair which was reserved for teachers, and a desk with a Chinese bell that looked like a tarantula spider wearing a World War I German helmet, poised to jump.

The girls in the class laughed, and the Horse wheeled on Ulysses and dared him to repeat what he said. Ulysses said, "You wear your blue suit like lunch wears a paper bag. I know three places near here where you can leave your suit overnight, man, and tomorrow at high noon, you will have a suit that fits." And before we knew it the Horse was raging, bellowing, throwing chalk and blackboard erasers at Ulysses. Maybe he was wearing exactly the kind of suit he wanted to wear, did Ulysses ever think of that? Maybe he was wearing this kind of suit because he wanted to tell the world of tailored suits that he had other things on his mind, did Ulysses ever think of that?

"What things?" Ulysses shot back. Amazingly, the Horse opened up and told him. He answered every question Ulysses asked. Personal questions. Embarrassing questions. Or at least as embarrassing as Ulysses dared. The Horse was a mathematician. He studied in Germany. He taught in Germany. He had thoughts on theoretical numbers and a reputation in binomial theory that made him some kind of relative of the inventor of the UNIVAC, which was a computer, not a vacuum cleaner. "Who cares?" Ulysses asked.

As the days and weeks passed, Ulysses started to use the names and stories about China and Korea and Vietnam he plucked from the newspapers and magazines that he had collected from the lobby of the Westlake Eclipse to provoke the Horse: Chinese brainwashing, MacArthur at Inchon, MacArthur and the bridges over the Yalu, Bo Dai, the Viet Minh. The three of us, Diego, Ulysses, and me were down the street at the new Big Alliance Chinese school talking with our friend, Porky Hop, who was sitting on a cinderblock wall.

I forget what we were talking about or who was talking, when Ulysses saw the Horse across the street, walking past the new school with his head down, lost in thought. Ulysses shouted, "Defenders of Dien Bien Phu!" and punched poor unsuspecting Porky Hop in the face and knocked him off the wall.

The next day the Horse stormed into the classroom and did not go into the back room and take his customary dump in the cramped little toilet and read the Chinese paper. How he could shit in that back room toilet with all of us waiting outside, I could never understand. It seemed very weird to me. I always had a strong aversion to shitting in public toilets. I had this unreasonable fear of unwinding a long turd halfway out of my asshole when someone would walk in and call my name, and there would be no toilet paper left on the roll.

The Horse stomped up to his platform and waved his rolled-up newspaper at Ulysses. "You will never guess what I saw yesterday by the new school down the street." He apologized to the class for lighting up a Camel and smoking in front of us. He had never smoked in front of us before. Only in the toilet as he read the newspaper and communed with his maker. "This boy here shouted 'Defenders of Dien Bien Phu!' and hit a boy and knocked him off the wall of the new school. I want no trouble with the people of the new Chinese school. And what do you know about the defenders of Dien Bien Phu?"

"The French Foreign Legion!" Ulysses said.

"The French Foreign Legion! *Hay yow chee lay!* What do you know about the French Foreign Legion?"

"*Captain Gallant* on TV. Buster Crabbe in a show where he doesn't have to show his belly. *Morocco,* with Marlene Dietrich dropping her high-heeled shoes to follow Gary Cooper on patrol."

"You're a kid! Kids do not talk to their teachers like this!"

"No, teachers don't take this kind of talk from kids. Big Wong didn't," Ulysses answered back. "He'd whip us with the *sah tung* or hit us with that ruler. What're you going to do about it?"

The Horse stopped as if Ulysses had switched him off, for just an instant, that electric instant we all saw and felt. None of us had ever heard Ulysses or anyone talk back to a teacher like this. The only way I could describe Ulysses at the time was to say he talked to the Horse as if he were the boss. Every day they argued. Sometimes the Horse picked the fight with Ulysses. And always it was to see who was boss. Ulysses never gave an inch, never stopped fighting once he started. Neither did the Horse. The blood surged into his face and scalp. His body hunched. The veins stood out on his wrists and the backs of his hands and up his neck like long balloons filling with air.

The Horse fought with real emotion. Ulysses seemed the one holding back, the one toying with the lesser opponent, the one amused and entertained by the shouting back-and-forth about Edgar Snow's *Red Star Over China,* the American annexation of the Philippines, Mao's Long March.

"I can teach you to read and write Chinese," the Horse said, "but you will never be Chinese. And by now you should all know no matter how well you speak English and how many of the great books of western civilization you memorize, you will never be *bokgwai,* white European Americans. The Chinese kick you around for not being Chinese. And the whites kick you around for not being American. Obviously you are neither white nor Chinese, but you tell me what does that mean? What is it? You are the stone monkey come to life. To learn the difference between stone idea and living flesh and blood, you must learn everything Chinese and American there is to know, you must master all the knowledge of heaven and earth, become The Sage equal to The Emperor of Heaven so as to see the difference between the real and the fake, the knowledge of what being neither Chinese nor *bokgwai* means." Just what pubescent kids in the early Eisenhower '50s needed to hear, right?

I had forgotten China and had felt no guilt. But for a moment the Horse made me feel I was missing something, having lost my memory of my life before I was ten years old, having lost my memory of China. The Horse made us feel special. Unlike anyone else in the world, we were neither Chinese nor American. All things were possible. No guilt. We were pure self-invention.

"'Self-begat,' as Milton's Satan says in *Paradise Lost,* denying that he was created by God," Ulysses said, which stopped the Horse cold.

"Where did you learn about *Paradise Lost?*" the Horse asked, shaking like something about to burst.

"CBS or NBC did Paradise Lost last Easter or Passover," Ulysses said.

"How old are you?" the Horse asked. Nobody had any idea what either of them were talking about.

Ulysses: Camping Out in Chinatown

Grandma and the aunts, who are all members of the electronic Buddhist church, decide I should go to the meetings. When Auntie and the fat doctor in the electronic Buddhist church have visions about me turning black, I know it is time to go railroading like Longman, Jr., The Hero. But I'm too young.

Once a month, after the Buddhist church meeting in the sewing factory on the Chinatown side of Kearny Street, Aunt Azalea drives past the Mother "i" on the way to the Bay Bridge. The Mother "i" sign is a wooden barrel painted black, with holes drilled through the barrel spelling out the name. With a light inside, the name is easy to read at night. What is it? I ask. "Bohemians" hang out there, is how Aunt Azalea explains the place, Wow, Bohemians right across the street from Chinatown. What are Bohemians? They wear French berets and grow beards.

Ma hopes I'll learn Chinese by staying up late and improvising with my baby-talk Chinese in the aunts' visionary, proselytizing, electronic Buddhist church. Ma never comes to the meetings herself—I ride with Aunt Azalea. The meetings let out after midnight, when we go for late-night noodles. Aunt Azalea drives back over the bridge and parks in front of the Hotel Westlake Eclipse, where she works the Saturday morning breakfast shift in the hotel dining room for Ma. After the ride home, sometimes I go upstairs to my room, sometimes I sleep awhile in the back of Aunt Azalea's car.

In the Chinese school under Chinese Nationalist Party Headquarters, our teacher, the Horse, spits on the words "Buddhist church," says the idea of a church is not Chinese, certainly not Chinese Buddhist, because Chinese are not religious. "Chinese morality, called Confucian morality, is not built on a foundation of faith, like faith in the Christian world, but on knowledge, on history. Life is war. In war it is what you know, not what you believe, that wins battles," he says in the middle of the Korean War. The four girls left in the school, oooh, in shocked breath, and wonder if our Chinese teacher, the university mathematics professor, is a

Commie, maybe one of the unknown spies who stole the secrets of the atomic bomb with Ethel and Julius Rosenberg.

The Horse, sweat shining through his thinning hair, says we will never be Chinese. That's good news.

The sewing factory on Kearny Street, where the electric Buddhists meet, is a store with fabric and clothes on racks and dressed mannequins in the large front windows. Next door is the oldest theater in San Francisco, the Bella Union, showing Chinese pornography under the guise of scientific documentaries. Some weekends I spend in Frisco sleeping over at Aunt Lily's, working on the church building during the day as a volunteer. I sneak out of the apartment when I hear Aunt Lily and Uncle Harvey squeaking the springs and singing like coyotes, oblivious of my cousins standing on top of the dresser in the next room, watching the shimmer and wobble of their parents' flesh through ventilation slats near the ceiling. I'd rather watch a movie if all I can do is watch. I can't see what they're doing through the slats. I want to see it all.

I sneak out and walk down to Columbus, where some of the Italian neon is still alive. The sign of the Café Tosca, with the smiling man in a Robin Hood hat and goatee, turns the valve of a cappuccino machine, and that brings the word *cappuccino* glowing in blue. On the way to sneaking into the Bella Union for close-ups of the male Chinese organ docking with the female Chinese organ, I pass the sewing factory storefront and see Ron, the oddly white-skinned, red-lipped, nearly hairless son of the factory owner, practicing kung fu in the dark around the clothes racks and dressed mannequins. He says he learns from the Chinese movies. We roast potatoes in the ashes of a fire we've built in an oilcan on the concrete of the last floor of the building we are tearing down brick by brick to build a Buddhist church designed by somebody's white boyfriend who Ron does not like. His little sister, Sharon, sits against me watching her potato in the fire. She likes me. I like her.

That night we all camp out in sleeping bags on the floor without walls around it or a roof above it. Outdoors in the middle of Chinatown. I haven't looked up from bed and seen the sky and the stars like this since I was a kid in the Mother Lode. I haven't felt something hard against my back and looked up at the sky since the redhaired acrobat and white-haired bit player let me out alone the night of my first lunar eclipse. When the huffing and puffing of the traffic dies down and next to nothing's on the streets, we hear the whistle of a steam locomotive hauling for the edge of town.

They say Ron was sent to Chung Mei Home. So the family that hosts the electronic Buddhists paid Baptist Christians to keep their own oldest son, Ron, out of Chinatown.

Uncle Mort says he was a Chung Mei boy before he became a San Francisco houseboy. The aunts say not to believe him, he's just talking smart. But I have the book by the founder and director of Chung Mei Home. I open it up and show Uncle Mort the picture of him in the back row of "the celebrated Chung Mei Minstrels."

"Where did you get that old thing?" He snatches the book out of my hand and hits me with it hard enough to knock me down. Some move he must have learned in the Army Signal Corps.

"I got it in an old book store," I say.

He says he's sorry for hitting me. He doesn't like thinking about Chung Mei Home. He hates the Chung Mei Minstrels. I can't tell if he's trying not to sneeze or trying not to cry. He tries to give me a ten dollar bill out of his wallet. "Here, I'll buy the book from you," he says.

"No, thanks," I say. "It's an old book about you, like The Sea and the Jungle."

"I know what they say about me. They say I'm crazy. Strange," Ron says. "But I just like to fight."

We roast potatoes with his little sister Sharon. Ron knows everything everyone says about him and he doesn't care. He is strange. He likes to fight. He says everyone in the church says I look and act like a nigger. He doesn't want his sister hanging around an oddball yellow nigger, if that's what I am. Is his sister hanging around me?

"I should be so lucky," I say.

"You got that right," Sharon says. Ron sits up straight and looks at Sharon and me with nothing on his face and watches us when he says he likes to hear the sounds people make when he hurts them.

We roll our potatoes out of the cinders through the slot cut in the bottom of the steel drum. The night is cold and I hold my potato for a long time before I feel it's too hot to handle, and let go.

One night late, walking around Chinatown after midnight noodles, I peek into the store front and see Ron with a staff, swinging and whirling in the dark around the display cases, clothes racks, and plaster mannequins, touching nothing.

Ulysses: Nights of the Electric Buddhists

Some nights it is members only in the factory behind the store, and I sit between my grandmother and Aunt Azalea. We get to see the woman everyone calls "Auntie" sit next to Dr. Larry, the physician and priest of the sewing-factory-become-a-Buddhist-church. Auntie wears glasses and looks like Ma twenty years older in a skirt, blouse, and sweater, sometimes a Chinese jacket.

On her right is a large green tank of oxygen with a silver valve and gauge on it. She lowers her eyes and puts on a transparent mask with a black bag underneath, and Dr. Larry stands, sweating already, the fat on his face bulging like clenched fists, and he grabs knobs and handles on the shining valve with his hands and turns on the gas. She breathes, the bag fills and empties. Auntie sighs, the insides of the transparent plastic mask fog up, and she has visions about different people in the room that give everyone but me the shivers, and we recite the Diamond Sutra from beginning to end, line for line, person by person, up and down the rows of folding chairs, each member, young and old, doing funny things with our hands in unison and taking our turn on the beat, chanting our couple of lines, *"Tai serng yert. Waw fook moh moon..."* to the beat of a pasty-faced old man bonking a wooden fish, with no sense of what any of it means, all night long.

A large framed and glassed picture of Buddha standing on a lotus, all in gold, hangs on the wall on the nights of the meetings. A large framed and glassed portrait of Kwan Kung, the god of fighters and writers, and Buddha Who Defends the Borders on one side of the Buddha. A portrait of Monkey holding a peach of immortality stolen from the Jade Emperor's garden, from the opera *Havoc in Heaven* on the other side of the Buddha. And over Auntie's platform, a long mirror to reflect beams of evil away.

On other nights, the shorter nights, Auntie (without her oxygen), Dr. Larry, and the elders of the church sit in chairs and take the parts of sinners telling their confessions in strange radio soap-opera soliloquies. Moral tales of things they saw and things they did.

One night Dr. Larry is a Chinaman grocer who bad-mouths Negroes in Chinese to his wife by the cash register, right in front of his black customers, and thinks it's smart and funny until one answers back in perfect Cantonese and tells him the story of being the son of a black father and a Chinatown mother, abandoned and raised in Chinatown, Sacramento, and happens to be visiting relatives in the neighborhood.

I look up and see myself in the mirror over the players, sitting between my grandmother and Aunt Azalea. They have tears in their eyes. And next to her, Ron, the strange white-skinned thin-haired kung fu-kicking Chung Mei veteran, staring at Dr. Larry, his uncle, with nothing on his face, nothing in his eyes. I see Sharon, Ron's sister, watching me in the mirror too.

I don't want Ron looking up into the mirror while I look at Sharon. I see how he stares at Dr. Larry, his uncle, and now and then swallows the drool in his mouth. I wriggle my eyebrows. She wriggles her eyebrows. I smile. She smiles. I frown. She frowns. I blink. She blinks.

Another night Dr. Larry speaks a low-class Cantonese dialect and English not too much more better into a *bokgwai*'s face. Drop dead, old man. Your day is done. And the bokgwai drops dead on the spot. They arrest that silver-tongued Chinaman and put him on trial for murder before a jury of twelve *bokgwai* men, the bokgwai judge says are his peers. "When the prosecutor stands and accuses me of cursing a white man in my highly improbable and disconcertingly perfect English, I call, 'Hey, Mr. Prosecutor. Drop dead.' And it's perfect. Every *bokgwai* in court grabs the arms of their chairs and pulls their elbows in."

All the rapt Chinese in the sewing factory laugh. I can't seem to get away from Chinese who act Hollywood and showbiz. Pa is Charlie Chan's Number Four Son and The Chinaman Who Dies. My Uncle Mort is a Chung Mei Minstrel when he's my age, the first all-Chinese blackfaced minstrel show in history.

Now the head of the electric Buddhists, who my grandmother and aunts have plugged themselves into, seeks to inspire by method acting. Most of the audience sitting around me fan themselves with paper they've folded or with cheap fans from the corner grocery. Dr. Larry crudes his Chinese on about his powers of superior English. "Mr. Prosecutor does not drop dead. I smiles and turns my face to the jury and points this finger at each member of the jury and intone, Drop dead, drop dead, drop dead, drop dead . . . twelve times, then I stand up in the witness box and looks straight in the judge's eye and growl, Drop dead. I wait a moment, look around, and says . . ."

I think his story is stupid, and butt in with, "And they all dropped dead," in spontaneous understandable Chinese.

Ma would be proud. The pomade is melting out of Dr. Larry's loosening hair and making wet, oily slime lines down the rolling hills of his forehead and face.

These meetings are free to lure folks in off the street. The old woman with gold teeth, a jade bracelet on each wrist and a red coat, who used to teach the early class of little kids in the front classroom, comes to the free meetings and weeps at every story the four or five church big shots tell.

When she dies, she leaves everything to the church in her will, and the Horse snorts and spits at the stupidity of the old and lonely in Chinatown. White boyfriends appear at these meetings with the young long-haired women of the church, including my Aunt Lily. Even the members laugh and Dr. Larry and Auntie do not like it.

Dr. Larry stays in character, whimpers and cries, and makes everyone feel guilty about laughing, and for no reason at all everyone in the big room is sniffling and teary eyed. "Nobody dropped dead!" Dr. Larry says. "And I told them, 'Nobody dropped dead. And nobody will, till the day I am convicted of a crime. Any crime. Any where. Any time.' And still they convict me of murder in the first degree, and sentence me to death in gas chamber. On Death Row in San Quentin I read the Diamond Sutra and I commit it to memory and chant it every day. Because of my good behavior on Death Row, brought on by my discovery of the power of the Buddha, the wisdom of the Buddha, the grace of the Buddha, they let me out to visit my dying mother, who is a member of this church.

"Don't worry, Ma, I'll be with you soon. Two months from now they'll give me anything I want to eat for my last meal. You might think because I speak English without an accent, I would want a steak or a fancy French meal. You know what I want?

"I want *ngau noh tong, hom yur jing jer yook beyeng, waw siew bok op, gawn jin tot sah, bok fon.* Beef brain soup, salt fish steamed with pork sausage, roast squab, deep-fried sand dabs and steamed white rice." A light cackle ripples through the audience. Dr. Larry got a nice little laugh of his own.

"Oh, yes, I could run away from here and maybe live a few more years, but I give my word. And I been tried and convicted, so I'll go back to San Quentin, eat the last meal, sleep the last night, wake up to walk into a steel room where they will strap me down into the only chair in room, and put a black bag over my head. Sometime after they leave and seal the doors, they'll throw a lever, a pill will drop into a fluid and mix, and the gas will knock me out in a matter of seconds and kill me in about ten or fifteen minutes. The moral of my story is a Chinaman can't beat a white man at his own game, because the Chinese are not white and this is a white man's country."

I am twelve years old and thanks to the Horse am able to see through Dr. Larry's version of Buddha. I see that this church has turned Christian.

There's a kind of confession after the show. The elders of the first family of the electric Buddhist church sit at little TV tray tables in the storefront, talking with the members and people who want to talk, separated from each other by the mannequins and clothes racks and display cases. I'm half-dreaming on my feet, piloting the flying machine of me from the wheel somewhere back of my eyes.

Suddenly Dr. Larry lays his face into me. He sweats. He smells like urine and chili oil. It's late. I tell him Ma has nicknamed her brassieres "Hollywoods." I tell him I pull them out of the hamper in the bathroom and smell the insides. Not only do I smell my mother's dirty underwear and put on her dirty girdle with the bloody crotch, I put on her dirty bra and stuff the cups with balled-up socks, do the whole ensemble, and look at myself in the mirror when I'm alone. The elders all hear. My grandmother, Aunt Azalea and Aunt Lily, hear. They all hear, and stop and listen. My confession is the best story of the evening.

Benedict Han: The Purple Heart

I would spend the one Friday night of the month Ulysses was out all night at the electric Buddhist church sitting at the end of the hall by the stairs where Ulysses' father, the actor Longman Kwan, had set up a console TV with a nine-inch screen, a record player, and a radio in a polished mahogany cabinet. The door of fake drawers opened to reveal the television screen and controls. The controls to the radio folded down. The top of the cabinet lifted up to reveal the record player. My mother and her opera man went out every Friday night to sing with amateurs at some opera club in San Francisco. Aunt Hyacinth, Ulysses' mother, often went with them. I didn't want to go. The dishwasher had a room at the other end of the hall next to the toilet and tub room. I sat deep into an easy chair and watched a wonderful world on the little television.

And there was Longman, so handsome and American-looking with his little pompadour, I knew from the start he would like the American bomber crew who had just bombed Tokyo and crash-landed in China. He wore his tie tied and suit coat buttoned. His name was Moy Ling. His father, a bald-headed whimperer with a false smile, slimy skin, and beady eyes, betrayed the American flyers to the Japanese and tried to use Longman to corroborate his lies at the showcase trial held by the occupying Japanese. As the slimy Japanese officer, played by a bald-headed Richard Loo, ran a movie projector in the darkened courtroom, Longman Kwan stuck a knife in his father's kidney. The old man screamed, the lights came on. Young Longman Kwan stood up, slim, combed, and buttoned, and announced, "I am a fighter in the Chinese army. I have sent my father to his ancestors to answer for his betrayal." He threw down the knife. A gasp in the courtroom. Uniformed goons took him away.

I was touched. I was moved. He was everything I could imagine my real father had been before the opera man killed him.

Longman Kwan, and the goons holding his arms, stopped by the cell holding the bomber crew. Dana Andrews the captain of the downed B-25, proposed he be made an honorary member of their squadron.

Longman took a deep breath and pouted, "I wish to explain why I did not act sooner than I did. It required much time to decide to kill my own father." The goons took Longman Kwan out and shot him.

"I'd have him on my team, anytime," Dana Andrews said. I cried. This was the greatest movie I had ever seen.

Ulysses: Lure the Enemy onto the Roof, then Take Away the Ladder

I am twelve years old and building model airplanes up in my loft with the radio tuned low so as not to wake Auntie Orchid's son Ben, sleeping below closer to the floor. From the top of the tall mezzanine floor window of my room above the kitchens of the Hotel Westlake Eclipse, China Brother is a shadow in a pea jacket and dark watch cap when I first see him. China Brother looks like a sailor. I see that. But he's not the kind of sailor who climbs masts or hangs over the side.

"*Ah-bah!*" he rasps up to Ma's window. How does he know which window to call under? I wonder. Has he been here before, calling while Ben and I sleep? Even when he tries to show his face up to the windows, I don't see China Brother's face. He climbs onto the roof of the little shed sheltering the garbage cans.

He crawls over the little roof on his hands and knees, picking the largest of the little stones out of the roofing tar. He stands and looks like he'll jump down but doesn't. He puts the little stones in his coat pocket and climbs down with wobbly knees. He's not far off the ground. I used to climb up there all the time. I watch the shadow toss the precious stones one by one up against the window and hear him call "*Ah-Bah! Ah-Bah!* Longman Kwan!" till a dim light comes on and Pa opens the window and tells him to be quiet and go away. Pa knows the shadow in the alley. The shadow's been here before.

"My ship came in early. I need someplace to sleep just for one night." How does he know Pa will be in Oakland when his ship lands? I climb down from my workbench and loft, down to the handles on the windows. The shadow is looking up hard into the light of the next window over. He won't notice my window opening wider in the dark. I push the window further open and duck back to peer just over the sill. The shadow doesn't notice. I know it's China Brother.

"Go away. You can't stay here," Pa says.

"I can sleep in the kitchen. On the floor," the shadow says. The kitchen floor is cement.

"Go away. Sleep in a hotel. Go away before you wake everybody up," Pa rasps, trying to shout him away and not wake Ma at the same time. But I know she hears what I hear.

"I don't have any money, *Bah,*" the shadow says, and Pa tosses some money out of the window. It flutters to the ground, bill by bill. The shadow stoops to pick it up and goes.

I had heard, from listening to Ma gossiping among her sisters and The Hero over mah-jong and midnight *juk* at Grandma's house, that the shadow is beyond a doubt my China Brother by a mama back in China. He's back sniffing and whimpering around for any scraps of fatherly love Pa might have left around for him. I have to shake my head in pity and disgust. China Brother expects too much of love in America. Love in the American Dream isn't what he thinks it is. What he bought in China, watching the movies Pa dies in, is Hollywood. Love in America is Hollywood. Pa is Hollywood. There is no love from Pa, except for Hollywood love, which you see only in the movies.

"Improve yourself, son," my father says whenever he's in town. "Better yourself," Ma says. Pa wants Hollywood Junior, the incredibly good-looking one women find irresistible, to follow in his footsteps to the Hollywood Walk of Fame. Hollywood Junior has the looks to be the first Chinese Hollywood star, Pa says proudly. That's why he calls him "Hollywood Junior." Junior is happy working as a conductor on the Southern Pacific and doesn't care for movies and television. Me? They want me to go to Cal, in Berkeley, stay near Ma, and become a doctor or a lawyer. He's for doctor, she's for lawyer. Sometimes, after a day of pacing around each other in our house avoiding each other, they decide to take me to a movie Pa neither lives nor dies in.

"Wuhay! Ah-Kid-doy, ahhhhh! Where're you gone, kid?"

"I go show! See a movie, man!"

"What movie?"

"East of Eden, waaahh! It's a Movie About Me!"

"Movie about you? Any movie about you, you die!"

East of Eden and *Mr. Roberts.* They ask each other if they realize that, in their desperately urging me to go to Cal, improve myself and stop killing Ma, and better myself, they are telling me I am no good. "Make something of yourself, son," as if me being nothing is why Pa stays in L.A. praying for stupid movies parts and is never home. When I am something and have gone somewhere, will Pa give up being The Chinaman Who Dies and Charlie Chan's Number Four Son? No one believes that.

We go out with Auntie Orchid, Uncle Buck, and Ben to see Pa in the movies. The war movies. The Chan movies. While they live with us, learning the restaurant biz from Ma, we have to go see Pa's movies to give him face in front of the opera stars, she insists, but she hates it.

"'Humane? What means humane?'" Ben quotes Pa's dying line, in *Keys of the Kingdom.* Gregory Peck is a priest. His mission hospital is burning from a civil war. He holds Pa 's bleeding body in one arm, and a Thompson submachine gun in the other.

Ma finds strange places to give Pa face.

"That's not bad," Ben says, "I take what he says in the movies as a personal message, Ulysses. Remember? 'Humane? What means, humane?'"

"At least Gregory Peck didn't shoot him, this time," Ma says. She doesn't like to see him die.

"'Beware of Christians and their missionaries bearing opium,' is one the things the Horse says, which gets him called a Communist and Pinko sympathizer in the Chinese school," I say, getting off the subject of Pa.

Diego Chang: Valentine

The best time Ulysses "got" the Horse was when we chased the girls into the back room where the toilet was and they slammed the door and locked it. Ben's sister was in there with that new kid, the F.O.B., "Valentine."

Ben named him Valentine because the first time he showed up at the school was on Valentine's Day, and Ulysses paid my little sister a dollar to give him a kiss on the cheek and say, "Be My Valentine." The kid was a young, scared, anxious-to-please immigrant innocently plunked into this little pond full of wicked American-born sharks.

We used to have these paperwad wars before the Horse came downstairs from whatever he was doing in the Nationalist Party Headquarters upstairs. He didn't live up there like the late Big Wong. We knew that because we'd seen him drive up to park in front of the school in his white two-door '49 Chevy. And we'd seen him drive away after school. Anyway, it was the girls and Valentine on one side, and the Three Brothers of the Oath of the Peach Garden on the other. I taught everyone how to roll nice tight paperwads, bend them, and shoot them with a rubberband stretched between their fingertips.

On this particular day, the girls and Valentine ran into the back room and slammed the door. Inside the back room they had this strategy. They'd open the door every now and then and all shoot their paperwads at once, then slam the door and lock it. It was a big tall door in that big old classroom, with the high ceilings and the lamps hanging down from chains over us.

Me and Ben wanted to sneak up to standing just outside, and when they opened up the door, we planned to push in fast and get 'em with our paperwads. But Ulysses told us to get out of the way. Then he backed up through the door into the empty front classroom with the ping-pong table in it, and trotted forward, toward the back room door, picking up speed, and ran and jumped and finally hit the door with both feet so hard he knocked it off its hinges. The door stood on the cement an instant but screeched. The girls and Valentine screamed. They laughed. They ran. And the door fell over slowly down flat and thumped up clouds of dust, clanging to the cement floor like metal rather than wood. Ha. Ha. Ha.

Just then we heard the Horse upstairs, on his way downstairs to go into the backroom with the newspaper, to take his afternoon shit.

The three girls and Valentine ran out of the room and climbed over the door to their seats then laughed, pointing at us. Ulysses and me propped the door back in place and got it kind of closed, but the screws to the hinges, which popped out when Ulysses kicked the door down, were all over the floor. When the Horse walked in with his newspaper, everyone was in their seats, and we were all looking into our lesson books, reading Chinese. Reading Chinese my ass! Even the Horse wasn't that stupid. He's had his suspicious eyes on us when he grabbed the doorknob on his way to his daily shit, turned, pushed . . . And the door fell and pulled him down because he didn't let go of the doorknob! Dumbfuck! He near shit his pants!

And as soon as the Horse got on his feet he yelled for Ulysses! He didn't throw things at Ulysses. He didn't pace back and forth up and down the front of the platform and rage at Ulysses.

He had *The Oakland Tribune* all twisted and choked to death in his hand. "I saw this headline, 'JOE,' on this newspaper," he sneered. "And I thought, what! Joe Stalin alive? And I see 'JOE DIMAGGIO MARRIES MARILYN MONROE!' This is what you nincompoops call journalism! This is *The Oakland Tribune!* This excuse for a newspaper is owned by Senator William Knowland who likes McCarthy, likes Chiang Kai Shek, likes Anna Chenault!"

"The Chinese widow of General Claire Chenault, creator of the Flying Tigers American mercenary squadron in China?" Ulysses asked.

"The China Lobby!" the Horse shouted, and shook his head. Then he called Ben by his Chinese name, *"Ah-Wah,* what do you do when you get home?"

"I watch television in the hall while Ulysses reads and listens to the radio," Ben answered. I thought he talked too much.

"What do you watch?"

"Baseball," Ben said.

The Horse asked me what I did when I was home. I said I listened to baseball on the radio and the dancing and music from the flamenco club next door to the family restaurant.

"Flamenco?"

"Spanish music," I answered. "Guitars. Castanets."

"Now, you!" the Horse pointed at Ulysses. "What do you do?"

"I get books out of the library on things I hear about from you, and listen to cowboy shows on the radio and read."

"Stop reading," the Horse said, "Be a normal kid. Play. Sports. Music. Forget reading. You're not ready to read books."

The Horse didn't sound like himself. Ulysses didn't smart back.

Ulysses: The Bird of Five Virtues

Auntie Orchid, Ben's mother, always picks Ben and his sister up from Chinese school to go off to some Chinatown testimonial dinner of one kind or another. I walk home.

I want to walk home. I like walking home, walking up Broadway past the arcades with the machines that have the dirty movies inside, past the used bookstores where I found the old model airplane magazines and some of the old missionary travel books that I can always use to get the Horse going.

The walks home are the most interesting part of the day for me, and a few times the Horse asks me if I'd like a ride home. He says he worries about me walking through the Oakland borderlands between the all-night fun-and-crime district and Chinatown and uptown Oakland.

One night it's raining. The Horse says it's too rainy for me to walk home. I agree, and get in his little two-door ivory white '49

Chevy and direct him through the streets of Oakland to the Hotel Westlake Eclipse. I ask him inside to have a restaurant dinner in the hotel dining room. Get the good table service by our white-haired German waitress or maybe Aunt Azalea in a nylon waitress uniform and apron. Aunt Azalea is in our goofy electric Buddhist church in Frisco that the Horse rails about every now and then. I think it will be fun for them to meet. Soup, salad. Choice of entrées. Dessert. Coffee, tea, milk, or buttermilk, the works. The food is good. Buck Han the opera man is a first-rate cook of Chinese and American food. All pastries baked on the premises. The Horse refuses. I tell him that if he doesn't like American food, the Chinese food is authentic, just how he likes it, but still he says, "Thank you, no."

I tell him I'm sorry for getting him all worked up over nothing, every other day. The things he yells at me make the girls in class think he's a Communist and I know they've been talking to their parents, and one is a muckamuck in the Nationalist Party circle, in the associations. From what the Horse has said, I've figured out that he was a math professor at Berkeley and was fired for refusing to sign the new loyalty oath. I figure I am partially to blame for him continuing to sound like a Communist fellow-traveler and want him to know I'm sorry.

He says he hates the Communists. When they came to power he thought they meant an end to the corrupt, self-aggrandizing bureaucrats that had been part and parcel of the Nationalists and the Imperial administrations before the revolution of 1911. He started a school of his own. He used his own method of teaching, his own curriculum. The Communists closed the school and put a price on his head. He escaped to Taiwan and started a school, and they closed him down and expelled him from the country. Hong Kong told him to keep on moving. He taught in Germany awhile, then his work in binomials and imaginary numbers brought him to Berkeley. Now the Americans end his story with the loyalty oath.

This dumb little remnant of a Chinese language school is his last school. We are the students of his very last school. And he has to be thinking of us when he says the failure is his, all his, not his students'.

Ulysses: July 4, 1955

Ma wakes me in the dark. We're not waiting for Pa. We're not going to the clan picnic. She talks fast and mutters, packs her things and packs my things. We take a taxi to the bus depot on San Pablo Avenue into the smell of barbecue, cheap Chinese grease, and the exhaust of idling busses. When we load onto a Greyhound bus a little after dawn and head for New York to live in rooms above Auntie Orchid's restaurant in Greenwich Village, she never says why. Six months later, Ma comes back to live in the new house with Longman Jr. She leaves me in New York for more than a year.

When I come back from New York for my last two years of high school in Oakland, I live in a room with kitchenette and bath over Uncle Morton Chu's garage workshop. Where I go, where I live, it's all planned, but nobody tells me the plan.

Ma has a new daughter, she says. Her name is Aloha. She says she and Pa are thinking of adopting. She wants a chance to raise a child. I was in the country where she couldn't raise me when I was a baby.

"What about Hollywood Junior?" She slaps me.

"What's that for?" I ask.

She apologizes.

Later Morton gets me sticky with a stupid conversation about how hard he tried to teach me and the cousins Morse code. We sit at his workbench in the garage downstairs where he's teaching himself how to build guitars, and he tells me Aloha is Pa's daughter by one of his many girlfriends. She's about Irma's age—Longman Jr.'s second daughter—born about the time Pa was shooting *Joey in Gobi*. Pa was bringing baby Aloha to Oakland for Ma to raise just before she took me to New York and left me in the rooms above Auntie Orchid's restaurant.

Ma is willing to raise her, but Pa can't talk her into adopting the girl. What does Pa expect? He hasn't lived in Oakland for years, he just visits.

Uncle Mort suggests that it would be a good idea to take my older brother up on his offer to get me a summer job on the railroad and stay away from "home."

Ulysses: Hollywood Junior Speaks Once

Ma's new house. I am back from New York, just beginning to understand what I'd been doing there. I have never been in this house before. Uptown. Out of Chinatown. It has a little yard. The sun is at one o'clock, light pouring through the big dining room window with a view of Trestle Glen, a woodsy little valley with winding narrow streets. All the houses are made of peanut brittle and have pitch roofs made of vanilla wafers.

The Hero and I are alone in the house. We paint the dining room with latex. We unroll a carpet and move a dining room table and chairs. He apologizes for never having talked to me. We were never pals. We never lived under the same roof, that I can remember. He was so much older and always on his own. We should talk. What do I want to talk about? We talk about The Hero. We talk about World War II.

World War II. That's you, Hero. I'm in high school ROTC, learning how to shoot a rifle, how to take apart an M-1 rifle, the manual-of-arms and close-order drill. You fought in the last war the U.S. fought clean and won fair and square. That's what we boys and girls around the world like to believe. The Nazi Krauts and the Tojo Japs were driven by evil, possessed by evil, mad with evil. They certainly had an eye-catching, terrifying evil sense of style. The ugly inverted gull-wing Stuka dive bombers looked like black widow spiders dropping out of the sky. The Nazis had twin-engine bombers that looked like Klansmen in black silk hoods and robes.

A Good Conduct Medal. Bronze Star for valor. Purple Heart with a cluster. No, no cluster. Whew. I hate to think of you being wounded twice. No wonder you're a patriot. Are you a patriot?

The one o'clock sun roasts the fresh paint all over the walls. The air is dry buttered popcorn and has a funny vanilla ice cream smell from the drying skin of latex sucking up to the walls. You glow, Hero. You talk like a drowning man seeing his life pass before him just before he dies in the art movies. Cocteau. Hitchcock. *The Seventh Veil.* You don't know those movies. You don't ask. You don't care. You don't sweat. But you look like you are melting. We unroll the rug and center it in the room. We lift and carry the table into the dining room, careful not to scuff the hardwood floor. You tell me a story no one has heard you tell. Ever. Why?

You got to England and passed ammo in the rain so long, you were stuck in mud above your knees when you were done. You had to be hauled out with a rope and a jeep. You and some buddies copped an ambulance and some willing nurses and drove around London orgying behind the Red Cross. You were afraid of VD and didn't fuck with the nurses and stayed behind the wheel, driving the fucks of others all night long. Sometimes with the siren on, sometimes with the siren off. There was a nurse who wanted you and offered to ride up front with you, but no, you say you said, and tell me of hitting the beach in real lackluster, emotionless prose, and of the German 88s opening up while you're behind the wheel of a truck full of ammo. You jumped out of the truck into a slit trench full of strangers' (perhaps German) shit and piss and stayed there until the barrage was over. And you aren't alone in the muck. I think you are trying to make the story funny, make me laugh. But you're sad, brother. You look sad. You sound sad. And you get more sad and shriveled up as you tell me that after the end of the end of the war, they gave you a month's leave to go anywhere in Europe and fart around before shipping you home for discharge.

Switzerland. You wanted to see the Europe untouched by the Stukas and 88s and B-17s and Liberators and Mustangs. Then a long, winding, dizzy impressionistic story of meeting a blonde German-Swiss woman one day, walking home with her from a bar, and being followed out by a couple of men, white of course, who, she said, wanted to beat you up and gangbang her for going out with a yellow man. But they don't try anything because they think you know judo. You lived with her, you say. You tell me what her body was like. She was married. Her husband was in the German Wermacht and hadn't been heard from since the end of the war. You thought her vagina should be looser, since she was married, and the thought of VD worried you, and you asked a doctor. The doctor told you if she hadn't fucked for a long while, she could tighten up. You liked it tight. So why did you want it loose? What prompts this veiled confession of the loss of your virginity and descriptions of the feelings of your dick inside her twat? You are still surprised you lived with her. Why tell me? Don't you have friends? Is this your idea of brotherly sex education, the proverbial man-to-man with you standing in for Pa? Did Ma put you up to this?

Uncle Mort doesn't believe you. Uncle Mort believes you jumped into the shit but doesn't believe you lost your virginity to a white woman or lived in Switzerland with a white woman married to a missing German soldier.

"Why should The Hero make up a lie?" I ask him.

"He wants you to like him."

"I like him."

"Your Ma is sure that a big boy like you who's been to New York is actively involved in premarital-type conjugal relations, you know what I mean?" Morton says.

The other sisters, including his wife Poppy, sneer at poor Uncle Mort, poke relentless fun at Morton's mangled high-falutin vocabulary when he talks about his inventions that never get off the ground and his other attempts to signal a superior education and intelligence that always crumble into gibberish at the family gatherings.

Ma says Mort is smart and talented but never finishes what he starts. Still, she loans him small amounts of money because he is kind to me, and she says he doesn't have to hurry about paying her back. Mort always pays her back.

The Hero drives me down to the railroad yards for the first time, takes me to the yard office and introduces me to the trainmaster, the yardmaster, and the freight agent. The freight agent gives me a job as a vacation relief clerk for the summer.

It's a great job. For two and four weeks at a time I take over for different damaged-freight claims inspection clerks while they're on vacation. I look at the shipped goods that companies on my route received damaged. If I look at them and say they're damaged, the companies get to keep the damaged goods to dispose of as they wish, and the railroad has to pay to replace them with new goods. The clerks who teach me their jobs before they leave on vacation teach me graft. "Don't fuck it up for me when I get back," they each say in their own way.

When the liquor warehouse wholesaler sends in a claim for torn cartons and damaged freight, I report torn cartons and damaged freight. But first, as instructed by the clerk I replace, I ask if they have Weller's Antique, 12-year-old 110 proof bourbon whiskey. No, they don't. I ask if they have Wild Turkey. No, but they want to give me a quart bottle of the finest bourbon they carry, the very fine Henry McKenna, 90 proof. I get cookies, cartons of baby food, toys, plastic model airplanes. I learn graft. It's crazy.

Ma slips into a special sadness that has her talking to me like high school creative writing teachers and Hollywood soap opera moms. "If you're going to become something in this world, young man, you are going to have to . . . to find yourself . . . to look for yourself . . ."

She wants me to look for myself in the bookish grammatical English no one but too sweet, too neat, straight A, student-government-type Chinese Americans speak. To look for myself around the house kept clean by my lonesome mom. To find myself in the Chicago-style Harvard-trained Christian-convert-subsidized punk dictators of captive banana republics, washing millions in U.S. foreign aid into numbered Swiss bank accounts.

Ulysses: Jason Peach

In high school ROTC I learn how to shoot. I go from the high school military to high school politics. I make high school speeches and go to high school conventions and tell jokes and run for High School Lieutenant Governor of the High School State of California

I tell stupid Chinese jokes about my father playing Charlie Chan's Number Four Son. The aunts love it and laugh when I tell them, and ask for more. Ma doesn't like it, considers it a cheap shot. But it works. I am elected at a weekend convention in the gym of a high school on the San Francisco Peninsula, where we have turkey for dinner. After the spontaneous speechifying and glittering self-advertising disguised as thank you's from the tables, a Japanese girl with a huge guitar strums and sings calypso songs that take me by surprise.

The peachy-keen high school club is paying her to sing. She's a kid. I like it. But she is not in Sacramento the weekend of the high school junior government. Instead, on the Capitol steps, a white girl asks me out and really means going out on a date, and I squeak weakly that I don't go out with Caucasians, and until just now, I did not realize that I do not think of white girls as real girls and wonder why? I cross the park to have lunch with the High School Governor and the real Governor and Lt. Governor of the state in the Governor's dining room.

"Oooh! Was it nice, boy?" Aunt Lily, the sexiest aunt, asks. "Tell us about the silver? Did the dishes have the state seal on them?"

"Oh, Lily! Who wants that thing looking at them out of a bowl of soup!" Ma says, "What was the menu?"

"Not soup!" Aunt Lily sings back.

"What do you mean, not soup! This is the Governor!"

"California squab stuffed with wild rice, nuts, and mushrooms."

"Small, huh! Not like Chinese squab. Did you tell him Chinese *bok op* is better?"

"Did you have fruit from the Governor's garden for dessert?"

"No. Baked Alaska."

"Oh, too bad."

I am the President of the Senate. Seated up high, looking down on a semicircle of desks, I recognize Jason Peach. I knew Jason as a Negro cadet major in high school ROTC at Oakland Tech. Now he is a high school state senator in Sacramento. The instant Jason locks eyes with me and pushes and I push back, we smile and see now, if we didn't see before, that we are both here for mischief. We both know at heart that we don't belong here. Being here is part of using everything we learned to make high school work for us. The look and the smile are as good as a blood oath. We have never really talked before, but now I know we have seen the same comic books and movies as boys, and we are allies defending the essentials of civilization: *King Kong. The Thing. Shane.* The Archie Moore vs. Yvonne Durrell Light Heavyweight Championship fight in Montreal. *Red Ryder. M. Les Enfants du Paradis.*

I learn from listening to fine-sounding resolutions written by smartass kids from all over California that Jews are white people who are not white people. Jews don't come from a nation of their own, like Frenchmen come from France. They are not a nationality but an ethnic group. What is an ethnic group?

A handsome, soft-voiced Negro in a white sweater stands to speak against a resolution favoring the creation of a Fair Employment Practices Commission and says he is a Negro and does not feel discriminated against and is against a Fair Employment Practices Commission, and there is applause. I never heard of FEPC before. But I see how to get applause. Then Jason Peach stands.

"The chair recognizes the honorable Senator from Oakland Technical High School," I say.

Jason takes the floor of the State Senate, which is more Hollywood than real. The marble pillars behind me are painted plaster. Nothing in the room stands a close look. Jason says he is happy he came to Sacramento this weekend so he could see for himself what a kissass nigger looked like. "The truth is, brother, you got here to these exalted chambers with these, the brightest and most hip high school hustlers in the bountifully hustling state of California, the same way I got here. You know what I mean, brother. Hard work. Making your mama work extra hard to put up the money for this trip. And also by kissing a lot of Caucasian ass. The difference between me and you is you pretend you don't join the whites in discriminating against the Negro when you kiss white ass, and I don't. I know I discriminated with Caucasians against my own kind to get here. I could have told other Negroes who know more about *Roberts Rules of Order* and all the stuff in these resolutions than me, and I didn't. I wish we were both here because of our talent, man. I really do. We should not have to kiss behinds to play high school legislature just because of the color of our skin. I shouldn't have to shame my people to be here. Anyway, I'm voting for the Fair Employment Practices Commission."

I am surprised at the hush, at the failure of the smattering of applause to catch. A kid rises to a point of order, "I pray the chair admonish the Senator to respect these exalted surroundings on loan to us and to refrain from the use of crude and obscene cursing."

I hit the gavel and say, "The Senator from Oakland Technical High School is abjured. There will be no more kissing of behinds in the Senate." The laughter is strange, not cleansing, not relieving the strain, not fun.

Later Jason phones, and we meet at the Il Piccolo in Berkeley for coffee. Ma was right about one thing—by growing up in the restaurant, bussing dishes, and waiting tables, I picked up table manners from the well-dressed old folks left to die here, eating off the American Plan. I know a cappuccino when I see one. Jason likes the café latté because it's big. He wears a black turtleneck and horn-rimmed shades. I wear a shirt handmade from handwoven fabric and sold in a shop smelling of soap. We have never seen each other here before. Jason asks me, "Are you living the part or playing the part, Ulysses?" without cracking a smile.

"I don't know what the part is yet, man. How about you?" I ask. "Are you playing the part?"

"No, Ulysses," Jason says, blowing smoke out his nose and mouth, "I'm living the part."

We talk of how we make high school work for us. He's been playing blues and old-timey music on the guitar and singing at Pepe's Pizza up the street two nights a week for twenty-five dollars.

I've been selling my paintings and pen-and-ink drawings to a Spanish teacher and a social studies teacher after school for five dollars each.

Other stuff. Yeah. The same comic books. The same movies. Sacramento was weird, we agree, but even though the high school FEPC legislation failed big, that speech got him laid.

"You say you got laid?" I ask, "Where?"

"In her room, where else?"

"Wow."

"You mean you went through all that and didn't get any quiff, man?" Jason grins. His front teeth look larger for the gap between them. "Why do you think I wanted to get to that bullshit high school state government in Sacramento, man? To make a fucking speech? No, man. To get pissed at a white nigger? No, man. Jason Peach went looking for the cream of this state's high school sweethearts, man. Where else are niggers like us going to find so many white girls on the loose and looking for trouble, man?"

"Was she pretty?"

Instead of answering, Jason says, "You didn't get laid, did you."

"Well, I didn't . . ."

"The reason you didn't," he says, "is because you have taste, Ulysses. I have no taste, and I get laid all the time." Jason is right. His words are like the last scene in Luis Buñuel's *Los Olvidados*, playing across the street at the storefront moviehouse next to the little grocery store with the green awning and the scalloped edges. What looks like Joseph and Mary and their donkey on their way to Bethlehem is the farmer's daughter and her incestuous father, unloading the dead body of a boy abandoned at the beginning of the movie, the only innocent in the movie, rolling like a joke, like garbage, down a hill of garbage, to a dead stop in front of the camera for The End. Jason says he's seen it.

"Great movie," he says with a shudder.

"I'm scared to walk on the same side of the street as the theater," I say, "Afraid it will give me bad dreams."

"That movie is such a mindfuck," Jason says. "By the way, the projectionist at that moviehouse is one hell of a classical guitarist, man. All he does is practice and run those projectors. The other night, after the last show of *Los Olvidados,* he walked across the street, and was so out of it, he didn't notice that the doors were locked. He walked right through the glass doors, man, broke the glass, noise all over the place. It was awful, it looked like there was broken glass all over him, and he didn't even try to shake it off, man. He just walked up to the counter and said, 'One cappuccino, please.' And everybody heard it and could not believe it, man. It's that movie," Jason says, and nods knowingly.

"Yeah," I nod. "Great movie."

Jason Peach is such a dark Negro that Ma shakes her head when she meets him, and my aunts come sit around me and try to talk me into telling Jason Peach we can't be friends.

Ulysses: The Mother "i"

During my last year in high school I meet Fat Jack, the fat cocky Chinaman who later teaches me how to draw, downstairs in the brick underground nightclub, The Mother "i", across Kearny Street from Chinatown, Frisco. I went to the "i" to show my drawings to Mr. Tucci, the owner, who was wearing a red beret that day. He liked my drawings and told me to come back that night and see "Fat" Jack Fat.

Fat Jack makes all the decisions about the art that hangs on the walls on consignment and takes a cut of the sale price when it sells. I'm told I'll recognize him because he's Chinese like me and looks like his name. He's short. He has a perfectly round head and face. He looks like the Pillsbury Dough Boy with slanty eyes, tweed jacket, brown slacks, sandals, and no socks. He stands behind a table covered with rings and bracelets, brooches and pins, all blobular and fungoid-shaped, in silver and gold, inlaid with wood and stone that looks like junk sifted from the ashes. He hates my drawings, laughs at me because I'm Chinese and wear glasses. "How old are you? You can never tell how old Chinese are, man. So tell me, how old are you?" he asks.

"Seventeen," I tell him.

He takes a pair of glasses out of his pocket and laughs. "All Chinese wear glasses," he shouts. His glasses have big lenses and big frames. "Humph," he snorts and sneers, pokes a cigarette between his little guppy lips, glancing at me and bouncing with the burning cigarette in his mouth and his hands in his pockets. "You look older than seventeen. It's the acne scars. My mother took care of my face. Russian and Japanese. High-class Japanese, you can see it in my eyes. High-class amber eyes, man. She taught me art. Took me to galleries. Played music in the house. Not like the other Chinese kids, huh? Ha ha ha! I'm not quiet and reserved like other Chinese, right? You tell her. How many Chinese friends do you have? Tell her," he says wagging his cigarette at the hair of the tall blonde woman sitting almost as tall as he stands in a chair next to him.

"I have a few," comes chickening out of my mouth at a crawl.

"A few! Ha!" he says, "Just a few, right? Like none! Am I right? Because you're a freak! You're an artist, like me." As he scowls, the ash falls off his cigarette, crashes on his table. He wags his head at the blonde, who doesn't look happy, then turns back to me. "But I never had acne, man! My mother never let me. A zit never had a chance. She gave me facials. How about that! Facials! You don't believe me? That's you. Turn your head that way. Yeah, you look younger than seventeen too. That's okay. You have time to get serious about art! Ha ha ha!" he laughs. "I bet you've never seen a Chinaman like me before! Ha ha ha."

He laughs his every "ha" as separate words, and shouts them one by one, reminding me of a toy wooden machine gun that cracked a hard click sound as I turned a crank, a toy I played with when I was a little boy with Aunt Bea and Uncle Jackie in the country, in the middle of the war. I remember being afraid of the big lumbering slobbery lipped crunching cows, and the clicking of the machine gun (made from nonstrategic materials and approved for sale in the Woolworth's in Placerville) was not scaring the cows, it seemed to be attracting them. When the cow shoved its head into the doorway and knocked my machine gun over, I picked up the toy and used it like a stick on the cow and chased it away, chased all the cows until someone yelled at me to stop, I was running the fat off them. I decide I like Fat's laugh.

A middle-aged woman holds up a ring and whispers "How much?"

"Lady, you are too stupid and offensive to wear any of my jewelry if you're going to begin a relationship with me with a stupid question like that!" he snarls without moving, his fat like a rock.

She recoils as if bitten by a snake, but he's more like a frog, skin smooth as rubber. Whiskey brown eyes like a frog. And he doesn't move very much. Like a frog. "I design and shape and choose the medium of the jewelry for the whole body and the personality of the person who is going to wear it. If you wear my jewelry, you wear it because you know art, you can see! You don't pick something up, and ask how much, you look at it, you ask if you can try it on to see how it looks on your finger or wherever you personally would wear something like that."

He introduces the tall blonde woman sitting behind the table with him as his apprentice. She says she hates him but that he's a genius. "And he's a lousy salesman!" she says and hits him on his shoulder.

"That's not true!" he says, "I am a great salesman. I know people. I have the instinct for public relations. But I don't have time for bullshit. I'm sorry, no bullshit for Fat Jack. That's me! Just me, that's all!" Fat Jack laughs that stupid laugh I start to like. He says he doesn't take many apprentices. He's not like other artists who take anybody with money, like giggly society brides looking for a little depth. He only takes talented people for apprentices. He likes talent. He asks me about my teachers. Teachers used to notice him in high school. Do they notice me? I tell him about the social studies teacher who says she's scared of me and dodges my eye when I'm sketching in class now.

"Mrs. Mitten? Mary Mitten! She was my social studies teacher at Fremont!" he says, and his Mary Mitten is the same as mine, so he can't be too much older than me, and he lives by making jewelry. He has a shop in Berkeley, professors with international reputations and Nobel Prizes are among his clients. He lives in an old Victorian house on the edge of Chinatown near the Nimitz Freeway in Oakland, where his Japanese wife, wearing very tight dresses, comes to spend the occasional night with him until their divorce becomes final.

"Why shouldn't she? I'm good in bed," he says, "Ask her! She loves the way I ball her. That's it. But I'm me. That's all." He is the last word on art. "What's Jimmy Dean's problem?" he asks. "He has his own car. Natalie Wood lives down the street. What's his problem?"

He teaches me to practice drawing with a stick, with a twig, with a rock, with my finger dipped in ink on wet paper. I find I enjoy drawing with a Chinese writing brush, a bamboo stick, and a fine steel pen. I sell my drawings for ten dollars apiece to two Spanish teachers, a social studies teacher, and the Girls' Vice Principal. Though I never took an art class in high school, the art teacher invites me to her room after school to go through her supplies. Paper, paint, pastel crayon, bottles and bottles of black India ink that smell almost like something to eat. Brushes and penpoints. I get my bamboo stick and Chinese brushes in a bookstore in Chinatown that smells of dusty shelves, brass ink boxes going strange, polished glass, and India ink. She enters me in competition for a scholarship to an art college in Oakland and asks me to put together a portfolio. I don't know what a portfolio is. She has one of her art classes make me a portfolio to hold my drawings as a crafts project.

She meets me after school to pose for me in her studio in the back of her house, with northern light. I sketch her as she undresses. The brush and ink. A steel pen ready, too. Fat Jack says I have a problem with hands, elbows, hips, knees. I don't know how to foreshorten. I can't draw a finger pointing straight at me, see the folding of shadow and flesh. She poses and I draw how the meat of the thighs falls round the bone and spreads to one side of the chair. I draw the toes of a foot pressed against glass. I draw the flow of musculature and soft bulges from the neck, shoulders, elbows resting on the knees down the thighs to her buttocks. I throw shadow and light on her to show up her shapes.

One day I'm surprised when she barefoots down off the modeling platform and unbuttons my shirt. "You have been sketching me in the nude for a while now. It's only fair you return the favor," she says and pulls my T-shirt up off my chest and licks my left nipple, then my right, with my head inside the bag of my T-shirt and my arms straight up. "I have never emphasized it, but I want you to know, I'm an artist too. I want to show you my work," she says.

We sketch each other naked and our fingers and our bodies are dirty with charcoal and India ink when she sits crosslegged right in front of me and starts scratching up a sketch of my dong in charcoal. And the thing changes shape, goes straight and throbs as she sketches across more and more paper, and it hurts, and I'm a little scared when she drops her paper and charcoal and crawls over and puts her tongue on the tip and slips her mouth over the whole thing. She lifts her lips, showing her teeth in a smile around my dick and looks in my eyes and inside she's licking. I try not to act surprised and say nothing so as to say nothing stupid, and let it feel good though I have no idea what's going to happen next. I hear my dick being gurgled and gagged and growled on like a bone in a happy dog's mouth, and come to know white girls are girls too.

My drawings win a state art contest, a prize at a county fair, and a scholarship to the art college. My drawings sell at the Mother "i". At first my work gets into the showroom because I am a friend of the house pianist. But soon, even though I'm not out of high school, I become a regular, a kind of fixture at the Mother "i", smoking dope on weekends under the Fat Jack's table with his apprentice and the house pianist.

All Chinamen think no other Chinaman has seen a Chinaman like them. Like all the Chinamen I know, all the Chinaman in my family: Pop, Charlie Chan's Number Four Son; my Uncle Morton Chu, the electronics whiz turned guitar maker; my older brother, Longman Jr., slowly rising in the railroad hierarchy; each of them are dead certain, that they, and only they, are so much more deeply and tangibly but inexplicably American than any other Chinaman who has ever lived that all other Chinamen who meet them will run hot and cold with jealousy and terror. And on that day with the art teacher, I feel that way too.

But Fat Jack really is different. Fat Jack is right. I never have met a Chinaman like him. He becomes a strange mentor, my brilliant twin in The Movie About Me. He is Orson Welles to my Mickey Mouse.

It is in his shop that I first hear Dylan Thomas reading elaborately worded children's stories, and the poetry of W.H. Auden riffing in a loping cadence fit to be sung as a country song. And today, Kenneth Patchen's deep, tubercular, egg-shaped rumblings to jazz about somebody's ducks on somebody's pond bounce off the black walls and clobber me. His phonograph is turned up too loud for Fat Jack to hear anyone step in from the street and shout his name.

"You don't care about them being homosexuals, right? Or do you? Yes or no?" Fat Jack asks, looks up from his hands on the worktable, lifts his magnifying goggles, and laughs at me.

"Who're what? Who're you talking about?" I ask.

Fat jerks his goggles off his head. "You're cherry!" he says. "You are a good Chinese boy after all! Seventeen and still a virgin. Ha! Ha! Ha! I see it, man. Am I sensitive, or what! You have never done it with a woman. But you've heard about it. You have heard about it, haven't you? You can talk to me." Patchen's voice fills the black walls of the shop like loud warm messy soup. The boyish-looking girl working next to Fat Jack looks up. She doesn't smile or look as if she cares what's happening.

"Come on, Fat," I say.

"So of course you haven't thought about men who might want sex with you, because you haven't found a woman who wants sex with you," Fat says. "Or is it something else? Don't be afraid of me, Chinese boy, I don't swing that way. Some people say I do, but that's them. If they want to think that way about me, that's them. I'm me. And I like Kenneth Patchen's poetry and listening to him read it, man, no matter what he is, okay?" Fat Jack's voice has the birdy nasal resonance of a banjo and like a barking electric saw, it cuts through Patchen's rumbling groaning boom about somebody once drowning in the water under the ducks.

"Well, in theory," I say, knowing it sounds especially stupid, because I have to shout it to be heard. I know he'll say, "Ha! Ha! Ha! Just like a Chinese boy!"

And sure enough—"Ha! Ha! Ha! Just like a Chinese boy!" he barks.

His short-haired apprentice who wears no make-up and has the sad eyes of a baby seal, smiles and spits up a little laugh. She wipes it off her lips with her fingers and makes a face. "My fingers taste awful," she says.

"So wash your fingers before I eat them," I say.

"I don't suggest you eat them raw," she says and stops me with a look.

Fat Jack introduces me to the sound of Spanish Gypsy flamenco guitar and singing in little clubs under the apartments where the Chinese live all over North Beach. Fat Jack takes me to the Old Spaghetti Factory to see the Flamencos de la Bodega for the first time and to hear Adonis El Filipino, a kid no older than me, play the smoked dry moans of beat-up boozy old men who've seen it all out of a guitar he Frankensteined together from old parts in the guitar maker's shop he works in as an apprentice, instead of going to high school. In The Movie About Me, I am raised by Spanish Gypsies.

Meanwhile, later that night, Fat Jack starts to really introduce me to his short-haired apprentice for the first time, as the three of us down cappuccinos at the Mother "i". She is the fifteen-year-old daughter of a professor at Cal, he explains, and works after school. "She's my dogfaced boy," he says nodding his chin at her.

"Fuck you, Jack!" she says in a voice sounding older, worn deeper, than fifteen. She turns and walks out of the Mother "i".

Fat bounces on his heels with his hands in his pocket and ash falling off the cigarette poked between his little Tweety Bird lips. I go after her for Fat. He doesn't ask me to go after her, but I do. She's on the corner angry, looking across Kearny Street up Jackson, into Chinatown, and across Jackson to Columbus and the espresso bars and pizza parlors of North Beach. I ask her if she feels like something to eat in Chinatown. "I know Chinatown. And it's just across the street," I say.

She's afraid of everything on the menu. She sounds like a kid the way she talks about food.

"Are you going to make a big fucking deal about what I eat with you?" she asks.

"No."

"I want something plain. Something not too strange, you know what I mean? Something I shouldn't regret putting in my mouth. Something meat and potatoes, like that."

"How about beef stew with potatoes?" I ask her.

"No rice?"

"You can have it on rice. You can have it with potatoes and rice, if you like."

"Really? In a Chinese restaurant?"

"It's Chinese beef stew," I say.

She tells me Fat showed her my poetry. "I think it's pretty childish, but I like it, because I'm a child too," she says.

Her voice and look curl my toes and clear my asthma. There's nothing I can say or do next. There is no next but eating and walking back to the "i".

Ulysses: Not Dating Sharon

I'm not in the wacky Buddhist church anymore, but Sharon still calls me. I haven't seen her since I was thirteen or fourteen. First she asks me to ask her out to her sophomore dance, a Sadie Hawkins sock hop, and it's too sad. I know her folks won't let her go with me, but she talks me into asking her. I have to ask her before she will ask her folks. If she tells them I asked, maybe they won't want to hurt my feelings.

Nothing stopped them before. Why should they not want to hurt my feelings now? But I ask her, the way she wants, and sure enough she comes back to the phone saying they won't let her go out with me. Now is when it would be nice to talk on and arrange to casually meet by accident someplace, like the San Francisco Zoo or at City Lights Books, and I'll take her to see my drawings at the Mother "i", which is really just across the street from her father's sewing factory but seems like a million miles away. She likes me when I talk that way. I hear her sigh, like Ma at the movies, reconsidering the sight of a dream come true.

Then a year later she phones asking me to ask her out to her junior prom, and it is a ritual chant now, a primitive children's ceremony. I ask her out, so she can say I phoned to ask her out and maybe this time they won't want to hurt my feelings. I have heard it before. I know what is coming, and she comes back to the phone saying her parents won't let her go out with me. I'm a year older now, and it's sadder this time.

Minutes later, she calls saying she has arranged a date for me to her junior prom with her best friend, a Chinese Catholic who wants to have a pre-prom date with me to see if we get along. It's okay, I tell her, I don't want to go to your prom if I'm not going out with you unless we're going to switch dates at the prom. But no, she can't lie to her parents, she tells me. Yeah, I know you can't lie to your parents, I say into the phone.

I agree to take her friend out this next weekend and take her to the prom if she likes me. Why is Sharon arranging dates for me with other girls? I go, feeling, hoping, that Sharon is just beyond her friend. Anyway, after this she'll owe me.

Sharon's friend has never met a Chinaman like me or been inside the Mother "i". She can't keep her hands off me while I'm driving her home out to the foggy Sunset District, where all the houses are the same height, have the same tile roofs, and are painted the colors of faded swimming pool bottoms. After making out a while in the front seat of Ma's Chevy under the streetlight gone milky in the fog around the car, I tell her I don't want to go to her junior prom. My thing is with Sharon, and she's nice, but I really don't want to go to the prom. She cries. She puts her hand on my crotch. She won't go all the way, but she will help me out, she says into my neck, as she begs me to take her to her junior prom. Her tears run down my neck under my shirt and down my chest and ribs. It's a long drive from the Sunset in Frisco to Bancroft Way in Berkeley and my apartment across the street from Fat Jack Fat's jewelry shop.

The whole Saturday night feels awful. As I climb the stairs to my little apartment over Uncle Mort's garage workshop to sleep it off, I hear groaning, a girl's voice inside, and the record player playing jazz, and I smell burning pot and incense like an ever-widening path to my door. Fat Jack Fat grunts the way he laughs, and I recognize the low voice of the girl he calls his dog-faced boy apprentice even over the noise and don't go in. Round and round I go. Back into Ma's old Chevy, back through the empty streets of Berkeley, and over the empty Bay Bridge to Frisco again, into Chinatown. The restaurants are closing. The garbage is out on the street. The only place open is the little Chinese-suey-and-American-food dive next door to the Times Theater where the whores socialize all night long and do their "office work." Boiled noodles and a piece of custard pie are on my mind as I open the door into the high ceilinged steam of the café, and all I see is Ron in a white T-shirt, with his hands on his hips, a mass of keys on a huge key ring looking like a weapon of some kind on one hip. "What are you doing here?" he asks.

"I'm getting something to eat," I say.

"Uhh, yeah? Okay," he says, and nods me past him. I sit at the counter and notice that the whores always pat Ron on the ass and say something to him on the way in or on the way out, and realize that the strange white-skinned older brother of Sharon, the princess of the Buddhist church, is some kind of bodyguard here. I stay, order donuts and coffee and watch until it begins to get light out and I can see the traffic begin to flow on Broadway to and from the Broadway tunnel just behind the movie house. I think of sleeping a couple of hours in the Times Theater like everyone else, instead watching the movies as I usually do. But no, Fat Jack and his apprentice have had my apartment long enough.

Ulysses: A Cooking Lesson

One day Fat Jack asks me if I've eaten yet, if I'm hungry, just as if he were a typcial Chinese host with a guest. He makes me a raw spinach omelette with sour cream, like nothing I'd ever seen made in Ma's restaurant. "French," he says. "A rolled omelette, not that airy puffy dried-up mess most Americans call an omelette."

It's delicious.

"You dig the different textures, man? The egg, and the cool sour cream and crunchy spinach? What a trip, huh? French!" he says, and fixes himself a bowl of corn flakes and milk. "Corn flakes and milk!" he says amazed at himself. "How Zen of me! Ha. Ha. Ha. My therapist is amazed, she says. I don't see things the way other people see them. I have insights, and artistic understanding, dig. She says she has never had a client like me. I'm a fucking genius, that's all! Ha! Ha! Ha!"

"There's this art teacher who thinks I'm a genius," I say.

Fat Jack jumps on me with, "No, *I'm* a genius. You're just very bright." He stops and makes a face all the way into his scalp, and says, "Maybe brilliant. My dog-faced boy apprentice is brilliant. I validated her brilliance. I began to culture her genius. They all say I was the one who taught her discipline. I helped her find her *art,* that's all," Fat Jack says, offhand, urgent, intimate. Beyond interruption. Beyond asking for sense or a sign of what he's talking about.

I don't ask for a knife. I try not to be awkward cutting and shoveling up pieces of the omelette with a fork.

"What happened is this," he says. "I became her lover, but I'm too much to just make love to her like that. I mean I *mean* too much to her to just make love to her. I am her *teacher.*

"But the way it happened. She says she wants to. She's not a virgin. She has a beautiful young body. But I do not take her body. She can do that with anybody. But I am special. I am an artist. She's an artist. We are. I see it in her work. Her sense of design. It's a gas the way we communicate, like without talking, just working together at the table together in the sour smell of pickling and polishing solutions, carving our wax, we are digging each other, man, grooving on each other's creativity, you know what I mean? Making *real* love, real communication.

"I never went looking for her. She came to me. Our eyes glommed on to each other when she first came in, tagging along with her father (the famous professor, up for the Nobel Prize in his field or I'd tell you who he is) and her mother (from up on the North Side, very classy) who had come to pick up a pair of rings they had commissioned me to create for their wedding anniversary. Gold rings. As I remember, they both had long fingers. Well, one day she came into the shop by herself, interested in making jewelry.

"I could have had her then, if I wanted. I knew it. I felt it. She wanted to. I could tell. And she was experienced . . . I could tell, didn't have to tell me. But her father was my friend, after all. When he came in for fittings, he had talked about her, and even then I knew he didn't understand her, he didn't communicate with her. But I understand, man. He's a genius, and deep into his bag, man. He works out.

"So she was fifteen and experienced. It happens. *My* father took me to a Chinese whorehouse in San Francisco on my twelfth birthday, but like everything about me, my father was not like other Chinese boys' fathers," he says, and laughs. "Wow, I haven't thought of that in years. My father was a hero in Chinatown! He was the best-dressed gambler Chinatown ever saw. A gassy Robin Hood hero kind, who looked like Errol Flynn to my mother. She thought he was low-class and a criminal, but he worshipped her, and we had money. If we did not have money, my mother was going to take me and leave.

"So we had money. Everyone else was poor where we lived, but we had money. We had a radio in every room but the dining room, where she kept the record player. We had a baby grand piano. We had French food. I tell you, I am not like other Chinese boys. I am not isolated in that cramped guilt-tripping Chinese-y thing, man. She knew Louis Armstrong, and Billie Holiday, and Trotsky. She was something else. Until I was three years old my hair was long, and she kept it in curls, you know, and dressed me in these Little Lord Fauntleroy suits and buckles on my shoes. See, there's no Chinese boys like me.

"I grew up devouring culture and art, with the nearsighted Chinese-y Chinese, the poor and stupid, all around me. And my dad was their hero. Every Chinese New Year's he used to leave a hundred-pound sack of rice at every door in Oakland Chinatown. My mother knocked him for being a pagan anti-Christ to humiliate her, in front of her parents. She's a Christian, of course, and the last couple years before he died, he passed out sacks of rice on Christmas Eve and Chinese New Year's, to make her happy. I understand people, man. I understand people because I am so many people! Wow! Wiggy thought! You don't have to believe me, you can ask her father.

"He says I'm a genius. I have insight. See? Lots of my clientele from Cal say that, not me. You smoke a little grass, right, you get high, you buzz with sensitivity, right? You can get turned on to things in your ears, in your eyes, in your mind, and buzz into them close up, man. Am I right? I know. I'm like that all the time. I see the Egyptians were great artists, man, but they only had two dimensions, man. No eyebags! The Greeks invented eyebags and the kind of painting that goes for the reality of the look only, and then the camera came and photographs had the reality of the look, and cats like Monet, and Toulouse-Lautrec and Van Gogh said enough of that noise, if I want to paint a face green because I feel the face is green, I will. And they did, and that's the fucking history of art, man, and why today I am me, just who I want to be, and not fucked up with guilt because I'm not somebody else. So when I smoke, man! Yeah, you know, what you're like when you smoke, so think of that supersensitive *you,* as *me,* just normal blowing me, wigging through the art experiences of the day, man, and then smoking! Whew! These professors who hang out here can't believe the things I say, man. It's like my thoughts are out there with Einstein and Aristotle, but I don't know *them.* That's just *me!"*

He smiles and looks like he's laughing, but isn't. "You know the dog-faced boy apprentice smokes some herself. I thought she could handle it. She smokes and she talks, talks about wanting me. But I didn't fuck her. And if I had I wouldn't feel guilty. No guilt. No guilt. Guilt is bourgeois."

Ulysses: The Stratagem of Running Away in Hopeless Situations

My big brother gets me a summer job in Roseville. It's in a big flat railroad yard and a little town with nobody on the streets most of the time. The summer's too hot. I am oddly within feeling distance of the country of my first memories as a lone yellow kid with Uncle Jackie and Aunt Bea, the retired vaudeville acrobat and the former silent-screen bit player. It seems as if Roseville is in a country far from World War II, and the old trains I hear in the Mother Lode, the sun shining on the rocks and dust, the dogs padding the shadows of low trees, and the cows resting in the shady garage, are of another time. Owoooooo! Hear that wolf? It might be the last one in the whole state of California.

I'm not ready to start my last year of Oakland High. When I come home to my apartment over Mort's garage, I find Ma's cleaned up my room and thrown away my poetry.

That's the only time I ever hit my mother.

"Remember it, son! I'll type it for you!" she shouts at me, screams to soothe the flesh I'd hit, and pats me on the back, bends to touch me rooting through the garbage cans. "I thought you'd like it. New curtains. A real desk!"

But I am not a poet, just a kid who's hit his mother and made her cry. She cruelly understands I am not a poet, that there is nothing I need to save in my room. That's why she cleans it and changes it, furnishes it so exactly. But it's not important.

Ulysses: El Filipino

Since we're two guys fresh out of high school, when Adonis and I glimpse each other in guitar shops, on the streets of Berkeley and San Francisco, in coffee houses, walking like James Dean in love with his car, like Marlon Brando yearning for his Harley, grinning like Alfonso Bedoya, trying to lure Bogey out of hiding with a pocket watch, we each think—Danger! This kid has seen too many movies. Our eyes are cameras filming the movies about ourselves in stereo. We see the shutters flicking open and closed in our eyes. We appear to each other as warnings, noticeably alike and uncomfortably dissimilar, as if we should each be more like the other or at least look more like each other. Especially considering the similar words people use to describe us, high cheek bones, thick oily curly black hair, long long slender fingers shaped like a show girl's legs with too many knees, and a dark olive skin that makes so many others take Adonis for me, and me for Adonis.

He repairs guitars in Harmon Satterlee's shop on Sutter, studies flamenco with Mariano Cordoba, and plays with Los Flamencos de la Bodega at the Old Spaghetti Factory on Green Street where Fat Jack has taken me. First impression, his looks say Spanish Gypsy or Mexican. But he's Filipino. An American-born Filipino Spanish flamenco guitarist. He is the ultimate gringo flamenco guitarist. His mother wonders if he isn't going through a phase.

Meantime I am the greatest poet in the world under twenty-five by evening, and on the late-night shift I work a job Hollywood Junior got me, mudhopping on the railroad. The lords of the road ride: the conductors and brakemen, the locomotive engineers and firemen. The low of the railroad are on the ground: the clerks, and the lowest of the low, the clerks who walk the yard, the mudhops. But high or low, the worst thing a railroader can be called is "college kid."

I'm back in Berkeley. Jason Peach lives here and preys on the young, hot, and liberal in his new guise as a well-rounded guitar-playing folkie. Jason, Adonis "El Filipino," and I see *Chushingura* together at the Storefront Moviehouse. Until it's time for me to head down to midnight shift mudhopping a railroad yard, we sit upstairs at the coffee house across the street from Jason's apartment above Buffalo Books, suck on espressos, talk about forty-seven samurai pulling up to the front of the movie house on forty-seven big Honda motorcycles. We line up at the box office for tickets and confess to wondering, What is James Dean's problem in *Rebel Without a Cause* and *East of Eden?* He has a car! What is he doing still living with his folks? Why doesn't Brando enjoy his gang biking over the rise toward the camera to take over a little town, like *Yojimbo?* Brando's answer to the question of "Hey, Johnny what'cha rebellin' against?" is just right, "Whaddaya got?" and we all slap hands and stick our tongues out in appreciation every time we recall it at the coffee house and sometimes attract a glance from a girl we've been watching. But what kind of white trash outlaw biker bandito is Brando? He's not a bandit. He's as scary as Ricky Nelson dressing up like Elvis. The bandits who ride over the rise at the beginning of *Seven Samurai*—those are righteous bandits!

Ulysses: College Kid Mudhop

It's early 1960s and I haven't caught on to TV news being rewrites of old movies. Gidget has become the ultimate white middle-class teen fantasy and Sandra Dee lets her adolescence get the best of her. My best friend, the TV, is teaching me the fine points of cracking wise, cutting low, grin 'n' bear it, cap it, and capper it closed, from the days of *Dragnet* deadpan high-contrast black-and-white, Napoleon Solo, and *Get Smart!* freaks talking "Would you believe . . ." All from TV. Blacks are Negroes. Hollywood Junior, you don't have a good word for Negroes or blacks on your TV, Hero, but you watch it all the time, even when blacks appear in their underwear in Fruit of the Loom commercials and drink wine with Burt Bacharach and Angie Dickenson in wine commercials. We work on the railroad. We watch TV.

I am a relief mudhop on the Western Pacific. I don't ride the engines or the caboose. I drive a pickup truck or walk the yard, up and down between the tracks of high walled steel boxcars on steel wheels that come up to my elbow. It's dark and shadowy between tracks of cars. Sometimes they leave the steel strapping used to tie a load of lumber to a flatcar dangling off the edges of the empty flat like spider legs. The crinkle of the flexing steel strap sounds a little like water trickling over stones and one night sneaks up on me on creeping heavy wheels, rolling on the flatcar, too low in the shadows to flash its steel tentacles in the moonlight. The track on the other side of me is loaded with cold boxcars. I hear the razor steel flex and whang in the air. I hear its tips slap the ground between tracks, and slice. If I fall on the ground like the old alcoholics I see I'll get all cut up. I run—too scared to scream—to a D/F refer boxcar and climb its ladder just as the leering and crinkling steel strap snickers by me.

I am not only a mudhop, the lowest of the low, I am worse—a college dropout. A "college kid" mudhop. The worthlessness of college kids has been proven by all the college kids grown old and bewildered as their lifetime is wasted writing down the road initials, numbers, kinds and contents of boxcars, and the names of the shippers and cities they rolled from, and where they're going. The college kid mudhops living through stupidity toward their pensions play chess with each other and become so absorbed in being intelligent in front of the cloddish conductors who are spitting tobacco juice in the wastebaskets that they don't hear the phone ring, and it's hours before anyone knows that a switch crew conductor, fresh with the news of a relative just dead in Vietnam, has shoved a flatcar loaded with a tank bound for Nam off the end of the railroad barge and into the bay, scaring off thousands of silvery anchovies which flash and add color to the huge splash.

When I am not at the railroad, I am busy at working becoming a great writer. I take a jumbo three-ring binder full of my poetry to Thom Gunn, the British cycle-riding poet in residence at Berkeley and expect him to be so overcome by my genius that he happily jumps out of his poetry chair and gives it to me. We chat a bit about my background. Chinatown. My high school. Two weeks later, after he's read my stuff, I come back. He seems nervous, which is understandable, seeing that I am a genius. He glances over a couple of my poems, raises his eyebrows here, bites his lip there, then swivels around in his chair, silently claps his hands a couple of times and says, "Mr. Kwan . . . do you have trouble with the language?"

Ulysses: Berkeley

I get a girlfriend when I am twenty-two years old, living in Berkeley and working on the railroad. Though girlfriend seems a maliciously deceptive word, "lover" is too scary. I am in a huge creative writing class, upstairs in a big hot room with all the windows open. The instructor glows. He is a poet working on his first autobiographical novel. The news his poetry has just been awarded the Pulitzer Prize is on the front page of the morning Chronicle, and everyone in class has a newspaper and a glow and gah-gah eyes for Mr. Pulitzer Prize.

Mr. Pulitzer Prize accepts our applause with a little smile, a little bow, and raises his hand a little to bring the applause down, then runs class as usual. He reads a story of mine. It sounds like how not to write to win the Pulitzer Prize. No sneering or jeering necessary—the story, full of Chinese in and out of the house, is too sorry to ridicule. He reads off the last awful lines, takes a breath, and puts his hand over the stack of pages. "What is this boy doing here?" he asks like he's found a fly in his tomato juice. The gah-gah eyes in the class go dim. "This young man shouldn't be in college. He should be writing!"

It takes me awhile to understand he's praising me.

She picks me off after class. Sorority girl. Campus beauty queen. Her name is Sarah. Blonde, brown eyes, a body dreamed up by Playboy magazine in a fuzzy black sweater. I see her close. I pant like a dog. I hold the dog of me back.

We get cappuccino at the coffee house. She likes discovering I know the dark man in a white shirt and no undershirt behind the counter pressing coffee. Pressing espresso at the Piccolo coffee house seems to be one of Adonis "El Filipino" Medina's many part-time jobs. She says an Italian man who took her virginity told her cappuccino is best in a round bottomed cup. The proportion of foam to the coffee stays the same that way. She pulls my cappuccino toward her and drops a half a teaspoon of white sugar in a mound about the size of a dime. "Watch," she says. We watch the little dime of sugar darken up with coffee, get heavy and sink slowly through the foam of steamed milk till plop! it suddenly drops into the coffee, and the foam shudders. She shoves the cup and saucer back toward me. "Sex education," she says. I nod. I walk her home to her sorority house.

I put in for a relief mudhop slot, working people's days off, two midnight shifts, two four-to-midnight, and one daylight, and try to grab some college three days a week. I come home from work and find her sleeping on my bed, a dream come true. A miracle. The room is cool. Her coat is cold. She's been here a while. She's moved in. A danger sign. A couple of nights later she asks me to hit her, tells me a woman needs to be slapped to her senses sometimes, and she scares me. I won't do it. The third time she asks, I begin to dread coming home and being asked again. I don't like her shaming me for not being up to hitting her.

Sarah's father is a fifty-year-old professor in the English Department who looks ninety. Mark Foot. He likes my writing and makes a fuss over me at school, as if he doesn't mind his daughter sleeping with me and is glad her sorority sister days are numbered. He becomes my drinking buddy and reminisces about Dylan Thomas and W.H. Auden, he recites Yeats, and Marcel Proust and Céline in French, and Shakespeare's *Midsummer Night's Dream* and *The Tempest* as one play.

We argue literature and bullshit. He worries about his daughter when he's drunk. He gets sloppy. His face caves in, and he falls and crawls, and I can't watch him melt into a puddle on the floor, but I do. And I listen to him ponder the same mystery in the same words. Sarah is beautiful, blonde, talented, the stuff millions of girls wish and pray to God for. Why, instead of following her beauty, blondeness, and talent to the light, where she will flourish does she stay hovering around him? Why does she prefer tormenting him for having been a slobbering slurring stumbling souse when she found him the night her mother died? She could be living a wonderful life right now. He can't understand her. The girl was eight when her mother died. She's been watching him drink since she was five. Everybody knows his wife hated his drinking. So it isn't his drinking that makes her hang around him wasting her youth, her looks, her love life, punishing him until the day he dies. Every time he visits, she calls after he leaves to apologize for him and say she's coming to spend the night.

What am I doing here? Where am I? This is better than The Movie About Me.

She talks about the old man. He was a writer. Heavy on the was. Bright boy of the department. Straight "As" from his start as a freshman to the finish of his doctorate. Where is his writing? she asks. Where is the writing he did while Diana—her mother—casually lingered and dozed a couple of years to death? She talks about her mother by name. No Ma or Mom or Mama. It's "My mother" or "Diana."

Ulysses: The California Zephyr

Saturdays I work baggage with an old man with button eyes and thin brown hair parted down the middle. He looks just like Dagwood Bumstead in the funnies, and Joe E. Brown, the old movie comic with the big mouth, who now and then comes to life on The Late Show. Dagwood reads out loud, talks to himself while he adds and subtracts, and tells himself what to do before he does anything. Mostly what we do when we aren't loading baggage is keep the rubber stamps of the railroads and the railroad stations of the nation in alphabetical order.

Dagwood talks to the rubber stamps. It's a wonder he finds something new to say to them every Saturday I work with him. Like fussy things to Provo, Utah, about visiting there with his wife and his car. Every rubber stamp has a distinct personality. We have a lot of small fussy things to do in this barn of a baggage room. Fake Spanish mission architecture on the outside, a two-story empty box on the inside. Mailbags are piled against one wall. Baggage carts and a jitney we use once a day to haul the carts of baggage off the inbound Zephyr in the afternoon.

"The inbound Zephyr was late. The baggageman had to wait."

One of the fussy things I do in the hours and hours between the morning outbound Zephyr and the early evening inbound Zephyr is write out my overtime slips in rhyme.

Among the kinds of baggage I load on Saturdays are the bagged, coffined, and crated dead bodies of American soldiers going home from Vietnam on the outbound California Zephyr. I don't know what's in the heavy plywood crates loaded on the steel-wheeled baggage carts. All I know is I hate working baggage in the summertime when all the Annettes, Ann-Margrets, Tammys, and Gidgets go traveling east together with well-dressed young men on the last of the great passenger trains. College students going home with their skis, good grades, and good looks. I'm jealous, and work on ways of revealing my brains to the college kids, make Annette swoon and Gidget want to fidget a strange baggageman's wang.

My job isn't much more than writing or rubber-stamping railroad initials on baggage tags, handing the stubs over to the passengers, tagging the bags, loading the bags on the carts, wheeling the carts out to the baggage car, and loading the bags off the carts onto the train. That's all it is. To make it interesting I get on the inbound Zephyr after all the passengers are off and race ahead of the porters through the train, feeling the seats for lost wallets, jewelry, coins, Colorado newspapers, and old magazines.

Some nights I ride the Zephyr through the washer and am on my way to Chicago in The Movie About Me. In the movie about my years as a fearless Saturday baggageman, a passenger comes into the baggage room expecting a counter and a scale, but sees, instead, me—in a smoking jacket, puffing on a pipe, seated in an overstuffed chair, with my feet wallowing in the fur of a polar bear rug. My fingers laze over a large globe. I offer the passenger a sherry, a cigar, and a seat. We talk of baggage through the ages, and the greater meaning of the railroads they will ride out of town. "The Bangor and Aroostook was always one of my favorite lines, but the last is the best. Yet alas, the mighty little Zug Line is a railroad of the past."

Instead, while Dagwood tells his life story and domestic problems to his powerful rubber stamps, I wheel the old baggage carts, one by one, out of the baggage room onto the street, next to the mainline, and wait for the California Zephyr to wheel out from the yard with a rested crew of ancient brakemen and conductor and a fresh locomotive. One of these old conductors I think is the funniest man in the world. Wednesdays I work daylight, and one of my chores is running the inbound conductor from the pad to the yard office in the company pickup truck to sign off his paperwork. This conductor acts like he's terrified of my driving. He cusses me out, and I cuss him out. I think it's great fun, until he has a heart attack in the truck. At least he doesn't die. I realize that he really does hate me and my driving. He really had been cussing me out. In a way, his heart attack was the best joke he ever told. I laugh when I understand how much the old conductor fears and hates me.

The passengers and their friends and family hang around for just one more last goodbye. They assemble in clusters down the track by rubber pylons marking where their assigned cars will stop and open doors and drop stairs, and porters step down to lay a steel first step on the ground, and tell you to "watch your step please." I always like being out on the street to see the outbound's effect on the people itching to ride her away. Even now, I know the California Zephyr, the train famous for sleek silver coaches and once upon a time headed by a silver locomotive born-and-bred to haul this train only, is doomed to die like the Twentieth Century Limited and the Santa Fe Chief. I hate being a menial to the Saturday passengers, but I love the train. The names of the coaches and pullmans speak of the Zephyr's class: Silver Cascade. Silver Juniper. The train loves the country it runs through from Oakland to Chicago over the Feather River route. The passengers *whoo* at the sight of the Zephyr's grimy orange and silver engine, floating on a growl out of an alley and curving to take the straight track down Third Street, past me and the carts, and right through the crowd if they don't step back. But I don't have to move. I know this train. I'm a part of it.

I step up onto the first cart and sit on one of the plywood crates and strike a match on it. I'm smoking my cigarette, squinting down the track, looking for the girls I'd like to turn and see me smoking, looking cool, while the huge cast-iron snout of the engine throws its shadow over me, across the sidewalk and up the walls of the depot and baggage room. I wonder if I'm not a little too close to the track and look down at the street again for the white line marking the safe distance from the rail. I don't see it. What if I'm sitting right in the middle of the track? I'm thinking when Dagwood pulls on my pants cuff and says, "They don't like to bring the remains out before the train gets here." Remains. I don't understand.

He sighs like Jack Benny, folds his arms, and tells me what "remains" are. Where they come from. What is inside. How they have to be loaded first. Dead soldiers. A passenger ticket for a seat they will never occupy. A serviceman of rank equal to the dead sits next to an empty seat—the missing man formation of the rails—and sees the dead man home to be buried with a flag, and gives some words to the family.

I hate working baggage on Saturdays more than I hate the war these days. Not because the work is hard. Not even because it's stupid. My brother's job braking off the brakemen's Extra Board is easier and stupider than mine. But you, Hero, you ride the big engines and get the view out of the snake eyes of the head end of the rolling train, and loll about the caboose and wave heroically to the kids standing by the right of way, throwing rocks.

After seeing Gilo Pontecorvo's *The Battle of Algiers* in Berkeley, Jason Peach, Terry (Jason's neighbor, a fast-talking Southern Pacific brakeman, a fellow college dropout with a fatal habit of getting drunk and loud in the wrong bar), and I go out for drinks to discuss how much we love the black and white, the low-contrast graininess, the close, midground, and distant objects all being in the same squashed-up focus. It makes the escape of the terrorist bombers through the crowd more tense. The splatter and scatter of the explosions are more dramatic crunched flat in telephoto shots. Terry loudly loves the idea of an Italian Commie making the movie about Algerians making fools of the bourgeois French Foreign Legion. He makes Jason Peach nervous, but "continuing on the theme of liberation," Terry tells Jason and me, "The Southern Pacific is hiring brakemen. You guys should hire on. They have to hire some blacks even though they don't want to. They hate the idea. But to avoid hiring some black guy, they're sure to hire Ulysses. And because they *have* to hire *some* blacks, they're sure to hire you, Jason," the brakeman says over a drink in the wrong bar.

He has a way of walking into bars where they don't want to hear anything nasty about any recently assassinated Kennedy, any Commie art movie, Mario Savio and the Free Speech Movement, the failure of the work ethic, God is dead, or anything else he has a mouth for saying. "Oh, Jason, I have to tell you, man, the most beautiful thing I ever saw in my life was you with Sarah in your arms at that candlelight vigil on the steps of Sproul Hall, man. What was that, who died? Anti-war? Student strike? All those candles, man. And there right in the center is this vision of perfection—Sarah's beautiful blonde head against your beautiful black body, and singing 'We Shall Overcome,' oh, man, I cried. It was beautiful."

"Cool it, Terry," Jason says, quiet and friendly. "Come on, I don't want to die in a bar where nobody knows me."

"How long you known Sarah, man?" I ask Jason.

"We all had dinner at La Fiesta, remember, and saw *Children of Paradise* together."

"Marcel Carné. Great director. Great fucking movie!" Terry says.

"Cool it, Terry," I say.

The brakeman is blond and blue eyed, and lives under Jason Peach's apartment above Buffalo Books on Telegraph. I remember him and his small, exquisite, straw-haired blonde blue-eyed lover making out on the lawn under the wings of the larger-than-life-size bronze pelican outside the Pelican Building. People on their way to the Faculty Club watched as their tongues went in and out of each other's mouths and her hand went inside his pants and his hand under her sweater. They are blond on blonde, beautiful as Hitler Youth poster children, no zits, no scars, no tattoos, innocent skin, like Hansel and Gretel. They are just so innocent, so decadent, so pink-skinned and blond, kissing and feeling each other up under the extended wings of that pelican, that an empty paper guitar case appears. People on the sidewalk, on the edge of the lawn, and in appreciation for the performance, toss coins arcing for the empty guitar case. Most miss. Many bounce off the bronze pelican, trickle off the extended wing, and drop into the lawn.

He gets buddy-buddy with me, becomes my cappuccino comrade, once he discovers I'm not only a railroad man but also in the union. He's a union junky. Hansel and Gretel and Karl Marx. He works as a brakeman to be a credible organizer in the Brotherhood of Railroad Brakeman, Conductors and Trainmen. But as time goes on, each great event of the Sixties, each assassination and controversial American move around the world, each escalation in the war in Vietnam, and even his declarations of love to Jane Fonda for talking against the war on the TV, contributes to the loss of a few more of his teeth, which keep getting knocked out of his head in the wrong bar.

Yes, there is Jane Fonda, speaking up, alone, throwing her career away with every word she says on every TV talk show on the dial, restoring Terry's friendship with his TV set for the first time, he tells us, since they took Nick Adam's series *The Rebel* off the air, back in the days of black-and-white half-hour action drama. She is on *The Merv Griffin Show, The Mike Douglas Show,* pushing a movie she's making with Donald Sutherland called *F.T.A.* (in print, *Fuck The Army*) behind the snickers and bleeps. The brakeman loves Jane Fonda so much he refuses to work jobs that service the military and military contractors. He wins the right and is bewildered by getting "Yes" for an answer. "I don't work any train that carries tanks or ammo or even K-rations. Fuck the Army. I love you, Jane Fonda," he declares.

I exchange a questioning look with Jason across the table. "Nick Adams?" we both say in the same key and rhythm. We start calling him "Johnny Yuma."

Jane's father, Henry Fonda, Young Mr. Lincoln and the nicest Wyatt Earp that ever stalked a gunfight at the OK Corral across the silver screen himself, guests on talk shows just to grump polite, distant approval of his daughter's moves leftward from her days as Mme. Roger Vadim. Henry Fonda worries on Johnny Carson. Comics seated on *Johnny Carson* after their sweaty pleas for laughs talk about Jane Fonda with Henry and Johnny and all worry out loud as we hear their minds drool out.

The wonder of Cassius Clay changing his name and religion, and as Muhammad Ali refusing the draft as a Muslim, and the wonder of Jane Fonda calling the government liars and the war in Vietnam criminal, American culture racist and sexist is that they do it on TV. They become the stuff TV talks about even when they aren't on the screen. They raise the national standard of American dumb allowed to walk the streets without a keeper. Before Jane Fonda and Muhammad Ali, talk against the war is neither tolerably dumb nor tolerably decent on the TV talk show American conscience. Jane is on the talk shows with Bernard Fall's facts and arguments against the war long before Fall himself. She makes TV ready for Bernard Fall and safe for Johnny Carson to nip and jibe at the war and the minds behind it.

The brakeman falls in love with talk shows that promise him Jane Fonda day and night. In a shrill, shrieking time of pressure groups raging to keep the level of stupidity on TV from getting more stupid, Jane Fonda is something new on TV. She dumps new knowledge and protest on the living room furniture at just the moment people are most vulnerable, in the afternoon, at the beginning of rush hour, and late at night just before sleep. On Merv, on Johnny, she is absolutely gorgeous to the railroad Johnny Yuma with missing teeth. A white Hollywood Princess throwing herself on the bodies of coloreds and pariahs to save their necks from the establishment white bourgeois axe. She is a long overdue Pocahontas in reverse. She gives herself to the coloreds, to the Third World, to the feminists, to the white man's enemy. The brakeman cheers whenever he sees another owner of a local station go on the air to editorialize against the war. He cheers for Jane Fonda.

Ulysses: Shangri-la

One night, Sarah's father returns to my apartment, looking a thousand years old sober. Before he sucks a fifth bottle of Eagle Rare rye whiskey dry and looks dead, he tells me he has written a poem about his habit of going out into the garden every day after his morning coffee, to clip all the dead and dying leaves off all the plants and flowers growing next to the house, as if he is snipping off the dead and dying bits of Sarah's mother, lying upstairs uncomfortably in bed. He says he would like me to read this poem after he finishes it. It sounds like an old poem that he had read to me when Sarah and I were sleeping together, but I don't say so, and yes, I'd like very much to hear the poem.

Then very straight, very serious, he tells me I can never return to Chinatown. The world I write about is too grim to bear. If I return, Chinatown will kill me, he says, thinking perhaps of Thomas Wolfe and Dylan Thomas and James Joyce, living and dying in exile as some kind of me.

Why does he think I don't live in Chinatown anymore? This isn't Chinatown? This is Yellowman's Shangri-la. Can't stand being a Chink in the white rat race? Stumble into Yellowman's Shangri-la, where, under the rule of an old Chinatown restauranteur who has become Archbishop of the Valley, the happy, innocent pastoral white folks grow their happy crops. In the Valley, any yellow man is manlier and more sexually attractive than the passive timid whites. All the music the white people of Yellowman's Shangri-la play is Chinese music. All the art they collect is Asian.

In The Movie About Me I just got here, and already I am being offered the absolute rule of Yellowman's Shangri-la.

I have the old Archbishop's daughter in my bed. The Archbishop is stooped over, bald on top with a fringe of thin white hair. He is wrinkled and hollowed out. His skin no longer takes a tan. If he had an eyepatch and a crutch, he'd be Blind Pew, the traditional prophet of doom at the beginning of *Moby Dick* or *Monkey* or *Momotaro* or *Treasure Island*. The Archbishop stumbles out of

Shangri-la, tries to go home again, ages a thousand years, and dies. Does that mean *I* can never leave Yellowman's Shangri-la, once I become high lama?

Ulysses: Railroad Nights

Then the long hot oily railroad night when everything goes wrong comes to the yard. The daylight train lists are marked up and switched out all wrong and left to us after-midnight crews to fix. Some cars are already out of the yard, spotted by customer's spurs. I walk every track, eyeballing the road initials and numbers of every car.

The local charges by me, the toothy steel wheels of thirty boxcars and a caboose laughing and chattering. The train seems headless, mindless, running on a dead crew. The the engine's overtones shriek up and past me and gurgle away, gaining speed, suddenly spitting flames six feet long out of an axle. Fire! Fire on a moving train. The twisting ribboning flower petals of flame shudder like lips and burn a long, soft, blood-red light on the slab side of a beefy brown boxcar. The flames burn from the hub of wheels snickering by. The journal pack is burning, the axle is burning. Hotbox! The wheels chuckle away into the dark down a track in the New Yard that is marked clear on the track lists when thunk! into the big hole, the screech of locked wheels sounds like a note played on a blue-grass mountain fiddle to my ears. The track *is not clear.* The crash thumps and crunches as the local hits something big and hits it fast.

A fight breaks out in the switchmen's shanty over a picture cut out from a nudist magazine showing a smiling white woman in her forties in full color, her lightly haired, meaty twat in the center of the shot. Dog teeth. Freckled low-slung medium-sized boobies with stretch marks and huge nipples sticking out like small noses.

She grins with her elbow resting on the door of a Buick convertible. And her vagina! Her vagina! Her legs slightly spread in front view, head on, her twat lips slung like the crops of roosters, make some grown men sick to look at that picture, they say. The longer they look, God! Makes you want to puke, they say. God! That's horrible! Shi-yet!

It starts as a little testicle, oozing, erecting, millions of erections unwinding in the tight layers of jock strap and panties, skirts and overhauls, a little eternal dance, a little Charleston-Charleston, hopscotch to work the thing unstuck from some slot. Eyes agog. Hands limp doing a hand puppet dance. Doing the dance.

Voices buzz. Oh, man! Look at that man-eater! Better keep your eyes off that, Kwan! What the hell you doin' here anyway? Get back on the mudhop's side! Man! That's awful! Terrible. Look at that thing. Make you want to go home and lay your wife, Bones? Go home and plank her? Wife's gone, huh? Off in a Rolls-Royce? I think you're fulla shit. Really. Beat the hell out of her. Take her back? Not on a bet. I'll be dogged. Lookie the nookie. Charleston-Charleston. Oh, my livin' God.

I hear them take it down, turn it around, tack it back up. Not bad on the other side. Smaller pictures. More variety. Looks like a nine-year-old girl. But it's in black and white. Hell what's that thing starin' you in the face. But wouldn't you like that in your face? Oh, man, that's sickening. Looka that thing there. Lotta wear and tear. See the stretch marks. Charleston-Charleston. That's art.

Their lanterns swing on their elbows. They all face west. I am between them and the west wall, whereon is pinned the spread from the nudist magazine. Savages facing a shrine. The cult of the great Mother Twat. She's married! She's got rings on. Rings! Get your oily nose offa that. A little snot to add realism is all. Realism, shit! The ink's gonna get runny! The paper will pucker. Will the paper pucker? Will it really pucker if you wet it? Christ! Wouldn't that be something! 3-D cunt. And real hair. I'll pull out some of mine and stick 'em on. You make me sick! Let's go to work. Charleston-Charleston. Bomp bomp bomp on the wooden floor.

Composition soles. Steel-toed high-topped work boots. The whole shaky building shakes with the five men dancing and muttering primitive hymns under their breath. It's 1960, the Year of the Dog. Hey, look at this here, Kwan. Tell us what you think? Her canines are crooked. Her incisors aren't real. You a dentist or something? Them's good teeth. I like 'em all pointy like that. Your girlfriend should have such good teeth. They all tromp and trod the rhythm of a giant's heartbeat, cussing and staring in strange and strained reverence, never asking who put the picture up and never taking it down.

The moon throws the shadow of the crashed local on the yard office. I answer a ring on the battery-operated yard phone. "Hello?" A woman's voice sobs. Her lips rub on the mouthpiece and creak. "Who's this? Yellow Pearl?"

"Kwan. Yard clerk."

"Who?"

"Kwan?"

"What?"

"Kwan?"

"Larry? Oh, Larry, call the police quick! Who am I? Who? Eullissa. Eullissa. E-U-L-L-I-S-S-A. Eullissa, yes, Larry, call the police. Hurry! He's hitting me! Hitting me!"

"Hello, Kwan? Yeah, this is Jack. Now, don't you worry about Eullissa. She's a little, well, she's soused is all, a little spat, you know how it goes."

Who's Jack? Who's Eullissa?

"Don't you listen to him, Fong!"

"Forget about the police, Fong. There's a good guy."

Forget it. Forget it. It's his wife. I don't ask. Out in the yard seventy-five cars are spreading out all wrong, ready for spur delivery. In the morning a cookie company expecting a tank car of coconut oil will find a refrigerator boxcar full of cheese. And the man expecting the cheese in Hayward, thirty miles away, will receive a boxcar labeled "Class B Explosives—Do Not Bump,ˋRide, or

Shove to Rest," full of small arms ammunition for the Army's Oakland Supply Depot. Eventual destination—Vietnam.

Ulysses: Failure to Failure

Three years out of high school, I am in a coffee shop after three in the morning, watching little lights from brakemen's lanterns sway as the brakemen walk in the dark of the flat trainyards of the old Southern Pacific and Western Pacific railroads. All the trains are in. The outbound trains are made up and ready to roll, the crews are called and the outbound times are set. Dead time. The deep end of the night. Someone caught a salmon off the Golden Gate, so this morning they have fresh salmon steak on special at the coffee shop, one of those restaurants built in a converted Key System train car. In the electric light inside, everyone looks like they're made of biscuit dough.

A Railway Express Agency truck pulls up and the driver hunches his fake fur collar up against his neck, sticks his hands into his jacket pocket, trots into the coffee shop, sniffles back snot, and swallows it. I recognize him. In Oakland High he was the black-leather, pimply, white-trash cartoonist and funnybook balloon philosopher, with vague ambitions to build on his high school fame. He glances at me, looks into his coffee cup, and slowly recognizes me. "Oakland High?"

"Yeah," I answer.

He goes on to describe an admirable Chinese fella who was a big man in high school, a fella who really had it. "Remember him?"

"Yeah," I say.

"I wonder what happened to him," he says.

"Couldn't tellya, bud," I say. "But I can tell you that this salmon was caught less than an hour ago. King of the fish, man. I recommend it."

He goes through a few names of classmates, describes his present life, wife, kids, job as if they are the saddest things in the world, speaking to me as failure to failure, neither of us ever asking the other's name or offering to shake hands. He says, "I wonder if anybody from our class will ever make it."

"Couldn't say, man."

"A featherbedder, huh?"

"Yeah, man, that's me," I say and leave, walk into the noise of the cyclical churning murmuring of a locomotive. Its sound climbs deeply into everything around it, and booms colossal, something calm and still inside the noise of terror, crashing past people's backyards, faraway from hearing of myself being so much less than what I was in high school that I no longer want to recognize myself.

Dawn. What a night! I drive back to Berkeley, up Adcline in a Studebaker Hawk of many parts, Frankensteined together by Jason Peach in his attempt to build the perfect Studebaker Hawk from the wrecks he's bought. The sun blasts rays of salty lemonade and cuts the edges of cold shadows on Berkeley by the time I get the car parked and find Sarah in bed, asleep, beautiful, just the way I remember her appearing to me that first night she was mine.

I undress and pull back the cover. Then I see my Boy Scout knife in her hand, but jump away too late and get cut when she slashes at me in her sleep. She slashed at me in her sleep! I didn't buy a ticket to this movie! Why is she waiting for me with a knife? This is the wrong movie.

Everyone is in the wrong movie. Everyone I know is going crazy and loving it. Sure, their genius soars and roars, but they still can't wag their arms and fly. A bright kid from my high school, son of the rich people in the hills, scholarshipping through Cal toward law school and a career in politics, sleeps on the couch next to my bed one night, listening to me talk in my sleep. Six months later he commits suicide because his parents discovered he was a homosexual.

A big black kid, a linguistic genius who they say burned his house down with his mother inside when he was ten, changes his name to something North African Arab Muslim-sounding, yeah, "Abdul," and he gets fat. Three hundred pounds and gaining. And he has a blonde sorority girl girlfriend, who, he says, laughs with him when they smell the sugar fumes in the air past candy stores, donut shops, and bakeries. He speaks every civilized language of Europe, Asia, and North Africa fluently. He speaks Cantonese. He knows the chants and rhymes I recited in fragments of Chinese school a million years ago. He doesn't resent learning. Learning for him is not a punishment, not an act of desperation. It is necessary, unavoidable, natural, like breathing. The lungs breathe. The brain learns.

And the body gets fat. In between several showers Abdul takes each day because he sweats so much, he recites the poetry of Rudyard Kipling in Cockney for fun. One night he roars it off the top of his lungs, standing on a car roof in the middle of the intersection of Telegraph and Haste. "Yes, Din! Din! Din!" he screams, all fun and laughs, swinging a length of chain around his head and slamming it against the car in a kind of rhythm:

> "You Lazarushian-leather Gunga Din!
> Though I've belted you and flayed you,
> By the livin' Gawd that made you,
> You're a better man than I am, Gunga Din!"

He's drunk. We get him down and calm the cops, who slip up in their car and look at us out of their windows. We thank them as they drive on. We get him home. The next morning, he borrows a gun, loads it with dumdum shells, walks into the Bancroft Library on campus, and blows his girlfriend's brains out onto the library table. Then he puts the gun to his temple and fires, but the dumdum shell is defective, and instead of expanding and exploding out of his head, the bullet whizzes around the inside of his skull and comes out his right eye.

"If you want to kill yourself, you put the gun in your mouth. Everybody knows that," Diego Chang says.

"Yeah, he was a romantic. Too many Hollywood movies," I say.

The last time I see Sarah's father, he's in the hospital. "He tried to commit suicide by swallowing forty-seven cents in change but his mouth was too dry to swallow and he couldn't work up any spit," I tell Sarah.

What can I say about the nobility of a man who is pronounced an attempted suicide because he has a quarter, a dime, three nickels, and two pennies stuck on his tongue? He dies anyway. An educated, pampered, unaccomplished alcoholic genius. A completely wasted life. "Don't try to live in Chinatown. It will kill you" is his last bit of wisdom. Clunky Thomas Wolfe. Zombie Proust. At his graveside, I seem to be his only friend.

Sarah sits on our bed and spreads out a stack of love letters from her father to her mother on the bedspread between us. Then another stack of letters, a smaller stack from her mother to her father. She says her mother's letters to her father are sad, adoring, loving—terribly in love. Her father's letters are long, several pages of wonderful ravings about everything and nothing, lavishing love in a mix of scholarly literary references and quotations, the linguistic joys of mathematical knowledge, and the only known examples of what she calls her father's wild lyric imagination. I don't want to read them. I don't want to touch them. I want them off our bed.

She looks for poetic passages and reads them out loud and tries to cry. But the letters are not that poetic. Her father's letters are pathetic. He'd kept all his letters to Diana and Diana's letters to him, their love letters, letters they wrote each other before Sarah was born. Sarah thinks she has to read the letters now. No, she doesn't. I wish she'd burn them and forget it. Her father tried to return to *his* Chinatown, and it drove him to a forty-seven-cent suicide. One quarter. One dime. Two nickels. And two pennies. Cheap. A bargain.

Ulysses: Too Straight for Berkeley

Jason rouses me out of bed to chase Adonis, "El Filipino." He's threatening to slash his wrists after catching his wife in bed with his best friend, "El Rubio de Pasadena," a blond surfer flamenco guitarist. Sarah freaks as I run out with Jason. El Rubio de Pasadena is a block down Telegraph chasing Adonis. I run with Jason. I'm no athlete. I never run when I can walk, never walk when I can ride. That's railroad. And I run. And run. I run with Jason and the worried "El Rubio de Pasadena" past U.C. Corner, past Larry Blake's restaurant, past La Fiesta, past the coffee house, and still we run. Adonis, with razor blades, runs past Buffalo Books, crosses Dwight, and runs. Jason runs like *he* was the one caught fucking Adonis's wife. We chase Adonis into Oakland but can't catch him. What will I do if I do manage to catch up to him? I'm no marriage counselor.

Five cops in Oakland finally bring him down, and his wife shows up with a car, and we follow the suicidal artist to Highland Hospital, and I'm back in my apartment wondering where Sarah's gone. I go by Jason's. No Sarah. Knives, bad dreams, disappearing. Sarah's scary.

El Filipino's wife shows up at *my* place, says, "Ulysses Kwan, you haven't kissed me tonight," and sticks her tongue in my mouth.

The campus is plastered with handbills advertising a French movie titled *We Are All Murderers*. Fat Jack is right. I'm too straight for Berkeley.

I hear Jack Fat is shot in the face in San Francisco in a dope deal gone bad. *"Yellow man's Shangri-la:* The End."

Ulysses: Brakeman on the Southern Pacific

Johnny Yuma remembers Jack Fat with me over cappuccino at the coffee house. He tells me the SP is hiring minority brakemen. He says the racist bastards need a Chinese for one nonblack minority out of the twelve they have to hire this month.

"You say they'd rather hire a Chink than a nigger," I argue. "But they're already hiring Chinamen brakemen, and my *brother's* made conductor."

"You're not white anymore," Johnny Yuma says and draws his thumb across his throat in the sign of cracking the air hose joint between cars. He gets some kind of thrill sitting in the coffee house on Telegraph Avenue in Berkeley, talking to me railroader to railroader with railroad sign language. "Until they get used to hiring Negroes, you are a minority *they* like better than the Negro minority. But one look at you and they won't like you that much better."

With that enthusiastic endorsement, I hire on with the SP as a brakeman. Extra brakemen to work empty slots or fill empty crews are called out to work off a list called the Extra Board. I do my student trips in two weeks and get listed on the Extra Board. The railroad's so fat they're running more trains than they have crews. I can get time off by calling in and having my name scratched off the list, and three hours later or three days later, put myself back on the list. I can time my call to position myself to be called at time I want and for the train I want. It's a kind of gambling called "shooting the Extra Board."

I'm glad to get out of the yard, off the ground, to ride with the view from the locomotive and caboose, good as my brother, The Hero. Now I can call a locomotive engineer a hoghead to his face, as an equal, and not feel embarrassed. I work every job the dispatcher calls me for. I learn the trains, learn the jobs, learn the routes, the sidings and the yards. I buck the board to get out for the fast nonstop freights, working chain gang and back and out again as many times as I can roll in the sixteen hours per day the Railroad Act allows me to work.

Hauling the tanks and personnel carriers chained down to flat-cars and inspected by the Army, the factory, and the railroad before rolling doesn't bother me. The extra pay for being held hostage by the Army and Navy's explosives for a hundred miles between terminals sometimes keeps me awake. The wind we make, the echoes we bang off the walls of the big cement and corrugated steel ware-houses and factories, sound different from the high wobble of the rectangular boxcars and solid, regular loaf-shaped loads we pass. The tank muzzles are covered with a kind of sock. The gun and the tank are chained down tight and stiff to the flatcar. On a bridge with a wind blowing and the train rolling, the muzzle socks flop-flop like drums, the chains whistle like kazoos, and the tanks and personnel carriers hum like harmonicas. The cars sing. Johnny Yuma is right about napalm. Nobody likes working a train hauling napalm. They scare me. But when I'm called out for one, I work it.

I move to Roseville, outside of Sacramento, to work the brakeman's Extra Board in another terminal district. I don't ask Sarah to live with me in Roseville. I don't ask her to move out. I keep the Berkeley apartment and drive in from Roseville twice a week for classes. Three weeks later I find she has moved out of the Berkeley apartment.

Roseville is a low, hot, stucco-and-cinderblock railroad town with dust blowing off the fields and collecting on the asphalt streets. Gold Country. Again I smell where I lived as a baby with the retired vaudeville acrobat and the former silent-screen bit player, Uncle Jackie and Auntie Bea, and wonder if I can find where the house used to be, by following the smell.

There's no Chinatown in Roseville. In the one Chinese restaurant in town, the mom and pop speak a kind of Cantonese with a lot of spit in it and print their menu in Spanish and English. A Chinese restaurant with no signs in Chinese! The ceilings are high, disappearing on the high side because of the glare from the light globes hanging from oily dusty chains decorated with ribbons of uncoiled flypaper. Yellow dust blows in thin streams and stringers.

Dust curls down the street and throws faint shadows twisting into the windows and screen door. The sunlight burns with a quiet yellow flame, licking the walls. The music on the jukebox is mostly in Spanish. The songs in English are "Happy Birthday," and "White Christmas" sung by Bing Crosby, some Nat King Cole and Elvis. I order the chicken-fried steak with chicken gravy, mashed potatoes, and green peas.

All of a sudden, I want to make money. I want to have enough money to make a big move, I think, but have no move in mind. Then Jason sends me a letter to my Roseville address that makes me laugh out loud. It says he's in love with Sarah, has gotten her pregnant and is marrying her. And then asks, "Are we still friends? I hope we are still best friends?"

Ulysses: Watch from Across the River

I am a brakeman on the yard switch crew, working with strangers off the Extra Board, and just happen to be called out this rainy midnight-to-eight graveyard shift in Oakland when the Yardmaster's speaker picks up Hollywood Junior, talking to the hoghead on the company two-way. His train is in the mountains racing through a shattering blithering rain down the Feather River Canyon. He says he is standing at the back door of the caboose looking off the rear platform, and instead of seeing where they have just been, he sees a mudslide peeling the face off the mountain, chasing the train. The tracks behind them fly off the mountainside and wave like ribbons in the air as they fall off down the canyon. I am the only other Chinaman brakeman on the road, and all eyes turn on me as we hear The Hero yell for more speed.

"The slide's gaining, Spider! More speed!" The Hero's voice crackles through the two-way.

"Spider Webb is the hoghead," Wild Bill Hancock, the Yard-master, mumbles for the benefit of another switch crew flopping rubbery into the yard office, slick yellow and dripping wet in their rain gear. I don't have to tell them that is my brother in the caboose of that westbound, racing home toward Tracy. The other brake-men and switchmen, everyone in the yard office moves back, giving me a little more room. As the mudhops from the yard's outer limits and engine men and firemen off their locos squeeze in, I find myself shuffled to the front.

The slick shine of our yellow rubber rain gear licks and slicks off each other like fish as we move. If we stood upside down in our rain capes, ponchos, and hoods, we'd look like bats crowding onto a cave roof. The conductors stand in a vague semicircle that includes me around Wild Bill's desk. The clerks stay at their desks and shove their papers and lists into tighter and tighter piles as the car-knock-ers, and Snake Eyes Ives, the Daylight Yardmaster, and others move into the little wooden yard office out of the rain.

The mudslide is gaining on the caboose, threatening to pull the track right out from under the train and send Junior and all the silver Damage Free refrigerator boxcars, the caboose and locomo-tive, the whole westbound, down a two hundred-foot echo. There is nothing I can do but listen. There is nothing any of us can do. The mainline is clear, green green green, all green blocks, all go, all the way to Oakland. Not a wheel on the Southern Pacific is about to take the main until the westbound passes. From the canyon to Tracy to Oakland we are all under the same plopping frog-eyed rain, and stare at the speaker, and hear Junior scream that a bear has rolled off the mountain onto the train, and the mike goes on and off.

The bear is groggy. The bear is pissed off. Junior says he and the conductor are climbing out of the caboose, climbing to the top and grabbing for the next car. Then we listen to the bear smash around the caboose, and the radio goes on and off. When they roll into Tracy, clinging to the top of a boxcar full of baby food jars, about five men jump onto the caboose with rifles and fire a number of shots before the bear chases them off. The conductor and Junior sit on top of the boxcar in the rain and watch their brother trainmen stand outside and shoot the caboose to smithereens for ten or twenty minutes and hope they've shot the bear in the heart by luck and accident. We hear it all over the Yardmaster's radio in the Oakland Yard Office, another district east of Tracy.

Snake Eyes Ives, the Daylight Yardmaster, clicks on the microphone, and says, "Tracy Yard, this is Yardmaster, Oakland Old Yard, over."

"We hear you, Oakland Yard."

"We have an official Southern Pacific company question for Grizzly Kwan, boss brakeman, who I believe just came in on your last inbound from the east, the Manufacturer's Flash."

"This is an official company communication from Tracy Yard to Oakland Yard. The next voice will be Grizzly Kwan: over."

"The next voice from Oakland Yard will be College Boy Kwan," Snake Eyes says as he stands up from his desk and hands me the microphone.

"Tracy Yard, this is Oakland. All the company employees want to know what it is about you that attracts bears in winter, brother."

Ulysses: Seattle

After trading jobs with a union brother brakeman, working the Union Pacific with comparable seniority, I move to Seattle. The railroad yards around Seattle are like toys on a tabletop around a tabletop toy town. The view out of my apartment window goes out over Elliott Way to Elliott Bay, across the bay to all the islands and beyond to every sunset of the year. Look out there far enough into the sky of any month and I swear I see the Big Bang.

Stand anywhere outdoors in Seattle, look around, and it's beautiful. But from inside my apartment, framed in the big window of my dining room, Seattle is a fairy-tale picture book world.

All the rain keeps the sky baby blue and all the sunshine shears clean rays off the ridges of the mountains, the lips of smokestacks, the sides of buildings. The sun shines lemonlight, flipping through the spokes of bicycle wheels. Nearest me at the bottom of the frame is a bit of yard and an upper branch of an elm tree growing up from someplace down below I can't see, up past the window. It's a tree with an instinct for seasonal ritual behavior. It buds and sprouts leaves. The bark changes color. The leaves change color, dry up, and fall. The tree looks dead in winter, a fossil of old petrified skeleton rasped and reshaped by wind erosion. Then a strip of blackberry bushes grabbing hold of the ground over the edge of the ridge, down to the pipe casting outfit in a yellow cinderblock building. Its asphalt lot is full of empty wooden bins, empties stacked against the building, and bins full of cast pipe joints and fittings standing against the retaining wall and feet of the blackberry bushes. A billboard facing north pushes Golden Lights, a cigarette that hopes to sell by pitching the line "Golden Lights / taste applauded."

"Who applauds taste?" Milton Shiro, my downstairs neighbor asks. We argue over movies in the hall and over dinner in Chinatown once or twice a week. Who reads billboards as literature? He takes my notes on recent movies to the editors of *Seattle City* magazine where he works selling ad space. Milton giggles like a Volkswagen engine. Now and then he takes a shopping bag full of groceries to Bob Crisp, a young writer from the south who Milton says is Mark Twain on acid.

Crisp lives in the University District where he's the center of a hippie anti-intellectual literary cult. A year or so ago Milton turned the magazine on to Crisp and they liked him and made him their art critic. The magazine is now serializing Crisp's novel, *The Washington Delicious Report,* and Milton shows me a copy. He insists I stand in the hall and listen as he reads. "'It's apple-plucking time in Washington. Not all pluckable apples are in the trees. Not all the best-tasting, most juicy or ripest apples are in the trees, according to the recent research in the basket. It has been found that most of the apples reaching the basket have been in other baskets. For connoisseurs of the Washington Delicious, the Golden Delicious, the Winesap, the Gravenstein, and other fine apples, it is the custom to choose apples that have been picked by someone else.'" Milton laughs. "Isn't that great?"

The magazine likes my writing. Now I freelance movie reviews every month. "Do the people who write the crap they put up on billboards sincerely believe smokers will applaud the tobacco growers of America after consuming a pack of cigarettes, like gourmets applauding the chef after a banquet?" Milton asks.

Next to the pipe casting outfit is an empty unpaved gravel lot full of everchanging lakes and holes where cops come to hide and where a few desperate or adventurous couples come to park late at night. "Foreigners," Milton says. "I bet they all have out-of-state plates."

Elliott Way runs by the big picture window. Across the street is a line of waterfront industry, a lumbermill and yard, the animal shelter, and parking lots. At night the animals inside the flat little cinderblock building all begin to howl and wail a little after midnight, before the phone rings and the dispatcher gives me my call, train number, and conductor's name.

Next to the animal shelter is the Darigold plant. The grain loader on the water. Waterfront park. Grass and joggers, cyclists and dogs. Then Elliott Bay, the island, the sunset behind the Olympic mountains. And every kind of boat imaginable is on the water, tanking, freighting, tugging, ferrying, sailing, cutting, and cruising. And between the waterfront park and the animal shelter and Darigold is the Great Northern main line and the grain loader's spur.

The great grain loader is a cement and steel machine disguised as a building and huge grain elevator. It has jaws that eat trucks and trailers. It has jaws that eat four oversized high-and-wide, sixty-foot-long railroad hopper cars at a time.

The tractor trailers line up and one by one drive onto a ramp to be embraced by jaws and held to the road bed, while the ramp tips up, pointing the nose of the tractor to the sky, opening the back of the trailer, and emptying it like a can. A little gas-driven switch engine switches cuts of articulated hopper cars out from holding tracks and shoves them, four at a time, onto a tongue of living metal parts that moves the cuts of four cars robotically into a hole in the side of the building. They're washed and dried just before they enter. Inside they are tipped over and emptied, then tipped upright and sent trickling out the other side. As the building eats the grain the traincars and trucks bring to it like endless lines of ants, the immense ships from Red China and Japan next to the loader, which start with water lines, rudders, and the tops of their props riding high out of the water, sink lower in the water every day, before my eyes.

All of Seattle lives in primitive performance and ritualistic display in my picture window, as if painted by Grandma Moses. I see it all. The fool from the building next door emptying garbage, birds in the bushes, cops howling down Cadillacs, the fleet of gold and orange Darigold milk trucks invading traffic like giant honeybees joining a rush-hour stampede of four-wheelers, the death house blues baying out of the animal shelter from too many dogs, all the little roadside vignettes—the Continental suddenly pulling up and a well-dressed man in his grayheaded years jumping out and walking along the walk to nowhere against the traffic. The woman at the wheel is old enough to be his wife. She looks comfy in a fur coat. She looks over her shoulder, shouts, backs up a little, but does not catch up to the man. The man walks away. She drives out of sight. He walks past the billboard, across the face of the parking lot, and out of sight. From here I see it all. My window is perfect for an invalid, an idiot.

The magazine gives me passes to all the movies in town and two or three hundred more dollars a month for talking to myself about the *cinema*. I have the seniority to bid in a regular job and ride out and in on the same train every day, but I like living off the Extra Board sometimes, shooting for all the fast money I can make in a day, playing my seniority to position myself on the board to work the fastest train out and a fast deadhead, or turnaround to home terminal and another hundred miles out for a total of three hundred miles before the mandatory eight hours off. Sometimes I shoot a local to get a look at the country, get acquainted with a trainyard working flats of chained-down lumber and plywood, and breathe the heavy choking breath of dying wood and rotting sawdust. Life looks and feels great from a moving locomotive and caboose. Everything tingles with noise and speed. Seattle is nice and tight for a railroader working off the Extra Board.

There's good eating all over town all day and all night long. Milton Shiro knows all the restaurants. The all-night places, the places with midnight special breakfasts served from silver carts by men in livery, the places where they serve wild game and dry, aged prime beef. Soul food, Chinese food, Japanese, Italian, seafood joints from Seattle to Olympia to the slopes of Mt. Rainier, on and off of I-5, Milton's tried to sell them ad space in the magazine. The women who are turned on by my columns in the magazine all seem to be redheads who get on my trail through the magazine, which is owned by the Dio family's KDIO communications empire. KDIO owns the top TV station in Seattle, an AM station, an FM Jazz station, and TV stations in Portland and Spokane in addition to the magazine.

The redheads usually find me eating with Milton in little restaurants all over Seattle. Seattle is magic for me. The redheads give themselves to me as if I am the fulfillment of prophecy or a dream. Some days I come back from the turnaround and have breakfast and sucky fucky and fall asleep with one, have another redhead and a nap around lunch, and a third for dinner, before I write for a while, then sleep again till the call from the dispatcher. This is the year of the women. I seem to attract certain beauties out of the crowd without doing anything. Is someone paying them to jump at me?

On an elevator in a building in Pioneer Square a young Chinese woman with warm skin and a rose between her breasts looks me in the eye and tells me I'm Ulysses S. Kwan. "I've heard about you," she says.

"Oh, what have you heard?" I say, too stupid to get the picture, then think stupidity may be an aphrodisiac.

"I hear you're oversexed," she says.

That summer I ride my union card from caboose, to caboose hearing railroad lies, divorce stories, middle-class dreams of do-it-yourself projects and a tractor lawnmower, and swap recipes across the country. Stories Hollywood Junior never told me spin into the night as I ride the silver rails across the brow of the continental United States of America to New York.

Auntie Orchid sits in the kitchen of her garish Greenwich Village Chinese restaurant with Uncle Buck, spooning a filling of ground pork and shrimp, bamboo shoots and green onions onto dry wonton skins, and folding the skins over the filling and sealing the edges with a wet finger. They wet their fingers in a bowl of water. Sometimes they wet their fingers in bowls of beaten eggs. I don't know the difference or the reason for wetting some wonton skins with water and others with beaten egg. Either way, the wonton skins stick when folded together.

Uncle Buck is always happy to see me. Always young and energetic, ready to fire up the stove and whip out a custom-made bowl or plate of noodles.

They no longer live in the rooms above the restaurant and let me have my old room for as long as I'm in town. Or any room I choose to use for a bedroom.

Upstairs is full of old extra tables and chairs and their restaurant supplies. I choose the room at the tip of the triangle. Auntie Orchid's old throne room. Her old dressing room. She liked being surrounded by light. The view out of the windows forming the point is like looking out of the windshield of a strategic bomber flying down Greenwich Village.

Auntie Orchid is not impressed, not happy to hear I'm working on the railroad. "I'm not a steward like my grandfather," I say. "I'm a brakeman, like my big brother, The Hero."

And she slaps me. I see it in her eyes before she throws her hand. Like *The Sea and the Jungle*. I don't forget. I don't stop her. I'm not that fast. I don't try. I want to ask her what she has against Junior, when she yells, "Your brother is a good man. Don't you pick on Longman Jr., hear me?"

"Huh?" I say. I don't get it.

She is not impressed that I get a couple hundred a month and all the movies I can stomach by writing movie reviews for *Seattle City* magazine. *I don't own a house.* I'm still moving around a lot. *I don't wear a tie.* I don't need a tie. I'm making money doing what I want. Money, Auntie Orchid. She admits I am making more money than her son, Ben. But he has security.

"Yeah," I say. "He has you for a mother."

"Me for a mother? He hates me for a mother. Your brother of the oath in the garden . . . you know what he did? Sure, you have to know what he did! He's your blood brother."

"What did he do, Auntie?"

"He learned that his biological father, the one who died in China, was named Mo, or Mao, just like Mao Tse Tung. And he was inspired! To get at me, he took the name of his dead father back. Just to spite me! Did you know that?"

She and Uncle Buck now own a condo in Chinatown with a million dollar view. They sponsor the Chinatown Chinese girls drill team. And they own Orchid Han's Han Dynasty Cadillac in New Jersey. The Chinese girls drill team appears in the Han Dynasty Cadillac commercials on TV. Auntie Orchid says she pays the girls drill team for each appearance.

Ulysses: Seize the Opportunity and Ask Lassie to Do Anything

Milton Shiro has a round face—the shape of a squeezable rubber bathtub toy—wears round glasses, his ears stick out, and he drives a white Porsche. He learned to drive in his white Porsche. It's the only car he's ever driven. He is an orphan raised by a stepmother who beat the evacuation into camp by voluntarily moving to Arizona at the beginning of World War II. He did two years at a fundamentalist Christian college, then joined the U.S. Marine Corps.

He was confused by his action in Korea but now carries a Zippo lighter with the Marine Corps eagle-and-anchor crest on it. He lights people's cigarettes with it in restaurants and bars and when they see the crest on the lighter they always ask where he got it. "Off a dead Marine," he answers with a smile, his round glasses and round face looking like the Jap of every World War II movie ever made. The moment passes with a couple of war stories like no one has ever heard before. Milton is an eccentric innocent who has been through baptism by fire. People apologize for being rude and prejudiced about a Japanese American with a Zippo lighter with the Marine Corps crest on it. "Do you want to buy it? I have another dozen at home," Milton says. I am invited to magazine parties. I have never had it so good.

I'm not sure when it hits me that at every meal I have ever eaten with Milton, indoors, outdoors, in a house, in a restaurant, he talks to his food. Less than a year in Seattle and I have sound flashbacks to a plate of steak dinner thudding into place in front of him, or even a steak sandwich on a platter, "Yum yum. Umm mmmm." Milton Shiro says, "Hello, steak. Boy, you look good." Worse, a waitress in basic black rayon uniform and white apron clanks a stack of pancakes in front of him, and he talks to each and every pancake. He names them "Eeny, Meeny, Miney, and Moe," as he butters and syrups their backs and bellies.

He organizes his ad sales for *Seattle City* magazine in his office in the basement of the old KDIO-TV Studios. It's December. The

Christmas issue is already on the streets and the race is on to finish the January magazine. He would rather be an eccentric dealer in used books in Pioneer Square. He likes writers.

Milton puts on an old aviator's leather skullcap with flaps over the ears and chin straps. It's December. Christmas is in the air at the offices of the magazine and TV station. Milton sings to himself, "Tum tum tummm!" as he adjusts his round glasses and picks up his little Japanese flag. *Seattle City* magazine is the nest of liberals and radicals in the old KDIO-TV building, and Milton is proud to be among them. He steps into the big office waving his flag and marches toward the stairs into the TV News room, asking, "Which way to Pearl Harbor?" Everyone downstairs looks up, everyone upstairs freezes at the sight of him. No one laughs.

He climbs into his Porsche. He's had it painted yellow with a red *umeboshi,* the meatball of the World War II Mitsubishi Zero fighter. "Do you need a ride?" Milton asks me.

"No, thanks, man," I say, "The Zero is a single seater."

Milton is wearing his skullcap the day Lassie comes to visit KDIO-TV. Lassie is in the lunchroom. Lassie's trainer offers everyone present the opportunity to ask Lassie to do anything and claims she'll do it.

I know Lassie's a transvestite as soon as I see him. What kind of breed are these collies who get big and strong, then let some fool train them to walk like girls on parade?

Milton likes all animals, especially low-energy ones. Animals that turn into puddles and stay there watching TV or dozing with him. I can see Milton likes Lassie but is shy. I can also see Milton doesn't know Lassie is a guy. After all these years of cherishing *Lassie Come Home,* it would break Milton's heart. It would be like telling me Annette Funicello on *Mickey Mouse Club* is a guy, or Shirley Temple in all those movies is a guy.

The trainer moves Lassie table to table and stool to stool along the counter, asking each and every one of people having morning coffee to ask Lassie to do something they might think she can't do.

Roll over, play dead, fetch, sit, stand, walk on your hind legs, recite the Gettysburg Address, Lassie does all that. The trainer and Lassie are moving on our table fast. Milton blushes. "Go ahead, ask Lassie to do something," the trainer asks me.

I point at Milton and say, "Kill, Lassie! Kill!"

Lassie lies down and looks stupid.

Milton laughs, but he is the only one laughing. He looks around the KDIO lunchroom at the stunned on- and off-camera TV people, stops laughing, and talks to his toast.

The offices of the magazine, TV station, and AM and FM radio stations are all under one roof in the KDIO building. It is July. It's been hot and bright for weeks in Seattle. The bright of things, pretty girls flopping themselves around inside summer dresses, chicks in bikinis lying white as mushrooms on lawns all over town, the pictures of explosions on fireworks stands, the hot greasy gleam of skin and hair—all seem mirages, all part of a terrific silence on the other side of the harsh clubbing of my heart, the tackiness lining the insides of my mouth and throat, my involuntary breathing, sounding like leaves being raked.

Ulysses: July 4, 1968

I drop by the magazine to pick up my check on the day before the Fourth of July festivities. The director of TV news, just hired to drive up ratings, calls me over to the group gathered around his secretary's desk just outside his glass office.

After four nights of black kids standing on a ghetto high school lawn chucking rocks, dirt clods, and an occasional firebomb at passing cars from afternoon rush hour till midnight, two of the many shots fired from the school lawn hit two white people riding passenger in passing cars, and three black kids shot by cops are now in the hospital. The militant activist black gangs call a community meeting. The place is packed with the community in lots of black leather, black shades, and different colored berets, observed by a swarm of smarmy white news people. One white TV newsman speaks up and starts pleading with his "brothers and sisters," talking more black than the blacks. Instead of turning the lights on him and lapping him up at 24 frames per second, the camera teams from the other stations feel the ugly rising funky from the crowd and quickly slink out, happy with what they have. Only one short bespectacled cameraman panics and pulls a gun. The reporter who had come to lead the blacks to peace and salvation before the Fourth of July and save the big boat races on Lake Washington from race riot has no film, but does have plenty of hot and cold ideas of who set his company car on fire.

The local Prime Minister of the Black Panthers, in black leather jacket, black gloves, black shades, and black beret, and a field marshal of the Black Immortals, in a leather overcoat, black wraparound shades, carrying a swagger stick, jointly issue a statement from the black community to white Seattle.

Herman Schwartz, a black man with a Jewish name who works in the Community Affairs Department of the station, says he is acting as a facilitator of communication between the militants and the Seattle press and TV news. He apologizes for his appearance, says he hasn't changed his clothes or slept in two days. As he rhythmically rasps on, now apologizing for being incoherent, his anger rises and falls the more he struggles to make himself understood. I sense Benzedrine twilight and can't believe this scene. Herman Schwartz says, "I have been delegated by several groups to ensure that the situation in the Central Area will be accurately covered by the news media."

"The TV news is out of control," the Black Panther and Black Immortal say, "The media is the pig! The very idea of July 4th in Seattle is an outrageous pig mockery of Independence Day. The presence of white pig reporters from the imperialist pig media will guarantee that the July 4th hydroplane races on Lake Washington will become one of the first great battlefields in the Third World

People's Revolutionary War. Therefore we, the Black Panther Party and the Black Immortals, in the name of the coalition of the liberation forces of the oppressed peoples of America, command the media pigs to exclude themselves from the immediate premises of our community's current events, or we will consider them as the forces of the enemy making a war of invasion!"

"Excuse me, I know this is all very important, so tell me what are you saying?" the news director asks. An Irishman with black hair, hired from back east, resented by everyone in the newsroom for being an outsider, is all bent over, crooked and gnarly from rheumatoid arthritis, which he suffers in stoic, conscientiously enforced silence. Visiting from New York, his much advertised girlfriend, taller than any man in the room, skinny, blonde, the first braless white woman in a transparent blouse allowing her nipples to show through ever seen in the KDIO newsroom and perhaps in all of Seattle, stands by his hunched-over form and looks straight into my eyes.

"Just for the stupid and illiterate among us, you are saying no more white reporters and cameramen in the ghetto?" the news director croaks. "Is that what you're saying, or am I wrong?"

"You hear us correctly, pig," the Panther says.

"Then please say it, so this pig makes no mistake," the news director says. "Do you mind if we film you to make sure we don't misquote you?"

"No, no filming," Herman Schwartz says. "Too often television has publicized the imposter and made all black people come to be judged against the likes of its creations. I mean: Stokely Carmichael and Rap Brown. We do not wish to make anyone famous. Turn off the white cameras in the ghetto, and the community can keep its own peace this Fourth of July."

"What are you up to, Schwartz? Are you nominating yourself for the Black Messiah of Month?" asks the news director.

"I don't know what this is, man. *You* do this suspicion on me because I'm black and don't want my community to burn down. While these brothers here don't trust *me* because I work for *you!*

They're ready to get down and bag this talking to the media: period! They want to beat me up, gang bang my wife for being a spy for the pig media, and I tell them I am just your token nigger, that you allow me to wear your necktie and sit in some little office with no windows nobody comes into but me. This *is* the way you treat me. I'm just about ready to say fuck it to all of you, man."

"I would still like to hear it spelled out for me. No white reporters and cameramen, is that what you're saying or not?" the news director asks.

"No white pig reporters or photographers in the ghetto," the Black Immortal says.

"Will you guarantee the safety of any nonwhite reporters and photographers the pig media sends into the ghetto?"

"What say?" the Black Panther asks.

"Are you trying to create job opportunities for nonwhites or declaring open war on the news media?" the news director asks. "Are you saying you want the news media to exclude the Central District and its people from the news? Are you asking us, the pig media, to discriminate against you, giving you gentlemen the opportunity to whip the community into a rage because the pig media is excluding you from the news?"

The Black Panther says, "Last night, the pig shot a tear gas grenade at point-blank range into the face of a black woman, clubbed kids, and flashed the bird at a black brother who happened to be a cameraman from Portland. The sister who was bombed in the face is at this very moment laid up in the hospital hovering on the edge of death. This is an example of the pig media waging a race war to make a few news pigs famous. The pig media can only make a high-pressure dangerous situation more dangerous. We do not care about your news, good or bad. We do care about the safety of our community."

"Right on!" the Black Immortal says.

"Even in these tense and trying circumstances, we are not barbarians," the Black Panther says.

"Tell him, bro'," the Black Immortal says.

"So, nonwhite reporters and cameramen who come without guns and knives and do not provoke the community are welcome," the Black Panther says.

"Right on!" the Black Immortal says.

"Ulysses Kwan here isn't white," the news director says.

"I don't think that's what they mean," I begin to say but Herman Schwartz throws his arm around me.

"Right on!" Herman shouts. "I know Kwan. We're like brothers! I've watched him. I read his column every month. Badmouthing all those pig movies in the *Seattle City* magazine. The badmouth that Kwannie lays on John Wayne I was sure was gonna get the niggah lynched from one of them bullshit plastic lanterns in Chinatown. Shiiii-yettt! He gives me strength in this pig corporation. We are brothers! He's *not* white. Yeah, we like him. You give him the guns and ammunition of newsgathering—a camera and a mess of film, a tape recorder and tape—and he'll tell it like it is."

And suddenly I have a Bolex camera, hundred-foot loads of Tri-x, a cassette tape recorder, three dozen cassettes, and a room at the Virgin Tropics Motel, which Herman says is perfect for our command post.

Our room has an old black-and-white TV. Next door, the door is always open and a man sits on an old steel and naugahyde kitchen chair in the doorway with no shirt on. Through the doorway I see a room full of TV sets, hi-fi components, and car radios stacked on top of each other.

I am not white. I am not Herman's brother. I only know him as a familiar shape and face I pass in the halls of the KDIO studios and offices. Now I am a cameraman and yellow companion of Lone Herman Schwartz. Lone Herman congratulates us both, gives me five, and goes home to his wife and baby. I'm alone in a scene of potential violence with a camera in my hand. I have an itchy trigger finger, but I can't kill. I can gel moments of life and death but cannot be touched by them. I am a professional bounty hunter of the Old West at last and feel no safety or comfort in my professional lack of involvement. If we're such brothers, why is it I know nothing about Herman's wife and baby till the instant he leaves me? It's a strange Lone Ranger who goes home to the wife and kid and leaves the guns and silver bullets with Tonto. I feel pretentious, icky, and had.

It's not the way Pa's friend James Wong Howe became a Hollywood cameraman. Not that he would call this being a cameraman—he would call this playing around and being a nigger. Pa always said I was a nigger. That's maybe number two or number three in the litany of excuses he uses to justify the fake rage that he says keeps him in Hollywood. And Ma takes him seriously. Pa stays in Hollywood because of my Negro friends?

I don't know this ghetto. This ghetto doesn't know me. I have no sense of where the railroad is from here. Patches of this part of Seattle still look like country. Lush grass in summer grows fat and so long it bends over, making green lips where the creeks still run. This is a ghetto with water and back alley dirty roads between the streets, lined with two-story houses pregnant with familiar porches. My grandmother lived in a one-story cousin of these Sixth Street houses in Oakland. But armed with nothing but a camera, in a motel full of burglars and their loot, I'm in the ghetto of a pretty picture-book city that looks nothing like drab Oakland, although I know everyone on Sixth Street is poor.

The people out on these porches aren't about to invite me inside and cook me breakfast. My first girlfriend, Sylvia, doesn't live here. I don't think people here will stand still while I keep them laughing, doing an impression of my father's impression of Stepin' Fetchit dying in the arms of Don Ameche playing Stephen Foster in *Swanee River,* asking, "Mazzah Stephen, you ever wrote that song you promised to write for old Black Joe?"

"Hey! Charlie Chan!" they call to me. I may be wrong. They may stand still long enough for me to make them laugh. They know Charlie Chan. They know Charlie Chan's honorable numbered sons. I know there was a songwriter named Stephen Foster and he did write a song titled "Old Black Joe." I remember singing that song in Lincoln School between Chinatown and the Hotel

Westlake Eclipse. For some reason I find *Swanee River* often on late-night old movie programs on TV in Seattle. And on cold nights, when they're inside these houses, up late watching TV, these people see *Swanee River* too, and Charlie Chan, and the World War II movies my father "Japs" and dies in. What if the stashman, standing outside his door with two large fans on stands blowing a kind of stereo tropical monsoon at his head, looks into my open door and sees me watching Charlie Chan or *Swanee River* and wants to watch with me?

I look up Willy Loman in the White Pages. Milton Shiro wanted his number unlisted, then learned it cost more to keep his name out of the book than to have it printed, then learned he only needed a name to go with the phone number for the book. The number was the important identity, not the listed name. So he uses the name of Willy Loman, a mythical traveling salesman, like Milton himself. Milton answers.

"Hello, Willy? Is Ulysses Kwan there?" I ask.

"No, I'm sorry, Ulysses isn't here."

"Then he must be over here and be me," I say, and Milton laughs his gagging Volkswagen laugh. "You know the Central District?" I ask. "Think of a decent barbecue rib joint near the Virgin Tropics Motel, and let's meet for some food. I don't want to hang around this room doing nothing but chattering my teeth all night. Name the place, give me the streets, I'll start walking as soon as you hang up, and you can give me a ride back after we eat."

"Don't walk with the camera! You'll get mugged!" Milton shouts and giggles over the phone. At last I connect his gagging Volkswagen to Peter Lorre laughing in *The Maltese Falcon* and Fritz Lang's *M*. "You'll get shot!" he shouts and giggles.

"Hey, I'm alone and empty-handed. If the stuff gets copped, tough shit, Kemo Sabe."

I walk like I know where I'm going, am obsessed with anger. Nobody better fuck with me. I don't look around much. People adjust their walk to avoid me a long way down the block. I haven't walked this way in years and am a little surprised I fall into it so easily. I take long steps very slowly, I am not walking like Henry Fonda in *My Darling Clementine*. I am walking like I did after Sylvia fought in the street defending me. If anybody stops me I'll start talking trash or go crazy, throwing stuff, breaking windows, until somebody calls the cops.

Milton drives into the lot of the Big Potato Barbecue Pit in his Porsche painted like a shiny new Mitsubishi Zero. He wears a blue blazer, khaki pants, and a fishing hat with little covers over the side vents that look like little ears sticking out of his hat, making his face look like the perfect teddy bear, except for his round glasses. He is such an odd bird here the pimps in their outrageous bright and burning custom-mades take Milton for a stand-out pimp on a first glance. We order two racks of beef ribs with the hottest sauce they have. A few half-watch to see if our mouths burn and stomachs explode from the heat. Most of the people here seem dressed for some nice summer dance. The girls wear gowns and little jackets and sit across the tables from each other next to their dates. The young men wear jackets and ties. The pimps are socializing among themselves. It's too early for the whores to come in for their midnight snack. This is a nice, brightly lit, glass-walled place whose insides are easily seen from the street.

It's summer. School's out. The boredom is hot twenty-four hours a day. Nothing to do. Nothing feels good. Nothing sounds good. Nothing tastes good. The restless hormones. No good movies. The air you breathe picks a fight with you. Your car's lost its snappy reflexes. All the smokes are burned. The cappuccino tastes like Lysol. Nobody believes the whores' moans and writhing moves. You want. You deserve. You should have. You wish. You should be so lucky. Nothing looks good. Only your anger grows like algae on your pond of boredom and what you have is no good. Everyone feels like you. That is the news commentary from the TV editorialist, who looks like an aging coked-up Tweetie Bird with his bong bong eyes seen through his big glasses and his semibald head with the pitiful lone tuft of hair sticking up on top like the Marines raising the flag on Iwo Jima while John Wayne, somewhere tiny on his head, looks on.

So where have these black boys and girls out of *Ozzie and Harriet* come from? What have they done? They seem to be in the wrong movie. Or is it us, me, Milton, the TV news and metro dailies? We're walking the streets of *High Noon, My Darling Clementine, Gunfight at the OK Corral.* But the movies are *A Summer Place,* and *Gidget Does Seattle.*

"Do you think those girls are attractive?" Milton asks, staring at me through his round glasses.

"Yeah," I say. "I think they're beautiful."

"I don't," Milton says. "I was brought up to see them as ugly and beneath me."

"Say hello to your ribs, Milton. Come on, talk to your food," I say.

Milton turns around. "Why? What?"

"You, Milton! You!" I smile, while snarling low and close. "If you're going to talk like that, be cool. Keep your voice down. I don't want to die."

"Why? What did I say? I'm telling you the truth."

"Where'd you grow up learning that shit?"

"After the war, my mom relocated us to Milwaukee, where we lived in a mostly Negro neighborhood. Mom got me and my brothers into a Catholic school full of Caucasians. I call them Caucasoids."

"Yeah, yeah. And dead Marines. Go on."

"She didn't want us playing with Negroes. Mom always sent my brother and me to school wearing a jacket and tie. And she shined our shoes every night. She said she didn't want Negroes for friends because they sat on your furniture and left a smell."

"This may be the time, but I don't think it's the place to talk about your childhood, Milton," I say.

"Do you know what your problem is, Ulysses Kwan?" Milton asks, in his Peter Lorre-as-Jap voice, giggling.

"I can't wait for you to tell me, man."

"You don't think enough about the fact that you are a yellow man. You think you're white. And that's why you're here with your camera and tape recorder."

"I'm here for some ribs in hot sauce and shallow conversation," I say.

"Your mother didn't discourage you forming any friendships with Negros?" Milton asks. "She didn't tell you not to wear green, because it makes you look more yellow?"

Milton lets me off and vrooms his little Porsche home. The night air is still hot and woolly, like breathing damp unwashed dogs. At the Virgin Tropics Motel, I stuff the oversized pockets of my jacket with cans of film and boxes of tape, pick up the camera and tape recorder, and drive over to the high school, where I see a group of black cameramen. Blacks, grown men in baseball uniforms, are playing baseball on a well-lit baseball field. A few families with children cluster in the bleachers, fussing as they watch.

We see each other with cameras in our hands, our jacket pockets significantly full. We avoid each other, lurking on the edge of the light around the grassy field. Grass surrounds the high school. I'm allergic to grass, especially hot flowering grass, passionate grass. Between me and the grass are a few allergy pills that have minds of their own. Sometimes they work, sometimes they don't. It's difficult to take the threat of danger seriously. It's too dreamy and adolescent to believe that these gestures, words, and half-actions I have seen so many times in movies are real. The kids wandering over the lawns are adolescents. We adults, hoisting our cameras like sidearms, are the dreamers, the prima donnas, the last romantics. Our cameras hang low. Nothing to shoot. Black teenagers wander over the lawns. They laugh loudly, trying to attract a group of girls. They sit in cars. They drive their cars around the school parking lot and honk their horns at each other. I get the feeling they're performing for us. They're taking their cues from us, the cameramen committed only to satisfy the camera's appetite for hot pix. But as for thrills and chills, as for a tense tingling undercurrent running through tonight's dull hot summer thud—we're it.

Loose groups of teenagers gravitate toward the cameramen. We move. They move. They ask what I'm shooting. Nothing, I say.

I'm a Chinaman. Why am I trying to feel like I've been here

before? Everywhere outside of the Mother Lode country I have been a stranger all my life. When I was six years old and Sylvia held my hand and put her arm around me on our way to Lincoln School, I seemed strange to the Chinese of my family and strange to Sylvia's family. I have been the stranger in town, the stranger in the family ever since. "Home," the way the Negro dishwasher standing at a urinal talks about "home" in New Orleans, is not the Oakland ghetto or Chinatown. Ma and the aunts don't understand. I don't know, understand, or want "home." Since leaving the Mother Lode, I haven't lived in a home. I'm not a homer, I'm a camper. I'm a boomer. Other than that, wherever I am, I don't *live* the part. I'm on location, *playing* the part.

I am trouble here with my camera, bulging pockets, and TV news license to drop the shutter. I keep the camera down and try to look stupid. What do I want to shoot? Hey, I don't want to shoot anything. I get paid by the amount of unshot film I bring back. I am the world's worst photographer. They send me out on stories and pay me extra when I come back with nothing, no pictures, no stories, nothing. I tell this to the kids around me and see that, for now, they are just kids, curious and arrogant about the adult stranger who has no chance of passing for a member of their student body, hanging out in jeans on their playground.

"Come on, cameraman, take a picture of this," a kid says, showing me a pack of firecrackers and clicking a lighter to fire. It's a picture. I quickly and unenthusiastically shoot it with pure guesswork about iris openings and light. Later a firebomb burns on a walkway. Another nothing picture. I see a gun in a teen's back pocket and follow him with the camera under my arm like Sarah's shinbone when I sucked on her toes. She didn't like being licked all over. She never allowed my tongue down between her legs. She did not suck me. No tongues in the mouth or the ears or on the face. No foreplay. What I gave, she wiped off. What I got, I had to ask for. Now she and Jason are expecting.

I imagine her here, on the lawn with her future kids, with mothers who say they are here to see their children stay out of trouble.

She would be beautiful here. An angel. But these are not the Negro kids like Jason Peach was a Negro kid when I was a kid. These kids run down the lawn toward the street with rocks in their hands. Running kids—that's a picture!

What if the kid with the gun in his pocket pulls it out and shoots it at a car? Will I aim at the kid's face? Will I get the shot that shows where the bullet goes and what it hits? I'm thinking stupid, thinking like a soulless machine, a pretentious camera-eye seeking the perfect man-machine relationship, something personal, satisfying, and famous, like the film of the survivors of the Titanic in the lifeboats in the water being taken onto the Carpathian, like *Triumph of the Will,* like the Zapruder film at the instant the bullet whacked Kennedy, and Jackie reached for him.

My viewfinder is turned up. I'm working so hard to be the legs and organs of the camera, I am slow to wonder at what I've been hearing for a long time now. The shouting grows thicker and faster, it sounds like old-time radio thunder. Boys who look no older than fourteen or fifteen have buckets of bricks and stones torn up from a parking lot across the street behind the drive-in. They throw them at passing cars and shout "Get Whitey! Kill the pig!"

The thunder flapping from one hollow tone to another is car doors caving in under the hit of a brick. A block away, the stoplights change from green to red, and the flow of targets stops. As cars from the cross street turn onto the street running past the school, the bricks and stones fly. American cars sound tinny, hollow, when a brick hits them. Seeing how little it takes to crumple a door makes me wonder what I want a car to do for me.

I aim the light from the sungun at Herman with my left hand, hold the camera under my arm, and look down into the viewfinder to see what I can see. Not much. I focus and see Herman Schwartz close up.

"Hey, man," he shouts, and points past me, "Hey, hey, man! Don't do that! He's with us . . ." I tip my head and camera back and have a personal point-of-view shot of a pack of firecrackers dangling from a spitting fuse over my face. I open my noncamera eye and sparks from the fuse crash on my glasses. Oh no! The Movie About Me is a Road Runner cartoon, and I'm Wile E. Coyote! No, I am both Number One Son and Charlie Chan. Bad movie. The kid with the crackers wants to drop a lit string down the back of my collar. Wrong movie! Herman keeps his finger pointed at the kid and bores his eyes into the kid's, until the kid turns away and tosses the crackers out onto the grass. If the film comes out, Herman is a hero.

A Coke bottle filled with gasoline and a flaming rag wick stuffed down the neck flies at a car, thumps the side without breaking, and bounces off to dribble and burn in the street. A shadow of a man dances against the firelight and headlights of passing cars. He waves his arms and shakes his head, shouting, "Hold it! Hold it! Don't throw no rocks unless you got a gun because the pig is going to come down here and shoot you!" I grab Herman by the arm and shove the tape recorder into his chest. He grabs it. I point to the dancing shadow screaming to kids about guns.

"Go get that sound!" I say and stop in the light to read the film counter. I look up and see the bomber with his pockets full of firecrackers dogging me.

"You needs a bodyguard," he says.

The lights change from red to green to yellow to red to green, giving the strange game being played between the boys with rocks and the cars a strange logical order: the cars accelerate by in groups, and the boys have time to rearm.

We quickly achieve a high-pitched calm in the regular noise of popping firecrackers and thumping door panels. We are alert on the edge of hysteria and boredom. Then a lovely girl, fifteen, maybe sixteen, maybe—a long maybe—eighteen, no bra, the fit of her T-shirt bulging, passes close by me, catches my eye, smiles and says, "Hi." I do not ask her name. She talks to the girl with her about me, as if I do not hear. "That's Ulysses. He's good. I like him."

The mothers stand between the baseball game and the teenagers who listlessly chuck rocks at racing traffic. No great excitement. No anger released. They don't look angry. They look more like kids, skipping stones across a slow spot in the river. A mother with a baby in a buggy asks where the parents of these kids are. "Do you think all this reflects racial dissatisfaction?" I ask. I should ask if these kids have ever skipped stones or seen a wide slow spot in a river.

"Yes," she answers abstractedly. But racism is beside the point to her. What she is watching is not a racial event but kids misbehaving.

The police arrive in three cars. Four men get out of each car, assemble, and show themselves. "Get on the other side of the cops and record their sound," I say in Herman's ear as another pack of firecrackers pops in the spongy heat. "I gotta protect you," Herman says. I shove him again, and he runs with the crowd to taunt, insult, and watch the cops.

"I'll protect you," the girl in the T-shirt says. "Want to feel my natural?"

"Sure," I say and run my hand over the edges of her hair. She tickles my hand as everything around me oozes off to chaos. "How about you, do you want to feel my natural?" I ask and tip my head to her.

"Yeah, I like you," she says, and feels the same hair my mother phoned about two weeks ago, to ask if I had gotten it cut.

The arc of a firebomb moving over our heads toward the street catches my eye. It doesn't smash when it hits the car, it lands whole and rolls down the trunk. Coke makes tough bottles. The car stops, a black man jumps out, strips his jacket off, and smothers the flames. I duck between a parked truck and a car to change film and find another man, a Negro squatting over *his* camera. He says he hears a black cameraman was hit by a cop and had his film confiscated. But he says he's been shooting among the cops, and from what he's seen, they've been keeping their cool.

"Look at that," he says, pointing. Across the street is an empty lot and an alley, and across the next street I see people looking stark on their porches in the harsh light of burning bare-bulb porch lights, watching the school through binoculars. This is the night before the Fourth of July. Summer in the city. I don't have a lens that can make my camera see that far.

"Reloading?" says a voice behind us. We look around and see a cop, in a crash helmet and raised clear plastic visor, flak jacket and short-sleeved shirt and gloves with a raised billy club. I expect to be hit. "Yes, reloading," we say, and the cop goes on his way. All the cops return to their cars, scatter, climb in, and drive away.

With the police gone and nobody shot, clubbed, or arrested, what little spirit they have goes out of the crowd. I come across an impromptu meeting on the lawn. With the dignified stupidity of the camera, I join other cameramen throwing light and eyes on a young man who says he's a member of a delegation sent out by Chicago's notorious Blackstone Rangers to "help."

He yells, "You jive asses! Throwin' rocks ain't nothin'! Get guns!" He whips out a fine-looking automatic pistol, pulls out the clip and strips off a 9mm bullet. He slips and clicks the clip back in handgrip and holds the bullet up for the crowd and cameras. "I tell you I fought for the stars and stripes, but from now on I am fighting for one flag only! The black bandanna!" He holds up a black bandanna. Whoever he is, he has a pocketful of props.

"Hey! Let's see that bullet again!" I shout, adjusting the light. Then, as I peep into the eyepiece and roll film on him, the man from Chicago turns and throws the bullet at me. Close-up in the close-up lens, he points into the camera, and says, "The next time you see that bullet, it'll be in your head!" Great shot. And a great line, even though it makes no sense. The kids rake the grass with their fingers looking for the bullet he threw away. The bullet he'll put in my head the next time we meet won't be that one. Assassins should be seen and not heard.

This one hasn't accomplished his goal. The crowd laughs instead of getting fired up with anger and rage. The crowd is loose, not unhappy, bored and looking for a good time, not angry. But what if they start happily chanting some war chant to burn one of the exclusive private communities of the wealthy and filthy rich a few minutes by car from here? Will I go along to lap up the images or call the cops?

In The Movie About Me I have a carbon arc searchlight mounted on top of the old two-tone green-on-green two-door 1952 Chevrolet. I have big outdoor speakers. I drive down the streets slow as a slow walk. I shine the light on the fronts of the houses of the exclusive, private, artificial, once-upon-a-time, long ago, and far away. I burn white light through their blinded windows, and call over the big speakers, "Whiiiiiiite folks! Oh, whiiiiiiite maaaaaan! I know you're iiiin there!" The white people jump out onto their porches with their guns and see a Chinaman in a ponytail and burst out laughing. When the happy black mob determined to burn down dreamland arrives on the scene, all the lights are on, everybody is out on the street, laughing in the middle of the night.

The man from Chicago holds up his gun and gets loud and hot, goes hoarse calling for guns, bombs, the revolution, but his performance has the opposite effect, calming the crowd. Then finally a firebomb flies through an open window into a blue four-door car with three or four people inside and burns. The car swerves to a stop, a door opens, fire rolls out, and a man stands up. The other people in his car are store mannequins. Was he caught taking his big Barbie and Ken dolls out for a ride? Is the moon full tonight?

As my camera runs dry, I look up. People are running downhill all around me. I get in on the run to ask people why they're running. They tell me the police are in the bushes, closing in with tear gas. I stop and look back. Sure enough, there are cops. There are little clouds of gas pooling and puddling in the air, slowly hazing out in the heat. I run across the street and make it back to the comfort and familiarity of the Virgin Tropics Motel.

The guardian of the midnight electronics motel room next door says no one went in or out of my room. I thank him and tell him the story of how I got here with a camera in hand. He likes the idea of me being a Chinese writing for whites about nights in the ghetto and offers me the loan of an electric typewriter (an IBM Selectric!), and a color TV. I can't refuse. He carries the TV in, plugs it in, and stands in the doorway, probably waiting to see me write. I think of telling him I have sentimental reasons for writing on the ancient little portable typewriter Ma used to type the ditto masters for the day's menus in the big kitchen of the Hotel Westlake Eclipse but don't know how to make it funny. Instead I load the IBM with paper and tell him I'll leave the front door open to ease the circulation of cooler air and conversation.

"Right on," he says and returns to his room.

Too late for the eleven o'clock news. The bug-eyed, bald-headed announcer, wearing a medallion and a polyester toupee, hosts All Night at the Movies on the independent Tacoma channel. Tonight's movie is *Flower Drum Song*. Tonight's All Night at the Movies guest is Tacoma's own 72-year-old go-go club owner and dancer, Granny A-Go-Go, in a bikini dripping with sparkling fringe. Granny A-Go Go's dancing fades into Nancy Kwan lip-syncing Pat Suzuki singing "I Enjoy Being a Girl" as she slips her stockings up her legs in front of six full length mirrors, and I begin tripping the keys of the IBM. Herman walks in with two six-packs and a baggie full of grass.

He invites the guardian in for a beer and a high. "Hey, Ulysses! Say, man, you remember that fine little sister in that nothing T-shirt following you around, man?" he says, putting a wet hand on my shoulder and handing me a beer when I turn. "I says to her, come with me and I will take you to Ulysses Kwan's sweet yellow ass, but she says no, she has to go home, and I say I will give her a ride home, and she says no. And a good thing too, 'cuz I'm so baaad, man, and she's so fine, man, and sniffing and wriggling around Ulysses so horny, man, I don't know how you resisted, man. I would've parked in front of her house and made her suck my dick, or I'd wake up her folks and let 'em catch her with my hands on her tits and her hand on my dick!" He laughs. The bare-chested guardian laughs. I don't understand the joke. Why should she feel guilty about his assaulting her? I know better than to ask out loud. I wait and listen, and feel my flesh turn to cottage cheese as I hear, with the absolute clarity of the stoned, watching from far away, that I am in the wrong movie.

"It would really hurt me if you called me anything but Black," Herman says, reading over my shoulder with the bare-chested guardian. Herman reaches over with a ballpoint pen—I hate ballpoint pens, I never use ballpoint pens—and crosses out the word "Negro" and writes in "Black." I rip the page out of the machine, tear up the pages of notes I've written, and stomp outside into the grin of the guardian of the room full of midnight TV and electronics, and walk off like I know where I'm going. After I take ten steps, I know that there's only one place I can go without feeling this walk is a big fake—to the Big Potato Barbecue Pit. Open 24 hrs. I have sausage and eggs over easy and hash browns.

I walk back to the motel past dark houses. The heat is quiet. Herman and the guardian of the midnight TV and electronics next door have Scotch-taped the torn pages back together. I laugh. I'm touched. I'm suspicious and laugh again. Contact high. Herman says, "I'm sorry I touched your papers, man. I had no right. You're a brother, man. You're an artist. I didn't mean to fuck your mind!" His eyes are bloodshot, stoned patty eyes. *Flower Drum Song* is off the TV and there's MGM's *China,* with Pa in Ma's least favorite scene. Pa is a young Chinese guerilla in China after Pearl Harbor, riding in a truck. Loretta Young, a missionary doctor, sits squeezed between Pa and the star Alan Ladd. Alan Ladd drives and does all the talking. Alan Ladd doesn't care who's at war. He only cares who's paying. Loretta Young is supposed to act like she doesn't believe Alan Ladd is so cynical. Instead she acts like Pa has his hand on her leg and she likes it better than listening to Alan Ladd shift gears and talk nihilistic. What would happen if Pa and Loretta Young were alone in this movie? That's why Ma doesn't like this movie. Pa is climbing out of the river holding a crate of dynamite to his chest. The Japanese machine-gun him and Pa disappears in an explosion, shouting, *"Aiiieeeee!"*

"I don't care about the notes," I say, "You're right, man. Throw 'em away. You made me think about it some more. And that's good." I sound stupid to myself.

"No, no, man," the guardian says, lifting his fingers from rolling a fat doobie to gesture with his hands. "I got all over my man Herman. Shiiit, man. You write what you feel like you feel it, and that's fucking beautiful, man."

"We had to read it to put it back together, you know what I mean?" Herman says.

"Yeah, lemme see that," the guardian says, taking the pages of typewritten torn and taped notes from me. "I like this here: 'I never feel more embarrassed, pretentious, and helpless than when I'm back in the Negro ghetto. I am still uneasy with the word *black*. I know they prefer to be called that now, but when I was a kid living with them in the Oakland ghetto, *black* was cause for a fight or a sudden offended tear down a lady's cheek. And we called them *ladies,* not *women.'* I like that," he says.

"Yeah," Herman sighs. He turns on the tape recorder and tells posterity he is unstrung without sleep. He looks as relaxed as he can be, but has to scream and shout just to hear himself, just to feel like he's talking at all. He shouts and screams the narration to The Movie About Him, running from his mother in the South, running from one marriage in the Midwest, running from a common-law marriage in Texas, running back to his mother, scuffling to raise the membership fee for the jive NAACP. He screams about TV ruining the NAACP by loving it too much, about police brutality in general, about black Christianity, and jive honky colonialist interpretations of Christ. He talks through the night.

Morning. July 4th is quiet. The Panthers and the Immortals are out all day in black leather, black shades, black Lenin moustaches and beards, black gloves, black combat boots tied with black parachute cord, in pairs and alone, carrying little black walkie-talkies with short, black-rubbered antennas wagging like toy hard-ons in their gloved hands, shoulder bags full of movement newspapers and flyers over their shoulders. They stop everyone they meet and press a paper, a flyer, a swagger, a handshake, a Black Power upraised fist. Just the look of them seems to keep people indoors and off the streets. Out cruising the streets with Herman later that night after the hydro races, we see the same pairs of black leather jackets and red and black berets, and once again, people get off the streets.

My attempt to capture the shadow man dancing against the flow of headlights, the flames of a dribbling bottle firebomb, and Herman pointing over my head leading the camera to that string of firecrackers about to drop on my face, actually come out on the film I shot last night, and KDIO airs it on the 11 o'clock news as a postscript to what they say has actually turned out to be an old-fashioned American Fourth of July.

I drive Herman back home after the sun is up. The shadows are still cool after another sleepless night. I feel divided. My senses, my skin, blood, lungs, all snap to a crisp awareness of the newness of the day. But at the same time, I am still choking for breath in the dark meat of the heat, watching The Movie About Me.

"I really did enjoy this," Herman says and holds up his right hand to give me five.

"So did I, man," I say.

Herman laughs and claps his hands, "You're funny, man. After two days in the ghetto you be talking like a blood, man. Shiit, I was marveling at how well you talk like a jive honky. Just marveling, Ulysses! I was going to ask for lessons and learn how to talk with them nice honky extra-credit vocabulary words. Now, here you are talking like a nigger, man! What is that?" He stamps his feet up and down, laughs and holds his palm bare for five. I give him his five and laugh. But it's not me laughing. I'm not happy.

Maybe it's frustration at having faced less danger than I'd anticipated and made too much of it. Already Herman is acting different because he's been on the TV news. He feels different, he says. He knows why. He sees why on every newsstand in the jellying gooey Seattle sunlight. A frame cut from the film I'd shot, a close-up of Herman saving me from being firecrackered to death is on the front page of the morning paper. I'm the hapless Wile E. Coyote, and he's the Roadrunner. We pass coffee shops full of people sitting at the counter and in the booths holding his picture up over their faces. We are sensitive to the lumps of rolled-up morning papers on porches, lawns, walkways all over town. Beep Beep.

"You made me famous, Ulysses! Famous! I can feel it! Every fucker who knows how to read in this fucking town is thinking, Herman Schwartz? Any nigger who saves the ass of some no-account Chink is some kind of moderate nigger arbitrator, negotiator, diplomat *I* can talk to without fear of having my throat slit or my pocket picked. Wow, man! Heyyyy!" He clenches his fists and kicks the floor of Ma's old Chevy again. "Whooo! It feels gooood, man!" Herman says and holds his palm up to give me five. I take his five, "You're goood, Ulysses. I thought you were just some jiveass rubber Chink token those honkies at KDIO stuffed into their affirmative action to cork the flow of blacks, but I see you' baaaaad, man.

"You know, Ulysses," Herman continues, "As a result of this experience I have this idea about a black-controlled, black point-of-view news service. We can, you know, provide film and sound for the press and TV!"

"Naw, man, you know all the stations are going to say their professional journalistic integrity blah blah blah prevents them from using stuff over which they have no editorial control and whose authenticity they cannot corroborate. You know what I mean," I say.

"Yeah. That's right. I didn't think of that," Herman sighs. Then he brightens up with a new idea.

"I want you to be my campaign manager for the board of education, man. We're a team. Then I'll run for the city council." Good old Herman. A part of us hasn't grown up. With our mock-vicious looks, riding around in a twenty-year-old car trying to look tough, I suddenly see us as the sham-tough scam boys of twenty years ago—the age my mother seems fixed in, waiting for us in another kind of Sixth Street, in a different Oakland, waiting for us to hang up our cameras and other toys, wash our hands, and ask for cookies.

I write about how I spent the Fourth of July with Herman for the magazine. Herman looks good in a fine tailored suit and new shoes on the cover. Next thing I know, KDIO calls me in to Herman's office and Mr. Dio, the station manager, the Director of Community Affairs (Herman's boss), a bruised, bandaged black woman in a gray suit, and lawyers and executives from rival KREP cram into the tiny Community Affairs office.

The night before, I was home in my apartment looking out over Elliott Way and Elliott Bay at the cars, boats, ships, ferryboats, helicopters, and airplanes playing in my picture window world and writing my review of John Wayne's *The Green Berets*. In the movie, my father, the stalwart South Vietnamese general, uses his wife, the luscious Nancy Kwan, to fuck the enemy general and suck the secret plans out of him. While I was writing about Pa doing his thing, living up to his rep as The Chinaman Who Dies, Herman Schwartz apparently took over a meeting of militants and accused this young black woman who works as a secretary at KREP of being a spy for the media. The result was gang rape. But Herman says he left and saw no gang bang. If he was there, if he was in on gang-banging her, she can't say for sure.

Inside, I know he did it. And I know he'll get away with it. I wind up writing about him as an old friend because he's black, because I'm not white, to make a good story, to take the easy way out. I am haunted by the lie.

He'll be the darling of the liberals and actually be elected to the board of education, and shuck 'n' jive happily ever after because of the picture I make of him in the camera and in the magazine. The black secretary will dead-end at the station, quit in humiliation, disappear, and be forgotten. And Herman will be beholden to his backers, laying on the concerned smiles and half-truths to cover his ass. TV has decided Seattle needs a heroic black moderate to celebrate, and thanks to my lucky snaps, Herman Schwartz is it. The Lone Ranger sometimes makes mistakes and rides out of town before The End. No one wants to thank the Masked Man. And there is no "Hi yo, Silver, awaaaaaay!"

Ulysses: The Star River Rock and Old Timey Festival & Pot Luck Fair

Now, over a rise, here I come in my yellow Volkswagen van toward the airport to pick up Adonis, his adoring gorgeous girlfriend of the moment, and his flamenco dancers, Marlon and Marlita, under thirty, dubiously self-improved high school dropouts, jingling bells, wearing beads and buckskins, clapping and singing. From Sea-Tac Airport to a barnyard near Rock, Washington (the first left turn after you leave Lotus), for the first annual "Star River Rock and Old Timey Festival & Pot Luck Fair."

But the Midnight Country Jock doesn't like it. The Midnight Country Jock has an echo—as if his head were inside a deep stainless steel pot—as he talks about himself in the third person. "Imagine a movie where the children take over the music industry, drop acid into the nation's water supplies, and elect an eighteen-year-old rock star as the U.S. President. Well good people, that movie has not only been made, but *Wild in the Streets* is playing all over Seattle, and the Midnight Country Jock doesn't like it. No, sir. The old Jock of the Midnight Road does not like it. It's too close to reality. Kids look on everything adult as the enemy. Even while Seattle sits complacently in the theaters watching *Wild in the Streets,* real live hippies, dippies, and yippies are descending on Seattle for a rock festival that's threatening to play amped-up, sonic-booming rock and freak music for seventy-two hours, three days and nights straight!"

I drive on, waiting for a country song on the way to the airport, but The Midnight Country Jock is not through. "All right, you yippies and hippies. You have howled yourselves silly at the Democratic Presidential nominating convention. And you'll be glad to hear that since your hero Huey Newton, of the Black Panther Party, has been found guilty of shooting a police officer in Oakland, hippies have taken over a building on the Berkeley campus. And the last straw is this Russian invasion of Czechoslovakia! You mindless and spineless yippies, hippies, and flower power children

out there! You call yourselves American and you call the establishment the enemy? What do you have to say now that the Russians
have invaded Czechoslovakia, I want to know?" he asks, and spins
two in a row: Merle Haggard's "Fighting Side of Me," and the song
from my father's current movie, John Wayne's *The Green Berets*.
Rumpa tump tump, tumpity tump tump, "Silver wings upon his
chest/ That's a sign he's America's best. . . ." Pa dies in *The Green
Berets*. A little Vietnamese boy who would have been played by my
father if this were a John Wayne World War II movie stands on the
beach as the sun sets in the east, tears in his eyes, sniffles in his nose
at the news that the American soldier who took care of him is dead.
Weepily the little Gunga Din asks, "Who'll take care of me now?"

John Wayne puts the dead soldier's green beret on little Gunga
Din's head. "That's my problem, now, Green Beret!" John Wayne
says, putting an arm around the boy.

And from nowhere, as if it were something I'd picked up on the
road, a premonition comes over me that the long-dead Fat Jack Fat
will be selling his jewelry at the festival. And I'm back in his shop,
ten years ago, eighteen years old, blooming late, immersed in the
thunder of wrestling consonants as Dylan Thomas's voice reading
Portrait of the Artist as a Young Dog piles out of Fat Jack's big speakers, bouncing with audible little flops on the linoleum tile floor.
What was it I became accomplice to, what was Fat doing to that
fifteen-year-old girl when I didn't understand what he said and
didn't ask him the obvious questions? I still wonder, and still feel as
if I had sold some unspeakable truth about a child to a monster, for
food. What truth, I can't believe, I don't know, and hope it's too
late to find out, to mean anything, to make a difference. . . . Some
days, I seem about to remember her name.

At the airport, and surprise! Who walks off the plane but Jason
Peach, my old friend from way back when, from Berkeley, bearded
and mustachioed, in a blue jeans jacket, wearing shiny red and
black watermelon striped pants like Burt Lancaster wore in *The
Crimson Pirate*, high-topped hiking boots, beat-up straw cowboy
hat, and lots of silver and turquoise? Dreamily he claps a rhythm,

one foot after the other, to the accents of a Spanish song. He acts unaware that he's quietly singing, in Spanish, a Fandangos de Huelva. He seems to vaguely realize he is in the wrong movie.

"Heeyyy! What's happenin'!" I growl at Adonis, holding hands with a beauty in buckskins and beads. The dancers, Marlon and Marlita, are costumed for dancing. Everyone's dressed as if they walked off a stage following a performance last night, got in a cab, went directly to the airport and took off. And now . . . no photographers. No star treatment. I ask, "What're you doin' here, man?"

"Adonis said he needed a nigger Spanish Gypsy flamenco singer who can play backup to help him save a little village in the Northwest from bandits," Jason says. "What's your excuse?"

"I am a man of no particular talent, but I have crashed many parties with my yellow gringo guitar," I reply. "And I have this empty two-story house, two bathrooms, a lot of beds, a fridge full of food, and you're staying with me, right?"

"Man, am I glad you said that! " Jason says, "I was afraid I was going to have to stay at some Americanismo Motel with them. Hear that, Adonis, man?"

"We're staying with you too, man," Adonis says, "Hey!"

"Damn straight. You all stay with me," I yell.

"Hide your women." Jason crows, "Samurai are here to save your village."

The spongy floor, rubbery paint, cushioned walls, spongy ceilings, spongy lighting, and spongy air-conditioning sponge up everything we say and do without a bounce or echo. We embrace. Out of the dismal synthetic quiet of the airport, breathing synthetic air, we round corners and head downstairs, Wyatt Earp and Doc Holliday, Henry Fonda and Victor Mature in *My Darling Clementine,* Burt Lancaster and Kirk Douglas in *Gunfight at the OK Corral,* through stares and titters toward my yellow vw van. Adonis "El Filipino" has a moustache and long hair in a ponytail. His girlfriend in white buckskins and beads is Doris Rainwater, a real Indian, Native American, no big deal, but with a New York accent. Yeah, she hears that all the time, but she has never been to New

York in her life. But that's what people say when they meet her. She sounds like she's from New York. Marlon Moreno makes jewelry and says he's a Spaniard born in Los Angeles. He dyes his blond hair and moustache black to look more Spanish when he dances with his wife, Marlita.

"You look tired," I say to Marlita when she catches me staring at her navel. Everyone in the airport up at five in the morning stares at her navel. It's the only exposed navel in all of Sea-Tac Airport.

"She's thirty-eight," Adonis says.

"You don't look thirty-eight," I say.

"That's because I'm tired," Marlita says.

"The Washington Delicious Report says the girls are nice here this time of year," Jason Peach says in the back of my van that has no back seats. They look like prisoners. They look like victims back there.

"They said summer has arrived in Seattle, the nice fresh town that smells of the mountains and the sea. The girls are natural here. Natural blondes. Magical redheads. Muscular girls. Girls who eat salmon. Jason Peach, the Black Grape of Berkeley blues, El Negro del Gringo Flamenco, has landed! Oh, ye mother and daughter girls swarming to the power of rock 'n' roll music and high times are doomed to be seduced with flashing fingers and my soulful Black Gringo flamenco song!" Jason Peach calls out, "Oh, ye girls with no shame, no clothes, no shaves in the armpits nor on the legs, and no mommies and daddies to say no no no—come! Come to Star River and marinade your sweet flesh in our music!"

Adonis climbs forward for a look out the windshield, as Seattle comes clearly into sight in the undersea deep of a cloudy, hazy dawn. "That's what it looks like, huh?" Adonis says, "Where's Juvenile Hall?"

"I don't know," I say, a bomber pilot at the wheel of the van, a Consolidated B-24 Liberator in the noise of accelerating speed, as we slowly go higher, up into colder air, up an incline on the freeway, past Boeing Field full of B-52s being painted green to look like slouching banana slugs with wings, climbing over the Pindus

Mountains toward a rendezvous and low-altitude bomb run over the oil refineries at Ploesti, Rumania. . . . "I was never a juvenile in Seattle. Were you?" I ask.

"I ran away from home when I was fourteen and started to hitchhike to Seattle. They picked me up in Oregon and brought me to Seattle. I was in Juvenile Hall for a month."

"Yeah? I used to run away all the time. Why didn't I think of running away to Seattle?"

"Yeah. It was cold," Adonis chuckles. "I saw snow out the window."

Only Adonis, "El Filipino," looks the part of the artist and lives the part of the star in The Movie About Him. I wonder, as always, at how he finds the women with the looks, the money, and the sense to know when to leave, which make his life so easy.

Driving through Lamar on the way to the festival Saturday morning, we pass a group of little kids standing in front of a church. They all shout and flash the "V" for Victory, "V" for We Are Liberating Paris, "V" for We Shall Overcome, "V" for Peace, for Hand Me a Joint, for the Number Two, "V" for the Fun of It. I flash the "V" back and they scream a laughter that goes up and down with their jumping. A dead cat on the highway and an old World War II truck on the outskirts of Lamar are to become landmarks, assuring us in our future drives in various depths and dimensions of psychedelic wickedness that we are going the right way.

From the bridge outside of Lotus on through to Rock, Washington, the road is lined with kids going to or coming from the festival. Parked cars and camper trucks line one side of the road. Some are in ditches. One bare-chested semilonghair with a can of green death shining in his hand dances around the slowly moving cars, sees the ARTIST sticker on our window, and kisses the windshield, giving us a glimpse of the insides of his mouth flattened on the glass like the sucker of a squid. "I love you," he says as we pass, and flashes the V.

To the left of the main entrance is the Open Door Clinic, a tent with a Cadillac ambulance in back, and the backstage area. To the right are the concessions. In one of the stalls, members of Seattle's Pope Bishop Ensemble are singing to recorded music and chanting invitations to the crowd to buy hotdogs. Behind them is a small stage where groups rehearse. Those moved by the moment burst into performance. The ground is mud, mud that smells like garbage. The grass that covers the ground does not last the first day. In front of the main stage, all the way to the hill and into the trees, all you can see are people. Some are in lean-tos and tents, some are sleeping in sleeping bags amidst the feet of spectators squishing from foot to foot to the music.

"Women!" Jason shouts, and spreads out his arms. They lean on their elbows, lean on each other's backs, shoulders, necks, legs, heads. Children run from a mud fight, run around our hips, push at our thighs, through the mud that splats under their little feet. Boys stand, staring at nowhere as they move one leg, then the other, and pat their buttocks clop clop with their hands. Shoes all over the place are moving up and down from toes wriggling inside. Girls' blouses are wobbling with live things inside. A chuckle is heard over the sound system, a soft chuckle making casual lunatic sense of all this. "Wow," the voice says, "I wonder if you know what you look like from up here, I mean it looks like one huge," he seems exhausted from the effort of absorbing what he sees, "gigantic, big hobo camp," and chuckles. "It's beautiful though, baby, wow. Groovy."

Backstage we come across Archie Tripps, the founder and organizer of the Berkeley Folk Festival, a large, curly-headed man who looks like the world's largest baby, with fat, rosy cheeks and big baby eyes. He's up here with his boys, who look older than their father.

"Hey, Ulysses!" he says. "You're a hippie, now, I see," and laughs "Ha! Ha! Ha!" which is Archie's way of laughing.

I flip his new beard and say, "I see you're acting like a kid yourself."

"Ha! Ha! Ha!" Archie shouts, one "Ha" at a time, almost too much like a slimmed-down Fat Jack Fat. And again, I'm back in

Berkeley, and Fat Jack has just given me a teaspoon of clear thick stuff for my cough, he tells me it's LSD-25 and falls asleep on the couch. I eat a Triscit and my tongue gets stuck in the weave of toasted wheat. The shower water goes straight through my body like bullets through a cloud. I know the streets are not covered with little yellow birds with black heads hopping up and down, but they still crunch under every step. A day later I don't know how I got home and I don't see Fat Jack for another long time.

Archie tells me the stage manager is named Buddha. I'm not sure which of the people back here is Buddha and I'm not sure I want to find out. Archie himself looks something like a bleached Buddha in cowboy boots to me. Anybody with a belly could be Buddha. Anybody bald. Or curly-headed like Archie. Or wearing a ponytail pulled back tight. Anybody at all. What if I look out off the stage and see nothing but the faces of twelve-year-old Chinese girls from the old Buddhist church?

"I think I'm going crazy," I say.

"That's bad?" Adonis asks.

"Beer?" Archie asks.

"Yes," Marlita says.

"Me too," Adonis says, nodding his head quickly up and down.

"It'll make you look thirty-eight," I say to Marlita to make her laugh and wink her navel at me.

Archie Tripps is blind from lack of sleep and proud of it. "Eyes full of music," he claims as we follow him to the artists' tent and the free artists' beer trailing his jackhammer bursts of laughter.

On our way we catch Adonis's brother-in-law, the producer of the festival, Douglas Parr, an Apache with eyes like flint arrowheads. Adonis hasn't seen his sister, Anna, yet. Douglas is the only man at the festival wearing short hair, a jacket, and tie. He is a history professor at the university but looks like Dick Tracy in the comic strip. Everything about Douglas Parr says "Don't fuck with me." The way he stands. He moves like a boxer, and I discover he has fought in the ring. He's wound up so tight, he looks shorter than he is. He puts his cigarette in his mouth and puffs when he looks at me and listens, pulls the cigarette out of his mouth with a pop, and snaps the ash off to the side. Wow, real George Raft.

Anna appears, so skinny and airy that every move of her arm and push of her hand on the bodies of people between us feels like a caress and draws a smile. She seems to swim toward us, all smiles, through the mass of people rolling in and out of the artists' tent. Pickpockets' paradise, but here all the rockers have their pockets by their crotches, and a small army of all-city football types are all over the festival with "Star River Rock Security" on the fronts and backs of their T-shirts. Anna has a long angular face like Adonis. They look like brother and sister.

Anna and Adonis touch people a lot, kiss with their hands. While they catch a few words and touch, I ask Douglas how an explorer of the Dark Ages and a Krishnamurti freak got the Star River Rock and Old Timey Festival & Pot Luck Fair together. Out comes the cigarette with a pop, and he moves, putting himself precisely where he wants, solid as a rock, his eyes free to watch me stumbling and slipping in the mud to keep up. "I got the idea one night doing something . . . I won't tell you what, because you probably know."

His voice is sweet and reedy and doesn't go with his glowering Dick Tracy eyes. He has a slight lisp which, I later learn, started when he bit off the tip of his tongue in a fight and swallowed it without thinking . . . and still went on to fight to a standup loss by TKO. Bleeding tongue.

"Anyway," he goes on. "I'd worked with Archie on the Berkeley festivals before, and each year he gave me more and more responsibility. Meanwhile people up here kept saying—Seattle! Groovy! Why don't you hold a festival up here? And I kept, you know, putting it off, until one night I said I'd do it, and suddenly there were people, all these fine beautiful people working and planning the thing."

The music from the outdoor stage pulses out of the dark spaces between the trees and cooks human flesh, squeezes arteries, and makes everyone a passenger of twangs, whirrs, echoes, and crashes.

Overtones hum out of the sky. Vibrations beat up out of the mud, sucking on bare feet. I feel the music buzzing out of the tent poles. The big sound includes everything, makes everybody a throbbing organ of its intelligence. Only the Apache's body is still his own, moving in his own rhythm, while everything he hears and sees and feels seems to eat through our soft tissue, to sizzle our bones.

The tent is full of guitars, amplifiers, and people waiting to go on stage. And every other minute more groups with their gear appear in the tent. Only a few hours before the star of the festival is supposed to perform, and the schedule is already a messy temperamental mystery. Only Buddha knows what's happening and like his namesake, the stage manager/master of ceremonies speaks in sweet riddles we are supposed to contemplate under the cloudy skies of Rock, Washington.

"Sounds like Charlie Chan," I say. Nothing. Our eyes have been looked into by thousands of diving eyes now, and mine are sore from seeing into the seeing of so many suddenly seen eyes, so many stoned out goofy smiles. Hippies. Hippies. Hippies. I am grooved out. "Do *you* look like *I'm* going *crazy?*" I ask Adonis.

"Yes," Adonis says. "I look like you're going crazy," and he does. His hair is high pomp Elvis Presley and his moustache is Caesar Romero. El Filipino looks more authentically Spanish Gypsy than any of us. I wear dark glasses to disguise my eyes. Jason Peach in his blue jeans, straw hat, silver and turquoise jewelry looks like he's in the wrong clothes, in the wrong band, in the wrong movie. Marlon Moreno has not darkened up the roots of his hair and moustache. Marlita looks like a belly dancer. They all look like I'm going crazy.

Outside the beer tent the Star River Rock Security, like hippie police, play touch football in the mud. "I love playing stoned," one huge short-haired baby-faced hippie policeman says, spooning the ball out of the mud at our feet. "You're the Spanish Flamingos, right?"

"Right," Adonis says, "Pink birds who stand on one foot." And we all stand on one foot.

"You look Chinese to me," the big hippie policeman says. "I'm stoned, though."

"I am Chinese," Jason says.

"Me too," I say.

"But you're a Spanish flamingo."

"He is a Spanish flamingo," Adonis says. "You must be stoned."

"Of course I'm stoned. I love to play football stoned. I was All-City and stoned all the time."

"Olé!" I say.

"Olé!" the hippie police says and splashes back into the game.

"Olé!" Marlon and Marlita say, clapping.

"Both ears and the tail!" I say.

"Groovy," Adonis says.

The blare of Buddha onstage, talking about his showbiz beginnings in burlesque between groups, catches my ear, and I step around to the wings to get an eye on the stage and stagger back at the sight of a large roly-poly Charlie Chan in white duck and Panama straw hat. No. No exaggeration. No hallucinating. And there's Pa, my father, my real father in the flesh, in the white duck, bowtie, and toupee of Charlie Chan's Number Four Son, talking to his father in an old movie.

"Gee, Pop! Even the apes are doing better in the movies than the Chinese. Apes have gone from *King Kong* to *Planet of the Apes*! And we have gone from Charlie Chan to *Susie Wong*, ping-pong, ping-pong. Pop, I see a movie. We are on the planet of the apes. Skull Island on the planet of the apes. The native apes living in grass huts have built this enormous wall across the island. The drums are beating. The torches are burning. The enormous gates give under the blows of something monstrous on the other side. The blows become heavier. Thunderous roaring and growling drives the native apes to shiver in fear. Bam! Bam! Bam! Huge fists beat and push. The gates give way, collapse, crash and there, in the gateway, they see, me, Ping-Pong! a gigantic naked Chinaman, beating my fists on my chest and roaring. I reach down for Cheetah the chimp, played by Annette Funicello, and roar, 'Gimme date! Gimme date!'"

I laugh. I don't like him. He's my father, but he's funny. I must be stoned. Contact high. Everyone is stoned. Ten thousand people in front of the stage are stoned slackjawed. They laugh. Pa is funny. Ten thousand other people, too stoned to laugh, grunt and moan every now and then.

"Please to contradict, daydreaming offspring, Number Four. Not possible. Not possible. Please, not to forget, you are The Chinaman Who Dies." Anlauf Lorane, Charlie-Chan-the-Buddha, says, and the festival crowd roars. Pa will never recognize me. He hasn't seen me since a big family dinner for Longman Jr. the night before he headed east for the race of the hundred-car freight train against one hundred trucks. He's never seen my moustache and goatee or my long ponytail. Even when Pa steps over to the edge backstage to grab a note from someone who is looking and acting like Billy Goat Gruff, he doesn't notice me. But he is funnier than I expect. I laugh. He shines onstage with Charlie Chan.

"Gee whiz, Pop! What a reception! I wonder if any of the gang remembers an old Richard Widmark World War II movie, *Halls of Montezuma*?" Scattered applause and a cheer rumbles up and down into the babble of the crowd. "I was a fanatical Japanese officer in that movie. My dying lines were, 'Sergeant, I am surprised at you. You say you have been a long time in my country, and yet you seem to have forgotten that for generations my people have thought not of living well, but of dying well. Have you not studied our philosophy, our military science, our judo wrestling? Do you not remember that we always take the obvious and reverse it? So we reverse the role of life. To us, it is death that is desirable. It is the source of our strength.'" And he makes the sounds of dying into the microphone and it comes big out of the walls and banks of speakers, sounding like small arms fire, a bombardment that brings the lily-white crowd up roaring.

"My Number Four Son, ladies and gentlemen!" Charlie Chan says without the fake accent, "The Chinaman Who Dies!" The Buddha is Charlie Chan. Too much! I want to laugh at the paranoid stupidity of what's real here. The path of enlightenment that leads from the high Catholic Zen Lama of hippie Shangri-la, Alan

Watts, and Kerouac's wracked and cultish homosexuality in Zen disguise, the Beats' brief colonizing of Chinatown, North Beach, the Dharma Bums, the very serious Gary Snyder speaking, reading, and writing more Chinese and Japanese than thou, leads all the stoned and sober alike to see that Buddha and the same old Charlie Chan of the movies are one. Forget Tibet and India and all the high lamaseries in the snows on the roof of the world. Go to Hollywood. Turn on your TV late at night and hum to the dots.

"A beautiful cat," a hippie stagehand named Jersey says. He's talking about Douglas Parr, who is downstairs in a basement where, underground, out of sight, we are smoking. Adonis practices the guitar, while Marlita moves in a desperate dance to the music, breaking her feet on the concrete floor.

Jason has collapsed, finally, fallen splat on a mattress, and sleeps until the the girls, like bushels of Washington Delicious apples with their stem ends and flower ends, are gone with a mournful "Oh, it's you," meaning us. Marlon Moreno chortles over an inoperable Czech machine gun and reminisces about the service.

"You see," Jersey says, "Like it's not only the Indians and black people Douglas is doing this for, but like the generation gap, you know? Like *Wild in the Streets* is all over town, right?" A chick snuggles closer to Jersey and hums her understanding. "And the riots at the Chicago convention? Dig? And, you know, people are scared of us. And Douglas sees this. You know in a lecture, right, to old folks, he got it all together. The Bomb. We grew up with that bomb thing, like, man, we were heavy with death and drugs, right? Drugs and the bomb thing. We got them pinned, grew up with them, experiences the parents don't have. Reason they can't understand, right? And they're ready for war! And there'll *be* war if they don't understand us. And this festival Douglas and Anna are giving is like Seattle's last chance to understand us, or it'll be war, baby!"

"But this is supposed to be annual," Jersey's chick says.

"First chance!" Jersey says giving up and kissing her.

Outside, included into the music again, Jersey looks around him, the press tent, the artists' tent with the wooden tub full of ice and beer, the stage, the rows of outhouses, all the work of his hands, seven weeks of it. "You don't believe forces were on our side, man, dig! A toad jumped out of the flames, man. Croak! A toad! And right then it started to rain, baby. Then later on, we started a fire of debris with a dollar bill, and the rain stopped. See, it isn't raining now!" It isn't raining now. "So, you know what toads mean to the Apaches, right?" Jersey asks, hilarious with conspiracy.

"No, what?" I ask.

"You don't know?" Jersey asks me.

"No. And I didn't know Douglas was Apache till Adonis told me a while ago," I say.

"I sure hope toads mean good things to the Apache," Jason Peach says behind us. "We don't need to offend anybody else with our Los Gitanos Gringos. We better rehearse, don't you think?"

"We don't go on until tomorrow afternoon at one," Adonis says.

Jason lets out his breath as if he's been kicked in the stomach. His eyes fix on a girl standing in one of the front rows. She seems to be responding to his panting. Her arms wind through the shapes of his moaning and sighing. Her hubcap breasts are there for Jason to seek, and he does seek them. The music and the waves beaming from Jason's eyes make all the girls around the one he eyes stand, bare their breasts, and writhe. Just in front of him a chubby chick wearing nothing but a fishnet fingers her fried-egg breasts. "She must have money," Jason says, as if to explain her flat chestedness.

Onstage, the singer of the hour, with seaweed hair, bare-chested, barefoot, masturbating his guitar, screams blood-splattering, eyeball-shattering hate and gore at people who drive to work everyday on the freeway and look at him funny when he passes on his Harley. He's against the war and for love, "69," brotherhood of the oppressed people, and kill the pig. Suddenly he spots my father in the wings, flips out, and chases him onto the stage. Seaweed hair wraps an arm around Pa and shouts into the mike, "My man! The Chinaman Who Dies! You deserve a song about you! Just you!" The crowd roars.

I put a standing rib roast from Safeway in the oven, and Jason and I practice the guitar in the kitchen with the backdoor open, letting the moonlight into the room. Adonis and Doris are upstairs in bed. In the next room, my friend the TV is alone, tuned to *Viva Villa!* shot by James Wong Howe, on location in Mexico, for director Howard Hawks.

Jason has not brought a girl home from the happy hunting ground after all. I catch a strange look in his eyes that worries me. Does he know I am the son of The Chinaman Who Dies?

Dark faces against the white hot sky. James Wong Howe does not like his cinematography of *Viva Villa!* likened to the dark faces against white hot skies of Sergei Eisenstein's monstrous montage bullshit, *¡Que Viva Mexico!* Yeah, I can see it. Jimmie's five years old, out in the dry hot flat and squat country of eastern Washington. Pasco. Just off the railroad, from Seattle, after crossing the sea from China. His high forehead, pinched sad little face is hot against a black background on his passport photo, shot in Toy Kong. His father sits with an Indian on the wooden porch of their wooden store, looking out onto the dry prairie grasses. Dark bodies against a hot dry cloudless sky.

Wuhay! Ah-kid-doy! Nay Hooie nigh, ahhh? Hey, kid! Where're you gone?

Cross the border, I go show! See a movie!

Oh, yeah! *Hur tie hay?* What show you see?

Ah-*Prisoner of Zenda* wahhhh! Ah-Ronald Coleman plays two different guys in love with the same woman. Ah-*Viva Villa!* Waah! Allaw good men of Mexico made outlaw by the corrupt government mount up to rescue the people and ride.

You craze!

Shot by James Wong Howe, man! Teach you how to box, man. You see a movie shot by Jimmie Wong Howe, man! Teach you how to fight!

Jason sighs, lowers his guitar, and tells me that the kid he taught how to play the guitar when he was a YMCA summer camp counselor just after high school has grown up, become a Black Muslim, changed his name to Abdullah, and now Sarah is fucking him. "She kicked me out of the house. She hates me, Ulysses. I don't understand. And it hurts, man. And you, old Kemo Sabe, you should know. 'You gots to know what dis lady can do to a man, man,'" he says in the quivering voice of Stepin' Fetchit we used to use for laughs.

Jason says he's going to sell his collection of vintage guitars, go to Japan, and study guitar building with a Japanese master, which is as far away from Sarah as he can get. But still it's not far enough away to escape the hurt she makes him feel.

"Why does she hate me?" he asks, "I'm not the one sleeping with a sweet young thing."

"Whaddaya mean, you're not!"

"Well, I didn't do it first," he says. "And now that she's kicked me out . . ."

I hear the floor upstairs creak to Adonis and Doris rocking in the big bed. "Did I tellya to fall in love?" I tap his shoulder with the backs of my fingertips. "You must have known it was dangerous, man. Any fool toting up the facts could see it was dangerous. Yellow boy tells black boy he's leaving town, leaving a gorgeous woman behind. And by the way, niggah buddy, she is blonde, tight, and from the American Gothic Midwest. Did she pull a knife on him? Great ingredients for a novel. A gothic novel in the midwest of California, but for a couple of nice Oakland ghetto boys like us— too much! Lucky for me Sarah was a lousy cook. If she had been a good cook . . ."

"She *was* a good cook. Just because she didn't cook like your mother doesn't mean she didn't cook like *mine.*"

"Yo' mama?"

"My mama!"

We laugh.

"You weren't supposed to fall in love. You weren't supposed to be a relationship. You were an affair. You were a rite of passage for daughters and the mothers alike. They let their precious little girls out of the family car, like a kitten out of a bag, to walk that space between Buffalo Books and Il Piccolo, facing each other across the street. On one side you and Crazy Edgar setting his hair on fire and spitting on you as he tells you the books you're buying are shit, and you'd steal them if you had any self-esteem, and on the other, the horny hippies and bikers and folkies singing,

> *Whazzat smell like fish, babe?*
> *Whazzat smell like fish?*
>> *Well, it smell like fish.*
>> *And it tastes like fish*
>> *And it comes served up*
>> *In a hairy dish . . .*
> *Whazzat smell like fish babe?*
> *Whazzat smell like fish?*

over their espresso, and nodding on hard drugs." I've got Jason laughing now. "Oh you were the black angel to the rescue, the voice of sanity singing the blues on an old Martin mahogany guitar. You had a closet full of women's bedroom wear in different sizes. You were supposed to pass her through the ritual, man. Not fall in love. You never fell in love."

"Well, man," Jason sighs. "I did have a lot of love to go around. Then I came home and found Sarah sleeping on the floor next to my bed, man. And it was about the most beautiful thing I had ever seen in my life. And you, my best friend, man, you left me alone with her!"

"Yeah, well, you wait man, it won't be long now. That kid you taught to play the blues will be limp-fingered, plunkless, sitting on the edge of his bed staring at the floor, praying for a way to keep Sarah, and praying for a way to get away from her, praying for the magic word. Whew!" I say, "Shiiiet! I'm going to start a home and set up a retirement plan for guys Sarah's burned up. We'll all wear satin jackets with Sarah in the nude embroidered on the back. All the nurses and staff will be blonde white women six feet tall and have deep voices."

"Brown eyes." Joason whispering. "They all have to have brown eyes."

We both muse on that vision. "I'm glad you're here, man," I say, "I'm sorry about your trouble, but I'm happy to see you again, man."

For now, Jason's romantic vision is as true as anything else. Sarah, the legendary Sarah, orbits the borderline of our sanity, is the center of our universe, and we are the stupid heavy planets in distant orbit around her fusion, fission, and radioactive glow. It amuses me to reminisce. But Jason loves her. Loving her, no matter what, means a lot of to him.

Ulysses: The Sound of One Hand Clapping

The next day, Sunday, it rains. The dead cat on the roadside is wet. Every raindrop that hits and wets it kicks its fur exploding off its body in the air, blue-gray with slobbering rain. Police outside Lamar detour us around their little city. We are lost until we see the World War II half-track. But Los Gitanos Gringos aren't scheduled until 11:30 tonight.

At ten o'clock, Number Four Son tells the assembled musicians in the backstage tent that we will go on at two in the morning, then smiles his asshole Number-Four-Son smile into my eyes. He clearly has no idea that I'm his son, his real son. Then he tells us three in the morning. Finally at eight in the morning my innocent father leads us up to the stage. He whispers the name of our group into Buddha's ear and the fat man in white duck and Panama straw hat turns, and for a moment I look into the eyes of Charlie Chan.

I look up and off into a landscape of skin and faces and an eddying streams of bodies. They move like leaves and petals floating on a winding river around fields of flowers. All faces. All eyes. A surprising number of my fellow hippies are wearing dark glasses in the rain.

"When I was thirteen," Buddha says several times, out of many speakers all around us throwing sound out into the muddy crowd,

"I would step out between acts, like I am presently doing, and sell things that were totally imaginary and had no real use. For instance: Ladies and gentlemen, while we are waiting for the next part of the show to begin, the world-famous Los Gitanos Gringos, may I direct your attention down front for just a few moments, please. One of the items we have on sale tonight is a pair of dice that were discovered in Paris during the first World War. After they were smuggled into the States they became a prized item among certain alleged mobsters involved with gambling, crimes of the flesh, and the importing and distribution of illegal alcoholic libations during Prohibition. I speak of course, of the famous French picture dice, first invented to entertain Napoleon's officers and discourage dueling.

"These French picture dice have now been duplicated and like the originals, you will find that the numbers on this set of dice, instead of being painted or printed, are actually tiny handset magnifying lenses. Yes! Each dot on the die is a tiny magnifying glass. To discover why, hold the die up to a bright light. You can look through each tiny little lens and see a picture on the inside. Inside the first die you will see pictures of a young woman, unclad, innocent, and unabashed. In each lens you will see a different pose, a different position of some dance she is doing. In the other die you will see a similarly unclad young man, pictured in different poses of a dance. Now when you put the dice together, one to an eye and look into them, a most interesting thing happens. The young man and the young woman appear involved in a dance or some game *together!* It is a dance you will recognize at first sight. It is a game everybody plays when they get the chance. You may be certain that Adam and Eve played this game after eating the apple. And it is not a game of chess or checkers, cheese and crackers, or one-handed pinochle! Now when you turn the dice to the side, one way or the other, you will find the young man and young woman change positions again. In fact, the more you move the dice, the more positions you see, and the more positions you see, the more you're gonna move the dice!"

We can't make it back to Seattle without food. We stop at a roadside A&W Root Beer stand converted into a whited-out, anonymous independent fastfood drive-in in Bothell. While we wait to pick up our food, a group of local teens walk in and ask us about the rock festival. "Yeah, we played out there," Adonis tells them. They nod knowingly and strike hip poses, looking at us and then looking away, making me feel like a precious specimen gathered into the laboratory of their senses. Because we are the real thing. Hippie musicians, glowing with the magic of this fated meeting. What will they do with us when we're just a memory? I wonder. Have they ever seen Charlie Chan on The Late Show? What would they make of the son of Charlie Chan's Number Four Son calling himself "Gringo," and playing flamenco in a rock festival, where his dad is off in a Charlie Chan movie calling a white pornographer "Pop" in public?

Monday evening a few drunks start a fight. The cops come. Then it is over. The music, the rock groups, folk singers, flamencos, bare-breasted girls, naked dicks with strings of helium filled balloons tied to them are all bobbing on their way home, making frog screams when they pull their feet out of the mud's suck.

Jason is off with a Washington Delicious, telling her he is looking for a permanent thing, tired of wandering the world alone.

"Rock, Washington was beautiful," Anna says, "Lotus was beautiful. Lamar was uptight for a while, but even they finally cooperated and let people drive through their town. No drug problems, no drug busts. The only real bad thing was the property Douglas tried to get for parking. He talked with that farmer for, like five hours, right? And the farmer refused. Well, his haystack caught on fire. The police say it wasn't our fault, that it was spontaneous combustion. You know, you pack hay too tight and then it rains? Well it rained, and his stack caught fire. But he blames us. Well, I just hope we'll be able to cover costs," she says after hugging her brother.

"But you had so many people out there! Thousands!" I say.

"You know, most of those people snuck in," she says and laughs.

208 : FRANK CHIN

"And people on their way home from the festival were selling their tickets to people on their way in for a dollar. But it was beautiful, wasn't it? So many people from all over came out here and helped."

"You know what you should have done about the tickets . . ."

"'What we should have done.' How many times have we heard that?" she laughs.

"Next year write us and we'll come up a few weeks early and help," Adonis says.

"And we'll stay a week over and visit," Doris Raincloud says.

On our way back from the festival for the last time, we pass two drive-in theaters showing *Wild in the Streets.* To Adonis the movie, already old in San Francisco, isn't about people like us at all. "But I liked it," he says back at my house. Last night already seems like a long time ago, as I sit here among the warm remains of food, coffee cups with drowned moths, and the lingering smell of barnyard mud drying on my boots. "I dug it as a kind of science-fiction thing, you know," Adonis says.

"Those kids are really the establishment, they're political activists," Marlon says. "We're the political dropouts."

"But you have to vote," says a stranger in my house. Who is this guy? Oh, right, Jason's in another room putting the make on this guy's girlfriend. "You have to do something!" the guy says.

"Come election day, surrender, man. Raise our hands up, go to the army, and surrender ourselves as prisoners of war," I say, and we hear over the TV news somebody's rioting in Berkeley where Adonis's mother lives. The Third World Student Strike? People's Park? Why?

"Mom lives down by Ashby. That's nowhere near campus. They're trashing the windows of the shops up on Telegraph," worries Adonis.

"Whyn't you call her up, man? Hear for yourself," I say.

"If I call her now, I might scare her. Better wait till after eleven, when the rates are cheaper," Adonis says. "But thanks, man."

"Hey . . ."

After three days of round-the-clock rehearsing, practicing, dancing, rain, and Charlie Chan, our bodies are all reminiscence, a reverie of flesh, everywhere at once, shrieking through the rain in my vw van, standing up to the boom of the music lobbing off the stage, throbbing in the trees and humming back, echoing a kind of shine out of the trees, over the heads of thousands of costumed, beaded, longhaired kids. The country jocks and *Wild in the Streets* are wrong. The rock 'n' roll rebellion has not led to the student rebellions on campus or the Third World Student Strike at San Francisco State. Rock 'n' roll is not rebellion, it's Hollywood. It's commercial. It's establishment. Big labels. Big radio stations. Freak boutiques, incense and paraphernalia shops, biker movies.

We all chuckle low, drinking coffee and Wild Turkey, and relax with memories too luscious for words. We chuckle, cleaning the mud off our boots, and chuckle till someone says my house sounds like a chicken coop, which makes us chuckle and cluck along intimately. The sound seems to be the sound of understanding itself. As chuckle, silliness feels its solemn way out from our mothers to warm the night 'round their babies.

In The Movie About Me, I am a young pimply pubescent whose luck ran out trying to score down at Edy's Ice Cream on Lakeshore Avenue. And I'm still too young to appreciate the fact that white girls are girls too. As the movie continues, I stumble into a cave across the street from a famous funeral parlor on the western side of Pill Hill, piled high with hospitals. Here, under an exclusive funeral parlor, is a huge grotto. Among the stalactites and stalagmites marking the open-mouthed cave roof and floor, is a forty-foot-high figure of a screaming tormented Christ on the cross with the ten arms of the Ten Commandments. A high priest dressed and made up as an exaggerated Charlie Chan in white duck and panama straw hat intones sinister scripture that echoes through the grotto lit by burning torches.

The high priest calls forth his Number One Son and strips him. As the young yellow Christians chant the Ten Commandments in somber mumbles, the high Chan priest nails Number One Son to a cross with sixteen penny spikes, lifts the cross up, plants it. And then Chinese nuns unsheathe their crosses and cut out Number One Son's heart. The high Chan priest gathers the blood running off Number One Son's toes and spattering on his white duck into a goblet, adds a little wine, and gives Holy Communion with the Blood of Christ and the Body of Christ.

Now the late news, read by the last newscaster on earth, who wears a toupee. He tells the world still up at this hour watching TV that he does not care. The rug doesn't fit. It looks like it might not be his. His own hair has a different coastline and a different color.

The TV says it is finally time for Adonis to call his mother and wake her up from a sound sleep in the middle of the night to ask if she's all right, the way she expects him to. He still throbs with the flamenco, he can't let go. In The Movie About Me, the screen is blank. How much longer can El Filipino ease from woman to woman up and down the West Coast, living here and there, playing flamenco guitar to occasional American flamenco dancers? What next for Jason Peach after being a black Spanish guitar maker in Japan loses its charm?

And me? My personal business is over. I'll put myself back on the Extra Board tomorrow at 11:00 A.M. and expect to be called by 10:00 P.M. Railroad Standard Time to meet a three-in-the-morning train.

I'll also put myself on the Conductors Extra Board and stand a chance of being called out as conductor on a job. It's late summer. Conductors like to take off in their monster recreational vehicles, big three-axle mobile homes with a Jeep in tow, in the late summer–early fall. I've been railroading so long, trying to make enough money to buy me time to write the way I promised, I finally took the conductor's test. I'm now qualified on this road to work as a conductor. And I have worked as conductor and enjoyed it. Yes, I did. Working on the railroad has become a little more than a summer job between semesters in my life. I think this monkey learned all the lessons the railroad has to teach me a long time ago. How much longer will I stay on the railroad before I realize we—me and my childhood pals like Jason and El Filipino, who were sure we'd die of adventure and fucking—have grown up and I have become another angry railroad brakeman and nothing more? If I tell no one I'm Charlie Chan's Number Four Son's son, if no one in the caboose or locomotive talks to me about movies or tells me what they think of Charlie Chan movies on the late-night TV, I can have a home on the railroad forever. The road to an end has become The End.

Diego Chang: American Rifleman

The Third World Student Strike strikes at San Francisco State. The avant garde of the Third World Revolution, the Revolutionary Black Panther Party, came to the park in Portsmouth Square in the center of Chinatown, wearing their black berets and black leather jackets and black shades and black jeans, set up their sound systems and mikes, and declaimed to the old men playing chess and the old women sitting together watching children play in the sandbox: "The Chinese are the Uncle Toms of the nonwhite peoples of Amerika!" And all the American-born Chinks suddenly mope about not having an identity like the blacks. Their identity as Chinese Americans is in some kind of crisis, a Chinese American identity crisis. Can they really be Chinese Uncle Toms?

I declare myself commandant of the Chinatown Black Tigers as a joke and find out I've become the leader of a gang of suburban Chinese-American kids determined to pay their dues, get their identity by shouting "Right on!" and "Free Huey!" in Chinatown. And the Black Panthers like me because they never read Mao's *Little Red Book,* even though they swear by it. They buy it at China Books in the Mission District for fifty cents and take it over to Berkeley and sell it on the street for something like three dollars, maybe five. They don't understand it, but hanging out with me makes them feel like they do. I help them sell it. I ask for a penny, just a penny for every book they sell while I'm out on the street in front of Cal campus pitching for them. I put the pennies in little red envelopes and sell them for five dollars apiece. "Huey gave me this penny personally . . ."

Ulysses' dad, the movie star, has an apartment in North Beach. The Chink's Swiss Bank. Big prestige in his tong and all that bullshit. He knows I'm bullshit and sneers that gigolo gold dogtooth of his at me as he trots out of one of the new stores in Chinatown that sell nothing but Danish butter cookies. People come out with shopping bags full of round tincans of Danish butter cookies. There must be a price war between the stores. Reactionary sucker, he hates the Cultural Revolution wiping out reactionary influences in China as we speak. "The Red Guards are my brothers and sisters, man!" I tell him. "I love all them Revolutionary operas. Ow! They really get me here, right here." I say, tapping my heart.

I buy thirty copies of *The American Rifleman* and have all the Chinatown Black Tigers fill out the coupon and send in their money order to join the National Rifle Association and get a new, free Garand u.s. rifle M-I-AI.

As Commandant Diego, I assert my authority and order the Black Tigers out to the San Francisco dunes for target practice. Close to a million people watch thirty Chinatown would-be punks in black tanker jackets, black jeans, and black hair pompadoured high, rounded, and shiny on our heads like sperm whales marching in our jump boots down the beach with rifles slung over our shoulders. And those same million people hear us sing:

> *"Who's the leader of the Party made for you and me*
> *Em Ay Oh, Tee Ess Eeh, Tee-eeh Yoo Enn Gee*
> *Mao Tse Tung! Mao Tse Tung!*
> *Forever let us hold our banner high! High! High!*
> *Come along and join the fun and march in our company*
> *Em Ay Oh, Tee Ess Eeh, Tee-eeh Yoo Enn Gee."*

We pop away at the dunes for about thirty seconds before the police helicopters and tac squad arrive and confiscate all our M-1 rifles. The next day the papers and TV news are full of stories about the Black Tigers marching out to shoot white surfers. Not my boys. They're surfers themselves. But Ulysses, my Minister of Communication, in his beret and silver shades and black leather jacket, looks great on TV. He announces that the Black Tigers have a fire perimeter set up around Chinatown and are now declaring a curfew on whites in Chinatown. No whites in Chinatown after ten at night. The tongs and every restaurant in Chinatown are pissed at us. The Panthers love it. The Tigers love it. I love it. The tongs and Chinatown Chamber of Commerce and the restaurant owners give me a little money in red envelopes, laysee, grace money to change the curfew to three in the morning. "No whites in Chinatown between three and four in the morning," Ulysses declares on the TV news. "The media's the pig! Right on! Free Huey!"

Ben Han: *Coincidence, Like Ancient Egg, Leave Unpleasant Odor*

Briefly, ever so briefly, I lived the part of the serious writer at Santa Barbara. Free of my mother and her legend, free of the clownish opera man, free of Chinese, Chinatown, and Chinese friends, I threw myself into an MFA program in Creative Studies.

There was an orgy on Mountain Drive celebrating autumn a week before my creative thesis was due. On the one hand, I had no creative thesis ready. But on the other hand, I had never been to an orgy. I was curious. So I went.

The Matriarch of Mountain Drive was a painter. Her big adobe house looked like the Alamo. Everyone was nude. There was a swimming pool. There was food. There were drugs. The punch was laced with LSD. The brownies were laced with hashish. The cookies were laced with marijuana. The scent of marijuana smoke breezed through the air. The lines of cocaine around the edges of the coffee table in front of the rock fireplace reminded me of the I-Ching. There was saffron in the rice and no MSG in the vegetable chop suey. Finally to wash it all down—decaffeinated coffee and herbal teas.

I kept my clothes on as I piled food from the barbecue onto a paper plate. I carried a paper cup full of nondecaffeinated coffee, kept my hands full, and smiled, telling everyone nice enough to try to strike up a conversation with me that I never did well at orgies. I was a loner, not a crowd pleaser. Actually I was not a loner, and I was a crowd pleaser, but neither as an athlete nor satyr. What was the sexual equivalent of brilliantly irrelevant observations and quips? High-class small talk? I wondered why the guacamole tasted like dirt until I discovered it was laced with peyote.

I thought by keeping my hands full and away from the pool and away from the vortices of bodies in orgiastic activity I would not be taken as a voyeur and had a reason for not taking off all my clothes. Having my hands full of stuff threatening to mess up my clothes, the velvet furniture, the antique carpets was suddenly a problem when a naked Caucasian man sat down next to me, looked at me with eggy eyes, smiled at me with dimples, and rubbed the inside of my thigh. Even here, where I had never been, where no one should have heard of me or my family, apparently rumors about me had spread. Not only was I the only Chinese-looking man or woman here, but rumor had it that I was homosexual. I tried to be civil. Polite. Hostility was never my style. All the food in my hands began to smell bad. I couldn't eat any of it. I was afraid to put it down and empty my hands. I realized that the painter who had built the Alamo on Mountain Drive had invited me to her orgy because she was sure that all artistic, intellectual, avant-garde, creative Chinese were homosexual.

One Spanish mission-style building looked like a barracks building. As I walked through the rooms of one building into another, smiling and trying to look polite with my plate of food, I thought I heard my name. I looked into the doorway and saw a Charlie Chan movie glimmering on the TV. I had seen this movie before. But not exactly this movie. Instead of Sidney Toler in the role of Charlie Chan on the screen, I saw Ulysses' father, Longman Kwan. Why was I seeing his dream come true, his dream of being the first Chinese to play Charlie Chan in the movies? But then I realized he wasn't Charlie Chan in this movie, he was "favorite son." The young Longman Kwan mugged, he mouthed racist stereotypes about East Indians, he rolled his eyes, he bumbled. And he said, "Gee, Pop!" in every other line.

I sat down and watched. Suddenly it was Longman Kwan, made up to look like a white man playing Charlie Chan, like a black man in burnt cork performing in a minstrel show. There was Longman Kwan as Charlie Chan saying "Scotland Yard Inspector Drake dead. Canary bird in cage also dead."

And there was Longman Kwan again as favorite son. "Gee, Pop! It might be a coincidence!"

"Coincidence, like ancient egg, leave unpleasant odor."

I asked if anyone in the room would mind if I changed the channel. I changed the channel to an old Bogart movie, *Treasure of the Sierra Madre*. But instead of Bogart, I saw Longman Kwan as Charlie Chan doing all of Bogart's lines in his Charlie Chan Chinese accent, white duck, and Panama straw hat. "If be mountain police, please to show honorable badges?"

"Botches? We ain' got no botches. We don't need no steenkin' botches!" the fat Mexican bandit in the big sombrero answered. No one in the orgy noticed anything strange.

"Contradiction, please! No one can pull fast one on Charles C. Chan," Longman Kwan said. I couldn't bear to watch, but I was afraid to change the channel. The Indians in white pajamas and straw hats came into the light of the campfire to tell Walter Huston and Tim Holt one of their little boys fell in the water and was not dead but would not wake up. They need help. Walter Huston translated for Tim Holt and Charlie Chan. "Yeah, tough," Charlie Chan said. Still no one had noticed Charlie Chan was in the wrong movie. I put down the plate of food and the cup of coffee and started to leave, when Charlie Chan called to me, "Ben! Murder without blood, like Amos without Andy!"

I turned to look back at the TV and he was in a close-up, as if looking out of the TV straight at me. "More stupid to know you have what people wish to buy and not sell it to them," Uncle Longman said, glorying in playing Charlie Chan at last.

When Ulysses drove down with Diego to visit, he said Santa Barbara was a big Hotel Westlake Eclipse, a big rehabilitation center. "Everyone seems so thrilled that they're able to make change, they have to take the rest of the day off to write about it in their journals," Ulysses said.

But Diego liked Santa Barbara. He immediately found the dopers and bikers in the hills and mountains. I hadn't known anyone or anything lived in the hills before Diego and Ulysses passed through. Now up in those hills, Charlie Chan was starring in Bogart's Academy Award-winning performance as a man losing his mind. "Try to pull a fast one on Charles C. Chan, will they?"

Writing to Ulysses wasn't a profession. It was fun. I took stacks of his letters, photocopied them along with one of Sax Rohmer's Fu Manchu novels, and rewrote and edited them together into the script of a three-act play, my creative thesis, "Fu Manchu Plays Flamenco." I phoned Diego to ask what he thought about me calling Ulysses' writing my own. "He has to do it, man," Diego said, "Your MFA is in danger and only he can rescue you. And anyway, as my Minister of Education, he says he's given up art for the people. So go ahead, do it, buddy!"

Ulysses liked the play. He didn't care what kind of scam I was trying to run. "One for all and all for one," he said. None of us had any thought that *Fu Manchu Plays Flamenco* would play in New York and give me my Warholian fifteen minutes of fame.

Ulysses: Yellow Minstrel Show

Junior has three beautiful daughters. I was already living away from the family when Irene, the youngest, was born. Imogene, the oldest, hasn't arrived on Planet Earth yet. She's working at the Odyssey Executive Massage Parlor. She's the closest to me, in part because we both live and hang out in North Beach and Chinatown. Since she and her kids are just a short walk from my place, I take them out to dinner now and then, and sometimes I baby-sit while Imogene's at work.

But Irma, the second daughter, is my favorite. She's a born smartmouth, inventing jokes when she was barely three. We were special pals, but suddenly she was gone and no one in the family talked about her. I haven't seen her for years. Now she's in her late teens, after several attacks of the Kwan acne. I am in my late twenties, the Power-to-the-People Minister of Education of the Chinatown Vanguard of the Third World Revolution—the Chinatown Black Tigers.

Irma drops out of Oakland City College to cross the bay and wear shades and stand on a Chinatown street corner passing out Black Tiger leaflets in Chinese that she can't read. She does it for months, day in and day out, religiously, though she can't speak Chinese as well as she does the high school French she has given up to be one of the people. Power to the People! Right on, sister!

How can I tell her the Chinatown Black Tigers and the Third World Revolution are all a shuck, a scam to cop War on Poverty chump change, a way to make a name doing the Chinatown Black Tiger show, calling white people names in the name of the people? . . . Power to the people! Right on, brothers and sisters! Right on! It's silly putty, easy money. The Chinese in Chinatown don't talk Right on! Free Huey! like us. But while I am a conscious and knowing clown, my little niece—more like my little sister—is a bitter and a true believer. She is pissed. She is wounded. The Chinatown Black Tigers are her refuge, her identity, she says. She scares me. She could get us all in a shootout with the cops.

She would rather be a Black Tiger than talk to her sister Imogene when she sees her walking through Chinatown, to or from the Odyssey Executive Massage. Knowing this, Imogene, in her make-up and siliconed breasts, crosses the street or turns a corner and walks around the block to avoid passing Irma in her black beret, black tanker jacket, and no make-up. I couldn't talk Imogene out of her boob job. And I don't try to get them to talk to each other. But I would like to talk Irma out of the Black Tigers.

Diego and me are all for fun, the Chinatown Black Tigers are nothing more than a yellow minstrel show, I want to tell Irma. But I don't know how to tell her to play the game without believing in the Third World Revolution. But there is no Third World Revolution. No Third World Revolution is about to scour the earth clean of all her enemies, whoever they are. The Third World Revolution is Marlon Brando and Jean-Luc Godard over in Oakland, holding the Black Panther Party hostage.

The Third World Revolution is my father, strangely holed up on the top floor of his North Beach apartment house, with Ma dusting his collection of eight-by-ten glossy black-and-white stills from his movies, and hoarding round tins of Danish butter cookies, and reading little pocket-sized Chinese comic books that he won't let me touch. Ma says she's happy to have Pa home for a while, loud enough for Pa to hear. And about Marlon Brando . . . Pa is sure he has a better chance than Brando at playing the lead in the next Charlie Chan movie. Brando's too expensive for a Charlie Chan movie.

"Yeah, Charlie Chan movies are cheap," I say.

"I got no money for a gift for you, so get out," Pa says, as if I'm here to ask for money.

"I don't come here expecting to see you at all, much less ask you for money. So why don't you get out," I say.

"Don't talk that way to your father, son," Ma says again—code for *Don't talk to your father at all*—and signals the end of this joyous family reunion. She slips me two twenty dollar bills on my way out.

"I don't need this, Ma. Come on . . ."

"Just take it, son."

"I'll pass it on to your granddaughter, Irma."

"Be a good boy, son."

I don't know how to tell Irma to play the game for fun, not for real, to feel good about the breakfast program for the old folks and Chinatown kids, even though it's not going to last. But the Revolution is showbiz. The Chinatown Black Tigers are bullshit. So Diego, my friend, the founder and Commandant of the Chinatown Black Tigers, tells her I am bullshit for me. That everything I say on TV news is bullshit. That giving up flamenco guitar for the people is bullshit. That the pledge to hunt down the last living white men to play Charlie Chan and try them before a People's Court is bullshit. The threat to burn the Chinese New Year's parade's Golden Dragon Lantern, the prize of the Chinese Chamber of Commerce, is bullshit. The Black Tigers manning a fire perimeter around Chinatown at all times is both comic relief and bullshit. Nobody really wants to start shooting anybody in Chinatown.

Anyway, time is running out. The Revolution is fading fast. When the chump change goes, so goes the noble social motives of the gangs. No more Black Tigers.

Ulysses: The Mandate of Heaven

Johnny Yuma, the college-boy brakeman, still hangs out at the Berkeley coffeehouse, sucking espresso, reading philosophy, sporting a new set of false teeth. He has become the boss brakeman on the Golden Gate Greengrocer and loves it, he says, railroader to railroader, college dropout to college dropout.

"The Jane Fonda I saw in *Coming Home* was a fucking impostor," he tells me. "She's *playing* Jane Fonda, acting contemptuous of the women she played in the early Sixties—the bouffant airhead cheerleader of *Tall Story,* the Bardot doppelgänger in ex-Bardot spouse Roger Vadim's *Barbarella.*"

The coffeehouse never changes. The same awful Day-Glo paintings of Greek gods, ancient boats, and the sea. The same people behind the espresso machines. Some of the faces are very familiar, faces I saw when I first walked in ten or fifteen years ago. They are always here. They never leave. Johnny Yuma is still here. I am still here.

"Sandra Dee should have gotten the part, wherever she is. Or Connie Stevens. Debbie Reynolds. Or Ann-Margret. Oh, yeah, Ann-Margret. But you know who really should have played Jane Fonda's part is, yes, yes! Annette Funicello. Yes! Yes! I could believe Annette Funicello loving a gung-ho Marine. Can you hear her wholeheartedly squeaking her Mouseketeer voice and closing her eyes under his heaving body?"

The thought of Annette going through Jane Fonda's changes in the '60s and early '70s brings a sadistic gleam to brakeman Johnny Yuma's eyes. He says, "Can you see a vet's pissbag bursting on Annette's leg? Oh, poor Annette! Anybody can believe Jane Fonda smoking dope, and no one cares. But Annette. Whoa! If she lit up, it would be an omen. Something awful has happened. No, Annette! No! No! Don't light up. I know it's just a movie, but don't do it, baby. Show your tits first!"

He sees the handwriting on the wall and is making the move over into the last generation of firemen to become a locomotive engineer in the Brotherhood of Locomotive Engineers. He owns a little house now. He does union work, even though unions aren't what they used to be.

He's right about Annette. Annette in a sex scene with wacky-eyed Bruce Dern . . . oh, no! and falling in love with a paraplegic and smoking dope would make *Coming Home* more real than it seems with Jane Fonda. Still, if there is ever a Movie About Me I will name a coach of the California Zephyr that runs sleek silver through my Sixties, the Silver Fonda. I always planned to ride that Silver Fonda on the Zephyr's last run.

And now I am, I'm in the dome of the Silver Fonda, riding one of the last inbound Zephyrs into Oakland from Sacramento. Sarah and Jason Peach's three kids are with me. He's in Hawaii, finding himself, away from the hurt of Sarah throwing him over for one of his students of blues guitar.

Sarah and I have stayed friends. I drop by her place, ask her what's happening, and get the latest news from Jason in Hawaii. I take her and the kids out for pizza every couple of weeks to get away from the life of a Chinatown Black Tiger. The guys she says she sleeps with scare me.

I drive Sarah and the kids down to the tracks to get them in the spirit of trains the day before we ride the Zephyr. I place three pennies on the top of a rail on the mainline, one for each of them. They watch me from the parked car as the afternoon Street Local hauls a cut of six empty boxcars over the pennies. I hand each of the kids a penny, hoping they will sense the power and meaning of the railroad. Look. Three pennies squashed flat into copper ovals no thicker than a strand of hair.

"What happened to Abraham Lincoln?" they ask.

"The train flattened him on the track," I answer, realizing I haven't touched what really troubled them about the penny. "The wheels are heavy and hot," I try again. "Rolling on the track makes them hot. When they rolled over Abraham Lincoln they rubbed him out hot and heavy," I say.

"Oh, he's dead," Jason's second son says. His older brother lights up and his younger sister nods. "Dead" they understand. An oncoming train, they don't.

So much for passing on my awe for the railroad.

The ride on the outbound to Sacramento holds their attention through the ticket punching, newspaper boy, and candy butcher. Then they all fall asleep. Sarah shows me a letter from Jason to the kids. He writes of himself in the third person, as "daddy" with a lowercase "d" and his adventures in Hawaii and Japan in a kind of storybook babytalk. Sarah catches me catching on to Jason's fairy tale about himself and says, "I hate him, that fucking hypocrite. I know he's your friend, but I hate him. I really do."

"You don't like his letter?" I ask.

"It's a piece of hypocritical patronizing bullshit," Sarah says.

There is no decent place to eat within a short walk of the Sacramento depot. We get hamburgers at a prefab steel short-order joint, and kill two hours walking in circles.

The kids are bored by the time the Zypher snakes off the right-of-way and runs back down Third Street, the last stop at the Oakland depot. I used to work baggage here, I want to tell them, but don't because I probably have already. They have the look of having been told too much today.

I step down off the seat platform into the aisle. An old man stands at the end of the aisle, barring the way to the stairs. "I'm not getting off at the depot. I'm riding down to the pad. I worked many railroads in my life, and twenty-three years on the WP, and have me a lifetime pass to ride this train!" He snorts and grabs the arms of the seats on either side of the aisle. "They can't take me off!" I hope he doesn't lead a cheer for everyone to ride the Zephyr another mile to the pad.

"I have a lifetime pass too," a plump biscuit of an old woman says. "My late husband was a conductor on the Zephyr before he died." She looks around, catching the eye of everyone in the dome. I realize all of us either work for the railroad now or once did.

From speakers set on telephone poles up and down Third Street, the stationmaster's voice booms tinny. "Will all trucks, all trucks please clear the Western Pacific tracks for the California Zephyr, inbound Train Number 17."

The tracks are empty. Third Street is empty. The stationmaster doesn't have to take to the public address. But he does. The last train is in. The last time he'll be dropping the stairs and unloading the passengers. The last time chalking in the arrival time. Passengers, porters, clerks, and trainmen, everyone works to make it special.

The old timers in the Silver Fonda with their lifetime passes to ride the one train that seems immortal, coming into Oakland for the last time, stay on for as long as they can stand it, hoping for a ride through the washer. All know the Zephyr died a long time ago.

Long before Walter Cronkite rode the train on CBS and said it would soon die, the Zephyr was already dead. Gone with the bald-headed dog-faced used-car czar of West Coast TV, Ralph Williams. Gone with TV spies and flying nuns, the Watts Riots, White Front warehouse stores, the hula hoop, and the Sixties. All gone, nothing but talk now.

I step past the old man. I want to show him the watch I wore, braking on the Southern Pacific, your railroad, Hero, but I have a sleeping kid in my arms. But I have to say something. I just can't shove past at a friend's funeral. "I worked baggage here on Saturdays," I say.

Part Three: The Underworld

Diego Chang: Orpheus

Out! I have to get out. I'm late. Fast. Stomp. Stomp. Taiko on the rim. Beat the beat of the dragon boat. Faster. Harder. Horses gallop on stones. Gypsies in black hats draw their black knives. Rasgueado. My guitar.

I'm too far from my guitar. Taiko's gotta go. Tapdance tease me flamenco. I want my guitar. Stomp. Go chips, down, stomp stomp. Three-in-a-row speed demons on the go-board. Bap bap bap. The house wiring whines like mice singing flamenco, like rats piercing sweet Cantonese opera, like blood in the walls. Owooo! Hear that wolf? Or is it the reds? Not the Commies, the pills. Owoooo! No, it's not the reds, it's the wolf! Run, boys and girls! Run!

The heart of the commune beats the beat of trenching Polynesian canoe paddles. My hands want the guitar. I want to feel the strings against the inside of the nails of the fingers of my right hand. My fingers tingle like naked boys and girls about to kerplunk into water to go skinny-dipping. Clark Kent wants an excuse to loose Superman on the world. If Superman is the Man of Steel, what's his piss like? Can he use a public urinal without melting it?

I was a hippie when I did my first skinny-dipping. I swung out over the water on a rope tied to a tall branch of a tree growing over the pond like Tarzan, like the nicely rhyming poetry about white men remembering visits to their country cousins on the farm, walking dirt roads, stealing apples or nuts off of neighbors' trees, white picket fences that they teach in my old Fillmore district junior high, where all of that is long-ago white folks' nostalgia, nothing but nicely rhyming words the teacher likes to read with a Patsy Cline throb in her voice, to the rhythm of a country song.

I like country music. George Jones and Patsy Cline sing like gringo flamencos with drumming shadows, rhythm ringing smoke, and dry heaves in their voices. My guitars want me. All my guitars. Their strings are all tense, clenching their teeth, anticipating my touch. Oh, they want me!

Play me. Play me, they all moan, like seductive vampires in their coffins. And Diego, the Comandante of the dreaded Chinatown Black Tigers by day, sits out on the deck in back of his house after the midnight hour and plays his Spanish flamenco guitar, handcrafted by Manuel de la Chica in 1963 in Madrid. In the court formed by all the backyards of the block with the houses forming a two-story wall around the block, Diego, El Comandante, plays to the trees and clotheslines at night.

Church bells, anvils, ringing anchor chains from John Huston's *Moby Dick*. Ulysses turned me on to John Huston. I am John Huston's father, the old man of *The Treasure of the Sierra Madre*, leaving Bogart and Tim Holt behind, leading them up the mountain of gold, building the fire, cooking the beans, eating heartily, and playing dance tunes on the harmonica. And I am Bogart and Tim Holt sputtering out, crashing and burning from too much hard work with my hands. Oh Lash LaRue! Lash LaRue! The other night I was watching this old Katherine Hepburn movie where she's a pilot like Amelia Earhart, and at this posh party, there's Lash LaRue in a tux kissing a blonde's hand, saying, "I love you. This is the first time I have fallen in love in four weeks."

The ache beats the drums of Kurosawa's bandits. They gallop noisy shadows to halt in my hands and tread the opening scenes of *The Seven Samurai*. Everywhere I go, they vibe hoofbeats to the ends of my space.

I see why blacksmiths, gypsy carpenters in old hippie folklore, knife fighters, sailors into tying knots, surfers—people who get high from the feel of working with their hands—have a feel for flamenco guitar. I used to own a commune in Berkeley. Got laid all the time. And flamenco was the music and the soul of the gypsy and the soul of the guitar.

Cowboy songs, country music, the blues, Polynesian lickety split, sea shanties, Sinatra songs, jazz, I like it all. But when I want to be loose and intense there is only flamenco. My hands turn it all into flamenco. Elizabeth Cotton's "Freight Train," Sousa's strutting "Stars and Stripes Forever," all turn into flamenco, brooding flamenco, raging fiesta songs. Owoooooo! I wish I had someplace to go and some reason to be there. But no. Did ya hear that wolf?

Water! Was I talking about water? Splash! A strong smell of fresh-cut spruce. My fingers strum empty space.

"Good one!" A kid. It's Raoul's kid from three houses up the hill. He's exploded my Manuel de la Chica with a fucking water balloon! What's a kid doing out throwing water balloons at his neighbors after midnight?

Time to bail the Revolution. Wrong movie! I *whoops* out of San Francisco and—on the invitation of acid-casualty friends in Maui—off to hippie paradise, where they do carpentry, and every day is a day in 1960, maybe 1965, but never 1968. 1968 and beyond never come to Maui.

The first thing I did when I landed on the island was sneeze. Palm trees and sand. I could care less. I should have heard the wolf when nobody for miles around knows what year it is. I'm allergic to the air. Smoking dope here gives me sneezing fits. I think it's cool—everybody's stoned all the time. Groovy. Everybody but my old friend Jason Peach, who doesn't do hard drugs or acid, and smokes the *pakololo* only after work. And then only sociable hits. I heard him playing blues in the Steppenwolf in Berkeley when he was a kid, using the name Blind Peach, and I found out he was friends with Ulysses Kwan.

One of the things that made it cool for me to fly over the water and dump myself on an island surrounded by thousands of miles of boring ocean so beautiful it looked like a planet of candied blues was that Jason said he hated the water as much as I did. I don't swim. I don't lie on my back on a towel in the sand and point my belly button at the sun and smile with my eyes closed and feel like I'm really living now, and this is paradise.

Mostly Jason's in his workshop, building experimental guitars he makes out of different kinds of woods after three years in Japan working with a Japanese guitar maker who lived on a little island. He's still Jason, the Blind Peach, and not some fakey, more-Jappy-than-thou Japanese-y. He still remembers Blind Lemon Jefferson playing the blues to the little round tables and black walls, black floor, and black ceiling at the Steppenwolf in Berkeley, a million trips and three radio stations ago. He's come back to Maui because, for him, this is the balance point between his dreams of Sarah and his dreams of working with wood, building musical instruments out of wood, playing the music of wood. This is as close as he can come to Sarah and as far away as he can go to get away from her without falling off the edge of the world.

As he'd found the Berkeley in Berkeley, he's found the Berkeley in Maui. He has a knack for sniffing out and attracting the talented freaks and freaky talents working in wood, working with cars and engines, players and singers, artists and actors frightening the local missionaries about the island. Everything of Berkeley of the '60s surrounds Jason, everything but a coffee house and a decent cappuccino and café latté.

He is everyone's best, closest, most trusted and beloved friend. An old lover from Berkeley has flown over from the mainland to sleep with him. His current squeeze, a blonde who looks almost like Sarah, gulp, takes it in stride with a smile and a cheerful saying for each new day. Serious flower child, I think. "Jason is my entire ecstasy," she says, like his mother did the first time I came by her house to meet him. His mother said I looked more like an Indian than a Chinese. What can I say? She's from Australia. What'd she know about Berkeley and Frisco?

Fatal Smith and Byron Fogg, the two carpenters with contractor's licenses, compete with each other to solely possess the illusion of dominating Jason. Acid makes them deep philosophers. Aesop was black. Socrates was probably black. Jesus was black. I don't care. I'm too stupid to care. Where's the drugs? Where's the food? Any women on this island speak Chinese?

I let it slip that Ulysses says that Jason is the only real Christian we know. And Ulysses doesn't like Christianity. Byron wants to know why. Because it's a religion. Religion demands a betrayal of the self, he says. Christianity is fascistic and works on self-contempt and betrayal.

Fatal Smith and Byron Fogg go crazy. Jason lies back in the arms of one woman and fingers his Martin steel string guitar, while another woman waits for him and watches TV in the other room. It's a Berkeley dream come true. For Jason, Maui is a kind of paradise. Meanwhile I hole up in a room with a TV and watch it, while rolling joints and eating them.

Jason can do mushrooms with me. He can't with Ulysses. He won't do acid because on his first acid trip with Sarah, Ulysses was his guide. And fifteen minutes or twenty years into the trip, Ulysses started reading scenes from this weird Christian ecstatic hallucinatory novel he'd found, *Place of the Lion,* by some English priest named Charles Williams. Ulysses started reading scenes of people turning into animals and dream women becoming real and melting into blobs, and he and Sarah started moving further and further away from each other, into other rooms, into different parts of the house, to get away from Ulysses' voice reading this shit that drives them crazy, and but they can't get away. After that, Jason never wants to take acid again. Never.

But now and then I do mushrooms with him at the back of his shop in an old Navy Quonset hut World War II warehouse, where he keeps his collection of strange old stringed instruments. We play music till China and Africa meet, till Jack turns Frisco gringo flamenco and sings the blues, till Jill stands on the half-shell and drops her bra and panties. We play strange strings out of his mysterious cases and sing inside this huge tunnel of corrugated sheet steel. The geckos dance while the gods sleep stony sweet dreams, and the righteous outlaws steal the birthday presents.

Mandolas, guitars with the bodies and bridges of violins meant to be bowed and plucked. Banjo guitars. Guitar banjos. Alto guitars tuned to scales beyond the fingerboards of normal guitars played by Chet Atkins, B.B. King, Sabicas, Segovia. He has their pictures on the labels of guitar strings. We play stringed relics and curios till the sea turns to swamp and the catfish come home. The sounds sing with the ghosts of rats who partied here when the tunnel was full of rice, during World War II. We play till we hear radio calls of Pearl Harbor chattering in the dark against the ceiling, and beyond. We play our way back to the time before Vienna sausage and Spam came to reproduce on Hawaii, eventually becoming a national dish with *poi*. We hear nothing but the grunt and crunch of the paddles of the first canoes digging into the water toward the islands.

Some of the instruments I take up bring the great guitarists out of the dark, and I feel them wanting me to play their licks. Niño Ricardo, Ramón Montoya call to me out of the warm depths of what I play, they want me to say their names with these strings. Zithers, dulcimers, a guitar made by a Chinaman that I have to play. I play and the giant sings motherly green-eyed honky-tonk to pasty-faced Jack, the Three-Headed Boy kisses Cupid on the lips, and Kwan Yin lays Monkey on his back and disrobes. Owooooooo! The wolf gets loose and pads out to party. Confucius, down on 'ludes, sucks the bones of the White Bone Demon dry and sings "Down by the Riverside" with his tongue on a drum. Peacocks fly alone. All the wild geese are shot out of the sky. The hens turn into cocks, all the peach trees refuse to bloom, the Peach Boy is a wood-cutter's dessert, and Kwan Kung does the plastic hula. Ukelele! Oh do I miss Flatt and Scruggs, bluegrass guitar and banjo songs in voices meant to hum in the roads of a continent!

But even stoned and blown away in Jason Peach's wonderland, I'm tired of the island. I was never that much for swimming. And there are no Chinese on Maui. It's like a bad trip. Here I am on the only island in the world where there are no Chinese. No Chinese girls. No Chinese food.

Meanwhile, on the job, in the house, all the time, the two black carpenters argue about their mainland union job experience. They hate each other. They drop acid regularly behind each other's back, each claiming that they don't need it. They have visions. And they each discover they are God. Oh, great! This again. They discover they are God. It's not that together they make one God. It's not "we all have some of God in us." They are each the one true Christian God. They denounce, deny, and try to outshine each other, carrying on a loud, stupid argument with lots of names and half-assed quotations from the Bible, and bullshit about God and humanity that certainly does not make believers of the rest of us, their fellow workers, as we build houses together.

Instead of experiencing salvation, everyone on the job carries a little pocket radio with a little earphone we plug into one ear, and stay worlds apart while whizzing our circular saws through precious redwood and cedar from the mainland. We have a job disguising a cement fortress of a bank branch building, making the inside and out look like a large wooden house. And as we work, the acid-propelled divinities compete for the honor of converting Jason Peach.

I get along with Jason, everybody gets along with Jason. It's the two acid-tripping experienced carpenters with contractor's licenses battling for the spot of "The One True God" while they also fight to save Jason's soul . . . they don't get along with Jason, each other, or anybody. "The One True God" is what Fatal Smith calls himself, "in all humility." A big light-skinned stud, he sputters with muscular mysticism against Berkeley intellectuals, white Los Angeles bullshit, and Atlantis Zen Buddhist monks. "He's like a man who deeply needs to be believed, because he doesn't believe in himself," says his young, white, blonde girlfriend fresh from the convent when she drops by the construction site, breasts firm and shuddering without underwear.

Fatal catches me eyeing his girlfriend's body and says, "I know what you are thinking, Diego Chang!"

"I bet you do," I say. "It's no secret."

"You're thinking, 'Why can't I have a young beautiful blonde white girl just out of the convent too?'"

"Yeah, man, that's exactly what I was thinking."

"You can't, Diego Chang, because you are not a Christian! You do not believe in God. You have no faith! You are a heathen!"

"Amen to that, brother! Now, how about some skanky white convent girl?"

"Diego Chang! I am the God of the Israelites, God of Palestine, God of the Jews, the God of the Pope and the Archbishop of Canterbury, the God of Joan of Arc, the God of Sister Theresa and Al Capone, the God of the Reverend Adam Clayton Powell, Billy

Graham, and Dr. Martin Luther King, the God of Little Richard and James Brown, the God of Elvis and Hank Williams! And I am the God of the blonde, beautiful, skanky convent girls. All of them! I am God Almighty! the God of your skinny yellow ass, Diego Chang! And I say: Thou don't deserve any kind of convent girl!"

"That's cool," I say.

"What do you mean, 'That's cool'? Do you believe you are black? You are the Devil in the flesh. You are Satan! Lucifer! Scratch! I know you!" Fatal says and tries to look crazy and possessed. "You! You are turning Jason Peach from the path of righteousness with your devilish tricks. I commandeth thee to stop it!"

To get away from it all, I listen to a country music station from Honolulu sponsored by the Columbia School of Broadcasting as I build big long fake beams across what used to be the front of the bank and the teller's cage. The others are tuned to other music, to talk shows, who knows what.

We almost have the place looking like some kind of Scandinavian Hans Christian Andersen ski lodge and pea soup restaurant. I'm working the table saw, an air-driven nail gun, and my Skil 77 wormdrive 7.5 inch circular handsaw, the Cadillac of handsaws. It's like having a motorcycle on the end of my right arm.

Jason the guitar maker is making all the built-in cabinets and bookcases out of clear redwood and redwood burl he's planed and squared in his shop by hand, with the tools he uses to build and repair his stringed musical instruments. He builds furniture and cabinets the way he builds his instruments. He builds houses the way he builds furniture. Everything he makes with wood has a sound, a voice that hums and vibrates anywhere near life, in resonance with the heartbeat of the mosquitos, of the mice, of the shadows cast by the moon.

He talks about musical instruments, especially guitars, with the same tense seriousness old men use when recalling the greatest fucks of their lives to other old men watching TV down at the tong hall during a commercial break. The lewd laughter is a little riff on the saxophone. I miss it.

I miss Chinatown most of all. There are no tongs listed in the

Maui County Yellow Pages. I like Jason for the same reason he likes me—we are both good friends of Ulysses, who's in Seattle working on the Union Pacific, and we've both seen a lot of old movies with him. As we watch old movies on late-night TV in Hawaii, we can't help but think about Ulysses, who argues with us about every movie ever made.

I learn a lot about tools and working with wood just watching Jason work on guitars in his shop. Tools nobody uses for what they were made for anymore. The spokeshave, I figured out, is a kind of two-handed chisel with an ever so slightly curved blade that carpenters used to use to shave wooden spokes for Conestoga wagons, buckboards, and stage coaches. Jason uses the spokeshave and a drawknife, which looks like a cross between a double-handled straight razor and a half-assed scythe, for shaping and shaving the backs of guitar necks. Since both tools cut on the pull, Jason made an old-time cobbler's bench with a Versa-vise on it. He straddles the bench and sits on it, holding the mahogany neck between his legs with the heel of the guitar upturned and tucked up to his navel, and the cut and glued piece for the tuning head angled up. He pulls the long, shiny, little hand-sharpened cutting edges toward his belly, and looks like he is carving a blocky wooden hard-on. I like watching him work but don't want to work those tools myself, I tell him. He is an artist, and I love watching artists work, but this isn't my craft.

As he works, we talk about going to the movies with Ulysses. "Did Ulysses ever tell you what happened when they were showing *Chushingura* at the Storefront Movie?" Jason asks again, smiling already and laughing with the same anticipation I've heard before but don't mind hearing again, like an old song at a Dead concert. "We drove up Telegraph Avenue on forty-six motorcycles and a Moped, wearing hapi coats over our leather jackets, dark shades, and carrying samurai swords and chains, stopped in front of the Storefront Movie, man, and backed our bikes to the curb, parked them, and lined up for tickets to the movie!" He laughs a roomful of after-hours smoke.

"The shit you did, man, or I'd have been one of the forty-six on my fucking Honda with the electric starter. Shiiiit," I say, having the fun time of my life on this stupid island.

"Yeah, but we like to talk about it, like it happened," Jason says.

"Yeah, I can dig it," I say.

Fatal Smith is dressed as close to naked as he can get, so he can look himself all over with love, a body more beautiful, more natural than thinc. Because he wants to be able to drop everything and go swimming whenever he gets the urge, he works in his swim trunks and blue-and-gray Japanese rubber sandals.

Byron Fogg, the other acid-fired One True God, is short, but thin and wiry like me. He has the habit of holding his shoulders up and his arms back and wide to keep his swinging arms from getting cut on his steel carpenter's combination square that hangs off his left side or the claw of his long-handled, eighteen-ounce hammer slung in a loop off the right side of his carpenter's apron. He walks like a cartoon cowboy gunfighter wearing a pair of six-guns from a couple years of framing houses.

We're building a deck and lanai behind the house, and Fatal and Byron are shouting their opposing gospels. Nobody else is righteous or devout or deaf enough to work with them and get included in their religion. Fatal Smith flip-flops his sandals against the floor and his feet back through the steel-framed sliding glass doors. Bobby, the car thief who's learned cabinet making in prison, is making an oak and beveled-glass bar while telling Jason and everyone working near him how peaceful and Oriental and mystic he has become, and how I am fucking him up by not giving him what he wants.

Bobby is on Dr. Ehert's "Mucusless Diet System" that makes him fart a lot and shit several times a day. His apartment in our commune has a newish small-size toilet he doesn't like. It's not big enough for him. He wants to come into my room and use my old porcelain toilet because it has a big bowl and a big seat. I don't want him trumpeting out of his asshole like an elephant in my toilet. "You're saying no, even though I am trying to better myself, man. How human is that? Tell me: How human is that?" he pushes.

Fatal comes in, cussing Byron out under his breath, misquoting the Bible, the Book of Changes, and Chairman Mao, preaching in a voice that sounds like big aircraft tires creeping through mud. As he goes to the tool table and begins sharpening a huge five-inch chisel on a carborundum stone, he turns to Bobby and bellows, "Don't bother asking him. He's an asshole. Just go in and take his fucking bathroom. I say you *can*. He's too chicken to stop you, you know that."

I think he's joking. Bad joking but still joking, so I joke back. "Say, God, why don't you drop your tools and go swimming in your deep blue sea?" I ask.

"Because the sea didn't ask me in, and you have not suffered!"

"What're you afraid of, Diego?" Bobby asks. "Huh? What are you afraid of? Be a man, brother. Is this your karma now, is it?"

"Yeah, far out, man," I grin and keep on at my work in rhythm to a happy country song.

"I am against violence," Fatal says, "But it's all right against an asshole. Sometimes that's the only way to teach him a lesson."

"You heard Fatal. He's against violence. So go use *his* toilet, Bobby. This is a commune, right? And Fatal's not an asshole like me, so just go use his shitter, man. You won't have to fight him for it. He said so. Right, God?"

"You! Diego Chang, you and all your yellow-assed squint-eyed brethren! You have not suffered at the hands of whites in America. Therefore the blacks who have suffered most are the most important American minority."

"Hey, you say you're more of a nigger than me?"

"That's right!"

"Far out, man!" I say and laugh. He drops his five-inch chisel. It swishes straight down, chomps through his big toe and his Japanese sandal, and sticks in the floor with a thunk. He yells, grabs his foot with the bleeding toe in his hands, hops onto a nail, and drops onto his ass with a foot in each hand. I hear the points of his hipbones hit.

"Wow!" Byron says and nods at the door, "Far out. The Lord is just. The Lord is great! Ommmmmmmm."

"You know why that happened?" Bobby asks. "It was Diego's karma. It started when you said you wouldn't let me use your toilet."

"Come on, Bobby," Jason says, "Be cool."

"You come on! Diego's sick, man. He's gotta be a man, he's gotta let me use his toilet."

Everybody takes a vote and I am elected to drive Fatal to the hospital in Kahalui in Byron's TR-4 Triumph that he bought for $50. Although it's a classic little sports car, it only cost $50 because it has no first gear and no reverse, and there are no parts on the island to fix it and no mechanic on the island willing to work on it. And you have to stick a nail in just-so, and twist it just-so to start it. Fatal Smith must be the eighth or ninth owner in the last three years. Jason takes one of Fatal's arms and I take the other and we heave his gloriously sculpted body up on his feet, help him walk on his heels out to his car, and fold him into the passenger seat. Then Jason helps me push Fatal's Triumph backward out onto the road.

We trust Fatal to put the car in neutral, ease the handbrake off slowly, and steer, while we push against the face of his little car. But he can't put his feet on the floor and keep his ass from moving when he works the wheel.

I have never driven a real sports car before. Just taking a deep breath twitches the wheel and sends me toward the edge of the Kaanapali-Wailuku road, hugging the edge of rocky cliffs on the right. I slow down, trying not to go faster than I can steer. But Fatal reaches his left leg across the car and pushes my foot down on the accelerator with his heel and suddenly I'm all over the road, driving in the wrong lane to avoid the edge of the cliff. Rounding one of the curves Fatal rolls against me and his mouth is against my ear, and he shouts, "Diego Chang! Why are you ruled by fear?"

"Because I'm scared!"

"What have you got to be scared of, with your scrawny chicken neck? Your skinny sticks of arms? Your hollow bony chest? What have you got to be scared of?"

I came over to Hawaii for a change, and this is it. This is where

the walking wounded of the Third World Revolution come to re-
cover from the '60s, and our falling apart keeps on keeping on. I
can hear the life of this house through the walls, in the pipes, in the
hollows of termite caverns. Bobby has a Filipina girlfriend, the wife
of a bearded white hippie who moved out of the flimsy, termite-
ridden, single-wall-constructed houses of the commune, and into
one of the many derelict cars abandoned along the side of the little
dirt road to our compound of old workers' houses. She and Bobby
snort hot and heavy together, in and out like some kind of yoga
deep breathing through their noses—in, out, snort, snort, reaching
a crescendo of leaky valves. Their breathing sounds like wood being
sanded by hand, feet scuffing on mats, a slow shoeshine. At first I
thought it was humping. But it wasn't.

One night I'm in the front room dinking on the guitar and
watching Fatal's convent girl, Byron's never-tanning blonde with
thin hair, Jason's two women, the blonde from Australia who looks
almost, kind of, just like his ex-wife Sarah, but she seems to live to
see him happy, loves him, idolizes him, worships him the way
Sarah never did. And she's friendly with the brunette who flew over
from Berkeley with her baby to share Jason. All gather in the kitch-
en to fix dinner, with nothing on under their summer flimsies. The
sweaty spots of the fabric stick to their bodies like saliva, making me
wish I had licked there. I groan and fade to my room, which is
attached to the other house, and lose my mind in an old black-and-
white TV I have commandeered. And wow, out here in paradise,
every movie Longman Kwan, Ulysses' father, ever made is on late
at night and weekends.

Bobby and his girlfriend, the other man's wife, in the other
man's apartment on the other side of the double wall, take turns in
their toilet, bellowing yoga farts and blasting mucusless shit while
the other man lives in one of the abandoned cars on the side of the
commune driveway, and who knows where he farts and shits.

I am coming down from watching Longman Kwan crashing,
when Fatal hobbles out of the main house with a big bandage
around his right foot and his left foot in a cast, carrying a bag of

trash out to the garbage cans, and slips. He falls and breaks his wrist and roars to split the night and destroy the singing inside the house.

"You want me to take you to the hospital, man?" I ask.

And he jumps in with, "It's because you drove me to the hospital the last time, I broke my wrist, you motherfucker. Keep away from me!"

"Yeah, man. Far out. I want to drive you to the hospital to see what's gonna break on you next, man," I say. He's still a giant next to his little beauty from the convent school, who worships him. She wraps his broken wrist in ice and kisses him where it hurts.

Jason retreats to his latest unfinished guitar awaiting perfection in his workshop, and I walk away to the one Chinese restaurant on the island, the Tiki Tasty Suey.

Diego Chang: The Tiki Tasty Suey

Signs along the wall read:

"All kinds of SANDWICHES"

"USDA choice STEAKS"

"We serve MARGARINE"

"Delightful COMBINATION"

"Tasty roast PORK"

"Steaming hot SAIMIN"

"Southern Fried CHICKEN"

Above is a corrugated sheet steel roof. Inside, dim lighting. Next to stacks of folding chairs in the back room, dust settles on a miniature mountain made out of lava flagstones, a little pond that hasn't had water in it for a long time, a bridge, a pagoda, a fisherman, a little plastic tree. The last of the Chinese blood on the island flows somewhere in the veins of the sixtyish old man Hong, who owns and cooks in this place. He and his wife and his cousin in her eighties love me. I am all-Chinese blood. Nothing but Chinese in my veins.

There are no other full-blooded Chinese on the island. The tongs are all gone. The family associations are gone. I wonder what happened to the Chinese on Maui? I eat alone on the old Yellow Trail. Old Man Hong shakes his head. When I ask for all the real old Chinese homecooking no one has ordered in his restaurant in years, he gets all shuddery with joy, steaming and wokking for me. His cousin, Mrs. Ah-Fong, fusses over me as soon as I walk in. A new teapot, just for me, tonight. And real chrysanthemum tea from China. Real flowers. Have I ever had real chrysanthemum tea before? In Chinatown, at dim sum brunchtime. *Gook far.* Don't the petals get caught between my teeth? Oh, Mrs. Ah-Fong you're such a joker.

Old Man Hong wants to know. "You like one salt fish tonight? Or *bumbye* salt fish too stinky ? You like stinky kine?"

"Sure, give me stinky. Can you do it with *jur yuke beng?* You know, chopped up pork hash?"

"Oh, stinky fish *jur yuke beng!*" Old Man Hong says and near dances on his toes.

"Yeah, *hom yur jing jur yuke beng!*" I say in Cantonese, because he likes to hear it, though he doesn't understand it all. He always smiles, as if me talking Cantonese brings back memories.

"Yeah," he says *"Hom yur jing jur yuke beng.* Yeah. Dat's da kine. *Jing!* Dat's it. Yeah?"

"Yeah, *jing* is steamed. Yeah," I say.

"Yeah, I like da kine salt fish *jing.* "

"Me too, Old Man Hong," I say.

"You mean, *ah Hong bok.* " Old Man Hong says.

"Yeah, *ah Hong bok,* " I say.

Old Man Hong and his wife and his cousin, Mrs. Ah-Fong, invite me over to the restaurant for Thanksgiving dinner with the Chinese Club of Maui. Old Man Hong is the President. The General is coming. I will enjoy meeting the General, they tell me.

They're going to pop a string of twenty thousand firecrackers. I smile and say it sounds good but don't say for sure I'll come.

After the little dinner, I go in back and wash my face. I think eating Old Man Hong's family's cooking makes them feel like Chinamen again, and wonder if I've gotten away without having to face them again. I haven't. They come to me at the cash register as I'm paying and tell me to go back to my table. The waitress has baked me a cupcake in a cup. The old lady of the kitchen has made me some guava juice, and old Man Hong offers "a fried Chinese sweet." They got me, and I don't like it. If people too moochie hate me, no problem. Too moochie nicey-nice makes me nervous.

Thanksgiving dinner with the Chinese Club? Why not? The Tiki Tasty Suey is washed down, swept out, and dimly lit by three rows of Chinese lanterns strung across the dining room. The signs pushing the specials are out. The folding chairs in the back room are unfolded and set up expectantly around little bar tables lit by candles burning inside little red globes. And rescued from the back room, the fake waterfall is working, and the lava flagstone pond is full of water. But the trickling of the water is all I hear in there.

I step inside. I brought my guitar, thinking I might play some Frisco gringo flamenco at their Chinese Club Thanksgiving. I smell punk burning, sniff it out, and see their Kwan Kung shrine for the first time. How could I have not seen Kwan Kung here before? Chinamen don't get so stoned they don't notice Kwan Kung in a Chinese restaurant, just like a Catholic can't go into a church and not notice the cross.

And mingling in the trickle of the fake waterfall and the hum of the pump recirculating the water, I hear a girl whimpering, sobbing, shuddering, snickering snot and tears up her nostrils on her inhales as she weeps. She's further into the dark end of the bar than I have ever seen before.

This is where all the Primo beer signs come after they die, a series of vacuformed color contour maps of the islands, one island at a time, with glowing streaks and explosions erupting out of volcanoes. Silhouettes of the islands against a night sky, deep and distant with stars that twinkle and planets that shine on and on. She's short. The first thing I think on seeing her is "She's just my size." She looks like a short strange Bette Davis with big lips, big Rolls-Royce goldfish headlights for eyes, big glasses, hair on her arms, and a reedy voice just between Eartha Kitt and Tammy Wynette.

She stands, lays her cheek against my chest, and her tears wet through my T-shirt and her big soft breasts press into my belly. "You're in such good shape!" she says. I like it but don't understand. "You're not so soft and flabby under your arms like other men. Yeah?"

"Yeah."

She says her family promised her to the General when she was eleven years old. She says she is Chinese. She went to Oahu to the University of Hawaii then did two years at the University of Texas at Austin, and has come back with a worthless degree in Chinese language and literature, and doesn't sound like a Maui girl any more.

She says they talk about her complexion. They say she has skin the color and texture of sliced Wonder Bread. I see they're right. I am the only one she has spoken Chinese to since she came back to Maui to fulfill her destiny.

She says they talk about how people who meet her take her for *haole*. Now she's twenty-one. The Maui people say she looks *haole* and sounds it too. The General has been good for what's left of the Chinese people. He was good for the Chinese of Maui—back when there were Chinese on Maui, she says, cold and bitter. He lives in Honolulu now, and only comes to Maui for Thanksgiving with the Chinese Club. His generosity allows them to live as Chinese as they imagine or dream they are, and tonight they want her to set the day of her marriage to the General and announce it at Thanksgiving dinner.

"Far out," I say, "I guess everyone is in the kitchen, or are we as alone as I feel?"

Then the General walks in. I recognize him. I feel his story slipping through armies in my head, but can't remember where I've seen him before. He's fat. He's tall and fat. I have never seen a man this fat before. A white man. He's bald on top, wears his fringe of white hair long and arty, and has a moustache and beard like Shakespeare, in fact he looks something like Shakespeare to me. A tall fat Shakespeare. But he isn't Shakespeare.

"Who have we here?" the General asks, meaning me. He wears a white suit and a tie and a Panama straw hat and makes me think of Truman Capote or the wimpy white guy in the white suit, Tom Wolfe, but isn't either of them.

"I heard about your Chinese wedding and thought you might like me to play some Chinese impressions of Spanish gypsy music on the flamenco guitar," I say.

"And you are Lucinda, my bride," the General says to the miniature customized beautiful Bette Davis of Maui. But when he reaches for her with his left hand, she suddenly has a knife in her right hand. She whips it in a nice curve and *ow!* slashes his arm. His thumb and fingers twitch and go limp. Some of his blood splashes on the pickled pig's foot, steamed chicken, rice, and tea set out as food for the dead.

"I want no more to do with my family. They love their dreams more than they love me. They sold me to you because you keep their dream alive, but you make them pay too high a price. This brave man here is a real man. He loves me and he will fight you to the death to keep me from marrying you. And I promised to be his woman for the rest of my life—even if he's married—if he kills you."

"Hey, mellow, man. Everything's cool. I came for Thanksgiving dinner and to play a little guitar and figured on getting all the free beer I could drink," I say. But the General runs out holding his cut arm and bloody sleeve with his right hand, his soaked sleeve dripping blood. He's very fast, light on his feet for such a fat man.

After a long time alone and getting turned on by everything strange and everything I hear and see of Lucinda, in walks Old Man Hong, his family, and maybe twenty old people of all colors from

Hershey bar brown to white as rice, and maybe five kids between ten and twentyish—the Chinese Club of Maui—carrying turkeys and hams.

"Where is the General?" Old Man Hong asks.

"This is a real man!" Lucinda says triumphantly, the happiness ringing in her overtones makes me smile, but Old Man Hong and the Chinese Club shy back and screech to a halt. From where I'm standing, I don't see that she's holding the knife in her right hand and the bloody pickled pig's foot in her left. I don't see her waving them over her head. I only hear her jumping up and down, which makes her sound like she's skipping rope when she talks.

"A real Chinese," she says. "When that fat beast tried to touch me with his hands, this man took this knife and cut the General on his arm," Lucinda says, and points at the floor with the knife. "See!" And there are spots of blood on the floor, a trail of little splashes of blood in the dust.

"Diego! You did that?" Old Man Hong looks betrayed. I don't know what to say. How did I get into this? Who is this Lucinda, who is this General?

"Diego is rescuing me from you! What kind of Chinese are you, selling me to Charlie Chan?" Lucinda shouts.

"Charlie Chan!" I shout. "Yeah, the General was Charlie Chan in the movies! I knew I'd seen him before."

"Without that nice kine Charlie Chan we Chinese of Maui would not know who we are," Mrs. Ah-Fong says, holding a plate of mooncakes.

"Look at you all, man," I say. "You're all sullen and moody. What are you thinking when you walk in as if this was a church instead of a party, man? This looks more like a funeral or some kind of pagan sacrifice in the movies than Thanksgiving or a wedding or whatever. How long have I been here? I got here on time, and I've been sitting around at least an hour already, and nobody's even offered me a beer!" I laugh alone. Am I part of the ceremony? "You do this every year?" I ask.

The Chinese Club decides to take Thanksgiving dinner to the

"General" if the "General" won't come to Thanksgiving dinner. It's too late to go back to the dump for Thanksgiving dinner with Jason and the Gods. Whew. And Lucinda is holding my hand and squeezing up next to me. Chinamen aren't this lucky! And this hum seems to come humming out of her body and vibing into mine, so I hang with them, and ride in Lucinda's vw Bug six or seven miles out of Wailuku to the General's house. It doesn't look like anybody has lived here in years. It's like mostly hidden in jungle. The windows are broken out and the window frames gone. The place has no electricity.

Inside we find plants growing through the floor and a big dead black pig lying in a pool of its own blood. Its left foot had been nearly hacked off and it looks like it had come in here to die.

"I don't think the General will be coming to Maui for Thanksgiving ever again," I say, and clap my hands together. "Let's cook this pig for Thanksgiving. He's fresh killed and already bled out. Shuck Charlie Chan! Stop sacrificing virgins to *that* pig every Thanksgiving. Let's eat *this* pig. Come on! Cooking and eating this pig is Chinese!" And as they stare at me with little smiles about to happen on their faces, I say "While the pig is cooking, we can eat the turkey and ham. Come on, it's time to party. Let the good times roll." And with that, I save and improve Thanksgiving dinner.

Lucinda moves in with me, and I move in on the kitchen at the Tiki Tasty Suey every night and do all the Chinese cooking while Old Man Hong and his family watch like kids at the circus. I have seeds mailed to me so they can grow their own *bok choy* and other Chinese vegetables.

Working under the warring Gods on a cedar house in Kihei from a kit shipped from the mainland, we somehow frame the first floor six inches short. And we've spiked the cedar tongue-and-groove flooring through with 30 penny spikes four and a half inches long. Anyone over five feet tall who stands up straight when going to the garage downstairs is going to get nailed in the head.

No kind of prayer or curse gives Fatal or Byron the answer to the problem of how to raise the first floor six inches without taking the house apart. But to keep the owner from driving up the driveway of his Hawaiian cedar ski lodge at night and seeing his headlights hit the roof of the garage and cast the long shadows of snake fangs sticking out all over the ceiling, Jason Peach suggests the tallest man, or whoever has the biggest hammer, bend those nails up and clinch them to the bottom of the tongue-and-groove.

Fatal Jones won't allow anyone else to be taller than he is. And his hammer is bigger than anyone else's.

Ben's play was being produced in New York. Since I was the model for the Fu Manchu who plays flamenco guitar in *Fu Manchu Plays Flamenco,* he needed me to play guitar. Just in time.

I fall by Jason's workshop with Lucinda, my guitar, and the last of the mushrooms. I tell him that all the signs—the accident-prone Gods and the way we could mysteriously build a house all wrong using a kit of pre-cut lumber—tell me it is time to cash in, forget Maui, and get off the island.

Yeah, Jason tells me, he feels the same. He's decided not to go out on jobs with the Gods after they finish fucking up this cedar ski-lodge kit. He's just going to work in his shop. I tell him to keep the mushrooms for himself, for when he feels like making a guitar in one night on pure uninterrupted feeling, and let's just smoke ourselves stupid, play music, eat fatty food, creamy food, and fried food, and sing one more time.

"Let's have a beer," Jason said, "Let's drink it from the can." He pulls a six pack of Primo out of the fridge and rips three beers out of it. We pop them open and toast ourselves. As I close my eyes, the beer is cold starry waters down my throat.

"When you two are back home, mainland side," Jason says, "do me a favor. Keep a beer in the refrigerator for me. Just one can. It won't take up much room. You can put it in the corner in the back on a lower shelf. Okay? A beer for Jason Peach. And someday, I'll come by and ask for my beer. All right?"

And Lucinda sings. Her voice flies to the twenty-foot-high top of the tin arch and sounds like a flute inside the large Quonset hut. At the very back of the building, far from his workshop and his instruments, Jason has built himself a little house without walls, on piers and posts with an old restaurant stove. While we boil water for *saimin* and Lucinda cooks up Vienna sausage and eggs, Jason tells me the story about when he and Ulysses lived together in the same building above Buffalo Books in Berkeley.

Ulysses had been working as a brakeman on the Southern Pacific and Jason had been working a series of carpentry and freelance auto mechanic jobs. They both spent a lot of time drinking espresso and cappuccino at a coffeehouse across the street from the bookstore and watched a lot of old movies at the old Storefront Movie up the street on Telegraph. Then Ulysses split Berkeley for Marysville to work Roseville as his home terminal, braking on the SP, and left behind his beautiful blonde old lady, Sarah. Jason was in love with Sarah from the first night he came home and found her sleeping on the floor next to his bed. I was in the Air Force then.

He laughs when he tells of writing a letter to Ulysses about falling in love with Sarah that began, "I hope we're still friends." Three kids later she went a little crazy and ran him out of the house. Now, years later, he still loves her, and all the women he has here in Maui, one at a time, several in a day, in orgy, all have something that reminds him of her, he says.

I remember them as a couple, I say. There was a picture in the *Chronicle* of people holding a candlelight vigil on the steps of the Administration Building the night after the People's Park thing on Dwight Way. Right in the center was Jason playing a guitar and singing, and Sarah and their beautiful children, light-skinned blacks with blond hair looking like angels, attending Jason in the candlelight. Sarah looked like she could sing, and that's all that counted on the front page of the *Chronicle*.

But no worry, no blame, no guilt, man. I'm not running off to New York with my guitar and leaving Lucinda behind. I don't worry about Jason or anyone on Maui nabbing her after I'm gone. She goes with me. One suitcase in the baggage, one little carry-on thing. That's it. I carry my guitar and one carry-on case with clothes, soap, toothbrush, razor, and brushes.

But I've been playing carpenter too long. My hands are muscle-bound. I can scarcely play anything in time, anything straight. Playing with Jason Peach in his private tin can, the mushrooms, weed, and beer is magic. But when I get to New York, I can't play a lick. My hands feel as if they are cramped around an invisible handle and trigger of a big Skill 77 wormdrive circular saw and tingle from taking the shock of hard hammer blows. I can't make the guitar go.

Ben's New York director is so pissed at me he throws his script up in the air and walks away in a huff, swearing in Yiddish. I've never heard Yiddish before. At first it doesn't sound that different from the Hawaiian pidgin that's been fucking me up on Maui. I didn't know I was supposed to act in this play of Ben's. I thought I was only supposed to play the guitar. And I can't play the guitar. I need a couple of weeks to get my chops back.

I feel so bad about making Ben look bad that I tell him I will pay for Ulysses' flight out from San Francisco and pay for his taxi in from La Guardia so *he* can play guitar and star in the play.

Lucinda says I should be the star, not Ulysses. She blames herself and says she loves me, and knows I love her, but she will understand if I want to sleep with other women now that I'm a little down. She says she understands a man with friends like Ben and Ulysses will have his fans.

"Cool, baby, groovy," I say, "Far out. Same goes for me and you. You want to get it on with Ulysses, I understand. You want to go off explore around New York on your own, go. You know where to find me. I'll be here till the show's over."

Diego Chang: To Be or Not to Be

Orchid Han's Han Dynasty Fine Chinese Cuisine is the only yellow building with red and green trim that screws up a whole triangular-shaped block in Greenwich Village. Taxiing along one of the three streets that shape the block and seeing Ben's mother's restaurant, I feel like a cartoon mouse charging a giant wedge of cheese.

Ben and Ulysses used to live in rooms above the restaurant, just the way they did in Oakland. We could have stayed there in their old apartment above the restaurant and eaten good Chinese food every night free. I liked the idea of a mess of Chinamen from the play walking into Greenwich Village every night and disappearing inside Ben's mother's restaurant. I love the place.

But Ben is, and at the same time isn't, playing Hamlet. He says he's promoting his play by writing what he calls an open letter to his mom about why he's not eating at her restaurant. *The Village Voice* tells him they're putting it on the front page. They put it on the front page, all right, just under an article by Pandora Toy. None of us ever heard of her, but there's a nude picture of her on the front page. I look at the picture. What's so special about her that makes front-page nude news?

A Neurotic Exotic Erotic Orientoxic

By Pandora Toy

I wish I were just a woman who loved sex. Instead I am a Chinese woman who loves sex. There are no men, or attractive, precocious, muscular boys in Chinatown. There are only Chinese who tell little girls the story of the beautiful princess whose father, the king, flayed her foreign sweetheart to the death, held a banquet to announce her wedding, and gave her hand in marriage to the prince who belched the loudest. My father and mother tell me it is famous in the repertoire of traditional Peking opera, and I simply haven't lived until I've seen it. But I cannot seriously believe Chinese women have ever found an evening of opera with all that belching sexy. And the marriage fairy tale as sex education leaves me cold. When I think of such a tradition, all I can do is sigh. With all the erotic exotic orientoxic women like me, past and present, I sigh.

But I have to be honest. It is nice to be exotic. Exoticism makes any man I want for a quickie or for a night mine, all mine. Not being the naturally humdrum everyday plain universal Caucasian woman makes me stand out in a crowd. And I was born to stand out. At times I worry about what effect my exotic birth and sexual temperament is having on the authenticity and honesty of my behavior. But how can I know, when I am truly and righteously as free as I can be, having been born a girl within the labyrinth of a sadly unmanly culture, a culture with a language that uses the same word for "slave" and "woman"?

The question is serious. But Eric, my well-muscled blond rocker, laughs. He only wants to make love. No one takes an exotic seriously. Sometimes it is sad to be an exotic. Oh, exoticism excites men to paw and pat with their macho auras, to drool on my Chinese neck. Men! First they tell me how exotic I am. But when I tell them my father passed the imperial civil service examinations and was a scholar in the official old China, they become electric with excitement. Yes, scholar officials of old China are the Ivy League, the Phi Beta Kappa, of exotica. Then they try talking my body into bed with them with Baba Ram Dass, Zen, bonsai, or other bits of exotic orientalisms. So dull. Oh, to be just me. Sigh.

Sometimes it would be nice to just be an ordinary woman with an ordinary man I happen to find attractive. I'm so tired of always breaking the racial barrier. It has been so difficult, so painful, so wearying to wrestle myself free of centuries of restrictions that have punished women who seek pleasure with a race of soft men. So I have become the lone scout of the exotic East meeting the beefy West, and I'm tired of it. I'm tired of rich hippies and their drugs, people who make a fetish of chemically rejecting reality. Of course some are very nice, but as my friend Agnes says, I would like to be a real woman and date a real man, instead of rich toads with hemorrhoids or ethnic trophy hunters.

Agnes is a beautiful Japanese woman. She also loves sex. Agnes has a daddy who refused to allow her to date white boys, because white people put him and the other Japanese into camps during World War II. "I kept telling Daddy that it wasn't white people's fault that the Japanese *are* Japanese," Agnes explains. Nonetheless, her daddy still wouldn't allow her to date white boys. But try as she might, she just did not find Japanese or Chinese men sexually attractive. And I second her feeling. Anyway, Agnes didn't date a real boy till she left home at 19. And we both agree that we will never marry an Oriental. And as we remember our fathers, as we think about all the oriental men we have ever known, all we do is . . . Sigh.

Why I'm Not Eating In Your Restaurant, Mom!

By Benedict Mo

Mom, it's a strange feeling to live in Santa Barbara a while. I never think of myself as Oriental here, the child of a Chinese father and mother, born in China. In Santa Barbara people ask me why I do not just write about people instead of the Chinese, whereas in San Francisco and Los Angeles, people ask me why the Chinese characters I write are not more Chinese.

Were Ralph Ellison, Richard Wright, James Baldwin, and Lorraine Hansberry capable of writing of themes and emotions and truths of character beyond the confines of their particular, unique Black Afro-American experience? Did writers Louis Chu or John Okada have any other color inside of them besides yellow? Real writers are rainbows. That is what I'm trying to say with my play.

Diego Chang: "Fu Manchu Plays Flamenco Guitar"

The American Face Theater throws War-on-Poverty chump change at Ben. The War-on-Poverty money that has made the Chinatown Black Tigers such a success for three quick years failed to assimilate the gangs. Now it is out to create journeyman whodat artists from the dinkiest, most neglected American minority ever to pay their dues with a token. *Fu Manchu Plays Flamenco* is ornamental Orientalia, making us the ornamental Orientals of the minute. I know it. Ulysses knows it. Ben knows it. No problem. Party time!

To make the play and the "theater process" relevant to the community, the American Face Theater makes a deal in the halls of New York City bureaucracy. We are auditioning, casting, and rehearsing with a pseudo-famous white director, two white stage managers, a New York Sansei Japanese-American boozer for a lighting designer, a white set designer, a famous Korean American costume designer, and a cast of professionals with portfolios and photos and résumés, in the gymnasium of a condemned public school building right in Chinatown. None of them has spent more than a couple of hours at a time in Chinatown and weren't comfortable being with yellows who don't even speak the language. But I have no problem. I speak Chinese. My father's tong is nearby. I am a lost son come home. Chinatown is mine. And Ulysses and Ben used to live here in New York. They're home. No problem.

Ben's really showing his stuff at first rehearsal when Pandora Toy shows up. She introduces herself to Ben and the famous playwright directing Ben's play. She walks up to Ulysses in his Chinese robe and Fu Manchu moustache and hat and says, "You don't remember me, do you."

Ulysses doesn't remember her.

"I happened to be in one of the audiences you postured in front of as the Minister of War of the Chinatown Black Tigers a few years ago," she explains to Ulysses. Whew! She doesn't recognize me. "I told you that I wasn't suffering from any imagined racial problems because I had real, pressing personal problems. You asked me to share one of my personal problems with you, and I told you that my parents didn't approve of my being engaged to a Caucasian boy. Even though I was over twenty-one at the time, you had no sympathy at all. You laughed at me, you asked the audience what they had learned from me. You said that when I put racial problems and personal problems in separate sentences, it showed that I took them to be different problems, when my problem with my parents and my being engaged to marry a Caucasian was obviously *both* a personal and a racial problem. I had never been so insulted and embarrassed. I ran out of the room crying," she says. "It was one of the most significant moments in my life, and you don't have the courtesy to lie about remembering me!"

"I'm sorry," Ulysses says.

"Would you be surprised to learn I have recently divorced my husband and that I am currently at the end of an affair with a black man?" she asks with her chin up.

"Astonished!" Ulysses says.

She came with a friend who, we assumed, came to audition. He introduces himself. Washington Ching Flores is his name, a Chinese Filipino American. He is insulted that anyone would even think that he had come to audition. True, he has been an actor. He has been an Indian with no lines in a margarine commercial, a Chinese laundryman with an accent in a spray starch commercial that was still on the air, and he has played a Japanese American teenaged boy in a series of American minority plays on PBS last year. Pandora says he is the resident Asian at *The Village Voice* and is "very important."

So what is the "very important" man doing here? we wonder. Waving a rolled-up copy of the script in his hand, Washington Ching Flores shakes with anger or nervousness, almost spitting his words at us. "You cannot put this play before an audience! I share your anger. I understand it, but this will destroy all the progress we have made. You cannot take a shit on a stage. I know it's Fu Manchu taking a shit, but you cannot have a Chinese say 'God Fuck it!' in front of white people!"

"How about a *pagan* Fu Manchu?" the director asks.

"What?" Washington Ching Flores answers back, flustered.

"How about a *pagan* Fu Manchu taking a shit?" Pandora asks.

"I know you don't like hearing what I have to say, but I know where you're coming from. And as an actor, I tell you you have written a part beneath our dignity!"

Ben listens patiently, then asks, "If I were to write your dream part, the part you want to play—any time in history or fantasy, any place, any kind of movie or play, western, tragedy, screwball comedy, classic—what would that part be? What would be the part that makes you a star?" Ben adds. "Just out of curiosity."

"That's a good question! By chance, I have been giving just that question a lot of thought. I'm a writer myself," Washington Ching Flores says. " And I have a play I happened to coauthor with a group of people, in the works."

"Oh, what a coincidence!" Pandora Toy says and sits down next to Ben.

"But this!" He throws the script down on the floor. "No one will ever put this on stage."

Who *is* this guy? I start strumming along with the bluesy gospel version of "Ching Chong Chinaman sitting on a fence/ Trying to make change for fifteen cents," and Ulysses starts singing, on his knees, to a statue of Buddha, like Ray Charles, like George Jones, like he believes in God and this is "Amazing Grace." "Ching Chong Chinaman sitting on a rail/ Along come a choo-choo train/ And cut off his tail," and we're laughing and howling, when Tom Tom Tom walks in, his fists clenched, his teeth clenched, shaking with rage, and tells Ulysses to stop singing that song.

Tom Tom Tom's gang, the Dragon Kings, squeaks in on the composition soles of their jump boots just behind Tom Tom. I put my guitar down, ease over to the director, and tell him to cool it. "Tom Tom is a killer. Right now Ulysses is the one he wants to cut. Let us Chinks handle it," I whisper.

"So, you don't like the song I'm singing?" Ulysses asks, in his Fu Manchu costume. "Why?"

"It's racist!" Tom Tom says, gnashing his teeth, staring a hole into Ulysses' face, looking as if he were about to slice Ulysses' throat. But Ulysses kept smiling under his moustache, his hands loose and down.

"Why do you say it's racist?" Ulysses asks.

"It makes fun of the Chinese people. I don't want you to sing that song in Chinatown."

"But that's why I *am* singing this song. I know it's racist. We all know it's racist and makes fun of the Chinese, that's why I'm singing it."

"You're singing 'Ching Chong Chinaman' because it makes fun of the Chinese?" Tom Tom says. "Are you crazy?"

"Kill him!" the fat face standing just behind Tom Tom yells, and everyone in the gang shifts position toward Ulysses. But Tom Tom stays put and stares through Ulysses, waiting for him to make the first move.

"Don't take any shit from these guys. This is America." Pandora Toy stage-whispers for everyone to hear. Uh oh, I think, she has just killed Ulysses. But nothing happens.

Finally, "Have you ever heard of satire?" Ulysses asks Tom Tom Tom and the Dragon Kings. Ulysses is crazy. What is he doing, dressed up as Fu Manchu, standing up to a Chinatown gang for his right to sing "Ching Chong Chinaman sitting on a rail/ Along come a choo-choo train and cut off his tail" . . . ? So what is he doing?

"Satire? You motherfucker!" Tom Tom says, wanting with all his heart to throw a punch.

"Kill him!" Fat Face says, throwing a finger toward Ulysses.

"Satire is where you make fun of how *they* think and what *they* say in order to make *them* look *stupid,*" Ulysses said, not too slow, not too fast. I don't know if he makes them understand, but he keeps them listening until the fight fizzles out. And suddenly instead of starting a fight, they find themselves chitchatting about old movies they have seen on late night New York TV. And before long, they drift away, no more sure of what has happened than I was. It takes us a few moments to realize they are gone, that nothing has happened, that Ulysses is still in costume and that the crazy fuck is ready to sing that stupid song again.

"Cut the song!" Ben says. "Cut the whole scene!"

"Yes," the director agrees, "that scene was always a little too didactic. A cheap shot. Thank you, Ben."

I bet Ulysses didn't know how to fight. I've known him since he was twelve and have never seen him in a real fight. He was always talking.

In the play, Fu Manchu tells the white captive to give up the secret to Kool-Aid or he will let his beautiful nympho daughter give him the dreaded torture of a thousand excruciating fucks and exotic sucks. But the white man defends the secret to Kool-Aid, and Fu's luscious daughter wheels the captive off to her silk-sheeted torture chamber. When the director sees Ulysses offstage watching, still in character, he tries putting Fu Manchu back onstage, reciting classical Japanese haiku of Issa and Basho, breathlessly watching his daughter torture the white man by seduction. Then Ulysses gets the idea to have Fu play the guitar in rhythm to his daughter's hips while badmouthing the white captive's sexual organs, skills, and style in Spanish, English, and three dialects of Chinese.

Ben asks Ulysses to tell his ideas to *him,* during a break or at home, before spilling them out to the director in front of everybody. Ulysses didn't think it mattered. I didn't think it mattered. One for all, all for one.

So who knows and who cares whose idea it is for Fu Manchu to end his flamenco in the torture chamber by ripping open his robe and showing his body in a bra, panties, garter belt, and black net stockings, licking his lips as he makes a move on the white man, while Fu's daughter straps on an eight-inch dildo? The captive American screams the secret formula, not only for Kool-Aid but for Bisquick and Crisco, too.

I liked hanging with the guys and seeing stuff like that happen. It's fun, it's goofy, but it's not worth fighting about. Ulysses doesn't want to fight about anything. Ben wants to fight. Ulysses is so good, he's making Ben look bad. Ulysses' ego is so big, he doesn't even know he's doing it when he's doing it. No, no, no. The play is by Benedict Mo. That's the way the credits read.

"No matter what, this is *A Play by Benedict Mo*. So, you are the first and last word," Ulysses says, trying to be real nonthreatening. And still Ben *is* hurt, and pissed, and intimidated, and humiliated. Nothing to do with the play. He is in love, instead of paying attention to business.

Pandora Toy takes up with Ben, and after a dinner at some cheap Cuban Chinese, they go back to the bedroom and fuck. Lucinda and me sleep on the couch that converts into a double bed, and Ulysses sleeps on a thick foam pad on the other side of the large front room.

There's a lot of furniture, and we move a Chinese screen to make a wall between one side of the room and the other. Lucinda brings women home from the rehearsal, and everybody brings steaks and chops and sausages, and we all party and play music. Ulysses could get laid every night, but often sleeps alone because he wants to. And at the same time, he doesn't want to.

"What's wrong with him?" I ask.

"Loner," Lucinda says.

Diego Chang: Replace the Beams With Rotten Timbers

Ulysses says it isn't good for Ben to badmouth his mother in public. Ben replies that it isn't good for Ulysses to badmouth his *father* in public. Ben didn't speak like this before he and Pandora became "a thing."

"Don't!" Ben snaps at Ulysses before he speaks. "Whatever it is you're thinking, don't say it. I intend to marry her," Ben says.

"What about when the *Neurotic Exotic Erotic Orientoxic* and

Agnes vowed never to marry yellow men who remind them of their fathers?" Ulysses challenges.

"Are you trying to talk me out of marrying her? Are you actually singing 'Those Wedding Bells Are Breaking Up That Old Gang of Mine'?" asks Ben.

"What about that fake marriage story with the belching princess that she's using to advertise her hatred of Chinese tradition?" continues Ulysses.

"That's not an autobiography. It's fiction. She explained it to me. That's just a character, not her. Her character is inventing this fantastic—but credible—Chinese culture, not her."

"Credible?" Ulysses snarls. "Remember all that shit we had to learn in Chinese school? Did anybody belch and win a woman in *any* of those stories? Huh?"

"Ulysses, come on, don't be that way. You know you've heard that said about the Chinese."

"You ever heard any Chinese say it's polite or sexy to belch at the dinner table?"

"Yes, of course. Pandora Toy and her mother!"

"You heard Pandora Toy's mother say it's polite to belch as loudly as you can at the dinner table to show your appreciation of the meal?"

"She says, I mean her first-person narrator, says she heard it from her mother," Ben says. "Chinese enough for you?"

"Hey, the first place that anybody, anywhere, anytime, in any language read such a thing was when Pearl Buck said the only good Chink is a Christian Chink, and that belching at the dinner table is good manners to the Chinese. Then the whites invented the Nobel Prize for literature and gave it to her. That showed us!"

"It's fiction. It's first-person fiction. A character whose thought processes show the effects of the diaspora."

"*The Village Voice* didn't say it was fiction. The publishers of the book don't say it's fiction. It's on *The New York Times non*-fiction best seller list. It is not presented as fiction, it's presented as autobiography."

"She explained that to me, man, listen. They would only publish her book as nonfiction. They didn't think it would sell as a novel. Fiction, nonfiction, that's marketing. Read her book. She creates a Chinese culture that is acceptable to whites by rewriting a little of of this and a little of that, in order to show higher truths, inner meanings. As far as I'm concerned, she's doing exactly what we're doing with the play."

"What are we doing with the play?" Ulysses asks.

"We are revealing the truth of the Chinese culture we reject and creating a Chinese-American culture that is more humane, more considerate of women, more . . ."

"Aw, bullshit! *Fu Manchu Plays Flamenco* is creating a Chinese-American culture that kicks white racism in the balls with a shit-eating grin," Ulysses sneers.

"You have to admit Chinese culture oppresses women," Ben says.

"No more than Christian culture . . . it's all recorded in their history books, scripture, and literature."

"What about foot-binding?" Ben says.

"Were your mother's feet bound? Did Pandora's mother have bound feet? It was never a popular or common practice. Nothing in Chinese folk tales praises women with bound feet or even mentions it because the folk didn't do it. To the folk, binding women's feet was always the behavior of perverts. And not one woman ever had her feet bound in Chinatown in the States. While white Christians drowned women as witches in Salem. There are more women with boob jobs in white Christian North Beach right now than Chinese women with bound feet in all of Chinese history," Ulysses says. "The fact is that Chinese literature—The Three Brothers of the Oath of the Peach Garden, *Sam Gawk Yurn Yee,* The Romance of the Three Kingdoms, Fung Sun Bong and Kwan Kung—has nothing to do with your fiancée's strange tales. The stories she says are Chinese aren't and never were. She's not rewriting Chinese anything, man. She's just doing a rewrite of Pearl Buck and Charlie Chan and Fu Manchu."

"Right, just like James Joyce at the end of *Portrait of the Artist as a Young Man,* man, she is forging the uncreated conscience of the Chinese in the smithy of her soul!"

"Are you saying substance doesn't matter, that she can suck off the white racist fantasy as long as she does it with style and makes money at the same time?" Ulysses shouts.

"That's just what I'm saying! If anyone deserves to profit from the white racist fantasy, we Chinese Americans do," Ben laughs.

"Excuse me, Gunga Din, but what you describe is sometimes called selling out," Ulysses says, looking ugly.

"Grow up, man!" Ben laughs. "The only way we can make it in America is to sell ourselves. No one wants to buy our folk tales. But they like buying exotic Oriental women and Oriental men who are either sinister brutes or simpletons. So why not sell it to them?"

Ulysses moves out of the uptown apartment the theater had provided Ben, and into the old rooms upstairs from Ben's mother's restaurant. Pandora Toy says she hoped it wasn't her fault. Ben says, "No, it's just Ulysses being Ulysses," and doesn't take it seriously. But they aren't friends anymore. I see that.

Ben asks what I think, and I tell him. "Ulysses is doing the play and hates it more and more, but he's doing it for you. He does the play thing and stands next to you for pictures, but that's it. He's your friend only in front of Pandora Toy and other people."

Lucinda says even she sees Ulysses is being loyal, and Ben should leave him alone when the three of us guys do get together.

Ben gives a half-assed smile and says that he and Ulysses shouting at each other sounds like the Horse, the old Chinese teacher Ulysses used to infuriate until the Horse couldn't speak Chinese or English and picked stuff off his desk and threw it at him.

"That pussy!"

"Are you calling Ulysses a pussy?" Ben grins.

"Aww, Ulysses, fuck, you can call him anything," I say. "But, no, man, I mean the Horse!"

"The Horse! Whatever happened to the Horse?" Ben laughs.

"What I heard from this friend of my father's I happened to bump into—he hangs around the Mah family association—is that soon after he closed the Chinese school, the Horse wrote letters to all his friends and told them he was withdrawing from the world."

"Withdrawing from the world?" Ben interrupts.

"Something like that," I go on. "He didn't want them to try to contact him for any reason whatsoever. Ever. He had his phone taken out of his house. And he drove his wife out and divorced her, gave her a big settlement. Don't ask me what they meant by big. I didn't ask, and they didn't say. But they do say she didn't want it. Who knows? And he withdrew from the world. No one heard of him again. That's it."

"He withdrew from the world?" Ben asks. "Why?"

"Don't ask me," I say. "I'm just telling you what I heard."

Lucinda and I move out the next day.

I like Ben's mother. She's tough, funny, and no one can drink her under the table. I really like her husband, the opera maestro. Nights, after closing, he always calls us down for a midnight snack before driving his Caddie home, trusting everything in the building to us. One night, Lucinda and I find him in the restaurant dining room with a stack of Danish butter cookie cans on the table. He opens a can, takes out a few layers of cookies, and replaces them with a couple of pocket-sized Chinese comic books in waxed paper envelopes. Then he puts a layer or two of cookies on top of the books, replaces the cover on the can, using a little machine to replace the plastic seal around the seam between the lid and the can.

"What're you smuggling, *Ah-Buck bok?*" I ask.

He laughs as if he doesn't understand my Chinese or my English.

After a little tea, while out of curiosity I help him seal a couple of cans with the machine, he explains. "Some friends are having trouble finding these funny-books of the stories we do in the opera. I want to help them out, but I don't want to get them arrested by the Communists. Understand?"

"What do you mean, Uncle?"

"All the Chinese stories are forbidden in China by the Cultural Revolution," Uncle Buck says. "That's why the Cantonese opera has been so good these last few years. No real opera artist will do that stupid revolutionary bullshit that they demand. So the real artists come here where they can sing and be Chinese without any Red Guard. You understand what I'm telling you?"

He is telling me this is real smuggling. Little books of cartoons with captions, the stuff I learned in Chinese school as a kid, have become real contraband and can get real people in China in real trouble.

"So what stories are you sending your friends?" I ask. I should apologize and tell him I always loved Cantonese opera, even when I was Comandante of the Chinatown Black Tigers. I loved the opera and will love it still, even knowing that the Cultural Revolution and Chinese Red Guard and Mao's *Little Red Book* and all that Third World Revolution bullshit don't allow it.

Buck won't let me touch one of the little comic books. I can see what it is. I read enough to read some comic books. I want to look at it, but Buck won't let me. "Oh, it's nothing, just kidstuff," he says. "You know, just fairy tales, boys-and-girls kidstuff."

"People are willing to go to jail and lose their families for kidstuff, Uncle?"

"The people I know are willing to die."

"What kind of people?"

"Chinese people. Being Chinese isn't just skin color and personal feelings. You American-born kids have always had everything. You don't even have to think," Buck says. "You don't know what you're missing."

"Does Auntie Orchid know you're smuggling books inside tin cans of cookies to Communist China, Uncle?"

"You never noticed since the Cultural Revolution in China all the stores selling Danish butter cookies opening up in Chinatown right next door to a new paperback book and magazine store? Have a Danish butter cookie," Buck laughs. "Help yourself."

Benedict Mo: Take the Obvious and Reverse It

I hadn't seen Pandora in three days and nights. No note, no call, her clothes weren't gone, nothing. I knew something was wrong. I knew it. An hour before the rehearsal was to start, I grabbed Ulysses and Diego and begged them to run with me to the Holiday Inn nearest Chinatown.

On a couple of beers and a hit of reefer, Diego sometimes achieved an effortless beatific calm and his every word soothed, made sense, spoke justice. Now was one of those times. "Ulysses," he said, "you stay and do the play, man. They really don't need me and Ben, so we'll go find Pandora."

So Ulysses left. What had I been thinking? Why had I thought if I couldn't be at the rehearsal, neither could he?

How did I know she was at the Holiday Inn? Diego gently asked, after we were in a cab. Was I Sherlock Holmes?

I didn't know how I knew. But she had to be somewhere. She had been babbling and ranting about the meaning of the Holiday Inn built on the site of the old Police Building on Kearny and Washington Streets in San Francisco. I opened up the Yellow Pages and went through "Hotels" until I came to Holiday Inn, found an address that made my heart jump, and knew where I had to go to find her.

We arrived. No Pandora Toy registered there. Her white ex-husband's name was Swan. No Pandora Swan. "Pandora Mo?" I asked, "Em oh. Mo." There was a Pandora Mo registered there. She had used *my name*. I began to lose it.

Diego put his arms around me and gave me a squeeze and smiled at the desk clerk. "This is Pandora Mo's husband. She left a note saying she was about to commit suicide, you hear me? We are here to stop that and see that she's okay, okay?"

The desk clerk directed us to hotel security, a short fat man in suspenders behind his desk in a little office with no windows. He put on his jacket and grabbed his keys and took us up an elevator to Pandora's floor.

"'Ludes and booze," Diego said as soon as the short fat man opened the door and pushed his way in. Pandora, looking limp and bloodless, lay on the bed. The bottles of Quaaludes and Jack Daniels were on the TV. Diego dragged her out of bed into the shower, hit her with cold water, and stayed there till the paramedics arrived.

"Ben, you saved her life, man," Ulysses said. "You knew just where to find her. You're bound."

"Yeah," I said. "I know."

Diego accompanied me to the hospital and stayed the night. He told me what to expect from 'ludes and booze—barbiturate sores, big blisters. If she did the 'ludes and booze the first night I missed her and she'd been out two and a half days, three days before we found her, she was going to be out a long time. It was going to be close. He told me that when she did come out of it she would be crazy for a while while coming up from the downer brought on by those pills. And that the city shrinks would want to hold her for 72 hours at least. He left some time after dawn. I stayed at the hospital waiting for Pandora to regain consciousness. Sometime as the opening night performance was going on without me, Diego came to the hospital carrying a canvas sports bag with a razor, shaving cream, soap, deodorant, and change of clothes.

"She's at least out for the night, man. They have it under control. She's alive. You have to get to the theater for the party and introduce me to the celebrities, dig?" Diego said, shoving the bag into my belly. "Now, find a bathroom, man, and get yourself together."

Diego counted three limousines waiting outside the theater. On hearing the jabber of a crowd, Diego said, "That's good. They must have liked the play or they would have all left." Lucinda ran up to us, grabbed me and kissed me. "Good play!" she said, and put her arm around Diego.

Diego said he saw Princess Lee Radziwell and Jackie Kennedy in the crowd. He thought he'd go get a better look and slinked between a few people who were wearing clothes I had never seen the likes of before. New York. Opening night.

But brighter than the celebrities the theater courted for their money was my mother in a blue-green silk *cheongsam* and red apron and her ballooning hair, behind a table of hot trays, serving glorified Chinese take-out grease. I'd forgotten Mom had been hired to cater the opening night party. "Hey! Where've ya been?" Mom shouted. "Everybody's talking about you!"

A haze began to lift. All of this was for me. The people out of *The New Yorker*, and *New York* magazines. The actors. The stage carpenters. The sewing shop. Everything was for tonight. And tonight was for me, and I'd missed everything but the party! Ulysses brought me a plastic cup of champagne and a plate loaded with a couple of fried chicken wings, a couple of greasy fried egg rolls, and a couple of deep-fried wonton. Then, having filled my hands with flimsy floppy stuff, he stepped back, threw his arms open wide, gave out a snarl that turned into a whoop, and we embraced as gingerly as I could without spilling anything on the lobby carpet.

I wolfed down the greasy stuff from Mom's restaurant and drank the champagne. It was the first food I'd had since we'd gone after Pandora. While I was still chewing on the rubbery insides of the last egg roll, this thin young blonde Twiggy skinny type I'd seen around the theater, wearing a thin white long-skirted dress tight as a bandage, caught my eye and seemed to stalk me, weaving past the backs of chatting first-nighters as if they were trees and brush, closer and closer. This was the script Fate wrote, I thought, not fully believing my eyes. I didn't hear her. I didn't smell her. No one else seemed to see her.

Was she joking? She had to be somebody's girlfriend, the stage electrician, or the shop foreman, or she wrote press releases in the office—I had never spoken to her and had only the vaguest idea of who she was. This party so overzapped my mind I wasn't sure this white blonde was real. I was so tired and she was too pretty. Was this a dream? Not that I had any reason to dream of white women—until I met Pandora I had only slept with white women.

Had she disappeared? I didn't smell her. I didn't hear her. Then I did. She stood up in front of me trembling. Her breath trembled.

Her sweat trembled on her trembling skin. She grabbed me. I grabbed her. She threw her face against mine, grabbed bits of my face with her lips and teeth, and let them bounce back. She tongued her way into my mouth. We slipped over to a corner, fell to the floor, and rolled to a corner where the white actor who's tortured into becoming a dope addict by Fu Manchu sat on the floor with another young woman I'd seen around the theater, exchanging prissy little kisses. Meanwhile, my waiflike creature encouraged me to feel her breasts through her thin white dress as she reached inside my pants, grabbed my cock, felt it grow hard in her hand, and squeezed me. "I can't resist talented men," she said. She licked her hand, looked me in the eye, licked her hand again, and was gone into the crowd.

Some reviewers liked the play more than others, but there were no wholehearted endorsements. The *New York Times* reviewer had never heard of Chinese Americans, had never given them a thought, and after seeing my play didn't know what the problem was, or why some people in the audience thought it was occasionally funny in places. And, oh! Surprise surprise! *The Village Voice* had Washington Ching Flores, their resident Asian—who'd visited rehearsals and tried to get us to rewrite the whole thing as part of his attempt to impress Pandora Toy—write their review.

Charlie Chan's Grandson Stars as Fu Manchu

IN BEN MO'S "FU MANCHU PLAYS FLAMENCO"

A LOT OF BULL BUT NO OLÉ! NO EARS NO TAIL

by Washington Ching Flores

The most dramatic aspect of Benjamin Mo's first play, *Fu Manchu Plays Flamenco,* is its casting. Irony of ironies, the actor playing Fu Manchu and the guitar, Ulysses S. Kwan, is the son of Longman Kwan, the actor renowned for playing the Number Four Son of Charlie Chan in the movies.

As a Chinese-American actor, as a Chinese-American writer, as a Chinese American sick and tired of living on the margins of American society, I would love to be able to say that I love the first Chinese-American play to represent us on the New York off-Broadway stage. Alas, this is a play with no new Chinese-American characters I was jealous to act, no lines that made me wish I had said that. Mr. Mo, an instructor of Asian American Stuies at San Francisco State, is no Chinese-American John Osborne, Tom Stoppard, nor is he a Chinese-American LeRoi Jones. What we have instead of a play is a sophomoric skit that is offensive to both Chinese and American art.

What we have is the first Chinese-American actor to play the part of Fu Manchu in public. This Chinese American is the son of one of the Chinese-American actors who still clings to the nobler ambition of becoming the first Chinese American to actually star as Charlie Chan in a movie. Longman Kwan was surprised to learn his son had any interest in acting *or* playing the guitar, much less was acting *and* playing the guitar in an off-Broadway theater in New York. He says he has had no contact with Ulysses in years.

Number Four Son is still acting. He is currently a regular on the ABC TV series, *Kung Fu,* starring David Carradine, playing a one-armed Shaolin priest and archery instructor. The shock and disappointment he suffered at the news that his second son was about to become the first Chinese to play Fu Manchu in the theater was apparent in his voice as he said, "I get sick and tired about the protests against *Kung Fu.* Shaolin Temple *was* an actual temple in China. Those who are complaining did not have to live in the times before Charlie Chan opened doors for the Chinese in America and led to our current acceptance in every part of American life. But it has taken us years to put the Fu Manchu image behind us. Those of us in the acting profession in America realize we are performing in American theater, Western theater, not Chinese theater. American theater, whoever makes it, is Western theater, the theater shaped by Chekhov and Saroyan and Arthur Miller."

Astonishingly, playwright Mo and his actor Kwan seem to be serious about their Fu Manchu's fanatical adherence to Chinese tradition, and the humiliation and subjugation of women. Do they seriously believe portraying Fu Manchu's daughter as a foulmouthed nymphomaniac, using sex to torture the American into giving up the secret formula for Bisquick, is funny? All those whose eyes have been opened by Pandora Toy's "The Neurotic Exotic Erotic Orientoxic" will be outraged and revolted by this two-hour exhibition of infantile ego-tripping and excess.

Even the lead-actor's father agrees. The Chinese civilization of Fu Manchu was so morally depraved and perverted, the only option left to the Chinese in America is to reject it, to free ourselves from it and kill it, as does the cutting-edge work of the ineluctable Pandora Toy.

Benedict Han: Festoon the Dead Tree With Paper Flowers

"You're not John Osborne or LeRoi Jones. I could have told them that," Ulysses said. Mom touched me with her pep talk about reviews and discreetly told me she was pleased at the way I stood up under some harsh criticism from the New York papers. I had done something by myself and stood by it without excuses and took the critics without self-pity. She was happy to see this side of me come out at last.

Pandora revived from her barbiturate coma two days after the play opened but was required by law to stay in the psycho ward for observation for 72 hours. She wanted me to bring her vitamins, but the doctors at the hospital wouldn't allow it.

She said my success depressed her. She couldn't help it. The attention my play and my writing were attracting depressed her. She admired me but couldn't compete with me. She couldn't compete with me and love me. What competition? I wanted to know. I talked about her writing, how *The Village Voice,* the hippest of the hip, the pacesetter, had front-paged an excerpt from her book and dumped on my play. I was shallow; she was deep. She perked up when I said I would probably never write another play in my life.

No Rivalry between the First Chinese-American Playwright and the Neurotic Exotic Erotic— We are Brother and Sister

By Pandora Toy

My friend, the brilliant Washington Ching Flores, has assumed that the simultaneous publication of my book, *The Neurotic Exotic Erotic,* which pleads the case for the courage and freedom of a new Chinese-American woman, and the debut of my friend Benjamin Mo's wonderful play, *Fu Manchu Plays Flamenco,* are an unhappy coincidence. I did not mean the excerpt printed in the *Voice* to be a declaration of war on Benjamin Mo's play. His play is the first play by a Chinese-American playwright in the history of the New York stage. He is a new Chinese-American man, as I am a new Chinese-American woman. Our appearance at the same time at the same place tells me that we are not enemies but that the time is ripe for us to be brothers and sisters in a new era in Chinese America. We are not angry. We have learned from the Blacks that anger does not work.

We herald the creation of a new, more humane, more graceful, more Christian Chinese culture. The Chinese culture that bound the feet of women at birth or otherwise drowned their daughters to please their men is dead.

Destiny seems to have cast this American-born male Chinese playwright and this rare American-born Chinese woman in a flesh-and-blood Chinese-American version of the Chinese creation myth. Washington Ching Flores, understandably but mistakenly, uses me to criticize Benjamin Mo's play in the prestigious *Village Voice.* It's not Ben's fault that Chinese men left their wives behind when they came to America. It's quite unbelievable how recent Chinese-American characters and events parallel the myth. I would not presume to criticize Washington Ching Flores for doing no more than his job as a theater critic for the *Voice.* Nor would I presume to criticize the *Voice.* But I would like to share this traditional story of the creation of man and woman, as I remember my mother telling it to me. Right now, it feels like prophecy.

The myth speaks for itself. Kwan Kung was one of the giants who inhabited the earth before the creation of human beings. He is known in Asia as "the Chinese Mars," and in the west as "the Chinese Prometheus." The Jade Emperor charged Kwan Kung's older brother, Lowe Bay, with the creation of man and the animals. Kwan Kung was charged with recording and cataloging Lowe Bay's finished work.

Lowe Bay proceeded to bestow upon the animals the various gifts of courage, strength, speed, and stamina; wings to the animals of the air, fins to animals of the sea, paws and claws for the beasts who hunted and scavenged prey, horns and hooves for the animals who were the quarry of the hunt. The best teeth and claws, the wings and scales, and keen eyes were all distributed among the animals. Then he created Chang Fay, the first man. Lowe Bay had no more gifts left to bestow upon man, much less a gift that would make man superior to the animals, so he sent his brother Kwan Kung to heaven to bring something back, something that would give man a little brother.

Kwan Kung brought back an immortal peach from the Jade Emperor's private peach garden. Lowe Bay and Chang Fay doubted eating a peach was good for making man superior to the animals. The peaches from the Jade Emperor's garden were reserved for the gods. Chang Fay devoured the entire peach and belched. Eating the peach had not made him immortal. But, quite suddenly, he asked for "fire." Before this moment he had neither heard nor uttered the word "fire."

Lowe Bay sent his brother to heaven to steal fire for his little brother, Chang Fay. Fire unlocked the gods' secret of the five elements. Fire made man superior to animals. With fire, man could forge weapons to hunt, and tools to break the ground to farm, or build a house to shelter himself from the wind. With fire, man could keep warm inside his house in winter.

But Lowe Bay had neglected to create the first woman and was not aware that his world was incomplete. The Jade Emperor took advantage of Lowe Bay's lapse of creativity. After he created the first woman, he sent her to Lowe Bay to be his wife. She was created to be a punishment for stealing fire from the gods. Her name was Kwan Yin. The gods who desired revenge made Kwan Yin beautiful to the eye, and gave her a voice beautiful to the ear. They gave her the arts of persuasion, seduction, and confusion. She presented herself to Lowe Bay with her eyes lowered, as a gift from the gods. Kwan Kung and Chang Fay cautioned their older brother to beware gifts from the gods. Lowe Bay brushed aside his younger brothers' cautions and gladly accepted.

In his house, Lowe Bay had a jar in which he had collected the gifts he found noxious and did not wish to bestow upon man. But over time Kwan Yin was seized with a fit of curiosity and lifted the cover. Immediately a multitude of plagues issued from the jar, surging off in all directions to ravage the body and mind of man. The lid dropped from her fingers and shattered. She poured the last of the contents of the jar quickly into a vase and plugged the vase with a small sprig of bamboo. Of all the terrible evils she had set loose to plague humanity, only one remained in the vase—mercy. Thus, Kwan Yin, who had been created by the gods as a kind of revenge against the three brothers who stole from the gods, became immortal and the goddess of mercy.

Diego Chang: Throw Out a Brick To Catch Gold

"This isn't Chinese. This isn't The Three Brothers. This isn't Kwan Yin. How does she get away with this bullshit?" Ulysses shouts and throws *The Village Voice* at Ben.

"What do you care, you're not Chinese, brother," Ben smirks. "You are an American of Chinese descent."

"She's faking it all, man, and you're not!" Ulysses' voice is getting louder.

"How like a Chinaman to defend the awful culture of our cruel fathers," Ben says.

"She says her father took the imperial exams and became a scholar official."

"Yeah, so? You're saying she's faking that?"

"The imperial exams ended in 1905."

"Aww, come on, you're making that up!" Ben says.

"No, we learned that in Chinese school, Ben," I say. "Remember the revolution, Dr. Sun Yat-sen, Borodin, Chiang Kai Shek, the overthrow of the Manchus?"

"So her father's a hundred years old, so what?" Ben laughs. "And who says *I'm* not faking it? Fu Manchu is not authentically Chinese either."

"I wasn't faking it. I'm not faking it," Ulysses says.

"It was a fake play to begin with. I'm faking it. But she does it better, doesn't she?" Ben grins. "You're just jealous because you can't write that well."

Ulysses doesn't argue back. He says he is quitting, and they have a little argument about that. Ben calls the director and the director calls the producer and Ulysses talks to them both and the producer announces that Ulysses has given his two weeks' notice.

Lucinda never says so, but I know she is happy I take the lead in the play. "The worst thing people can say is you're playing yourself, but you shouldn't mind because you like yourself," Lucinda says when I ask her what she thinks. She says she loves the play because it is both about me and not about me. A hippie. What can I say. I blow her mind, she says.

Ben asks me if I think Ulysses is hurt. "No," I say. "Nothing hurts Ulysses."

So I stay drunk and stoned and do it in a happy fog. The cast rehearses with me in the daytime and Ulysses teaches me three things to play on the guitar by rote. I get it down note for note, line for line, word for word, cue for cue. It is kind of like kung fu or judo.

It's like sets. I memorize. I recite. I trip on the reciting and get into it.

Diego Chang: The Stratagem of Beautiful Women

This is New York. Pretend. Play. This is not for keeps. These women making slurping sounds around Ulysses aren't throwing themselves at him because they think he's a *chump*. Fuck like a star while you can, man, before you turn into just another horny Chink, I always say.

Ulysses offers to fly his folks out to New York and put them up for a couple of nights at the Americana Hotel so they can come to his last night on stage, but his father will be up in Oakland for a tong dinner that night and wants his mother along to give him face. And she won't come to New York without the original Hollywood Kwan.

Ben's mother phones us around six in the morning at the apartment after we get home from the cast party for Ulysses. Ulysses hangs up the phone and looks up at us. "Charlie Chan's Number Four Son was behind the wheel of the new Chevrolet I bought for my mother. On the way to his tong banquet in Oakland, a drunk ran a stop sign, crashed into the passenger side of the Chevrolet, and killed Ma," Ulysses says.

I'm not enjoying New York that much now. And the play keeps on going and going for almost a year.

Diego Chang: Asian American Studies

Lucinda lives with me in San Francisco and gets a job and keeps happy around me. The play in New York turns Ben into Mr. Asian American Studies. He asks me to tag along as a counselor in the program, help lure Chinatown gang kids into Asian American Studies. Soon Asian American Studies is where gang kids come to fence their boosted electronics and auto parts, to begin their higher education, to get into business courses and start on their way to become the managers and bankers and brokers of the banks, savings-and-loans, and holding companies owned by the tongs and tong alliances.

Old Chinatown bakeries and stores are going down and banks and savings-and-loans are going up on tong land. For the young Chinatown, proud with Detroit iron and nowhere to go but around the block in a Chinatown war to shoot 'em up or deal Chinese fantan in a floating tong game, Asian American Studies is a big step up on the way to a new set of choice Brooks Brothers, Hickey Freemans, and Toy Kong tailor-mades.

Hawaii, the Maui madness in Paradise, the near yearlong New York party, was never anywhere near real life. It was all once-in-a-lifetime fun. It was all out-of-town bandits on the run and Lucinda was my amazing luck, a gorgeous slut of my dreams fooled by my out-of-town bullshit. As long as I was out-of-town, I was bullshit, and it was okay. I brought her home and she took care of herself and said she was happiest loving me and making me happy. Every year, Easter through the summer we scoured the land for country and folk music festivals in the South, and loaded up on bluegrass, fiddle, and old timey music, in Carlsbad Caverns, or the Grand Canyon, the Petrified Forest, some natural American wonder like that, and all the time she was too good to be true. It began to bother me. Every day she loved me felt as if I was telling another lie. I was not the heroic rescuer. I was not a star. I would never be any of that. New York acting was not acting for me. New York was pals, not stardom. I wasn't about to get myself posed and snapped and portfolioed and go out for readings and auditions to get myself liked and bought. I didn't want to be too well liked. She didn't mind. Ben and Ulysses were the stars. I was the entourage, the family drunk.

Ulysses tries his theater workshop, gets it going with the help of people who read the New York reviews and take Ben seriously as a writer and Ulysses seriously as an actor. Then PBS comes along with the *Great Performances* series, taking Ben and *Fu Manchu Plays Flamenco* very seriously. Ben and Pandora want Ulysses to play the guitar and act Fu Manchu on TV. He can't do it, he says. His theater. They understand. No more need be said. No pressure. No argument. He doesn't want to go to New York again with me and Lucinda, even to hang out and party, he doesn't want to go. No thanks.

We are in New York for a month, casting, rehearsing, shooting, and editing the play over the summer. *Fu Manchu Plays Flamenco* airs the next April while it's also running at Ulysses' dinky theater in the New Chinatown growing in the Richmond district. Again, they want me to play Fu Manchu.

When the play opens in Ulysses' theater, it gets snotty reviews from the San Francisco papers. They like their Chinese in the image of Charlie Chan, and say Ulysses is trying to create an unrealistic macho-butch image of the Chinese man, accuse me of playing Fu Manchu as an angry black man. They quote Pandora Toy's book to put us down: "Chinese men do not get angry." They do not quote her saying "Blacks learned anger doesn't work." When the PBS TV version comes out a couple weeks later, the San Francisco papers suddenly know Ulysses is Charlie Chan's Number Four Son's son, run pictures of his father saying "Gee, Pop!" and quote Longman Kwan saying his son Ulysses has it all wrong. Chinese want to play Charlie Chan, not Fu Manchu, and Ulysses being serious about any kind of Asian-American theater is a big joke.

Ulysses: July 4, 1973

My niece, Imogene, the divorced single mother of two, takes the day off from working outcalls at the Odyssey Executive Massage. She looks a lot like me. They say I look like Ma. Some of Ma's old childhood friends still recognize me as her son. But Imogene looks more like me than Ma. It is strange when she comes by with her boys, asking my advice on having her breasts enlarged. Though she is my niece, she feels closer to me in age than to Longman. I can't tell her to stuff or not stuff her tits. To convince me it's okay to mutilate herself for larger tips, she assures me that she gives only straight licensed massage, no locals, no unwritten extras. The Odyssey Executive Massage she works for is straight, she says. She assures me there's no self-contempt in facing the fact of life—that bigger tits get bigger tips in the world of massage for men. It is not mutilation. It won't hurt.

"Nobody dies from breast enlargement, Uncle Ulysses!" she flutters, "It will leave only a little scar under each armpit."

Oh, okay, and I find myself driving some backway I last drove a long time ago. Perhaps riding back, the way you and Pa drove me away from Auntie Bea and Uncle Jackie. The big dog named Guess and the rooster we raised from a crippled chick and ate the night it pecked me. I drive that way again, feel my way. I can show them where all the wooden buildings of my happiest days used to stand, as I pick the old main roads of memory though the new streets of cinder block and stucco buildings, trailer parks, and vacuum-formed plastic signs lit from the inside, searching for the remains, the foundations, the physical evidence of my first world.

Imogene talks, fascinated, all the way through Placerville. "Uncle Ulysses! I never knew! Isn't this a treat, boys? Remember, today is the day Uncle Ulysses exposed himself."

I park the car by the Irish Gypsy Mercedez' recently stuccoed house. She's long dead now. I wonder if anyone lives here, year-round, the way she used to. A big chunk of the big oak tree's cloud of little twigs and fingertips have been cut away to lay electric wires into her house and clear a space over the house for a TV antenna. The big oak tree is bigger now. The blackberry bushes go from the edge of the house all the way to the where I can't see the creek. The mounds of shale tailings are hidden in the thorny, matted bushes. Imogene and the boys climb out of the car, and I lead them down a path to Auntie Bea and Uncle Jackie's house that I remember as longer, darker, deeper, with spotted shadows.

It is a tarpaper shanty. I don't remember tarpaper shanties. I remember houses. Two-room houses. Everyone cooks, sits, sews, plays cards, eats, drinks, talks, whittles, sharpens and oils tools, listens to the radio, some roll cigarettes and smoke in one room, while some sleep in the other. I don't expect the happiest days, the richest memories, the best stories of my childhood are inside a tarpaper shanty, but I recognize it as the real thing. It's so small. I can't stop saying, "It's a tarpaper batten-and-board shanty house. A tarpaper shanty," and the twin boys and Imogene stare.

"I think it's cute," Imogene says. The Peterbilt tractor, parked where the yard lined with white stones used to be, dwarfs the house and little covered porch where I made my stand with a toy machine gun against curiously munching cows. Where I stood when they called me over to have some watermelon and see the king snake (that was as long as I am now tall) swallowing a rattlesnake, there's a rusting engine block now. Behind the house where there used to be a path to what used to be the new outhouse, I find the scattered remains of the cast-iron coal stove Auntie Bea cooked on. The front of the oven door with a little porcelain trim on the handle is by the toe of my boot when I look down. I pick it up.

"Excuse me, do you have business here?" says a big man without a shirt, as tall as the doorway, stepping out into the hot light. He wears biker's tattoos all over his chest and arms. A .22 automatic pistol dangles in his right hand.

I smile, all my gestures are slow and sweeping and open handed. "I was raised in this house during the war," I say. "World War II. I was out for a drive with my niece and her kids, and I just got the feeling that I was near this place, and I found New Penelope Mine

Road, and here I am. I used to eat food cooked on the stove this comes from," I say, and hold up the little oven door. And I nod toward the remains of the coal stove partly covered by years of grass roots and ground erosion.

He doesn't raise his gun. I keep on talking. "The Conroys built this place. There used to be a creek over where it's all blackberry bushes now."

"Yeah, there's a creek over there."

"I'd like to keep this piece of the stove, if you don't need it for anything."

"Hey, take it!" the biker says. "You and your family like to come in out of the sun for some lemonade?"

"No, thanks, man. I told them I'd take them back to Placerville to the Blue Bell Café for some oysters Hangtown-fry."

At Aunt Mercedez' house, a large fat man wearing a greasy baseball hat on his head, rimless glasses over his eyes, and galluses to hold his pants up is walking around the car looking inside the windows and windshield.

"Hi," I say, all smiles.

He asks us what the hell we're doing around here.

"I used to live here," I say.

"Oh, yeah?" He looks skeptical.

"Old woman with orange hair I called Aunt Mercedez used to live here, raising a little Mexican girl my age back during the war. Little girl, name of Mary Susan. And Aunt Mercedez used to tell people's fortunes with the cards. And she'd make you a cup of tea and read the tea leaves at the bottom of the cup after you took a couple of sips," I say with a smile on my face, my hands harmless in my pockets, and my eye on the big fat man in galluses. He nods slowly, drops his gaze briefly to the ground. He isn't looking for trouble.

"I see she finally got that road paved, and a little bridge over the creek so you don't have to chuck rocks into it after every rain to make a crossing," I say.

The fat man's eyes are a little gummy behind his glasses. He knew Mercedez. He may have heard of me. Mary Susan lives here now. She's visiting friends in Oakland right now, and he saw my car. Mercedez' daughter died a couple years ago. And Mercedez' son-in-law fixed the place up for Mary Susan and was last seen loose and looking for another woman.

"I lived in the house down the short path, with the Conroys. Up that road over there lived a guy named York, who had rigged his little house with electric lights from an automobile battery."

The fat man is convinced, and looks at me the way people look at me when I am four years old, telling people I am an American of Chinese descent and not a Jap kid. Yes. He seems to have heard stories about me and the Conroys.

I wonder where they're buried. His wife would know. She's from around here. He's only been here the last twenty years. He's lived and worked in the city, but he was overwhelmed with a need to live in the same kind of lone house off a country dirt road that he lived in as a boy.

We drive up the road to his place. The house is surrounded with big white boxes, soft-drink coolers, box freezers, refrigerators, stoves, all dead, gutted, rusted. All the refrigerators and air conditioners of the Gold Country come here to die. An air conditioner blasts away in every window. The house sounds like an old fleet of biplanes in *The Dawn Patrol*. The old man brings an old bony woman out of the house who says, "You must be Ulysses the Chinese boy they found in the same foundling home as Mary Susan."

"Yes," I say.

So Imogene and her twin boys are there in the Gold Country with me when I first hear I am born in a foundling home. And Ma's not here to answer a few questions from Charlie Chan's Number Four Son's bastard son.

"They used to call you their little Chinese dolly," the old woman says.

Diego Chang: "Planet of the Apes"

Ulysses tries to get his theater workshop thing together in San Francisco. He does Ben's *Fu Manchu Plays Flamenco,* his way. I do the lead again. But, I'm sorry, it isn't my fault the Chinatown activists and assholes won't come to Ulysses' theater. San Francisco audiences—Chinese, Japanese, and whites who know Charlie Chan's grandson runs this theater and is directing this play—don't see anything funny about *Fu Manchu Plays Flamenco.*

Meanwhile yellows join his theater because he is the son of Charlie Chan's Number Four Son. "They take me for a Priest of High White Supremacy of the Church of Our Lady of Charlie Chan," Ulysses spits.

"If I become as famous as Keye Luke and Longman Kwan, I'll be happy, I'll be satisfied," his actors say, pissing Ulysses off. And the women all want to be famous for suffering and despising other Chinese, like Pandora Toy. Their idea of Asian-American theater is a production of *Jesus Christ Superstar* with all Asian-American cast. *Ahmal and the Night Visitor,* with an all Asian-American cast. *Hair,* with an Asian American cast. They don't want to do *Flower Drum Song,* because they don't want to be typecast as Asians.

Ben and I fade after the first play. I don't like rehearsing and I hate the people that want to be actors. Ben says Ulysses is burning himself out trying to prove something about Asians that isn't true. Why doesn't he learn from Pandora and just make money?

But Ulysses wants Asian-American actors to commit to creating an Asian American Theater, and keeps spouting off, like Capt. Kirk talking about "humanity" on Star Trek, as he expounds on the adventure of inventing Asian-American theater as W.B. Yeats, G.B. Shaw and Lady Gregory, James Joyce and Sean O'Casey had put together the Abbey Playhouse in Dublin and created Irish Theater where before there had been only the British stereotype of Irish as the niggers of British Isles. No one knows what he is talking about, and no one cares.

Friday night is boys' night at my house. Play the guitar. Get stupid. Talk shit. Ben comes over from his place in Marin sometimes. He puts his little girl down for the night in an upstairs bedroom. When Ulysses carries on about how fucked up his theater group is, Ben takes it as personal criticism.

"Fame and money are the only truths American yellows respect. They don't want to act. They want to be stars. They don't want to write. They want to be stars. They don't want Asian-American plays. They want stardom. No swearing in front of whites. No criticism of white racism. No railroad stories or Japanese-American concentration camp stories that do not confirm the stereotype and reassure whites. Yellows are a pathological victim people. They don't want Asian-American theater. They want the secret of the stereotype. The want to learn to be the Keye Luke, Benson Fong, Victor Sen Yung, Longman Kwan, Anna May Wong, Nancy Kwan of their generation. This isn't a theater," Ulysses says, "This is a meat market."

I tell Ulysses I feel the same way watching *Planet of the Apes* with my mother. She has lived here most of her life and had never been to a downtown first-run American movie. So I take her to see *Planet of the Apes* at a Market Street movie palace, the one with Art Deco all over it and some Art Deco pre-Columbian Egyptoid Popsicle people in universal profile, marching all over the walls to the lintels of plaster columns, wearing loincloths, feathers, and animal parts. Others with wings and arms fly in profile across the ceiling in some kind of religious ceremony or college pep rally. They all come together in the outstretched arms of a winged full-front Popsicle cheerleader wearing the head of a bird, a necklace, a loincloth, and nothing else. There must be at least a thousand seats and maybe six people in this theater. "What kind of place is this?" Ma asks me. She laughs and talks all the way through *Planet of the Apes.* I want to laugh myself. Ma makes the movie very funny to watch.

Luckily my new phone tweets, and Ulysses gets off the subject of his Asian-American theater and says, "Why don't you get a phone that rings, man, instead of sounding like a three-year-old boy pissing against the window?"

We laugh while I get up and answer the phone. The conversation is in Chinese and is serious, souring my stomach and sobering me up.

"The Horse is in Highland Hospital in Oakland," I say. "That was a man from the Mah Family Association. They tracked me down, looking for you, Ulysses. The Horse is dying and asking for you, Ulysses."

"The Horse?"

"The old Chinese teacher?" Ben asks.

"The guy said you'd better go see the Horse tonight, man. He's not going to make it."

"Tonight?" Ulysses asks.

"Fuck it," I say. "It'll be midnight by the time you get there, and you're stoned. Fuck it. He's a chump."

"I'll be glad to drive you," Ben says.

"That's okay," Ulysses says, "I can drive. You say he asked for me. So only I have to go. I might as well. I have nothing else to do till midnight."

"No, I will drive. My car is more likely to get us to and from Oakland in one piece, and in comfort. It has a working heater/defroster," I say.

"Sure, we'll all go," Ulysses says, "Chinese school's back in session, boys. The Horse is calling class to order."

Highland Hospital at midnight looks like Dracula's castle in the fog, rising from the woods. It's a castle, with battlements and turrets, everything but a moat. The Oakland streets form the moat. The grounds and woods and gardens around the castle are an artificial island, rising voluptuously from a straight wide Oakland street like the wobbles of a fat woman posing on a rug for Rubens with a castle on her hip. We walk a long, slowly rising staircase up the island through the soft humped lawns, the little strange woods, through a section of the castle with gates on either end and slots for weapons on either side, into an eight-sided lobby with high ceilings and fake medieval architecture. By the stairs is something that looks like a brass teller's cage from a more modern period, an old bank of the Roaring Twenties. Inside the cage an old switchboard with rows of switches looking like small lollipops in slots with sticks sticking up as fat as pencils, and rows of big old phone jacks, like silver crayons standing on end. On the face of the upright cabinet is an old patchboard. Rows of holes with phono jacks stick in some of them, and out of the ends of the phone jacks thick rubbery snakes dangle. A fat woman the color and texture of styrofoam sits in the cage. "I hear my Chinese teacher is here, dying, and I should see him tonight," Ulysses says.

"Are you a member of the family?" the receptionist asks.

"Yes, he's my uncle," Ulysses says.

"What's your uncle's name?" the receptionist asks.

"Mah. Emm Ay Are. Or, Em Ay Aitch." Ulysses says. He turns to me across the lobby and asks, "Mah what? What's the rest of his name?"

I blank. He sees it in my eyes. I am along for the company, not to work.

The receptionist finds no Mar, no Mah. Ulysses asks her to look for "Horse," then to look under the *C*s, the *L*s, and *W*s. She says she can't do that. She isn't allowed. Okay. "If the patient is your uncle you should know his name, sir," the receptionist says.

"Yes, I should," Ulysses agrees. I have never thought of the Horse's name before. None of us has ever asked. Our Chinese teachers never had names. Only nicknames. Each was a phase of our childhood. Each was a chapter in the book of our childhood friendship. "The Emperor Wong." "The Horse." I refuse to phone the Mah Family Association man and get a name, saying, "His Chinese name wouldn't be the same as his American name anyway, if you can't find it under Mah or Mar."

"You're right," Ulysses says. Ben might protest, but still, I personally feel stupid, and am a little sad that Ulysses isn't yelling at us. He leans against the marble countertop with both arms and says, "Okay, I got a name for you. Look under Chan."

The receptionist starts thumbing the index file. "First name?"

"Charlie. Charlie Chan," Ulysses says.

And there he is.

"He registered himself in the hospital as Charlie Chan," Ulysses explains, and points out Ben and me and says, "These are my brothers."

"That's okay," Ben says quickly, "You go on up, brother. We'll wait down here."

Ulysses glares at him and says, "If this is all a large practical joke you and Diego plotted together, I will be very pissed."

"Delusions of grandeur are often accompanied by delusions of persecution," Ben says.

Then Ulysses climbs out of sight. "He climbed out of sight up the stone stairs of a castle built from the confectionery imagination of a WPA Maxfield Parrish in the '30s—to his fate, or his punchline. Hamlet, to the tower to meet his father's ghost or the Fun House," Ben says.

Then Ulysses unexpectedly walks out of a hallway while we're watching the shadows where we've last seen him. Are Ulysses and Ben setting *me* up for a joke? If I were setting them up, I wouldn't go this far with them watching my every move. The joke still might be on me, I think on an intake of breath.

Ulysses says, "He was all tubed and wired up to bottles and machines. He looked awful, what I could see of him in the plastic tent. He looked dead already. What could I say? I couldn't tell if he could see or hear me, so I said, 'Hi, Uncle Charlie.' It didn't sound right, man. It didn't even sound funny. *'Ah-Mah Sin Sang,'* I called him. I didn't even know what he was sick with. I asked him, *'Nay ying duck ngaw muh?* Do you recognize me? How come you're using the name Charlie Chan? That's not your name,' I said. And the Horse's right hand, man, I swear, pinched my sleeve and tugged. And he droped this in my hand. A wadded up piece of paper about the size of a walnut," he says, opening his hand to a vaguely cone-shaped lump of clay with Kwan Kung painted on it. Green for his robe and hat. Red for his face and hands. Little stripes of blue and red painted along the hem of his skirt and across his boots.

"I look down in my hand and I unwrap this little kid's Kwan Kung. Just then this nurse walks in and starts unplugging him. I ask what's going on. She says 'Excuse me,' and that's it. She covers his face and leaves the room. The Horse is dead." He nods at us instead of saying more. We all look down at the floor.

"Diego, take a look at this and tell me what it says." Ulysses hands me the paper that had wrapped Kwan Kung. "Does this Chinese read Shurn Gee, grandson, in Chinese?"

"It's Shurn Gee in Cantonese. Sun Tzu in Mandarin. Maybe he's saying you're the grandson of Charlie Chan," I say.

"Shurn Gee, the Grandson, was the pseudonym of the famous Chinese strategist," Ulysses says.

"The what?" I ask.

"The *nom de guerre,*" Ulysses says.

"That I understand, asshole!" I say. "They liked that *nom de guerre* stuff in the Air Force. Everybody had one."

We all follow Ulysses back across the bay to my house the way we came. The *jook* is ready by the time we get back. It's good, hot, sweet and creamy. As late as it is, we play a little guitar and stay up a little longer. It is the least we can do on the occasion of the Horse's death, even though no one says anything about it. We just stay up a littler longer.

After three years, everyone in his theater group blames Ulysses for holding them back from stardom. "Fame is not a civil right," Ulysses says, and splits. They think he is bluffing. Ulysses will try to talk you out of shit, but he does not bluff. The theater calls his bluff and he splits. I see some of the actors from his theater doing parts on TV and some movies, becoming the Keye Luke, Benson Fong, Victor Sen Yung, Longman Kwan, Anna May Wong, Nancy Kwan of their generation before I hear from Ulysses again.

Benedict Mo: Switch the Guest and the Host at the Table

Ten months of performances later, and *Fu Manchu Plays Flamenco Guitar* was a memory in New York. The marriage became easier after Pandora became the most famous and beloved Chinese American ever for her first book, *The Neurotic Exotic Erotic Orientoxic.* I kept my promise not to write another play, and instead began a contemplative expressionistic Christian confession wherein I wondered if I had lost myself, along with my real father, in my amnesia and hatred of China. The piece was a muddle, and I enjoyed wallowing in it a couple of hours a day. Pandora took it and turned it into her memoir of a girlhood in Sacramento, *Conqueror Woman.* Mom would see through the disguise and know Pandora's book was about me, Mom, and her opera-man lover. In the book, Mom and the opera man were so vile that they murdered my father. Except the "I" in Pandora's book was Pandora, not me. The opera star was Pandora's father, the opera star who got involved with a young opera starlet. Together, they murder Pandora's Christian mother. The story of my life worked better with a female protagonist and a male villain. The reviewers all agreed. Pandora's father could not have gotten away with murder anywhere else but in male-dominated, misogynist China.

They couldn't say enough about her courage and rising above suffering and the centuries' old horrors of being a woman in traditional China. When someone corrected her and said the ban on Chinese women entering the country was not because Chinese men wanted free rein to chase and marry white women but was a result of the Chinese Exclusion Act of 1882, Pandora shot back that Chinese men drafted the Exclusion Act and "The Gentlemen's Agreement." Newspaper book editors and reviewers didn't know what to do with history and facts—sounded too much like work, and work was boring, as opposed to autobiography, where all they had to do was take Pandora's word for what was what.

When Pandora went out to be feted and courted by the famous and those who wanted to make her more famous—publishers, producers, interviewers—she always left doggie bags and little white boxes of leftovers in the fridge for me. French, California cuisine, nouvelle this and that, Chinese, Thai, Japanese. I saw what she ate but rarely saw her.

One night after a difficult time putting little Martha to bed and tucking her in, I went to the kitchen and opened up the fridge to make myself a little supper and saw nothing but white boxes, pyramids of white boxes and white cartons and white bags from restaurants all over the Bay Area, with bits of this and pats of that from all over the world. I realized I was sick of leftovers. I had a tantrum like Orson Welles in *Citizen Kane*. I grabbed bunches of boxes off the shelves and threw them at the stove, at the double sinks, at the breakfast nook. Food dropped out of my hands as I pulled the boxes out. I couldn't pull them out fast enough or throw this tantrum with sincerity and conviction. I stepped in the mess, stomped in it, kicked it over the floor, and could not lose control. I could weep. I could shout but not too loud. I didn't want to wake Martha. I'd worked too hard to get her down for the night. I could hit things but couldn't hurt anything or hurt myself. I couldn't break windows or glass. It was a chickenshit, bullshit, horseshit tantrum. I was a bullshit playwright. A bullshit Hamlet. A chickenshit chair of Asian American Studies. I'd have to race to clean the mess up before Pandora got home with more little white boxes.

Pandora was not home for long stretches of time, weeks on end, touring, guest teaching, giving readings. Of course I could not travel with her. A Chinese man in her company, even her husband, would blow her image as a new, free, and free-thinking Chinese woman. I understood. And, of course, she did not use her married name. Out of the house and away. The arguments ended. Ended.

And that's the way our lives continued for the next fifteen years. She never met the man who took Martha's virginity. She didn't have the time. It was halfway through Martha's second semester at Iowa City. She phoned. She had a job in one of Iowa City's two Chinese restaurants, waiting tables and growing bean sprouts in the basement. She was in love with life, in love with nature, in love with an older man and living with him, but knew we wouldn't approve. She flooded words out without noticeably breathing, but this soft pathetic accusation that Pandora and I were prudes . . . it was too much. I laughed.

"Baby, believe it or not, I was a kind of hippie when I was your age. Your Uncle Diego was a super hippie. The first house he bought was a commune in Berkeley. And your mom lived with her first husband for years before they had a wedding ceremony. And even your mom and me, within a few hours after meeting, did our thing in the huge bedroom of a New York apartment while your uncles Diego and Ulysses played flamenco, and I think held orgies in the front room while we were rehearsing and performing *Fu Manchu Plays Flamenco.*"

"Okay, Dad, um hmmm, you were a hippie. That's what I need to hear right now."

"Listen, baby. If you're happy living with a man outside of marriage: sounds good to me. If you get unhappy and can't get out of it, or he beats you up, Uncle Diego will kill him. No problem."

"What about Mom?"

"Your mom is very happy for you."

"I don't want to strain your morality, you two, so Rudy and I are going to get married."

"Oh? When?" I asked, gulping down my surprise, and speaking slower and easier than my wildly sputtering heart, and she was suddenly waffling, wishy-washy, fumbling for words, which was not like her. This had to be a call for help. I said I would come to Iowa City and help them make the arrangements for the wedding. As the father of the bride I was footing the bill, so I had the right to be in on the plans. And while I was there I could do the parental thing and fill their fridge and cupboards. Shouldn't I be interested in the man she was in love with, living with, going to marry? She could write me about him. I didn't want to pry. Whatever she wanted to tell me I would listen to. How soon was I thinking of coming to Iowa City? How soon would she like me? I asked. No sooner than Easter Break, I said.

"And once there, I can stay an extra week before or after. I'll get Diego to cover my classes for a week. They'll love him. These kids need a shot of worst-case reality after a week off for Easter."

Rudy, the son of a Chinese father and Nisei mother, was short—no taller than me, and I was short. He had a round head. His eyes turned down his cheeks, giving him a look of perpetual, inexplicable sadness. He stood at an ironing board with a hot iron and boxes of Christmas cards warped and curly from having been wet. One by one he ironed the Christmas cards and stacked them up on the end of the ironing board. An unusually robust robin flew about the apartment and both Rudy and the robin seemed comfortable with the robin perching on the top of his head. The robin had claws for digging worms up out of the dirt, I supposed, and the robin hanging onto Rudy's scalp with its claws looked like it hurt.

"Yeah, it hurts," he said.

"Oh," I said. I watched him iron another Christmas card. They weren't extraordinary Christmas cards. I watched him iron a couple more with the robin on his head.

"Can I ask what it is you're doing there, Rudy?" I asked.

"I'm ironing our Christmas cards."

"Why?"

"They got wet in the bathroom and ripply, you see? And we couldn't send them out last Christmas. And I saw they're really still perfectly good, you know. So I thought I'd iron them up and send them out next Christmas, and now would be a good time to do it, okay?"

"Oh, yes," I said.

He was Vietnam-era vet, though he never got any closer to the war than Saigon, where he was run over by an army garbage truck his first day there. The garbage truck was big and beetle-shaped, with the front hooks that picked up dumpsters the size of small houses, swung them over the cab and dumped them, then put them down again, whirring and cranking and thumping all the time. A big garbage truck ran over his head. His head did not pop and squirt like a stomped grape, but it did change shape, and he spoke a little slower than before. More natural than before. He was in the Master of Fine Arts program in the Art Department, and Martha told him I knew how to draw.

"Your Uncle Ulysses is the one who knows how to draw, baby," I said. "He used to hang his ink drawings at the Mother 'i' when he was still in high school." I wasn't about to let Martha lock me into some kind of Oedipal drawing contest with Rudy for the right to marry her.

"People in the Art Department ridiculed me, they told me to learn how to draw people with their teeth clenched," Rudy grumbled as if in a trance. "Or they ask me in this fake baby talk if I know how to draw. I wonder what I just said means? There is a difference, I suppose," Rudy mumbled, and slurred a little like a punchdrunk boxer.

". . . a difference?" I asked with genuine curiosity and confusion. "I beg your pardon, I must have missed something." His eyes told me he was burning too low to run a sense of humor. I stashed the corny Iowa jokes about expecting a view of cornfields, windmills, and wallowing pigs from their downtown windows.

"But it all meant the same thing, huh. They're all telling me I'm not a real artist if I don't know how to draw. The department's making me take this drawing class or they're going to hold up my MFA. And if I don't get my MFA, I lose my job teaching art at University High. The drawing class is for pigs. Draw a hand. Draw a foot. I don't like drawing. I don't mind being told I'm wrong because I like the wonder of the question instead of any direction toward an answer, you know. Drawing defines things. Things can be too defined and limiting. You define one thing and it leads you toward wanting more definitions of things. That's boring. I think suggestion is better than definition. That's what I think is very Buddhist about me, you know. I like formlessness."

"But to suggest well, you have to know what it is you're suggesting before you can suggest it with any telling effect, don't you think?" I said with genuine concern and a little panic.

"Yeah," he said. "The search. I was just talking about that with somebody. It's kind of interesting, you know? What's going to become of my life? Maybe it's kind of interesting, you know? Maybe it's just, you know, human nature that you just don't know. So that's why I don't look for anything. I just like looking. I'm not looking for any direction toward anything. Any place. Any meaning. Maybe I'll miss something important if I get that direction. Don't you think that direction makes you narrow sometimes?"

"If you don't know what it is you're looking at, and you can't relate it to anything other than yourself, how can you tell it's important?" I asked. "Things, occurrences, people, places are not important as themselves. They're important because of their relationship to something else, other things, a coincidence of things."

"A baby. Like, you know, important to an innocent baby. Things are important to babies too."

I could not believe my ears. This had to be Martha's first and brilliantly executed practical joke. This could not be the man she fell in love with, not the man who deflowered her. I was glad Pandora wasn't with me. In her own way, she sounded like this Rudy. She'd take to this young man. But at twenty-seven he was older than I was ready to accept. Martha was a gangly smartass mere eighteen. "You're an artist, man," I said. "You take risks about importance, or you're supposed to."

"There are great, famous artists who didn't know how to draw," Rudy said.

"I'm sure you're right, but right now my memory fails me," I said.

"Keep your disillusionments to yourself, and I'll keep mine to myself, and we'll get along fine, okay?" he said.

"The word is delusion," I said, and asked the way to the bathroom. I went expecting nothing confounding or especially memorable. It was an old overheated building. The tub was old, large, and heavy. It had a juryrigged shower with a curtain that had to be hung all the way around the tub to keep water off the tile floor. No sooner did I sit on the pot and commence my posterior monologue into the porcelain bowl of water, than I saw no one could shower or bathe in there anymore because Rudy had filled the bottom of the tub with dirt and earthworms and grass to make his pet robin feel at home. And when I returned, Martha encouraged Rudy to tell the story of his Robin. No problem. Nothing bothered Rudy. He was mellow. He was natural.

He had found the robin as a featherless, bald, bony little baby in a broken egg under a tree as he was walking home. He had thought of putting the little bird back in its nest. He had actually tried, but the little bird was so little and looked so cold and seemed so cozy in his big warm hand, he had carried it home to talk over the next step with Martha. Then the bird had made this horrible little hissing sound. How do you feed a baby bird? You chew up worms and bugs and spit into the baby bird's mouth, Martha told him, and he was giving it serious consideration, she saw, when she suggested buying an ear syringe and filling it with mashed worms and milk to stuff the little bird's mouth. Yeah, he liked the idea.

Martha loved him because he pondered the profundity of the simplest things and made them glow with Zen poetry. Pandora would love this. Our daughter and Zen poetry. I wanted to puke. He mashed the worms with condensed milk, squeezed the bulb, and let it go to suck the stuff up the rubber beak, stuck it in the baby bird's squawk, and squeezed a little in. The robin was fat, flying, and friendly now, and would not leave the apartment.

Martha used my agreeable presence to persuade Rudy that the robin was a wild bird and belonged in the wild, and it was time to set the bird free. It flew from room to room, from person to person, dropping dust, tiny insects, odiferous gusts of the robin's feathers, smelling like dirty laundry and sweat, and everywhere it puckered its asshole and dropped wet birdshit, perched on a shoulder or one of our heads or in flight. I never knew robins shat so often. The whole apartment smelled of wet robinshit. It flew over and shit on the turkey I was stuffing for dinner.

Perhaps Rudy's worms were giving the robin diarrhea, I suggested, a prelude to suggesting we go out for dinner. Martha laughed, but Rudy seemed to be out of his body—his face didn't change at the sound of our laughter. I offered to open a window, throw the bird out, and slam the window shut.

"That would be cruel, wouldn't it? It's not the robin's fault this apartment is all the world and sky—it wants to fly," he objected.

I could see Martha was impressed by the profundity of what he had just said, and I realized I had no more ear for the Zen of Zen poetry than I did in the '60s. It sounded stupid and pretentious then, and it sounded stupid and pretentious now. I dumped the turkey fouled with robinshit into the garbage along with the wonderful fruit dressing I had been making.

I think that even for Martha, the robin had become an annoyance, that the charm was over. The robin smelled like a wet dustmop. The ripe gasses off its wet and hardening droppings all over the floor, furniture, and books reactivated my old childhood asthma. I slept in the front room on the motel furniture couch by the window, with the window cracked open to the cold and the snow, hoping it might blow away some of the birdcage atmosphere Rudy had created. If the robin flew out of the open window, all the better. My apologies the next morning would be profuse, sincere, recurrent, generous.

But the bird liked the bathroom, it kept to its perpetual spring in the bathtub. To get to the bathroom I had to pass through their bedroom. I wasn't ready to knock on their door while they were balling, but I had to take a leak. I wasn't ready to see Martha in bed with Rudy. I wasn't ready to have the robin splat on my head with joy while I was standing at my business, trying not to splatter on the floor.

To walk around this house I had to wear shoes or step on little wet and partially set robin splats. If I were going to go to the trouble of putting on my shoes to take a leak, I might as well get dressed and go piss in the alley, where the statistical chances favored me not getting birdshit on my head, hit up by a panhandler, rousted by the cops, or hit by a car. But why mark up the night with my footprints and melt a hole in the white marshmallow snow?

I hadn't been in a college town frosted with snow in years. I got more pleasure watching the snow change on the ground, in the street, on the sills and tops of two- and three-story buildings, than doing anything to change the snow myself. I slept with my feet by the old steam register and my head away from the noise it made. I heard the cars driving by with chains on their tires, chattering on the wet pavement, chewing on the snow, and eventually giving way to a cold, icy, gemlike silence. No breeze through the treetops. No solitary barking dog. No watery undulation in the air. Outside the building was the silence of waiting snipers. I heard the gurgle and growl of the snowplows, shaving the streets with dull razors, and the trucks carrying the sandman spreading sand on the streets with shovels.

Rudy woke me before dawn and farted as he mumbled and slurred his rage and mystery. "There's sand in our bed."

I stared at him blankly. My face and head were still asleep. My feet were hot.

"How'd sand get into our bed, Mo?"

"Your feet," I said.

"My feet! Somebody put sand in our bed."

"You did. You put sand in your bed with your feet."

"Yeah, sure. It looks like a goddamned sand pile in there."

"Look," I said and nodded to the street. "They put sand on the street and out on the walks when it snows, right?"

"Yeah?" he said, with a grunting belligerence.

"And you walk on the walks that have sand on them, right?"

"So?" he opened his eyes on me and forgot to close his mouth to breath.

"And the sand gets on the soles of your shoes and you track sand into the house and all over the floor, right?" I asked. "Am I making sense so far?"

"So, how does sand get into our bed, hey?"

"You take off your shoes and socks. You barefoot around the apartment floors and pick up the sand you left from the soles of your shoes. And you take your feet to bed with you. The sand you picked up on the soles of your feet and between your toes comes off."

"Oh, between the toes," he mumbled, and the lids drooped again, the eyes dimmed. "Between the toes," he mumbled to himself.

The college town padded with snow was oddly quiet and refreshing during Easter break. Like most college towns, the food within walking distance of campus was awful, but anything to not have to eat with the robin happily hopping and flying about. At the gourmet hamburger place, Martha pulled out a photocopied page and told me this was why she had first fallen in love with Rudy. I reluctantly pushed aside my little plastic bowl of blade-cut semi-wilted iceberg lettuce, pinched a wad of paper napkins out of the dispenser, and wiped my hands before touching the copy of this significant document. I thought it might be poetry. Martha liked poetry. She had a good ear and grew up with everyone, virtually everyone, talking and writing books, strong opinions, art, race, and politics. I didn't expect the coffee to be any good. It wasn't. I didn't expect my wise, literate, talented daughter to fall in love with the author of a letter to the Treasury Department. "Is this for real, baby?"

"Just read it, Daddy, will you please?"

The letter was typed and began without capital letters. "dear treasury dept. of the United States of America," I read to myself, but moved my lips purposely, in case Martha wanted to sing or chant the words. "I found this check which you sent to me in 1959 amongst things like love letters and pictures of old girl friends and notes from girls I used to go with in high school the other day and I said to myself the reason I didn't cash"—the *c* in *cash* had first been typed a *w*, spelling *wash* not *cash*. His changing *wash* to *cash* by striking over the old *w* several times with the *c* was one of the very few indications that this letter had been written by an intelligent human being—". . . the reason I didn't cash it right away like it says to do on the back, was that you spelled my name wrong, which is not *Ysni*, but *Tani*. But I knew the reason for the misspelling was that in 1959 I didn't write my name too good and you made it worse by on your form asking me to sign my signature instead of writing my name real plain, so like it really came out bad, so I don't blame you for writing *Ysni* right on the check. And then I was scared that if I went to a bank where they would ask to see my driver's license and see that I wasn't Rudolph Ysni that they would think I was trying to con them or pull a fast one on them by forging or something like that, which is why I was scared to cash it."

I took a sip of the coffee that tasted like water boiled in old sweatsocks and brown mud, and doing my best not to offend, asked Martha, "Is this letter for real?"

"Everyone who reads it asks the same thing, Dad. I thought you'd at least be original, see something Asian American about it or something." She sighed dramatically and said, "Yes, it is for real."

"He actually mailed this letter to the Treasury Department?"

"Yes," she said, rolling her eyes and melting into a heap. "He sent it."

"I guess that was the next question everybody asks," I said.

"Yes."

"Can you guess the question I am dying to ask now?"

"Here is a Xerox of the check he found and sent back to the Treasury Deptartment with the letter," she said, handing another sheet of paper across the table.

"Three dollars and nineteen cents?" I asked the Xerox copy, as much as Martha, and read on . . .

"Now I could have changed my name to Ysni which has more ring to it than Tani, more zip and powee, but no, I thought, my mother's feelings would be hurt when she saw me change my name and then again I thought it might be a good thing, as I've been knocking up quite a few girls I used to go with in high school so Ysni is a pretty good name you made up for me, but then I thought about my biographer when I get one someday, which I will because I'm going to be a great artist and philosopher and be great and a great name but they will think it funny that I didn't exist until 1959 and will have a hard time tracking down the sordid details of my childhood as Rudolph Ysni was never a child so I gave the idea of changing my name up and was still scared of being called a forger and I was scared of some T-man coming in to look for the check which like the directions on the back said I should cash quick before the money ran out that I moved and changed my address several times which is why I'm not where you sent this check to me anymore. But I am really Rudolph Tani and you did really send this check to me and I need the money to get an abortion for this chick I knocked up last month before she calls the fuzz and gets me publicized in front of my mother who is a wonderful woman and loves me and just back when I got the check warned me to watch out for being called a forger and looked at me funny as if I had stole this check from Rudolph Ysni, and I looked in every phone book for every city in the country trying to find Rudolph Ysni and see if he got my check for Rudolph Tani but no such name existed but I did find out by looking through the school records for the year 1875 that in the town of Bridalveil, KY (pop 44) at the time that a boy named Rudolph Ysni, the of Hickory Ysni and Sarah May Carter died of scarlet fever at twelve, but upon more checking it couldn't've been him you sent the check to because he doesn't or didn't live where you sent the check to in 1959, in fact, he didn't even have a job, in fact income tax didn't exist then, so I thought I could sign his name and endorse in my real name like he gave me the check but my mother said that would be forging, but I really need the money for this abortion for this chick and she won't take the check because it's so old. You will notice in all these years I have not folded or mutilated it."

"I can see how, if I read this letter as anything other than the literary masterwork of my prospective son-in-law, the Albert Schweitzer of fallen robins, I would find this very amusing. And think it very bold and audacious of him to send this stupid letter to the Treasury Department."

"They sent him a new check and he cashed it, Dad."

"Oh, they did!" I said, "And is that why you fell in love with him? Was it you he got an abortion for for $3.19?"

"That was a joke, Dad."

"What was a joke? You falling in love with him? Or the abortion for three dollars and nineteen cents?"

"Daaaadd!"

"Okay!" I threw my hands up. "I had to ask. That's all. I asked. I give up."

"Oh, Dad, don't be that way."

"What way is that, baby?"

"You don't want me to marry Rudy."

The third or fourth day there, I woke up to blue shadows, blue snow, and remembered things Martha said as a baby, as a kid. "The butterfly clapped the sun with its wings," when she was four. "Sometimes when it's dark blue in the morning, dark blue is a sad color," when she was drifting to sleep in the back of the car one night, when she was five. That my daughter spoke wisely about sadness and was only five years old made me sad. Sadder because I could only wonder why. She was always a happy baby.

Rudy went off to his studio early. Martha took me out for a walk around the campus, this Old Capitol building, a memory of when Iowa City was the state capital, the theater by the river, the river. The river was flowing, but not all the ice had melted. Snow was pocketed and pancaked like a huge Dalí, melting watches all over the broad little hills around the campus. We seemed the only people out in the open in all of Iowa City. It was as if everyone left town for Easter except the Chinese. We stepped into and browsed the occasional open shop, and I bought a coffee mug with the school seal and a visored cap with the Iowa Hawkeye mascot on it. We stopped in the five-and-dime for coffee and hot chocolate before making any decisions about returning to the apartment and the robin. The place was empty. Very Edward Hopper *Nighthawks*, but it was 11:00 A.M. and the sun was shining. Two other people were at the large double-horseshoe-shaped lunch counter, with space for the waitress to work inside the horseshoes. Only one waitress was on duty. The large fat man with very short hair sat alone at the bottom of the far horseshoe. A fortyish woman wearing a hat sat a few stools away from Martha. She called the waitress over and we heard her ask the waitress to call the police because the large fat man was making suggestive faces and offensive expressions her way. The waitress went to the front to call the police.

Martha and I looked over and I saw immediately the fat man wasn't coming on to the woman, he didn't even see her, he was an epileptic or a diabetic winding up to throw a grand mal.

"What's that?" the waitress asked, and the woman glared at me.

"He's about to throw a fit. I suggest you get him a glass of juice with a lot of sugar in it to possibly bring him down and call an ambulance or the paramedics or whatever you have in town to come and get this man," I said, begging pardon for interrupting, and Martha slapped me on the shoulder and said, "Daddy, what would Uncle Ulysses say! Begging pardon for interrupting please?"

Yes, I agreed, I did sound like Charlie Chan in an old movie. It must be the Midwest. I instinctively take cover in the movies Hollywood blames on the tastes of the all-purpose America of the Midwest. By the time the waitress had consulted with the manager and the manager had asked the blinking outward-bound young fat man if he had a problem, and the waitress appeared with the juice, the big man made a few strange moves. I asked for a spoon quickly, please. And they handed me a five-and-dime lunch counter knife. He was lurching off the stool now, and from college ROTC at Berkeley thirty years ago I followed the drill. I jammed the handle of the knife into his mouth, pressed his tongue to the floor of his mouth, wrestled him to the ground, and kept him down as he flipped and swam at nothing. I looked up and saw a short wiry man, barely taller than me, in a white jacket chewing gum and watching me intently. "Are you from the ambulance?" I asked. He nodded.

"I'm the driver."

"Where's your attendant?"

"There's no attendant."

"Get the gurney in here and take him to the hospital."

"You help me get him there, and I'll give you a ride back," the driver said.

Martha and I rode in back with the big man, who was strapped down on the gurney. By the time we arrived at Mercy Hospital a cop was pulling up in his car, following us in. "I wonder who he is?" the cop said.

"Why don't you see if he has a wallet?" I suggested.

He had a wallet. The policeman knew the young man's father. "We should call his father up and let him know about his boy," the cop said.

"Why don't you look him up in the book?" I asked, feeling as if I were in hot conversation with Ulysses and Pandora, talking Ulysses into trusting me with the first volume of his bound journals and notes. They were thirty years old now, the experimental works of the wonderful Ulysses in his teens and early twenties. "I want to show Pandora that even at eighteen you were the best writer we ever had," I said. "Come on, one volume! You have so many! Loaning me one won't hurt. You're a big boy now, don't be a baby."

I enjoyed reading the letters and notes of the unformed Ulysses Kwan. There was a fashion spread featuring a high school girlfriend out of *Teen* magazine pasted in. A deep eyed, Slavic blonde. He wrote about her. There was a letter from his black friend (he still called him a Negro in 1961), Jason Peach, asking if they would remain best friends after this letter. Jason said he was in love with Ulysses' old girlfriend, Sarah, had made her pregnant, and wanted to marry her. There were very Zen brush-and-ink and stick-and-ink sketches of trains and trainyard scenes that surprised me. I remembered from our boyhood in the rooms above the Hotel Westlake Eclipse and the Chinese school where the Horse threw blackboard erasers at Ulysses when the back talk got too much for him. Ulysses' writing had always had a way of bringing back memories, making his prose sound deep and shimmering personally, privately, as if addressed just to me. His writing in this hodgepodge of word games, pretentious philosophizing, and just stuff still had the same effect on me. Then I found the letter from the Berkeley NAACP, asking about Jason Peach. Ulysses must have been in his early twenties. The NAACP asked Ulysses if he could verify Mary

Hudson's memory of sitting in the box office of the Storefront Moviehouse, while the owner told Ulysses he would not give Jason Peach Ulysses' job as doorman and ticket taker because Jason was Negro. The letter from the NAACP was followed by a carbon copy of Ulysses letter of reply. I was shocked. He wrote:

"Miss Mary Hudson was the cashier on duty that night. My exact words were: 'I have a friend that would like the job of doorman after me.'

"Mr. Blanchard did not answer immediately but said finally: 'Bring him around.' For a reason that I cannot translate into logical terms, I added: 'He's Negro.'

"Mr. Blanchard said, 'Well.'

"I answered him, 'All right,' with a pause.

"'I don't think it would look right in front of the theater, Ulysses,' he said. He then went on to refer to the fact that he was a businessman trying to draw a clientele consisting of all elements of the surrounding community including those elements that are, unfortunately, racially biased.'"

Why didn't Ulysses ask Blanchard if he booked movies especially appealing the racially biased? Instead, Ulysses sailed on, "I might point out that Mr. Blanchard never blatantly in my presence refused to employ a Negro, nor did he, even at the time that he implied that the employment of Negroes as doormen might be detrimental to the business, ever blatantly or through suggestion express a personal bias either in favor of or against Negroes. The fact that I am Chinese inadvertently might have affected his conduct with me."

God, Ulysses was a pompous asshole when he was young. "If the Storefront Theater actually does depend on a clientele composed in large by racially biased elements of the community and not, as I had supposed, by the immediately surrounding student community of the University, for its support, I would deem Mr. Blanchard justified in not hiring those people who in any way might threaten this means of support." Ulysses bought his boss's rejection of Negroes as a business, not as a racist decision. I was saddened. From the moment I met him on my first day this side of the Pacific, this side of my amnesia at eleven years of age, I thought Ulysses rubbed people the wrong way because he was ahead of his time. I had never thought of him being right on time, or behind his time. Why didn't he quit? Of course, he wrote this letter to keep his lousy usher's job.

"I also might add that I submit this statement reluctantly, as I have the sense that this along with other statements will be used collectively to coerce. I have never trusted groups, even groups that had aims and opinions similar to my own, because within the group, these aims and opinions, the ideals which are the group's definition, become sacrosanct dogma. In the case of the NAACP, although my best friend *is* a Negro, one who might marry my sister with my blessings should he and she wish to marry, I do not think the Negro sacrosanct."

Oh boy, I sighed, depressed and fascinated. Reading his letter was an experience rich and juicy with embarrassment, like flossing my teeth with a violin string. "I do not agree with the omission of the word 'Black' from 'Little Black Sambo' or the abolition of minstrel shows, or the suppression of D. W. Griffith's *Birth of a Nation*. Such action to protect the Negro against discrimination seems ludicrous, even patronizing to the Negro." Oh, no. Delicious. Worse and worse. I was sure Ulysses had forgotten this exchange of letters. What would happen when he found this letter between his hard covers? What would happen if I told him I had found it and read it? If he were a politician, the exposure of a letter like this could destroy him. But nothing hurts him. People believe he's passionate and angry because he's loud and big, but he's a cold, pretentious . . . a cold pretentious . . . I couldn't think of what he was.

On our way back to the five-and-dime, the ambulance got a call on the radio. An accident on the other side of the river. Pick up the victim and take him to University Hospital. "How about helping me out with this one?" the driver asked. "Of course, why not?" Martha said, and we were off with the electronic siren and howler, flashing lights and speed. The driver trembled and flashed sweat as he drove. He breathed hard and I wondered what I had gotten Martha into here.

An old Buick had driven into the blade of a bulldozer set at the height of an old Buick's windshield. The windshield was gone, along with the steering wheel. The driver was in the back seat on the passenger side. He was bleeding or had been bleeding, from the left eye, the nose, mouth, head, chest, and groin. People were pulling at him through both back doors. The ambulance driver stopped and breathed hard. I calmly yelled for everyone to back away from the car so we could take the driver out. We didn't look like it, I shouted, but we were from the ambulance.

The bottoms of his top teeth were all sheared or broken off. One of his eyes was open and bloody. Martha helped me get the board under his butt and roll him back down the board. I had to ask the driver to help me move the board out of the right rear door onto the gurney. Martha and I rode in the back again. I thought I felt a pulse. I asked Martha to feel.

With a couple of interns helping and a doctor directing, we slipped our arms under the back of the victim to lift him off the ambulance gurney onto a hospital gurney. During the process, all his blood flooded out of his back and splashed on the ambulance gurney and the fronts of our coats. The driver went with his gurney to hose it off. While he was gone, the doctors, by a vote of three to five, decided the man was dead and announced the time. We washed up, and on our way back to the five-and-dime, Martha asked the ambulance driver for a job. He suggested checking with the owner, who had a garage next door to the five-and-dime. The owner of the ambulance company also owned the taxi company and had a cab up on a rack and looked like he was gutting it when we walked in, and Martha asked him for a job.

He was a one-eyed man who didn't wear an eye patch or glass eye, and held his pants up with suspenders. He still had eyelids and eyelashes, but no eye inside. What was inside that I could see, suggested fungus. I didn't want to see any more. He said he had hired an attendant that morning who was supposed to be working but hadn't shown up for some reason. The job was taken.

Martha said, "The man you hired missed his first day of work. He doesn't seem very dependable. I have proven I can do the work on two calls he missed already. I did the work. I should get the job because I have done the job." She spoke very well on her own behalf, I felt, but the guy wouldn't give the job to her.

We finally got back to the five-and-dime where the manager shook my hand and said, "I could tell you were a gentleman," and thanked us profusely. He said his "staff" had guarded my plastic bag of souvenirs "with their lives," and grinned. If he wondered at the huge blots of blood on the front of our coats, he didn't say. The manager, a thin man whose neck rattled around the inside of his collar like a flower stem wobbling in flower pot, not only did not ask us to pay for the cups of coffee and hot chocolate we'd left on the counter but offered us fresh cups and anything we wanted off the menu, on the house. "Your consideration is the perfect end to a perfect day," I said, and Martha smiled, but didn't laugh.

I slept late into the next morning, not wanting to break out of my bad dreams until Rudy or Martha let the robin out beyond the bedroom. The bird was bold, king of the boxed world Rudy gave it. In this world it had grown up without knowing predators: hawks, falcons, kids with BB guns. Martha took out the little guitar I'd bought for her and sat in the kitchen, but the shitting bird didn't allow playing the guitar. But she tried. She broke a string while tuning up and went out to buy a new one. She returned home, went straight to the kitchen, and discovered the string was too short for the guitar. She was uncharacteristically nonverbal, slowly packing the guitar back in its case. Then just as carefully, she uncased her portable electric typewriter and set it on a placemat on the kitchen table.

She sat and began to type with the strangest look on her face, then suddenly slumped into a sigh, realizing she had been sitting on birdshit. I suggested going out to a late lunch at one of Iowa City's two Chinese restaurants that advertise in the Yellow Pages, possibly the one where she grew the bean sprouts and waited tables. For the last three hours Rudy had been reading George Santayana's *The*

Sense of Beauty deep in his easy chair, oblivious to the flitting, searching, perching, pecking robin. He wanted to keep reading. We said we'd bring him something from the restaurant. Martha knew all about The Plum Garden. It had a sixteen-year-old baby-faced pudgy white boy cooking the American food, and a short wiry Chinese from Hong Kong cooking the American-style Chinese food. The Chinese lived in a room over the Greyhound Bus depot, saving his money to bring his family over. The sixteen-year-old white kid dreamed of joining the Army when he turned eighteen, and embarking on a career as an Army cook.

We ordered off the American menu. The Chinese food smelled too sweet and looked awful. I ordered the chicken-fried steak, hoping they took some pride in their fresh deep-frying of an American legend. Martha ordered a crab Louie salad. I wondered what kind of crab they would have here, so far inland? The waitress, a biker's dream of a biker's mama in a red stylized Chinese jacket with a Mandarin collar and fake frogs on the front, brought us a pot of tea. The sight of the teapot seemed the last insult, too much to bear, and Martha broke down sobbing. "I hate this place, Daddy," she said, every word making her cry more.

"Is there someplace we can go, baby?" I asked softly.

"Go!" she shouted. "Where do I have to go? This is it. This is the only place I know to go." She grabbed my arm and led me through the swinging doors into the kitchen and down the stairs to the stone basement where she grew the bean sprouts for the restaurant. She sat me down by the potato peeling machine and paced along the long wall of sinks and crocks of bean sprouts.

This morning, she said, she woke up and didn't remember I was there and was so angry and lonely. She felt it was her against Iowa, toe to toe, tooth and nail. Iowa was not America, it was another country. Iowans didn't think New York was in America. They thought it was full of foreign spies wanting to take over Iowa. People here didn't hear that she didn't have a Chinese accent. She had no real friends here. She didn't want to be a problem for me. She didn't want to come home. She wouldn't let Iowa beat her. She cried it out, babbled it out. And then showed me how she grew the bean sprouts.

"You know, baby, you are not obligated to marry Rudy because he's the first man to introduce you to sex. You are not obligated to marry him because you love him, either. Not even if you get pregnant and have a child by him, understand? You have options."

We took home an order of the Plum Garden special, a lurid concoction of chicken, roast pork, bamboo shoots, canned baby corn, snow peas, bean sprouts, and fat crisp noodles. "Your Uncle Diego would be in hog heaven," I said. "The great question of his life is: What ever happened to fat chow mien noodles? The fat noodles are Chinese America's great contribution to world civilization. To him, it's a disaster that the new thin Singapore-style noodles have driven the old Chinese-American original fat noodles out of existence in his home town."

Rudy was just where we had left him, with Santayana's *Sense of Beauty* in his hands. The robin had splatted the phone and my suitcase. Both were endangered species in Rudy's singular three-room habitat with terrarium bathtub. He was about halfway through the book. "Wow, man, I have to hand it to you, Rudy. I tried reading that book in college, and it took me a week to read the first seven pages. That is the most difficult book I ever attempted to read in my life."

"Oh, hey, I'm glad you said that. I thought it was me. Somebody said I should read this book, so I'm reading it. I don't know what this guy's talking about, you know. Every now and then something sounds nice to me. But then I forget it as I read ahead."

"Yes. That is a problem," I said.

Rudy was asleep in the bedroom and the robin was awake. Martha brought the portable black-and-white TV into the front room, set it up on the desk, and sat on the bed with me. She wanted to cuddle. I was shocked. She wasn't a little girl any longer. I did not go into the bathroom when she was in the bathroom. I did not dress her or undress her. I did not hold her against me like a woman. I piled up layers of blankets and sleeping bags between us and we eased into a kind of cuddling, watching the late-night movie.

The Million Dollar Movie of the night was *Walk Like a Dragon,* written and directed by James Clavell. Oh, boy! It's Jack Lord, McGarrett of *Hawaii Five-0* playing cowboys in the old west. He looks so young. Ulysses' dad, Longman Kwan is in this, so we had to watch.

In the movie, Jack Lord gets grouchy and moralistic about the Chinatown slave market in old San Francisco, then sees a Chinese Cinderella on special, buys her and tries to set her free. But she won't go. She is too Chinese to understand freedom. "Freedom? What means 'Freedom'?" Martha and I echo together.

"Uncle Diego would love this movie on acid," I said.

"You still do drugs, Dad?"

"Nah, just a little grass when I'm with the boys."

China Boy wears a black skullcap with a stupid tassel on top. He sees Cinderella and is in love. He offers to buy her from Jack Lord. Lord won't sell.

And here is Ulysses' father in a stiff Chinese robe and fancy hat, talking a very funny ching chong that makes me laugh. I like Ulysses' father. He is China Boy's wise merchant uncle in Sacramento. Alone in the back of his store with China Boy, he speaks perfect Yul Brynner English. China Boy is breathless with surprise.

Ulysses' father tells China Boy it's not good for a Chinaman to speak English too well in front of the whites in America. "Play dumb and keep your true self secret."

"Oooh," Martha said, "Keep your trooooo self seeeecret."

"Guess who gets killed," I said.

Cinderella is in love with Jack Lord. What a bore. We knew that. Boring. Then Mel Torme appears, the famous crooner called "the Velvet Fog." Martha used to think he was called the "Velvet Frog," which sounded perfectly sensible to me. Mel Torme, famous for fogging or frogging a velvet rendition of "Route 66", is the gunfighter in black.

"Is this actually being broadcast from a station in Iowa?" I asked.

"What an awful movie!" Martha agreed. "Yeeeooooooo! It feels like the movie I deserve."

It ends with China Boy calling Mel out. His right hand is still sore from an earlier gunfight with Jack Lord. China Boy gets his gun out but Mel shoots him in the belly. Jack Lord steps in for the final showdown with Mel Torme and the final humiliation of China Boy. Cinderella is left with a broken heart and a broken ineffectual China Boy she pities but doesn't love.

Leave it to Hollywood Kwan to come to me in a vision, in Iowa City, when I need him, I thought. It was just as Ulysses used to say, "God in Heaven gave up a son in the image of the perfect white man to die for the white man's sins and lead whites to salvation and the Kingdom of Heaven on Earth. And so white men in Hollywood gave up a son in the image of the perfect China Man, to lead the yellows to acceptance and assimilation, and Charlie Chan was his name." And we were all the sons of the sons of Charlie Chan.

A few miles down the road from Iowa City was Amana, an Amish colony with a couple of restaurants open to the world. Martha suggested we go. Rudy drove us in his '77 Honda CVCC and managed to get us to Amana after the town's closing time. *Town* may be the wrong word. I saw nothing. Our headlights reflected off a few shaded windows. A couple of wooden buildings near the road. Rudy mumbled and muttered, stopped in the middle of the road, backed up and turned, cramped the wheel the other way, and almost successfully completed the turnaround, when the little car slipped off the road onto the soft downsloping embankment that seemed to go down to a field. It was dark and the little car could not climb out. Suddenly a light as a door opened on the other side of the road. Big young men in white aprons came jumping and running out of the door, whooping and yipping like five-year-old boys. Two-hundred-pound five-year-old boys. Four or five of them. They ran across the road playing with each other. They were giggling, but at the same time restrained, as if to keep their parents from hearing. Did Rudy or Martha say something about the Amish not talking out loud to anyone after a certain hour? Or was my ego playing mindtrips with me?

The giant five-year-old boys in aprons ran and slid down the embankment to the Honda. We were still in it. They picked the car up without a word or a wave to us. They grabbed parts of the car in their hands, picked us up, ran us back up to the road, set us down gently on our tires, and ran laughing and whooping back into the building, slamming the door. Rudy didn't for a second consider thanking them . . . he just started up the car.

I enjoyed the visit to Amama. What I found perplexing was Martha's absolute silence in the car. No slippery wit, no irony at Rudy getting us to Amana too late to eat or see anything. No exchange of funny faces with me, at Rudy's emotional and whimsical way of driving. No urgent grunts and eeks of surprise when the five giant five-year-olds ran out and picked us up—car and all—like a piece of sports equipment, ran us up the embankment, and put us back on the road pointed in the right direction to go back to Iowa City.

By Good Friday, the snow had given way to rain that melted the snow and cleared the sidewalks and then moved on. Returning to the apartment through an alley and listening to the skins of rainwater dripping off the fire escapes and the drainpipes dripping onto the old worn brick of the alley, Martha and I stopped before crossing the street to watch Rudy standing in front of the doorway under a dripping awning, holding the robin. The sun was low, the shadows of the buildings crossed the street and folded up the faces of Rudy's side of the street.

There was no real traffic, no continuous flow of cars. The traffic light changed and blinked up and down empty streets. Rudy walked out into the middle of the street and tossed the bird into the air and dashed for the door. The bird braked in the air, flipped over, and flew back to his shoulder. Rudy stepped out into the street again, looked both ways and tossed the robin up underhanded with both hands as if dumping a pan of water, and ran for his door. Again the robin stalled and turned in midair for Rudy and caught on to him before he reached the door. After five minutes or so, it looked like a game they were playing with each other. A dance between man and bird. The robin flew higher, and Rudy took fewer and fewer steps out from under the awning, till once he threw the robin up, and it went up and up, while he made it into the building and slammed the front door. The bird came down and Rudy was gone.

Martha and I stepped back into the alley, fast, before the bird recognized us, caught each other's eye, and burst out laughing. I hushed her. "Robins have extraordinary hearing. They hear worms under the ground," I said. "Shhhh." It was the first real laugh we'd had together this trip. We walked hand in hand around the block, window shopping, returned to the alley, and entered the apartment building by the back door without being seen by the robin.

The next morning the robin was gone into the gray skies and drizzly air. Rudy wanted to be alone and went to his studio on campus to paint. I helped Martha dig out the pale lawn they'd been growing in the bathtub, scrub out the bathtub, and wash the bathroom floor. We washed clothes and cleaned house all day long. The place smelled less of the robin. Just a little less. The closed windows and steam heat had cooked the smell into the walls and furniture. As the guest, I graciously accepted my daughter's invitation to be the first to soak in the tub in over a month, possibly two months.

The next day, Easter Sunday. I thought of giving Martha and Rudy a day alone and was looking forward to enjoying a little walk out around the town by myself. I put on a suit and tie and was on my way out early in the morning when Martha asked me where I was going.

"I thought I'd do the tourist thing and walk around a little and watch white people go to church on Easter Sunday. And to sort of blend in, I put on a tie to look like I'm on my way to church too. That way maybe they'll think even though I'm not white, I'm trying to be."

"Hey, that's a good idea, Mo," Rudy mumbled, as he slapped

around the house wearing his untied shoes like slippers, brushing his teeth with a lot of foamy stuff bubbling between his teeth. "It's about time I see what this Easter stuff every year is about. Wait up, and I'll go with you."

I said nothing and smiled. So all three of us went out for a tense little walk on a crisp cold sunny spring morning, all dressed up and combed down, among the unsuspecting churchgoers of Iowa City. Everyone walked quietly. Real church bells beat and throbbed with electronic doppelgängers.

Rudy looked sullen, sad, suffering, a vampire in need of blood. He and his robin had lived in a sunless Eden. It was good for him to be out in the world, to see that birds survived in town without him. The people were drab and disappeared before my eyes in their own environment like chameleons. Trees lined the streets. Old trees. Elms. Oaks. Not the wild, imported, fast-growing weedy eucalyptus and spindly palm trees of tropical fantasy all over California. I was looking at the sagging roof of an old house, wondering at the wavy line of the siding and the roller coaster of the porch, seeing the scenery without the people when Martha said with a nasty snarl, "Okay, you don't like us on your street, we are going to church with you!" And she turned us around. I asked what had happened. She said a mother, son, and daughter had glared at us and curled their lips as we passed.

With Martha leading, we followed a family of four into a stone church that was spacious and magical, full of a bright wonderful light that passed through tall stained glass windows I had barely noticed outside the building. They made the interior mysteriously dim and bright at the same time. We followed the family up to a second balcony and sat right behind them. Martha, who had a very sweet voice and a perfect ear, purposely sang off-beat, off-key, and very loudly. They sang a lot in this church. I was at a loss to understand what Martha was doing. Rudy didn't seem to care and tried to sing in time and in tune with Martha. The sermon, being broadcast all over the Midwest through a microphone I saw with my own eyes, linked Easter and the Resurrection of Christ with the declaration that the theory of evolution had not been proven.

The whole visit with my daughter in the American heartland affected me as a kind of punishment. Her punishment. Let's fuck, with Dad awake on the other side of the thin wall. The robin who expressed its love and joy with shit fits. The prospective son-in-law whose head was run over the by a garbage truck in Vietnam. Christians endured great suffering. Like Wong Sam and Assistants said in their *Chinese-English Phrase Book,* I was a Christian by temperament and Western prejudice, by personal belief, more than by any church influence or doctrine. I was a Christian, but this was ridiculous. Perhaps it was homesickness, self-pity, or mid-life crisis, but I felt I was experiencing torment in Iowa City, a silly torment, too stupid for words.

Martha phoned home. Pandora was on a State Department tour of China. Martha said Rudy came home in the rain smiling and said, "Guess who came running out to me when I was walking home! Yes, the robin is back."

She didn't marry Rudy. Pandora never had any real cause to meet him and never did. "It's best she have no idea what I've spared her," I told Martha and we laughed.

It has become natural, even virtuous of me, to not be sleeping with Pandora anymore and to not be writing anymore. And I'm too old to move on any young thing who flutters the lashes of her twat at me. They're all younger than my daughter these days. I just can't get enthused. And Martha's baby, Justin, is home with me, while she's going to school away in Portland, Oregon, where all the bridges across the Willamette shine like the braces on my daughter's teeth did when she was starting junior high. I like Portland. Someday I'll sit down at Jake's Famous Crawfish with Baby Justin and Martha, a wad of money and nothing but time, and eat a dozen of every kind of locally grown oyster they serve, raw, fresh, on the half-shell. Until then I am "Good old Ben," as Ulysses calls me. "You always know the right thing to say at just the right time."

I hate this life. I never dreamed I would still be teaching Asian

American Studies at San Francisco State twenty years later. I thought I would be tucked into a comfortable writer-in-residence creative writing professor's cushioned chair in a corner office of an ivy-covered, reinforced brick or limestone or even granite building on the grassy and wooded campus of a private university on the coast of one ocean or another, or the shore of a great lake, to bald, to write *New Yorker* stories, to meet with eight or nine select students twice a week, and to furtively ogle the women in the supermarket twenty years later. Instead I am trapped by emotional blackmail, moral laziness and the wish for just one more minute of peace and quiet. Little Justin is the only thing that keeps me interested in staying alive a minute longer. And I daydream a lot.

And then there is my great daydream. Sometimes when Pandora's gone on a State Department tour of the great cities of Russia, and Baby Justin is where he belongs, with Martha, and the house is empty, I stop by a sushi bar I have noticed doing business in the most unlikely place, in the most unlikely part of town. Someplace like Grove Street in West Oakland, where the Black Panthers had their headquarters when we were all in Diego's Chinatown Black Tigers.

And I stop, because the house is empty and nobody's going to be back for days, and I have time, and I'm curious to see if sushi in this part of town can be any good at all. And the place inside is clean and tasteful. The case is full of fresh fish, roe, squid, oysters, shrimp, octopus. The place is bright, well lit, empty. I sit, and the sushi man is friendly, an artist with his hands and knives. Everything I order looks and tastes of art. The composition of textures and flavors of each piece and the orchestration of the pieces together. Yes, it is a joy to sit in this place. Then a car pulls up outside the window. This sushi bar is in one of the ugliest corner minimalls imaginable. But a beautiful young Asian girl gets out of an old perfectly kept Mustang. She comes in, silhouetted in the doorway, wearing a fuzzy angora sweater and tight designer jeans. She sits, leans over to look in the display case, and sighs. The back of her sweater hikes up a bit, and I see the small of her back sweep away under the rim of her jeans. She doesn't know anything about sushi and wants something-to-go for her roommate but doesn't know what to get. She's only eaten sushi a couple of times and then her roommate did the ordering. I could smell her and stare at the small of her back for hours. And my dream stalls there. I can't imagine what happens next. I can't take her to my place. I'm too old to go to a student dorm. I'm too responsible for anything to happen next.

Part Four: Home

Benedict Mo: Sex and Death

I never thought I would end up becoming "Good Old Ben," meeking around the same old Asian American Studies department from which I'd hoped to make good an escape to a classier scene with classier digs not so close to people like Ulysses and Diego. Good old Ben was Diego Chang's best man at his wedding to a rich girl from Hong Kong who'd done acid with him and had never quite come down. Diego and Ava got married in papier-mâché masks they'd made themselves. Ava made a very nice alligator-crocodile-looking mask for Diego. with what looked like cigarette filter tips for teeth. For Ava, Diego made what looked like a rice sack covered with chicken feathers and fur that made me sneeze. No one asked what Ava's mask was supposed to be. They made a mask for me too. No one had bothered to find Ulysses and tell him about the wedding because no one believed the marriage would last the day. It lasted years.

They had a daughter. Diego was a doting father. Good old Ben made the arrangements for the red egg party marking baby Vanessa's first month of life on earth and her introduction to the greater family and friends. At the end of the banquet, plates of hardboiled eggs dyed red came to the tables, and the guests took an egg and lay a red envelope containing gold or jade or money on the plate in place of the red egg they'd taken. In my resignation at being "old hat" in attitude, if not in actual age, I have to admit to enjoying Chinese red egg parties. Good old Ben's grandson, baby Justin, and Diego and Ava's little girl, baby Vanessa, become pals, cousins.

Good old Ben was the first one Ava phoned when Sheila showed up at the house and told Ava she ran a Korean massage parlor, was Diego's girlfriend, and had come to claim her man. "Hi Ben," Ava said to me in her low reedy voice, "How about we get together for a barbecue and contribute our fair share to San Francisco's smog?" she asked.

"Since when is Diego interested in barbecuing at his house?" I asked. Then remembered. "Oh, George." George, the handyman who traded work for a room in their apartment house, was going to do all the work, of course. He's from the south and into cooking and it would be wonderful! "Just say when, we'll be there," I promise.

"Do you remember that oral history project you and Diego did for Asian American Studies?" Ava asked.

"Uhhh, what oral history project was that?" I asked.

"You wanted oral histories of Korean massage parlor girls."

"Korean massage parlor girls?" So I was Diego's cover for visiting Korean massage parlors?

"Well, I would ask Diego about a barbecue for tomorrow, but one of those Korean massage parlor girls has been his mistress for the last five years, and she's outside on the sidewalk talking with Diego about life."

"Now take a deep breath and slow down. His who?"

"His mistress."

"What is she?"

"A Korean massage parlor madam. I don't know what else to call her. She runs a Korean massage parlor. She wrote me a letter saying she has fucked and sucked Diego off every night for the last five years. That's the way she writes me. Language like that. Five years is longer than our marriage. You want me to read it to you?"

"No, that's okay."

"She says since we both know exactly what we're talking about when we're talking about Diego in bed, we're like sisters. She said if I really loved him, the two of us would get together in bed and make Diego happy. But she says I can have Diego for myself if I buy him from her for $50,000. Can you believe that? Then she phones me up! No man is worth $50,000, not to mention the fact that I don't have that kind of money. I must have been crazy. You should hear how she talks about how Diego's prick acts when she does this and that, and what it looks like."

"Please, I don't want to hear about that right now, Ava. Just tell me what is going on? What are you doing right now?"

"We bargained over the phone, can you believe that? I have the girl, our daughter, Vanessa, and the real estate, that's his legacy, and I didn't know what else to do! I'm such a chicken sometimes. I said I would think about maybe $5,000."

"This is nuts, Ava. Don't do it," I reply. "Now, you say they are both outside on the street?"

"I tried to commit suicide and kill our baby."

"You what?" We had come a long way from an invitation to a barbecue.

"I confronted him with it, and he said he's going to kill her and shoot himself too. He's got a gun."

"He's got a gun?"

"At first I told him not to do it. Then I found out she paid for the gun, so now I don't care. You'd think he could buy his own Uzi if he wanted one that badly. It's not like we're destitute or have bad credit. But he's so crazy now, I think the gun should be unloaded, but I don't know how to unload an Uzi. Do you know anything about guns?"

Whoopee time in Asian America again. "I'll be right over, Ava. Just be cool, be nice, stay away from him if he comes in the house. Don't start anything."

"It's my house too!"

"Just do nothing till I get there. I'll park in the driveway, make a house call, unload your Uzi for you, and you and Diego and the massage parlor madam can have at each other without fear or hope of being machine gunned, okay? Listen to your uncle Ben. I'm on the way. Be cool!"

Luckily for everybody, I belonged to one of the last generations of university students required to take two years of ROTC. In addition to learning to march, I discovered a passion and instinct for form and function, for the tactics and strategy of engineering in the classes on the M-1 Garand rifle. A perfect machine for an imperfect man. Semiautomatic. The relationship between the gun and the man was reciprocal. Gas-operated, blowback-operated, recoil-operated firearms were a wonder I could master. I had been so determined *not* to become an engineer or a doctor or a lawyer, occupations from every Chinese parent's Column A, or a pharmacist or dentist from Column B, that I did nothing but write. I tried to become a writer, a poet, a novelist, a writer of short stories, and instead wound up teaching Asian American Studies. I might now be designing and engineering guns, or I might be a gunsmith, a solid, recognized, respected craftsman, rather than an uncomfortable professor of a dubious subject. I hate this life. Little Justin is the only thing that keeps me interested in staying alive a minute longer.

I packed Justin into the car to ride this rescue with me. When I got there, I expected I'd have to take care of Ava and Diego's daughter, Vanessa. Since Justin and Vanessa had grown up together, I hoped they could keep each other occupied and away from the action.

The car did not break down or run out of gas down the hills and around the curves of Marin County or over the Golden Gate Bridge. Good old Ben did not crash into another car or run over a pedestrian or have a flat tire. Justin and I walked past a dark car, with a yellow woman who looked fortyish and hard in the sepulchral purple glow of the streetlight. I found the Korean massage parlor madam hunkered down on the sidewalk just outside Diego's iron gate, looking longingly up into his face. Diego's hands were in his pockets. Shoulders hunched up. A new punky haircut with a lot of jelly. A muscle shirt. Diego introduced the Korean. Yes, she was beautiful. And her sister was parked in the dark car up the street.

Turned out his massage parlor sugar was married. Her husband split the scene with *her* quarter of a million dollar bank account built up by her booming massage business. He blew it all in Vegas and Atlantic City and was long gone.

"I'm his mistress five years, you believe that? Five years!" I realized that she and Ava talked about the same things in the same way. When I could, I eased off with Justin to see Ava and Vanessa inside the house.

Ava had all of Diego's clothes packed up in boxes and shopping bags. She had washed, dried, and folded all of them first. She told me the Korean had had an abortion last Saturday. Diego's child. He was with her, attending the abortion of his child in a grotesque parody of birth and family. I sent Justin off with Vanessa to pack something. She and Auntie Ava will come back home with us for the night, I explained.

Ava wondered where Diego scored the thousand dollar designer Corum wristwatch, and why he'd bought the RX7 when he hated to drive. And the Uzi. Ah, the Uzi. Cocked and loaded and somewhere in the house, was it? Great. Ava said she tried suicide with over-the-counter sleeping pills and threw up.

"Oh, no! Thank goodness," I said. She then tried a suicide-murder while Vanessa was asleep, closing all the doors and windows, turning on all the gas jets, and lying down to sleep, but a fly buzzed about her face and bugged her, so she got up and opened the door to release the nuisance—after all, it too was a living thing—and then the cat came in. She chased the cat around until she got it out of the house, but a butterfly fluttered in, and so on, until she gave up the idea of gassing herself and Vanessa. That's when she thought of calling me.

A live machine gun on the premises gave the old eternal triangle a spooky rush. The Uzi was about the same size as a large flashlight, and unloaded weighed about the same as a flashlight with batteries. The thing dared me to touch it. I looked it over for the safeties and the magazine release. It was like nothing I saw in ROTC thirty years ago. This was no nine-and-a-half pound Garand rifle. The Uzi looked like it would kill somebody if I just touched it wrong. It had been years, twenty years, since I last handled a real gun, a loaded weapon.

I removed the clip, cleared the chamber, and slipped the loose round back into the clip. I was amazed that Diego never tried to cover his tracks. All the stupid things a married man could do, he did. The massage parlor's number was all over his telephone bill. First drafts of his love letters were in his journals. Her love and kisses all over his body in the form of jewelry and classy dap-medowns like he'd never worn before. One lie after another to his Ava, a beauty from a Hong Kong banking family, an artist, an independent woman, and crazy about him.

Of course Diego's marriage crashed after that. It was all too public. Ava had to divorce Diego, which was what Diego had wanted all along. She went back to Hong Kong to the family banking business. Surprisingly she didn't want their child, Vanessa, and this actually delighted Diego. A couple from China were living upstairs in return for keeping house for him and helping him with Vanessa. He was an indulgent father, and proud of it, which surprised me. But on the other hand, Diego did fuck around with students, which worried me. And I told him he should worry about it too.

"Nahh! I'm not worried about that. I think she wants me to be her old man, or to live with me, and I don't want that. I told her that. I had that and got rid of that. I don't want that. She knows I don't want that, but I think that's what she wants."

"I don't know how you do it, Diego, at your age," I said.

"I can't stand fucking old white women, man. Their bodies are all fucked up with fat and they smell funny. Young white girls don't smell like old white women. And, man, I know I look good. My body's still tight, I can still pec up, man. Why should I fuck something old and ugly when I don't have to? There's young stuff in the world who will do anything to get in bed with me. Right?" Diego says. "All the Chinese ladies my age on the loose are divorcées or cheating on some old man, and I don't want relationships with trouble, man. Fucking is supposed to be fun, it's not supposed to fuck up your life. At least, that's the way I look at it. And when I get so fucked up I can't fuck and look like shit, fuck! It's checkout time at the Big Hotel. This life has been all visited out. I know how I'll make my last fade too, man. Yeah. That's how I look at life, man. Once it stops being fun. It's time go go."

"Man, if that's what fucking young girls does to an old man's mind, I want none of it," I said, laughing. "Sex and Death, man. You're Woody Allen."

"Yeah, I like Woody Allen," Diego said. "He fucks a lot without marrying anyone anymore. He's cool. I figure, I'll go out with a party, like this. Open house. Maybe a Superbowl party or World Series party, Martin Luther King's birthday, something hip like that. "

"I like the World Series," I said.

"We cook up about eight of our favorite foods, with the two soups included. One from the land. One from the sea. Like the bandits, man, we banquet on beef and horse. The banquet food of hard times, when even rice is a luxury. And all you assholes with your ugly old squeezes and all my young sweethearts are watching the Superbowl on the monitors I have in every room of my house. My kid will be maybe eighteen, and away to Spain for the summer with one of my sisters. I don't want to fuck her up too much. And I'll break out all my drugs, man. I mean, *all* my drugs! I can ride out of this world on the Indian visions of magic mushrooms, like a Native American becoming a bird and flying away, man. I can go out snowballing my brain with coke, traveling by nose, needle, blasting, like white yuppie types about to fall for insider trading. I can King Kong out on PCP. But I've decided I'm going to ride a mixed ticket home. I'll drop a tab of acid in the morning. Smoke some good California Green, play guitar with my friends, have farewell fucks with the ladies, and cook with the housekeeper. Then the end of the Superbowl, and I'll hop on the old horse for the last time, creamed with the Green and snapped with the coke, mystical on mushrooms and architectonic on acid, I'll take up my primo flamenco guitar and play a fucking Soleares that'll make you fall down on your fucking faces crying, man, getting cold nipples and hard-ons it'll be so beautiful. And ah-Ulysses S. Kwan, that pig buggering monkeydick motherfucker, he will beg me to forgive him for ever calling me a fucking dilettante, man. You hear that?

"You will see Kwannie beg me to forgive him. I don't do a hot-shot, man, that's not my horse. I mean for a nice smooth long ride into the sunrise, man. I needle light into the night, and smoke me some sweet gooey opium. You have to smell it to believe it, man. A whiff of the air this smoke touches inside of twelve feet lays you back for a dream of your junior prom, man. I'm playing a deep Seguiryas, man. All the frogs croaking in your guts shut up and tense and chant their Buddhist croaks. You're all looking at that big print of El Jaleo over my shoulder, with the pudgy gypsy dancer in the footlights, and the cuadro flamenco in chairs against the whitewashed wall. There's an empty chair. When I die, you'll see that chair fill up with a Chinaman guitarist winking at you from under one of the hats off the wall." Diego took a breath and toked, and said through the smoke, "And that's how I'm getting out of here. I'm not going to linger and fall apart like my folks, man. I won't do that to my kid."

"Wow!" I said, a little stoned and genuinely awed by my friend's strange plot involving the Superbowl and suicide, all to get Ulysses to apologize for badmouthing his guitar playing.

"If you weren't so chicken, you'd do it yourself, man. I think it would be good for you. How long has it been since you had something stashed on the side?"

"Never, man. Personally, I always planned to linger. So I never fucked around on Pandora, man," I said. Then bringing it back under cover of flattery, "And you are the one who taught me to find peace playing the guitar in the bathroom, by candlelight, instead of womanizing."

"You're just saying that because you want me to die right now, right?" Diego said, shaking his head. "Fuck you! *Diew nay gah hoon.* Fuck you in the ass, man!"

"I guess this means you're gonna live, huh?" I said, and we laughed. "You have strange daydreams, Diego. Beware!"

Diego Chang: The Stratagem of Self-Inflicted Injury

I should have married Lucinda when she wanted to get married and have kids. She said she'd love me always, no matter if I married another woman or she married another man and had his children—I would always be first. She left, I married the wrong woman, and had a wonderful kid. She was crazy. Now she's gone, and it's the kid and me. Me and Vanessa. All the women I had before and after Lucinda were hard to get along with, crazy crazy women. Lucinda was the only one who was perfect. Perfect. She was just my size. Had just the looks that made me tingle. Her color, the taste of her skin and sweat and cunt, especially her cunt on my tongue, were perfect. Sweet, spicy, warm. Every moment she was with me she was everything I'd always wanted. She was perfect. That's what scared me about her. And she was the only one who wasn't crazy.

I live my life as if I were trusting a movie I'm watching. Not like Ulysses. He sees the microphone pushing into the top of the shot. He sees the top of the set, the pack of Salems on the pilot's table in the World War II movie, the vw in the background of Napoleon at Borodino, two hands locked behind the head in one shot, the gun in the hand in the next shot. He asks if, between shots, the cop had put the gun in the dead man's hand. None of that bothers me. I'm heading for The End, man. I just don't let that stuff bother me if I see it. And if I see it, I don't remember it. And that's the way I live. I paid for it, man. I want to enjoy the thing. Ulysses is too Sherlock Holmes. He doesn't enjoy things. It's like everything's a murder mystery and he's out to solve it. Big fucking mystery, man. A movie is a movie. So he sees the microphone in the shot and the wrong car in the background. Didn't he know it was a movie when he walked in?

Sometimes I think of calling Lucinda up and saying, "Come back."

She writes me letters. Two or three times a year. They're great letters. She writes me about all the Chinese and Japanese fairy tales she's been reading and how they're all just like us. I keep them open for weeks on the kitchen table where I drink my coffee and watch the morning take to my pear and peach trees. Every time I read them, even just a line or two, all the happiness of her being with me comes back. I never answer. I don't know what to say. I never write back. I maybe send a card at Chinese New Year or Christmas. But I'm over fifty, so fuck it, I don't send anybody any kind of cards anymore. People send *me* cards. But I'm not worried about kissing up to anybody or making anybody happy.

The way I live is like, one day watching this movie, I want my kid to see why the good guy is the good guy and why the bad guy is bad. Another day watching this movie with my sugar, all I want to do is fuck and suck. But she's young, a rich little nostalgia tripper riding the '60s, living the part of a hippie. And I am her guru with the authentic '60s dong. It's all a little girl's kid game, playing like she's free and outrageous with an old bull Chink.

She says she doesn't care if her folks walk in on us with her hands inside my clothes in the faculty lounge of the faculty club on Parents' Day. The open doorway and the thin unbroken silence makes my hard-on stiff. But her parents don't walk in. She wants to believe she's more than a fuck to me when I let her come over. I don't let any girl, any woman, move into my house. I got the house the way I want it. This solar heat thing keeps the basement warm. The street level is the front room, the dining room, and the big kitchen, with the big window and sliding glass door to the deck. The kitchen is tile walls and floor and marble tops. I like playing the guitar in the kitchen and sleeping in the front room on the couch for a change. Upstairs is Vanessa's room and the couple that keep house, watch Vanessa, cook for me and don't nag me.

Diego Chang: The Stratagem of Shedding the Skin Like the Golden Cicada

I am up too early in the morning, working with my hands again. Fifty-three years old. *Fifty-three!* Working outdoors, building redwood and cedar decks with gang kids to make up for what I used to make in Asian American Studies. Benedict Mo could have made a stand and become chair of the department again or even threatened Washington Wong with that, intimidate him into keeping me on and giving me my tenure. That's supposed to be what friends are for.

But Ben has problems of his own, I guess. I'm not married to his wife. I don't owe Ulysses my fifteen minutes of off-Broadway New York fame. But I thought we were friends.

Tom-the-Pigeye and Lippy How slop termite-proofing water-sealing horrible smelling chemical oily twenty-dollar-a-gallon stuff all over the lumber. If I had my way, we'd wait a couple of days before touching the stuff, but I promised the dean of Third World Studies we would have his deck finished and ready for barbecue and partying before next weekend.

Tom-the-Pigeye boosts five or six diapers from a passing diaper service truck. They wipe every redwood four-by-twelve, four-by-four, two-by-twelve, two-by-six, two-by-four with cotton diapers before I touch them, cut them, drill them, bolt them, nail them up. I am termite-resistant and waterproof up to my armpits. I smell like the insides of a blown engine. Nothing washes the smell off.

Instead of this I would be teaching Asian American Studies to white girls who want to get me off alone and lick me all over with their young tongues, and young sugars from Singapore, Malaysia, Hong Kong, they would all loved me—if Ben Mo wasn't such a tightass.

Tom-the-Pigeye and Lippy want sushi for lunch. I'm not going to eat anything I have to touch with my hands. I come home sore. The muscles of my back and my legs are hallucinating on fatigue, like José Ferrer on his knees as Toulouse-Lautrec, trying to commit suicide by gassing himself in John Huston's *Moulin Rouge.* I remember him dying beautifully in this movie, with Zsa Zsa Gabor dancing in and out of a Lautrec poster, as the whole crew of the *Moulin Rouge* dance in, do the can-can, say goodby, and fade away. I remember the movie being an upper. That's why I rented it along with the Ray Harryhausan shot at animated Greek mythology, *Jason and the Argonauts,* to watch at a distance with baby Vanessa. She's too young for termite-resistant skin.

I didn't remember Toulouse-Lautrec climbing up on chairs to turn on the gas. He lies down and looks around his studio, his paintings covering the walls up to the ceiling. An incomplete painting of the can-can dancer at the Moulin Rouge sits on his easel and dominates the room. He sits up to add a few strokes of the brush, gets into his painting, turns off the gas.

"Why did he want to kill himself?" my Vanessa asks.

"He thinks he's ugly and nobody likes him, and the girl he loved more than any other human being hurt his feelings," I answer, wondering if the short French artist really did that or if Huston made it up.

The Chica that Raoul's kid smashed twenty years ago gets a new top, and I find out the hard way that happy Mexican guitar makers cannot fake a flamenco guitar. The Chica used to snarl and growl at you if you just looked at it. Everything that comes out now is loud but small, sweet and cute. This is a flamenco guitar for Bugs Bunny, and I can't stand playing it.

I call a dealer in vintage guitars and old timey stringed instruments from this ad in the classifieds of *Frets* magazine, and it's my old friend, Jason Peach. Jason is back in Berkeley, still beating himself up over Sarah, who has married again and moved out of Berkeley, out of California. He has several flamencos. And he has his own personal favorite in his collection. He might sell it. An Aguado y Hernandez Flamenco made in 1962. Everyone who has ever played it says it's the best flamenco guitar they have ever played. I play it . . . and although it's good, I am not ready to say it's the best *I've* ever played. He has a nice Conde Hermanos de Esteso for under a thousand, as good as the de la Chica with the new top. He has a very nice-sounding guitar that handles well and smells more and more like hot hide glue as it warms up to my body from being played. I play till I can't stand the smell.

Then he shows me what he calls his mystery guitar. It's the guitar Morton Chu made in one night on acid in Jason's shop on Maui. Good old Uncle Mort. It's still bare wood. Morton hasn't French polished or lacquered it. He hasn't even put his label inside. The guitar is anonymous. The thing snarls and tries to claw me for breathing in the same room with it. Everything I play on it sings and smolders. That scares me. This guitar makes me feel like King Kong.

This guitar is too good for me. It tells me I'm not ready to play it. But I want it. "How much?" I ask Jason. He isn't ready to sell it yet, he says. He'll have to have it finished and wants to talk to Morton about adjusting the neck and about a label. Am I interested?

"Don't sell this to anyone else but me," I say.

I let the trees in my backyard, a peach tree and a pear tree, grow wild while I practice on my Chica with a new top, hating the big macho high tension Mexican bridge. It's hard to play and sounds like shit. The bass notes don't plunk and shiver the stiffeners of my cock. They ooze and pool like warm syrup. I hate the sound. The highs now sound like scared mice in a big tiled bathroom and make me want to shoot this guitar.

I strengthen my fingers and hands practicing flamenco on this disgustingly happy guitar. Every finger gets ears, working a near flamenco sound out of its sweet happy disposition. The branches of the trees grow tangled in each other and wall out the view of the back of the house that fronts on the next street. The ivy that's wild in the backyards of this block grows with nobody taking responsibility for it, and climbs toward the sun, twisting round and round an old clothesline post that still has the pulley wheel for the clothes line, but no line. The ivy finally covers the pulley and grows on, coiling around and around itself, up and down. The physique of my right hand is changed in a couple of years. Curling my fingers like arms, exercising the biceps in the moonlight, I see the ropes of muscles of my palm, tying my fingers to my hand like rigging ties tall masts to a sailing ship .

My little white girl hippie dippie comes over to have me take her out to Chinatown for dinner and a movie—she just has to see the whole double feature. I'd already seen both of them before. If she wants to see two movies in one night, why not some variety? I ask her, and say we can see one of these kung fu swordfight things and then go down to the Bella Union and see some Chinese porn. She likes to shock people and be out of place. The last of living legends of the bachelor society would love to watch dirty movies with her.

No, she wants the experience of a Chinatown double feature.

After the first one, the lights come up and she looks at me funny. I see some of my father's old friends sitting around the old theater with their wives. When I first saw them they came with the wives and children and had more hair. Now some have different wives. The old men dye their hair. Just a few years ago on a night like this, only old folks would be in the theater with me. Now it's young couples with their babies, whole families with their bags of snacks and take-out dinners. It's like when I was a kid again. Very young, before I gave in to my curiosity and checked out the source of all the stomping I heard from outside the Sinaloa Club down the street from my cousin's place, near Chinatown. Before the Air Force and the student strikes, before the Chinatown Black Tigers and good old Ben Mo's play about me playing the guitar—before all that, Chinatown was like this. Young families. Lots of kids. Is it more than a coincidence that when I pick up the guitar again, Chinatown is shuddering with life that I haven't seen in years? The question itself makes me want to play.

"Morton Chu made this guitar in one night, on acid, man, can you believe that? It's weird. It's just weird. There's no other word for it," Jason says, laughing his coughing smokey laugh.

"Yeah," I say, "I was there, remember?"

"Wow! Yeah! That's right!" Jason is an expert on weird. Jason is weird. He's the only black vintage guitar collector and dealer I know, for one, and he knows flamenco and classical guitars made around the world, from Spain to Japan. He knows weird. He knows the guitars and strange instruments sold through the Sears and Roebuck Catalog in the twenties and things weirder than that. He's had the fingerboard and neck reset, and a French polish finish put on the mystery guitar, and I'm the first one to play it since. He hasn't played it himself.

The first chord I strike scares me and tingles my toes. The sound is dry and wise. "One night on acid, huh? I remember this guitar. It sounds better than I remember." This is the only guitar I ever played that scares me, the only one that's worth fighting for. It's the only guitar ever made that turns me on and makes me want to become a fucking guitarist. It feels like it will fall apart or explode at any time. The whole thing vibrates when the strings are breathed on. I feel the vibrations in the friction pegs when I touch them. The neck vibrates into my thumb as I move my left hand up and down, stomping the strings to the frets, and I have never felt a guitar sing into my left hand before, never felt the notes hum in the neck and the tuning pegs. Jason still isn't ready to sell it. He's keeping it as part of his personal collection.

"I didn't know Chinese men took so much shit from women," she mumbles into my sleeve.

"What shit, sweetheart?"

"The hero let that chick kick his ass."

"Yeah, she knows how to fight," I say. "That's cool."

"Don't you think that's unusual to the Chinese? Insulting to their manhood?"

"Why? It was a fair fight. He lost. He knew when to quit. Maybe he'll even learn something."

"You mean a girl beating up a man is no big deal?"

"Not if she's a better fighter."

"And you still think she's sexy?"

"This one? No. I don't like her giggle. I've seen better."

"Where?"

"In the movies. What're we talking about?"

Nice, happy people cannot make good flamenco guitars. Perhaps the wood the makers use and store in their shops absorbs the old air and gasses of their personalties, and that's why the new top made by three generations of happy Mexican guitar-makers makes for too nice a sound, too sweet a voice for my old de la Chica flamenco. To sound like I'm playing in a dark alley, I would have to take this guitar to just the right dark alley. The dark alleys are already in the mystery guitar. Every note off this guitar is nasty, mean, obsessed. There's nothing nice about this guitar Morton Chu built by feel out of his mind, crazy running from the terrors of acid nightmares.

"Don't take these movies that serious, sweetheart. They're like Chinese fairy tales. Once upon a time a girl disguised herself as a boy to make traveling through the woods to grandma's house easier. Most of grandma had been eaten up by the big bad wolf. She hits the road looking for the wolf and meets a boy. They fight. They join up with people with their own personal case of revenge against the same big bad wolf who's eaten her grandmother. The wolf's crazy with some superpower thing, an invincible killing genius in one-on-one combat who kills five or six of them, and the two or three left have to push themselves over the edge and work together to get him. They fought a war and won, that's love. The end. You'll see. It's a love story."

Yeah, it's the same old story. She says it's because I've seen this movie before.

"They're all like this," I tell her.

"Are you making fun of me?" she asks.

"I'm trying to, sweetheart," I say, smiling soothingly, already on my way out of the thought, as if talking to my Vanessa. I feel like a dirty old man for the first time in my life. She's too young, working too hard to win the little push with me to hear that what I said was funny. She takes my little laugh at hearing myself as a slam. I'm not smarter than her, just way older. My little white sugar is younger than Ben's daughter, and Ben is younger than me. Soon I'll be getting my hair dyed in Chinatown too, I think. And that's funny.

"You are making fun of me," she says, tapping me with her fist.

"What kind of pussy punch is that, sweetheart? A Chinese girl would hit me and make me feel it, baby." I can't stop treating her like a little kid.

Lucky for everybody Ben Mo's daughter Martha looks too much like Ben for me to like her looks. But I love her body. Long legs. Long arms. Round in the tits and ass. We were all over in Marin, in Ben's neighbor's pool. And we all had our glasses off, and near-sighted like all Chinks, all me and Ulysses could see without our glasses was shapes. Just shapes. And we saw a very nice shape walk-ing toward us, and oooh, we both snorted like mustang stallions and commenced to harden up till she got close enough for us to recognize Ben's daughter, and Ulysses says "Ooops!" for both of us and is embarrassed. I'm okay. I have nothing to be embarrassed about. All my friends expect me to get horny for their daughters. I'm the animal of the city, the black Chinaman, the urban aborig-ine. I laugh it off and tell them their daughters look too much like their daddies for me to seriously lust after. We all laugh, but I mean it. I don't want to fuck women who look like my best friends.

I look around the old moviehouse in the old light as dim as memory, and am moving a thousand miles an hour away from the blonde.

There are more people in the movies on the weekends than there were ten, even five years ago. The gangs are different than when the bad boys we were tight with gave me things they stole, asked my advice, and I knew all their nicknames. The Chinese from Indo-china, the Viet and Thai and Singapore Chinese who all call them-selves *tang yun,* Tang people, like us, are changing the look of Chinatown. These bad boys don't look like the gang kids from Hong Kong of my day. These bad boys dress like K-Mart Filipino pimps. And their bad girls are not Annette and Gidget gone wrong, these bad girls come from the movies my shock-hungry hippie sweetheart of the '80s is taking as my personal attack on her. The Indo-Chinese have changed the look of this movie house just by being here. These old-fashioned movies make them real and they make the movies real.

Chinese New Year in Chinatown doesn't look the same either. There's been a bombing, a strange robbery and beating, a botched murder in Frisco, some funny business with doctor's bag full of money behind the restaurant owned by the local Boom Boom Tong's head man in Portland but nothing like a tong war. Only a lot of people gritting their teeth.

These new Chinamen from Vietnam, Laos, Cambodia, Thailand, Burma, Singapore, the descendants of southerners who kept going south into the jungle and swamp rather than become Chinese, know how to use everything they see, everything they learn, as a weapon. They know how to keep their pride and their identity and make their way and make their moves. I see my father as a young man, my mother as a young woman, myself as a baby here. I can't believe Ben was born and had any kind of childhood in China, that he didn't come to America till he was ten or eleven. Maybe twelve.

Kung fu in Chinatown was always middle class. You have to have a little money to pay for the membership in the club and the gear and the little things that go with doing martial arts. And you have to have the time to work out. So the lions that come every New Year to dance in front of friendly businesses, to collect the bribe to tell the Emperor good news and to keep the taxes low, were danced by clean-cut middle-class Chinese Americans and businessmen's sons and daughters for a civic activity. And the kung fu clubs were like the Chinatown Boy Scouts and Girl Scouts. The lion dancers all wore clean club sweatshirts, Chinese trousers, and shoes. No drinking. No smoking. No sex.

The Cameron House and St. Mary's boys and girls and the goody-goody Christian kung fu clubbers, who used to gag on the word *tong* and put me down for reading too many cheap Chinese funny books and who promised to use their kung fu only for good, are getting theirs now. The Viet Chinese are teaching them they haven't read enough cheap Chinese funny books to read the shrines, swans, birds, dragons, and phoenix birds on the walls of Chinese restaurants.

The Viet Chinese lion dancers are street fighters. They are a gang. They dance and play stoned, carry four or five six-packs on the drum cart with the drum. They smoke. Between sets they flop in the closest nook or cranny and grab a girlfriend by a tit, toke on her long cigarette, stick a tongue inside her mouth, and blow smoke out of her nose. And if they happen on another team of lion dancers—the seriously taught white boys who dream of China being TV's *Kung Fu* and the nice middle-class Chinese American kids in their silk pants and white sweatshirts who never forget the "American"—the Viet Chinese lion dancers drop everything and beat the shit out of the kung fu clubbers, who were taught to use their power only "for good."

The last few years, the old timers' lions have come out on one day and the Viet Chinese lions on another. The movie houses and the operas, when they come to town, are like Geneva peace conferences in the Chinatown cold wars. I love watching it. It's the funny books come true. Everyone is bumping up against everyone else. The old timers watching TV in the tong headquarters don't like what they see. The big Boom Boom tong sponsors the operas to flash their prestige. The wives of the Indochinese tongs can't stay away, and they bring the kids. The Indo-Chinese families come, the tongmen come. The operas tell the same stories as the funny books. They are funny books. Raw, nasty, smoky, noisy, long long long comic books. The old timers and the Indo-Chinese meet at the opera. They speak the same southern dialects. They all call themselves Tang people. They invite each other to their tong's New Year spring banquets. Now the old timers are beginning to give.

"Is there always a woman warrior in these movies?"

"Yeah," I say, "At least one."

"That's something new since Pandora Toy Swansdown's Conqueror Woman, right? It must really bug the old timers. They never saw women warriors in the Chinese movies before Pandora Toy invented them."

"Naw," I say. "That Pandora Toy is bullshit. Her women warriors are pussies. As bad as these old movies are, the women fight pretty good."

"Please don't dump on that story. It hits me very personally."

"It's racist, but that's all right. Pandora's that way," I toss.

"Racist? It's feminist. It speaks to me personally as a woman," my white sugar says in such a sweet breathy voice and with such a nice little touch of my arm, so warm and loving, it gives me the creeps. But I'm the Chinese. And this is Chinatown.

"Yeah, a white racist woman, sweetheart," I say and shut up. Why am I so angry? she wants to know. Am I so angry? Nothing for me to get angry about. No fuck is worth this shit at my age, man. "At least you've eaten already, kid," I say. I get up and go. I leave her there in the Chinese movie alone, if she's such an expert.

Fuck it, the '60s are gone, man, the new parade of old young honeys are gone too, along with my Strategic Thinking class in Asian American Studies, and I'm gone. Gone to build decks with gang kids growing old, or maybe I am the leader of a Chinatown gang known for ruthlessly building redwood decks in black jeans, black T-shirts, black shades, and high black pompadours.

They hope to learn American English and the uniform building code from me. I do not carry a hammer too heavy for my wrist. I do not sharpen my chisels in my bare feet.

After hanging out in Sacramento with a Chinese doctor I used to know in grammar school, and getting the contract to build him a three-level deck around his house with my gang, I drive Vanessa through rain that the radio says won't break the drought, back home to Frisco.

"I have a joke, Daddy."

"Okay, honey. I like jokes."

"Why did the chicken cross the road?"

"Oh, I know that joke. To get to the other side."

"Right. Now why did Jaws cross the road?"

"I give up. Why did Jaws cross the road?"

"To get to the other tide."

"Say, that's pretty good, sweetheart!"

"Now, why did the deer cross the road?"

"To get to the other side?"

"No. To get to the chicken!"

Did my Vanessa really make up that joke? I laugh. It's a funny joke. "I love it," I say.

We roll across the Carquinez Bridge around 4:30 P.M. and the rain seems to have cleared. I stop in Berkeley at Blind Peach Music to visit Jason. I find him on the phone, long distance to Spain.

"Ah, España!" I say.

"Heyyy! Diego, man! You haven't changed a bit!" A familiar voice in a beat-up face calls mellow from the workbench. I recognize the body bent over the workbench. I haven't seen Adonis Medina in years. Ten years. Maybe twenty. Maybe twenty-five. Adonis Medina, the Filipino flamenco guitarist–guitar maker I've known since high school, "El Filipino" around North Beach in the '60s.

Adonis looks a thousand years old. His face is toothless and burled by a thousand years of fights and hard living. His silver hair is veined with black. It's thick and wild, pulled back into a ponytail but fighting its way out. He's thin. Wiry. Bare armed. He's setting up to shape a fingerboard on a guitar he's made. He still has the mellowest voice and flamenco sound ever. There is still another new beautiful young woman spending all her parents' money on him and living with him in North Beach. North Beach and Berkeley. The myth continues, the legend lives, I say, pleased, amazed, back in the company of gringo flamenco. I ask Adonis why he has no kids for all the women in his life. He says he has kids by three women. Oh? I'd like to meet his kids. He never sees them and doesn't want to. I grunt. The magic isn't dead, only a little dimmed. I've loved these guys all my life. I can't waste them for not being any better than me.

Vanessa has never seen such a mess of musical instruments before. Guitars hang on the wall next to each other above the display cases of guitars. Above that row is another row and above that row a third row. Guitars are stacked on guitars. Cases are stacked on cases. Guitars, guitarrons, requintas, banjos, banjo-guitars, guitar banjos, mandolas, mandolins, mountain dulcimers. Electric guitars. Vintage electrics. Jason Peach has a '63 Nakade flamenco that is very live, very good, very tempting. He has a half-sized guitar that is perfectly sized for Vanessa's hands and body. El Filipino has a big bruise on the left side of his face. He says, "I got caught between the cops and a robber. The cops threw me down so they could shoot at the robber, man."

This is the Adonis I know. I laugh. Home again. "Damn! You're too straight for Berkeley! I don't believe it," I say.

"This happened in New York," Adonis says.

"That figures," I say, "Everybody's too straight for New York, man."

Vanessa plays every conga in the shop. I apologize for my daughter's lack of musical talent. I pity the guys in this shop when they're wired on a hundred cappuccinos and someone with no sense of rhythm walks in and beats on every drum in the house. Vanessa does have a sense of rhythm. She's not offensively loud. She seems to be comparing the tone of the different drums. She practices a lick Ben taught her on the piano. She tries the marimbas and looks at a huge stand-up bass.

"Hey, Diego," Adonis says, sanding the rosewood fingerboard of a classical guitar with sandpaper tightly attached to a jointer planer. "Come with us to Mexico. A bunch of us are going down to do a flamenco party. Come with us."

"When you going?"

"This Friday."

"Who all's going?" I ask.

"We're all going," Adonis says. The whole shop. Jason and his son. All the flamencos in the area, the guys I know always knew how to play. Singers. Dancers. Can I really go back that far to when it all came so naturally just by going to Mexico this Friday?

A week of American gringo flamenco in Mexico. This is the kind of party Lucinda would hear about and smooth into. I could play both American gringo asshole and Spanish flamenco Gypsy asshole and sop up a lot of music and inspiration to play. It sounds too good to be true. Can I still be the guitarist I might have been if I'd kept playing in the '60s? Can I really play with the likes of Adonis El Filipino and Davey Jones, who have never stopped playing, playing in North Beach bars and productions of *Man from La Mancha,* playing even in Spain, getting better and better all these years and sounding great? In a world where flamenco is nothing, still playing and sounding great means something.

It is too good to be true. I have a gig in Sacramento building a deck next Thursday. I have to drive up Wednesday afternoon. I'll probably take Vanessa with me, as the teachers look like they're going out on strike. I'm not a Spanish Gypsy flamenco guitarist or even a good gringo flamenco guitarist. Vanessa's not ready for a Mexican adventure yet. But Jason has that half-sized classic that is just Vanessa's size. The price is right. But not right now. Right now I have come to buy the mystery flamenco guitar made by Morton Chu while stoned on acid. Jason tells me it still has no label. Mort hadn't even put a finish on it. Jason did the French polish finish. "It's like Morton cast off this guitar, like he put this guitar in a boat and sent it down the river out to sea and never wants to talk about this guitar again," Jason says. "But man, this is almost the best flamenco guitar I have ever played."

"You still play that fat guitar that smells like a boiled horse?" I ask.

"Gypsies like the smell of horses."

As I'm leaving, a longhaired steel string player asks me if I'm playing around here. He'd like to listen in. He says I sound great. This shop is unreal. For an instant I have a fan, an audience, a following. I am the great Chinaman flamenco guitarist I never was. I thank him and say no, I'm not playing anywhere around here soon. I'm so happy Vanessa was with me to hear that. She speaks English and Chinese better than I do. I'm sure I'll be famous someday for being her father. And when Barbara Walters or Connie Chung interviews her on her show and asks her about her daddy, she'll say I played a hell of a guitar.

Some nights I play the Morton Chu mystery guitar alone with Vanessa in my resonant kitchen or out on the deck. Some nights I play across the street at the Three Panchos. I play alone a little while in the near dark of my kitchen and think of what I'll say to Lucinda when she calls. The small light over the stove fills the steam curling above the housekeeper's husband's stockpot.

And I hear chains and hammers and anvils and church bells and the moaning of the penitent and the sweet songs of the sorrowful and grieving in the gringo flamenco I play. And sometimes I play well enough to wonder what would have happened if I had played this well in New York twenty years ago, and I expect Lucinda to call. No matter the hour. No matter where in the world she is. No matter who she's with. No matter how old I am. I don't look any different. I'm still limber. I play the guitar better than I ever have. It could be better. It's good enough to make the old Spanish farts who used to tell me I'm no good clap and dance and sing Fandangos de Huelva, and my Vanessa claps and sings and understands the words. Not me. I just play.

Ulysses: The Mandate of Heaven

I wake up in The Movie About Me. Night. A zombie movie. I am the corpse of the last white man to play Charlie Chan in black and white. Ma and Pa never dreamed they would be the parents of Charlie Chan when they died. They never dreamed they would be remembered as the Chinese mother and father of a zombie. I dream the same dream over and over and never wake up in my grave. I dream I am a better white man for their sakes. I am Superman. The Man of Steel. Blue suit with the red "S" in the yellow triangle on my blue chest. Red cape. I can't wake up. I can't wake up. Where's my body? Where's the big toe of my right foot? Am I back dreaming from the poppy?

The sweat chills me with real cold that scares me awake. Oooh. I am dreaming myself in zombie movies now. Good. Gooood.

If Eldridge or Stokely could only see me now! They were right about no one taking Chinese-American Third World revolutionaries seriously. No one remembers me from the late '60s, early '70s. No. Today, people take the picture poster of me in the wraparound silvered shades, Fu Manchu moustache, Charlie Chan centerline beard, black turtlenecked sweater, chrome bayonet fixed on the muzzle of an AK-47, "Power to the People!" emblazoned in exclamatory Chinese across the top and "Chinatown Black Tigers" in English on the bottom—as a *joke*. Everyone is too embarrassed to remember when the TV news took the Chinatown Black Tigers and me wearing a black beret and silver shades seriously. For a few weeks before the photos for the posters were snapped, silver shades were part of our look. But on TV they looked stupid.

Although there are advantages to being a minority no one takes seriously, no one is afraid of, no one stands up for. I mean, no one in Hollywood is about to give Eldridge, Huey, or Stokely a job writing zombie movies. The Pope of Universal City would say zombie movies are beneath the dignity of the great ones of the '60s. They are trapped in the little moment of history they made because people take them seriously. That's what Hollywood would send some old guy to say.

But nobody remembers the Black Tigers, so I got lucky and landed a job writing *Night of the Living Hollywood Dead*. Something about writing scenes about the remains of all the Hollywood stars of all my favorite old movies, in their jackets with the collars turned up, in their negligees and silk chemises, while shambling down Hollywood Boulevard at night when the Los Angeles air is thick with the gasses of yesterday's hamburgers and falafel, inspired me to achieve a divine stupidity in my writing. After the stupid movie, I wrote the stupid novel. The novel is about to come out and surprisingly got rave reviews in *Publishers Weekly* and the *Kirkus Review Service*. But I don't think I can write that perfectly stupid again. The movies is still keeping me alive. The Four Horsemen want the new zombie movie, storied and scripted by Leroy Mono, to be based on the Orpheus and Eurydice myth.

"I like the idea," I say, hating the idea.

The Four Horsemen ask me to use my personal experience. Orpheus travels south with a Greek formula for raising his wife, Eurydice, from the dead. His recently dead wife, along with the remains of presidents and war heroes, rise from Arlington National Cemetery. Malcom X, Martin Luther King, freedom riders long forgotten in unmarked graves, the consciences, the folksingers, and memories of the '60s, and all my brothers and sisters of the Third World Revolution Power to the People politics from the barrel-of-a-gun days have been secretly buried in Arlington by the FBI for the usual FBI reasons of patriotism and paranoid schizo banzai gung ho arrogance and loyalty to the Bureau. Now they all rise from the dead. Even if they're not dead yet, they rise from the dead.

Eurydice and the Third World zombies wreak havoc on Norfolk, where they board a nuclear submarine and stalk the crew by the light of red bulbs. Orpheus follows, determined to rescue Eurydice. They show up at a Star Trek convention where the President of the United States is giving an address on the peaceful uses of nuclear power in space. Once again the fiction and print rights are mine, and I have already sold the novel.

No more doing it for the people. No more agonized poetry. If *The Night of the Living Third World Dead* brings in just $30 million, I can quit writing for the Four Horsemen and be rich enough to be forgotten, to wander Chinatown, anonymous even to the Chinese, for the rest of my life. If it makes $35 million I won't even have to worry about catastrophic illness. If it makes $40 million I will write one more stupid movie for the Four Horsemen, but only if they contract me to direct it. If not, I'll never have to work again in my life, anyway, and I can go back to writing art that goes nowhere, without ever again worrying about eating out and paying the rent. Yeah, I have plans.

The phone rings. The box answers. I'm awake looking at the ceiling at night. The voice sounds like my father's, only it's thick with phlegm and fatigue. Pa would never call me sounding lousy like this. He's too vain. He'd have someone else call for him.

"This is your brudder, Joe Joe Chu!" the voice writhes every syllable loose and painfully wrenches out every word dripping with blood. China Brother, the son of China Mama and a "paper American." Chu.

I haven't thought of Joe Joe once in more than ten years. He has to tell me he's calling on his cordless touch tone phone from the million dollar home he hasn't had a chance to tell me about till now. The sucker for the American dream tells me his dream has come true. But I hear that still nobody respects him in the difficulty of his voice. I know I don't.

I switch off the box and am on the phone with the touch of a key.

"I don't want to hear your American dream again, man," I Lee Marvin into the phone, then jump into cruel mimicry of his voice and accent. "I come Americker got nutting. My own fodders trit me worse he trit a dog. I supports my modder. I marry, raise tree kids. Bring China Mama Americker. I make lots money now. I got one million dollar house all pay up. I give college education and new cars to allaw my kid. I drive Cadillac car!"

"I drive Rolls-Royce," China Brother barks into the phone. "My wife drive Cadillac."

"Gee, Joe Joe. I sure am glad you called," I say, "Your sense of humor is like sunshine down in the dark of my coal mine."

"Your Pa is dyin' in a hospital in San Francisco. Polly Jade ah divorce-ed him. She bankrupt him. The bank is foreclose his house Monday morning."

"Hey, Joe Joe. What're you talking about? Pa's dying? Which hospital?"

"You want to save any inheritance from him, you better come up here with some tools and I break his door down with you, and you get the books and papers and maybe find a will before Polly Jade steals it all."

"Hey, you are the first son, not me," I say. "I'm not even the first American son. Junior, The Hero, is."

"You seen Junior lately? He dying of cancer. He can't walk, can't eat, can't go to take a shit or piss by himself. He can't break down anybody's door. He can't live that long to inherit anything."

"Oh, have you seen him?" I ask.

"Auntie Orchid tell me don't bother him. "

"So you haven't seen Longman Jr.," I say. "I didn't think so."

His voice is hard and tight, and hardens and tightens as he speaks. As I listen to him, I think of how it must hurt his throat to talk like that all the time. "You don't know you and Junior come from different mothers, like me. Pa has no two sons from the same mother."

"What? Ma wasn't Longman Jr.'s mother?"

"You are Hyacinth's only son," he says. "You never heard that before?"

"You have a strange sense of humor."

"With you I have no sense of humor, so stop it. I am sure your Auntie Orchid will talk to you about who Longman Jr. real mother is."

"Is?" I ask. We were never that close, Joe Joe. So what's it to you, if my mother is not yours?

"One thing sure," China Brother says. "She going to tell you not to let those old tong guys talk you into big Chinatown funeral for the old man. Nobody knows if Polly Jade leave enough money in his estate to pay for it, understand me? That's why if you want to find a will, you come up right now. You can stay at my house. I don't want anything from him now. I got it made. I am a millionaire! Junior, he's got his railroad insurance. You, you never worked a day of your life, what're you going to do without money from Pa, huh?"

"What? Pa never gave me money!" I say.

"Don't tell me, you tell Auntie Orchid. I told you, I don't want anything. I got money. I put all my kids through college. They want a PhD, I tell them go ahead, don't worry, I buy the books, pay the rent, everything. For graduation I buy them all any kind of car they ask for. I don't want anything of his after he's dead."

"It sounds like you've been talking to Auntie Orchid yourself."

"Sure, I told you why," he says, explaining nothing. "When your Ma died, I told him come live with my family. We treat him like he the king. Or I built for him a mansion. He laugh at me for that. Called me craze and laugh. I invite him for Christmas dinner with my family and good friends and he come. No presents for my kids. His own grandchill-drennds! And he turn on the TV and watch football by himself instead of come sit for dinner with us. My house! My Christmastide dinner! I cooked one whole roasted prime ribs!"

"Hey, Joe Joe. I agree. No argument. He's a lousy father. He's a rotten man. A shitty husband. A treacherous friend. So what? Tell him, not me. You told me before."

"Not this. . . !"

"Then stuff like this. Since when did you tell me anything else but the bad shit Pa's done to you? What else have you ever talked about?"

In the morning. Turn left onto the on-ramp north on I-5, and hello, lonesome road.

The son of Charlie Chan is dying, Ma.

Ulysses: Let Him Die

"Let him die," China Brother says at lunch in a horrible Korean-Chinese-Japanese place he knows near the hospital. It says a lot about China Brother's taste that he'd bring Auntie Orchid, a heroine of his history and people, here for lunch. Is this his way of punishing her for being fatter than his dream can stand?

He burns his eyes dry glaring at me and says, "Who's going to take care of him, if he lives? You?" He snorts and sneers. "You tell me. He got nothing leave him after Polly Jade bankrupt him. That's what bankrupt means, right? You tell me, is that right? So you going to take care of him if he live? Let him die."

"If he lives, that's his problem. I'm going to ask for the second opinion without you. If he's got a fifty-fifty chance, I'm not going to fuck up his benefit of a doubt. If he lives through this and hates it, it serves him right. I'd rather he die wide awake with all his wits and all alone the way he deserves than stroke out and coma away," I say.

The food is greasy, too salty, brittle with MSG. No matter how we try to eat just a bit of it, we can't. It's not food. It's prop food. Set dressing. But Joe Joe likes the egg rolls. "These aren't bad," he says.

"They're awful," I say. "Look, every time you bite on it, grease oozes out from everywhere all over your fingers. Why're you eating those awful things with your fingers? You want to lick them afterwards?"

"What's it to you?" China Brother blurts back, grease all over his fingers and lips. "It bother you or something?"

"Oh, this restaurant gets nice light through that big window," Auntie Orchid says. "Very nice light." She lays a chicken wing as crunchy as old dry bread back down on her plate.

Today is Monday. The Hero wants to see me on Friday, dinner early with the family, Auntie Orchid says, as if it will cheer us up. She kicks me under the table hard with one of her short fat legs. Her way of saying cool it and play along with her. This is a performance.

I hem and haw. Hollywood Junior, The Hero, is dying. The doctors say six weeks. Why is she so close to my mother's family? It's not because Pa was that great an opera star before the war.

She tells us The Hero is trying to live till his sixtieth birthday in October. The tenth day of the tenth month. The day Dr. Sun declared the end of the Manchu Empire and the beginning of the Republic.

He is my brother after all. The whole family expects me. When

The Hero dies, I will be the oldest male in my mother's family. The oldest male of direct blood to the madam of the largest whorehouse on Stockton Street and her daughter Rose, who married a railroad steward named Kwan. He took the family to the opera in San Francisco every night he was home from the railroad, on the turnaround.

"You never worked a day in your life," China Brother says right on cue.

"Hey, come on," I say, my eyes on Joe Joe as he bites into a deep-fried shrimp that squishes oil through the crust of the breading when his teeth press closed. "Last year I made more money than you made in the last three years, I betya, Joe Joe. Wanna bet?"

"Doing what?" he asks.

"You ever see a movie called *Night of the Living Hollywood Dead*?" I ask.

"That's the one with Frank Sinatra and Marilyn Monroe zombies . . ." China Brother says before I cut him off.

"We don't call him Frank Sinatra, okay? He's not even dead yet, so how can he be zombie?"

"Wait a minute, that's his question, stupid," Auntie Orchid says, batting my shoulder with her fingers.

"I wrote *Night of the Living Hollywood Dead.*"

"You really wrote that movie? Nawww! If I see your name in the credit, how many Ulysses Kwan, in the world, huh? I would remember it, but I don't," China Brother says.

"I write under the name Leroy Mono. It's incorporated. Leroy Mono, Inc. Check it out. Rent the cassette of the movie. Or better yet, buy it."

"I'm proud of you, boy," Auntie Orchid says, "Your mother would be proud of you too. You stuck with it. And now you've made it."

Ulysses: The Heroic Tradition

Three Aztec warriors sweat, bounce light off their skin, and press forward up Mission Street. I slow my walk to let them pass. The long feathers of their headdresses snake and float a long way after their thrusting heads. They load a half-naked Aztec maiden, either dead or asleep, into a shopping cart from Safeway, and shove her along Mission past the big window of the Los Tres Hermanos Salvadoran-Peruvian-Mexican Restaurant. I look through the glass for Diego Chang and into the frightened desperate eyes of a thin man who looks enough like me to make me want to laugh.

The Four Horsemen know where to reach me with notes on my latest rewrite of *Night of the Living Third World Dead,* and they know where to reach me.

I take another look at the caricature of me being served a long dish of *platanos fritos,* sour cream and black beans, just what I would have ordered. He looks down the front of the waitress's blouse as she bends over his table with the hot plate of golden, oil-fried ripe plantain bananas, just as I would do if she served me. All the waitresses have black hair and dark eyes and wear white blouses with red, yellow, green, and blue flowers embroidered on the sleeves and the yoke. The colors and patterns look Chinese. They dress like the Kwan sisters just before Junior came home from the war.

The Aztec warriors shove their shopping cart full of a very young, luscious, and vulnerable-looking Aztec maiden off the Mexican beer calendars past the old woman smacking her tortillas. The building façades leer cool neon Popsicle flavors on their skin, and the world is pastel on black velvet.

The pneumatic steel elbow gasps and keeps the front door open behind me, and the sound of the shopping cart clatters and rattles in. No one blinks or says a word or acts as if they have seen anything strange. The glass and steel-clad iron-barred door squishes shut behind me.

The walls are white enamel on white simulated plaster and brick.

The upper wall is balcony scenes. Happily imaged tableaux of the Mexican revolution. Pancho Villa wanted posters on the wall. On the back wall a mustachioed store mannequin in white pajamas and bandoliers of ammo sleeps against a wooden keg of blasting powder marked xxxx, his rifle against his cheek, a stuffed chicken by his feet. The stuffed chicken looks real. The stuffed man does not. In a room through arches cut in a bearing wall, Pancho Villa rides in a huge painting, and neon glows higher up the white enamel.

The ceilings must be sixteen feet high. The air is so tropical in here that the stuffed toy parrots and plastic tropical birds dangling from the ceiling might as well be real. The shrieking of brakes, gurgle of scooter engines, and chirping and buzzing alarms on city buses make the same jungle bird sounds. A red, green, and very cool yellow, sultry candified blue neon sign zigzags a few Spanish words I can't read backwards, reflected in the window of a city bus stumbling away from the curb.

And there he is, Diego Chang. What a relief. His back to the wall of the restaurant, back in the '60s playing flamenco guitar. No, not like the '60s. He plays better now. He plays like the very best guitarists of twenty years ago.

He wears amber-colored shooting glasses low on his nose, and a Giants baseball cap. He sees me and gives me the gringo flamenco cold shoulder, and cool as Jell-O clangs into the Fu Manchu Seguiriyas, from when we both played Fu Manchu in Ben's old play. He sings,

> "Oh, rice! They say I don't eat you!
>   Oh-ohhhh, riiiiiice!
> They say, ay ay ay I do-oh-on't eat you!
> Because all the Chinese in Charlie Chan
> Fu Manchu Big Bijou eat rice!
>   Ay ayyyy ayyy
> And that is a racist stereotype!
> So, to avoid the stereotype,
> I do not eat rice.
>   Ay ayyyyy ayyyyy!"

I join in when he sings again,

> *"Oh, rice! That is a lie*
> *such as to break my heart.*
> *Oh-ohh-ohh, ri-ice! That is a lie*
> *Ay ay such as to break my heart.*
> *I love you, rice. I eat you more than once a day.*
> > *And heat you up.*
> > *And heat you up.*
> > *Ay ayy ayy*
> *Alone, I like to wash you,*
> *Till I see your every grain*
> *Till I see your every gray-ay ay-ain*
> *Clear and sharp through an inch of water.*
> *Then I like to cook you up fluffy.*
> *Oh! Oh! Ohhh! Rice! It's you and me.*
> *Ay ay ayyyy! Oh, rice! It's you and me!"*

In Diego's kitchen I am no longer nobody. I have an identity for a while. The two women who've followed Diego home know I am the son of a dying tong big shot who used to play Charlie Chan the Detective's Number Four Son in the American movies. They know all about me. What does the son of Number Four Son think of Pandora Toy's Charlie Chan? The first Charlie Chan scripted by a real Chinese-American writer?

Yes, the first Charlie Chan movie in two decades is being scripted by the hottest yellow writer going, Pandora Toy. She is making movie history with the first Charlie Chan going big studio, big budget, with a big-name Oscar-winning producer—director Ozzie Clay, taking a little R&R from romanticizing the killing of yellow men who deserve it and yellow women who deserve only pity, in fantasy war movies set in the Vietnam War. Ozzie Clay and Pandora Toy promise "a more authentic Charlie Chan, not the stereotype," and the producers trumpet that *the big* first will be Charlie Chan played at last by a Chinese actor.

"No thanks. No comment," I say.

"That sounds cold, man," Diego says. "They know your old man, Number Four Son, is dying with his eyes half open. I mean, Charlie Chan is like your grandfather, man. You have to have a comment, man."

"If Charlie Chan uses first-person pronouns, does not walk in the fetal position, is not played by a white man, and looks and acts like a real Chinese, he's not Charlie Chan anymore."

"Isn't that progress for the Chinese?" asks one of the women.

"Yeah, sure it is. And putting a black man in a white sheet makes the Ku Klux Klan a civil rights organization."

"You write zombie movies. That's a stereotype," the other answers.

"Zombies are not about to picket or protest anything Ulysses writes," Diego says.

I laugh. "Diego, true to form is proving himself to be more of a grieving son for a Chinatown big shot than I am," I say.

"You're going to have to do what I just did, man. When he kicks, you're going to have to go down to the tong with the white candy and sit with the old men awhile," Diego says, stretching his legs out on his deck and toking a doobie of good California Green.

"Yeah, let's talk about something cheerful for a change," I say.

The dark is dense with the shadows of his trees and the ivy grown wild, winding round and round an old clothesline post, and spacious with moonlight. "You have tea with them," Diego says, "Ask them for their advice. It makes your father look good, like he raised a decent filial son instead of some asshole like we really are. Though my father wasn't a member of our West Coast tong, they respected him as an older brother because he was who he was. Everybody knew he knew lots of secrets. I mean lots. Everybody's secrets. He wrote their letters home. He kept their records, like he was their clerk and letter writer. Your daddy was big. Playboy, right? They'll run it down to you. They ran it down to me this way: My daddy wasn't a tong big shot, but he was a respected elder statesman. I had to give him a Chinese funeral. So, you know, the tong big shots are going to say your dad deserves the show of Chinatown big shots spending the better part of a whole day honoring his dead ass. You know what I mean? You better find out if there's enough in your old man's estate to pay for the kind of funeral he wants. And they'll tell you. You gotta have the Chinese Lady come in and wash the body. Fifty bucks."

"That's kind of poetic," I say. "A Chinese lady washes his body. It's too good for him. I'll get a dog to come in and pee on him."

"Six hundred bucks for what they're gonna call special services or professional services—embalming the body and shit like that. Then the coffin. For your dad—you have to go buy at least a $1,200 box, man. You don't want painted wood and plastic handles. Naw, naw. Look too cheap, so the $1,200 box. That way you also get two free limos and one free flower car. Oh, yeah. Limos are $150 each. And you have to have limos for the tong big shots to ride in. Flower cars $115 plus the flowers. You will have to have the pillows and the blanket. The pillows are $250 each. One for each of his children. The blanket is $500. The clock is $250. The heart, you have to have the heart, is $250. The band is $2,000. The cops to stop the traffic are $130 each and you have to have 'em, man. Fuck, man, they were so cool we never stopped, from the mortuary to the cemetery. They were good. I tipped them $50 each. Yeah, you're going to have to have someone pass out a little white envelope with a little piece of plain sugar candy in it to the people going in, and coming out you pass everyone a red envelope with a new nickel in it."

"I have enough money to live without panic, but not enough to throw forty or fifty thousand into Pa's funeral."

"You have to, you're the first son, like me," Diego says.

"I am not. China Brother is the first son."

"Anyway it comes out of your old man's estate. You don't pay. That's right! Your China Brother. You ever meet your dad's China Mama?"

Ulysses: Borrow a Corpse to Capture a Soul

Irma's house on Ithaca Ave in Oakland is all black enameled wood trim and red flock wallpaper on the walls. Red wall-to-wall polyester deep pile on the floors. It looks like a whorehouse from an old TV western. Everything about the place is swiped from an old movie. Nobody uses the front entrance. Everyone walks up the driveway and knocks on the side door that opens to a snarling pit bull pulling against a chain in the little hand of Irma's six-year-old daughter. She's no taller than the dog is long. When Auntie Orchid trills "Irma's daughter Yumi is a little Japanese doll," over the phone, I get the creeps and shudder, depressed. It's too much like hearing people call me a "a little Chinese dolly." When I was a kid it was okay. It's not that I hated the retired silent-screen bit player calling me her little Chinese dolly. It's that other people remember and lie in wait to tell me. That makes for the bad memories. The family is all here. It's larger. It's different. It's been almost twenty years since I've seen them.

Auntie Orchid is right. Yumi is a little Japanese doll. She has Irma's eyes. She looks a lot like Irma as a little girl of six. A fine white jade, gem-quality skin that makes me fear the raging acne that runs in the blood of the Kwans. Little Yumi is a brief memory of her mother in her little white Shirley Temple dress, perfect porcelain skin before it was hit by acid rain, the long straight black hair, the little heart-shaped lips from a print by Hokosai, the pit bull's choke chain in her hand, against the red and black insides of a TV show Dodge City whorehouse. This is kabuki. This is puppet opera. A mythic vision from the opening of *Whatever Happened to Baby Jane?* Will my pretty little grandniece grow up to become a pockmarked elderly harping Bette Davis in a large Shirley Temple dress tormenting her sister in baby talk?

"Not even our great grandmother's Frisco Chinatown whorehouse on Stockton Street looked like this in the old photos taken before the 1906 earthquake and fire," I say, to announce myself. The first complete family gathering in more than twenty years. I expect Randolph Scott and Joel McRae to walk in any second now.

Longman Jr. doesn't suit my smile. He's down to 90 pounds. I look away into the eyes of family members I have never seen before.

"Close the door! Yumi-ko! Close the damned door! Sheee!" I hear Irma shout out of sight from the kitchen. And the door slams shut. The door opens a crack, and the dog punches his snout through and barks and shows his teeth. "You can't come in, Uncle Ulysses, because Cerberus doesn't like strangers."

"Yumi! Close the door!"

"I am! Give me a chance!"

"Put the damned dog out back. Then let Uncle Ulysses in! Can you do that?"

"Yes, Mommy."

"Then do it! Come on, move it, girl!"

The birdy old ladies pant for air at the top of the stairs, flashing their gold teeth. Storks and penguins in black overcoats. Their thinning black hair is pulled back into buns, gold and jade rattle on their wrinkled skinny wrists, the last widows dignifying the dead of the funerals of my Chinatown childhood are all gone. Instead my aunts are the new elders, with their different colored overcoats piled on the good couch, bodybagged, as always, in clear plastic.

Everyone who isn't talking to anyone is suddenly talking to me. We have come to Irma's house to keep Longman Jr. company while he dies before my eyes as surely as the pork I smell roasts in the kitchen. Without saying so, all want Longman Jr. and me to see each other while the sun is still out lighting the world like a picture postcard from California.

The floor around The Hero is alive with children I don't know. I used to be the kid nobody knows at the family gatherings. These are the kids of Irma's husband's sisters. I forget this is Irma's husband's house. She's married, a Yoshi now, not a Kwan, and this is Chester Yoshi's house. That's why his father is not out of place here. All the pupils in their eyes pop in the blast of light through the side door, watching me step into their shady electric light through the front room and into the kitchen.

The Hero looks like a pile of French fries sticking out of a bag. I see the bones of his face, the seams of his skull through the skin. There is nothing on his face but skin. The skin doesn't look like it belongs to him. The skin looks borrowed from a raw turkey. His papery eyelids barely keep his eyes from falling out of the sockets. The eyes don't move fast. They float in oil. I burst into tears at the first clear sight of him and turn away, making for the kitchen by smell. Always the kitchen. Refuge in the kitchen. Listen in the kitchen.

Irma is slicing roast pork. Another generation, mine this time, makes another family potluck. I pass three or four different variations of lasagna, chow mien, aluminum roasting pans full of differently treated chicken parts. A recipe from *Vogue* that no one knows what to think of, and no one, not even Auntie Orchid, knows how it should taste. A large drip pot of weak canned ground coffee shows me what a phony I am for being here. I hate the stuff on sight. But it's dark. They got it just for me because they know I'm a nut for "dark" coffee. Irma grabs a towel, wipes her hands, and shoves me through a swinging door with her wrists. I try to get my eyes to focus on a segment of the flock pattern on the wallpaper, dizzy away and drop my eyes to focus on the toe of my right boot, for a bombsight view of the prow of a battleship, a black leather dreadnought at anchor on a red pile sea. The thick mindfucking cartoon stomach-churning red pile quiets things down, I hear not one of Irma's steps as she walks out of her kitchen into the hallway after me. Thick carpet. She puts her hands on my back, "Would you like a jay, Uncle Ulysses?" she asks. I don't understand. I can't catch my breath to speak one intelligent thought. I can't explain myself. "A jay?" I ask.

"Would you like to smoke a joint?"

At last, something I understand. "No, that would make it worse," I answer.

Ulysses: The Eight Immortals

Eight is the number of invincibility. I take Irma to the eight-sided room with the round table by the unused front door, where people go to speak Cantonese, smoke their cigars and pipes, and sneak quiet farts.

All the desserts lie naked and virginal, glossy, frothy, wobbly, and gooey on the big oak table. The aunts don't have foam plates stacked with food on their laps yet. It will be a while before anyone comes in searching for dessert. We sit by the liquor cabinet and turn our chairs in to face each other, keeping one eye on the round table and the aunts.

Great Aunt Willy Hum, the aunts, and Uncle Jim are settled into high-backed chairs along the wall. They sit tight and upright against the backs and conscientiously leave a path between their knees and the big round table covered with colorful desserts.

Only Uncle Mort sits with his chair pulled up to the table. He slouches and smiles. The children run in playing tag and nibble at me and Irma with their eyes without slowing their conversation as we sit on the far side of the table. Irma grits her teeth and starts telling me what she can't tell her father.

The long gut-wrenching war of whining snipes and subtly coded innuendo between her and her sisters, The Hero's daughters by his first wife, and Virginia, the wife of his old age, continues. I promise to talk to Imogene about what Irma wants me to talk about, I promise to talk to Irene about her freed gangster boyfriend, and nod and nod as she worries and mumbles on, a grim child reciting her grim list to my grim Santa Claus.

"I see you're wearing green tonight, Ah-Ulysses?" Big Aunt Poppy says sweet and sickly, holding her glass up to me. "Weller's Original, 108 proof."

"I remember you said green makes me look yellow, Big Aunt," I say. "I thought Weller's Original was 107 proof."

She smiles wanly, and sighs, "Oh, no. 108. And that was brown that makes you look yellow. I told you not to wear brown."

"No, green!" Aunt Azalea sitting next to her says. "Don't wear green because it makes you look yellow."

"No, that's not right. Brown makes you look yellow," Big Aunt Poppy says. "What are you doing these days? How long has it been? You have a job?"

"That's right, Ah-Poppy!" Aunt Azalea laughs. "Make sure his money is honest!"

"I write zombie movies."

"Night of the Hollywood Dead wahh!" Auntie Orchid says slapping my arm for happy emphasis. "He wrote it. Didn't you! Tell her!"

"Zombie movies?" the aunts lift their faces, adjust their glasses and refocus on me.

"It's a job," I say. "You probably never saw it."

"Now, not so fast." The words pass from Big Aunt Poppy's mouth, soft, wispy, just a little more audible than a breeze. "Is that the one that has these whatchamacallit . . ."

"Zombies *Wahhh! Haaa!*" Aunt Azalea hurries irritatedly from her mouth. "You speak so slow it drives me crazy, you!"

"That's right, zombies. Zombies of uhh, Rudy Vallee and Tex Ritter? dig themselves out of their graves all rotten and go to Beverly Hills at night," Big Aunt Poppy flutters and pants beyond exhaustion. "And Elvis! Yeeeh! He was all maggots."

"Elvis! How could that be?" Aunt Azalea scolds. "He's not buried in Los Angeles. Not even in California, right?"

"And Frank Sinatra," Poppy sighs. "They chase this Sunny Ninja—she's a television news reporter—all over Los Angeles."

"No!" Aunt Azalea whooshes the word out like a gush from a firehose. "Frank Sinatra's not even dead yet! How can you make him a zombie?"

"That's what I told him," Aunt Poppy struggles to flutter in a ghostly harmony. "Frank Sinatra is not dead yet. He's still alive and singing, *hie muh.* Right? See, I told you. If only you had graduated from Cal."

"And he sounds gooooood, too!" Aunt Azalea says. "You

wouldn't think he was so old. You wouldn't think he was even as old as you, Ah-Poppy!"

"If I were him I'd sue," Big Aunt Poppy sighs.

"You mean you actually saw the *Night of the Living Hollywood Dead?*" Uncle Mort asks. One of the rare occasions of Mort directly addressing the wife he left thirty years ago takes the family by surprise.

"Yes, Christopher took me to see it at a drive-in," Poppy says.

"He did?" Mort shoots back and sits up. Oh, oh, both are possessive of their own privileged, mutually exclusive rapport with their grandson.

"For his Pop Culture class," Poppy sighs, fading fast. "Elvis and Frank Sinatra, and Rudy Vallee, and Bing Crosby . . ."

"You said 'Tex Ritter,'" Aunt Azalea pops.

"Yes, Tex Ritter too, and others too. Judy Garland, Marilyn Monroe."

"Marilyn Monroe?" Aunt Peony moos up. "Her too?"

"All singers and movie stars. All dead, and you know. . . . Decomposed, and ugh! Their tuxedos and gowns all dirty from all that digging themselves out of their graves, and they shuffle and stagger out of the cemetery into Beverly Hills, and Elvis and Bing Crosby and them see one of these neon signs on a boutique, I guess. It says *Heaven* and all the zombies stop, and Elvis says *Heaven* and Bing Crosby says *This is it. We've made it.* And Frank Sinatra and all the zombies sing *Heaven. I'm in Heaven* . . . Right? Huh, Ulysses. That is the movie, right?" Aunt Poppy says, as if these were her dying words.

"Well, since this isn't a court of law, and I'm not being sued for libel, slander, or violating anybody's trademark," I say, "yeah, the zombies in the movie, who are never named, do bear an uncanny and putrid resemblance to the people you mentioned. Yeah."

"I should have known you wrote it, you," Aunt Poppy seems to be dying tragically again and again. "How come your name wasn't in the credits?"

"I use the name Leroy Mono in the biz, Aunt Poppy," I say, "But

I wrote the novel *Night of the Living Third World Dead* under my own name. And the novel version of *Night of the Living Hollywood Dead* is coming out in a new edition under my own name too. But the strange thing is no one is taking them seriously as zombie novels. Everyone's reviewing *Third World Dead* as not just a serious Chinese American novel, but Ah-Sin, as the Chinaman man's answer to Pandora Toy.

"I can't believe you actually saw Ulysses' movie!" Mort says, leaning back in his chair. One arm is draped over the back and one arm extended with the hand resting palm up on the table between the pies and cakes, gesturing with his fingers. I hadn't told him about the movie or brought him down for one of the previews. Now, posed in his deceptively off-balance slouch, speaking through his tense little smile, Mort is making the stupid zombie movie a family issue.

"We even went to see his father's movies, huh, Azalea. Isn't that right?" weird-eyed Auntie Peony smiles and sneers at the same time.

"But Longman, that *kie die* was in the movie. Why not be a star like your father?" Aunt Azalea taunts.

"I'm a writer, not a star."

"You should talk to your friend Benny," Azalea says and nods in agreement with herself. "You could be the first Chinese to play Charlie Chan in the movie his wife, Pandora Toy, is writing. Did you read about it?"

"I mean, you really understood the existential gizmo of the dialogue Ulysses wrote?" Mort asks in a big voice.

"I don't know what you're talking about," Aunt Poppy sighs. "I saw it at a drive-in with Christopher, I said. I think you did a good job, Ulysses. The look of the meat when the zombie people came apart was very realistic."

"Thanks, *Ah-Dai Yee,*" I say, calling her Big Aunt in Cantonese.

"That's probably because your father, Longman Sr., was a butcher when you were young." Aunt Poppy's voice lofts like a leaf catching a warm thermal off a hillside.

"No, Poppy-aaah!" Aunt Azalea grins. "Don't be that way," she says and sings insincere sugar through a smile of brilliant false teeth. "It is because your father, Longman Sr., was a movie star in Hollywood, wasn't it, dear."

"He was always Charlie Chan's Number Four Son and—that's Industry with a capital "I"—the Industry's reliable Chinaman Who Dies, to me," I say.

"You got that right," Aunt Azalea mumbles under her breath. "Not even Number One Son. Just Number Four. *Say yeah.* Excuse me while I take out my teeth to laugh," she garbles as she loosens her teeth.

"'You dead thing' in Chinese sounds like an old hippie saying 'Say, yeah!' Don't hit me again, Orchid. Everything's groovy."

"Auntie Orchid to you, bozo!" Auntie Orchid says, punching me again.

"Say, what do you hear from your daughter-in-law, Orchid?" Aunt Azalea asks.

Orchid ignores the question and continues, "And now he's written a novel of the movie and that is being published."

"It is published," I say.

"Oh, pardon me! It is published!"

"And *The Night of the Living Third World Dead* is about to be published," I say.

"Oh, two novels."

Imogene sweeps into the octagonal room without her gold silk Chinese jacket. Her tight fuzzy black sweater fits with the red flock wallpaper and black woodwork that keeps this house closed in perpetual night life. "Ah ha! I knew I would find you still in here, holding court, as usual," she says. "I bet you haven't eaten yet either. And you know, your Uncle Mort made a roast prime rib just for you, and you haven't even looked at it. You can't hurt his feelings like that . . . So I cut you off a bone, because I know how much you love to chew on bones."

Imogene sits in the place just left by her father's second wife and says, low, righteous, and treacherous, that she wants her father to stay in the hospital where he can get the rigorous round-the-clock care and diet control he needs, rather than staying at home making the family feel inadequate and guilty. I cut her off. "The decision is made," I say out loud, making sure no one mistakes who I am talking to. "He has maybe six weeks! He's going to die. That's it! Whatever Virginia says is right! And we all help her. No more argument. No criticism. Period." Imogene gives me another hurt and betrayed look. "That's it!" I bark. "Any disagreement will wait till after."

She pouts and glowers at me like her younger sister. It's the look of the hour. For Auntie Orchid and Big Aunt Poppy I tell Imogene to go to talk with her sister Irma, "Just to let your father see his daughters looking like they love each other before he dies. Just give him something to look at. He's not going to ask for a lot of truth when he's nothing but a fiction himself. Go!"

The voice of authority makes her rage for the sport of rage: Peter Lorre in Bette Davis drag. And the war is on. "You know Virginia is just an atrocious housekeeper. Atrocious!" The aunts lean back, mumble to each other, and listen our way. "Dad always complained to me that he had to do the housework, he had to vacuum every night and do the shopping and all the cooking. Yeeh! It was horrible to hear him talk, and the kids don't know which end of a vacuum cleaner is up and don't know the difference between soy sauce and cough syrup," Imogene chants breathily to the table of desserts. Her jaw set, cheekbones up, neck extended, shoulders back. The chant is to the rhythm of a Shirley Temple song from a Shirley Temple movie.

"The decision is made! No more argument," I bark again, blasting death rays out of my eyes.

"Dad said he was vacuuming one day, and she came home and used five different glasses, opened a bottle of pop, and left it half full, made herself a Vodka gimlet and left the Rose's Lime and Vodka out and the caps all over the place, left the glasses all over the house on the arms of the couch and the dining room table without using coasters, all in one hour . . ."

"No one expects your dad to vacuum the house now. And the aunts are taking turns keeping the housework done and the family fed, so—no arguments! The decision is made. He wants to be home. He's home! Whatever Virginia says till the moment he's slid into the crypt is it. No questions. No arguments. No backtalk. It can wait. Now get out of here and look good for your dad." I hear what I say after saying it, as if I'm a looping dialogue, and wonder what movie this is.

"I can't," she says.

"Fake it. You don't have to believe it. Just do it. Fake it." She opens her mouth to speak, and I barge in, "Fake it!"

"Ai-yaaaa! Ah-Imogene!" Auntie Orchid sings, "You're still a little *moong moong day* in the head, a big girl like you. What's the idea of bringing your uncle all this food and no fork or chopsticks? How do you expect him to eat, huh?" Auntie Orchid joshes and bullies Imogene with her smiles and a few pokes of her pudgy fingers, prods her out of the chair and herds her out of the room and closes the door.

"You know, Ah-Imogene used to be such good friends with me. But it's as if her whole personality changed with her breast enlargement," Big Aunt Poppy says.

"There is something you should know before Longman Sr. and Longman Jr. pass," Big Aunt Willy says.

Big Aunt Willy, the living flesh of our family history and protocol, looks faceless. Her eyes are two round fishbowls with dark and still fish inside, waving their fins. Her fingers in her lap toy with a red and gold sleighbell-shaped tone box called a "wooden fish," tapping little sounds out of it with her fingernails, like scrabbling crablegs. She has the complexion of a cooked crab. Is she bald under her wig? Her lips are the same fleshy puckering swollen guppy lips pressed shut in a disapproval that is better expressed without words. How old is Aunt Willy?

Next to Aunt Willy is an empty chair with a crutch leaning against it. It's the crutch Ma used after she broke her ankle the night I was burned with a gallon of boiling water.

Big Aunt Poppy, still a blooming beauty in her seventies, sighs and waves a fan under her face. We used to call her "Chihuahua Eyes" when we were kids. Her eyes were the secret of her beauty, we thought.

Big Aunt Poppy's thin hair is still long, more like the hair of an old man's beard than anything on anybody's head. She still wears it in some picturebook Chinese style, braided and rolled up into spiraling earmuffs on each side of her head. She refuses to divorce Uncle Mort and refuses to talk to him directly.

Mort sits with his innocent boyish pugnacious grin from the days of early Jimmy Cagney, belly up to the table of desserts. He fingers a dried lotus pod and stem, holds it like a telegrapher playing a speed key out of an old habit. Did I know he turned seventy-five this year? Mort asks.

"How about that!" I say.

Aunt Peony, the weird-eyed, once-upon-a-time otherworldly beauty of the family, looks like a career traffic lady with her stretch slacks and sweatshirt, hiding behind the basket of flowers on the table between us. Aunt Azalea, Myrtle's mother, clicks a pair of wooden chopsticks like castanets next to the youngest of the Kwan beauties, Aunt Lily, in her sixties now, widowed for the third time. Every time she married, she married money. She still yowls and radiates the cats of sex. Her first husband, an elder in the electronic come-and-get-it sutra-thumping Buddhist church invented by his family, gave her a jade flute she wore around her neck on a gold chain after he died, through her next two marriages, and to this day.

Orchid in her *cheongsam* tailored for a baby elephant, wearing a silver sword in her hair, runs this family as if it is her own. She is the general, and Azalea, the late Myrtle's mother, is the strategist. Big Aunt Willy, the ancient agelessly old old aunt, is the book, the family's Confucian historical conscience.

Big Aunt Willy says, "The red envelopes with the symbolic nickel wish for joy and prosperity will never be dealt out to people going into the funeral of one of our dead again. The wish for continual life comes after the funeral, on the way out, not going in. Now you are the oldest living male with direct blood to the Kwan of this branch of the Kwan family. Before you say anything about being the head of the Kwan family—"

"Head of the family! I'm the black sheep of the family, the skeleton in the family closet. I'm a member of this family in name only, what're you talking about head of the family?"

"Don't interrupt Big Aunt Willy," Auntie Orchid commands.

Big Aunt Willy says evenly, "We have to tell you a couple of things before your father and Longman Jr. leave this world."

"Is this some kind of ritual where we all drink blood and piss in a pot? If I'm just a rent-a-patriarch, showcase head of the family, I'm happy, because I don't know everybody's name out there, and I don't really want to. I don't mind having no real power over people. I don't care, really, if Irene has the guilts over betraying her gangster boyfriend and letting him rot on Death Row. I don't care if she marries him, either, now that he's out. I'll be happy to give her a speech out of *Ozzie and Harriet,* but I don't want to make anybody's big decisions for them. It's not up to me to bless marriages and births, okay?"

"Who's asking?" weird-eyed Aunt Peony pipes up. "You just have to make us feel good about whatever happens, that's all. No one's going to listen to you anyway, so don't you worry about it."

"So you're not out to do something to me to change my life forever? Convert me to Christianity or make me see into the fifth dimension?"

"You know Longman Jr.?" Orchid sings. "He's your father's son, but not your mother's."

"Ma is not Junior's mother? But Pa is his father? Is this a trick question, or a trick answer?" I ask.

Orchid sighs and continues, "Junior doesn't know. You can tell him if you want. He doesn't know your father's dying. If he knew his father was in a coma and dying, it might be the straw that breaks the camel's back. It is your place to tell him, if he's going to be told."

"My place to tell him? Tell him what? Ma is not his mother? Ma is not Longman Jr.'s mother? Who is Junior's mother? And why would Ma raise another woman's baby as her own? Is that what you want me to tell him?"

"With all my awe and respect for your father's talent and charm and intellect and all of that," Big Aunt Willy Hum says in a voice that sweeps the leaves off the street, "Longman Kwan Sr. was never a good man. He insinuated himself into a home-cooked family dinner with the Kwan sisters, and your mother fell in love with him at first sight. One night your father was drunk and seduced your grandmother."

"What do you mean seduced my grandmother?"

"Do we have to draw you a picture?" Auntie Orchid snaps.

"Your grandmother, still pregnant with your father's baby, offered your father money to start a business in Chinatown if only he would stay away from your mother, Hyacinth, and the rest of the family. He promised, took the money, started that big meat market. Ten years later you were born in secret, outside of Oakland, so your birth wouldn't be in the Oakland papers. *Your* mother had already been raising Longman Jr. for *her* mother, and when *you* come along, and when your grandmother found out about you, she knew the opera star had lied and stolen her money. So she kicked your mother out of the family. She never did like Longman Sr. She kept calling him the Snake."

The Movie About Me is not a movie at all. It's a comic book. The family secrets the aunts are trying so hard to make me accept as my own are like the Four Horsemen's forgotten series. Who The Hero's mother is has nothing to do with me. I'm not his mother, that's all that counts to me. Longman Jr. is The Hero, not me. I see myth under a different and grand sun. What is it they see happening to me that I don't feel? These American-born Chinawomen, well-aged and oiled princesses, are mummies of the dazzlers they were in the Depression '30s, when their beauty made the most down-and-outer smile as if the sun were shining and dream as if under the light of a bright and private moon. They live in the dark of today's Christian stainless steel, ceramic tile, and neon composite Shangri-la, where every suey shop is deep in the land of the heathen, and every white and semiassimilated yellow is a refugee from the rat race of Western civilization, escaping into gobs of sweet 'n' sour hoochie-koochie eaten with chopsticks.

"This doesn't make any sense," I blurt before the silence gets glassy. "You're telling me Junior is Ma's half-brother and not her son? Uh huh. Why are you telling me this?"

"*Wuhay!* Hotshot!" Aunt Azalea says. Her voice is more resonant with her false teeth out of her mouth. "This just old Aunt Willy, remember! Not Ah-Sigmund Freud *wahhh! Teng gin mah?* You hear me? She's old! Don't yell at her!"

"I wasn't yelling. I'm sorry if I was yelling. I'll eat all of Imogene's brownies because I was yelling. I'll take leftovers home because I yelled at you, Aunt Willy. *Dir um jur ahhh!*"

"Come on, don't overdo it," Auntie Orchid plays a smiling sneer in her voice. She looks like Oliver Hardy without a moustache. "I don't trust you when you try to be charming."

Aunt Azalea laughs and nods, then all the aunts nod. Uncle Mort smiles, as if he were dreaming. His glasses make his eyes look smaller than they are, like insects in amber. I can't tell if his eyes are open or not through his thick glasses. I can't stand the trembling still fish waving their fins in Aunt Willy's thick lenses. I lower and relax my voice, having trouble finding other words.

"I'm sorry. Wrong movie. Wrong movie. But why did Ma live a lie? If Grandma didn't want her baby by my rotten father, why didn't she get rid of him? Why push him on Ma?"

Big Aunt Willy sings the song of a gate with rusty hinges working back and forth in the slow lick of an occasional breeze. "Your grandma did not appear to be pregnant to any of us. As I remember, she was always stout."

"As I remember she had the figure of an orangutan," I say in the breath she takes to pick her next words.

"Careful, now!" Aunt Poppy sighs. "That is our mother you are talking about, buster!"

"Whaddaya mean buster?" Aunt Azalea says in slow shock. "Nobody says buster anymore. Where have you been?"

"I would like to answer your question without any further interruptions," Big Aunt Willy says. "I hope you can keep your personal remarks to yourself."

"I am the black sheep of the family, I'm the skeleton in the family closet. I have the right to live down to my rep, right?"

"Your Grandmother and Hyacinth, your ma, she was only fourteen at the time, took the train to Seattle where Longman Jr. was born. They came home claiming Hyacinth, your ma, was his mother," Big Aunt Willy creaks and burbles. The aunts listen, sigh, and nod. "Everyone believed your father, the Chinese Rudolf Valentino, had swept her off her feet and taken advantage of her girlish adoration of a famous Chinese movie star."

"That's true. She was crazy about Pa," I say. "But why did Grandma make her keep the baby?"

"Because he was a boy, stupid!" Aunt Azalea says, *Her baby boy. She had to keep him in the family."

"Your grandmother," Big Aunt Willy continues evenly, as if resuming a recital of the alphabet to a dull boy, brings everyone's eyes back to me.

"What's my grandmother to you, Big Aunt?" I interrupt.

"She was my little sister, and I am your great aunt. The oldest great aunt."

"And what if your little sister had had a daughter by the Snake, instead of a son?"

"Who needs another sister? There were five of us already," Aunt Azalea half jokes. "Ma had already lost two boys. One before we were born, one after."

"I remember him," Aunt Poppy says, almost too soft for hearing.

"So who was going to be the head of the family if we had no brother, huh?" Aunt Azalea fires at me.

"Oh," is all I can say.

And Big Aunt continues, "Everybody believed your grandmother had taken her fourteen-year-old daughter off for a few months until she had her baby and then brought her back." Aunt Willy creaks on, swinging to the rhythm of some unseen wind, "And everyone understood why your grandmother would give your father money to stay away from your mother."

"Why not give him money to marry her?"

"Because he was already married in China, stupid! *Chie!* Where do you think Ah-Joe Joe comes from?" Aunt Azalea snaps and raps her wooden fish.

"You never wondered why your father and grandmother have the same family name?" Big Aunt Willy asks. Her voice is a little brittle and cracking.

"As I heard it, Pa's a paper Kwan. He wasn't a big opera star, he was an apprentice. So Grandma sponsored him as her brother-in-law after he bought papers belonging to somebody named Kwan, right?" I recite the ten thousandth time.

"Your father is not a paper son," Aunt Azalea says. "He's the real thing, you might say." The aunts fidget and gurgle up a little nervous laughter.

"What do you mean the real thing? The real what?" I ask

The family stares at me. "Don't you get it yet, man?" Uncle Mort asks from his slouch.

"I'm supposed to guess?" I say.

"Your father was not Grandma's *paper* brother. He *was* her brother," Aunt Azalea says.

"That's right," Big Aunt Poppy sighs ever so softly.

"My father is my grandmother's brother?" I ask, with a dull thud.

"You got it, man! How about that!" Uncle Mort says.

"That means Pa is Big Aunt Willy's brother too, right?"

"That's right," Big Aunt Willy answers. I wonder what she looked like when Pa was fresh off the boat, sixty years ago, but I don't ask if Pa-the-lech ever put his eyes on her.

"Naw, man!" I protest and shake my head. "She married a Kwan. She wasn't born a Kwan. She couldn't be Pa's sister."

"We were born Kwans, and my sister married a Kwan from

China," Big Aunt Willy says. The living record. The last word on who's who.

"So you're telling me Longman Jr. is the result of brother-sister incest."

"Well, that's your point of view on the subject, as Mort would say," Aunt Azalea says.

"I wouldn't say that," Uncle Mort says.

"Well what would you say, then? Say something," Aunt Azalea shoots back.

"Ma is your mother and father's daughter, right?" I ask the aunts.

They nod and mutter a few kinds of yes.

"So I am not the product of brother and sister incest, right?"

"Oh, no!" Big Aunt Poppy sighs.

"I'm the tainted love child. *That's* why I was born in a foundling home in Berkeley, so I wouldn't make the Oakland papers." I'm not bitter. I'm just finding the proper place to file this information.

"Well, you are definitely not insects!" Aunt Azalea says.

"That's incest! Not insects!" Uncle Mort yells.

"I can't help it! I know what it is. It's my teeth," Aunt Azalea says.

"Except your mother is your father's niece, see?" Big Aunt Willy squawks.

"Whoops! I guess I am incest!" I cheer.

"Not so loud. You want everyone to hear?" Aunt Azalea hushes.

"You know what? I'm fifty-one years old, folks. And I don't care if my mother was the first successful sex-change operation of the 1930's and I'm a product of her test tube womb. I don't care." I shrug. "So I was born of an incestuous union between my mother and a man with a compulsion to whip it out, stick in the family, and keep it in the family. Well, if I was going to be a pinhead or a cheerful goof, I think it would have shown up by now."

They seem to be looking at me to make sure.

"Oh! I see! I'm being anointed figurehead head of the family because I'm less 'insects' than Longman Jr., The Hero."

"If he were in good health," Aunt Peony yelps.

"Of course. Of course. I understand." I shake my head. "Incest. That's the big secret?"

The tiny old woman with the big wax lips out of a gumball machine and the unconvincing wig that raises more questions than it answers about the old woman's hair puckers up and shifts her weight. The black finny fish dart away, then rush back and tread water. "That is why, when you were born and everybody learned Ah-Hyacinth had secretly married your father in Reno, your grandmother banished your mother from the family."

"Banished?" I ask.

"Don't you speak English?" Big Aunt Poppy asks. "Our mother kicked Ah-Hyacinth out of the house, told her never to call us on the phone, never to write us, never drop by the house. Is that banished enough for you?"

"She was banished," I agree.

"Because of you," Aunt Willy said. "I know that doesn't sound fair."

"No, no. I agree. Pa agrees. It's all my fault! If I hadn't come along, who knows? Ma would have had Pa and the family too. So my father, being a wise, cultured, and Christian man, sacrificed me to fix up his relationship with *Paw Paw* and Ma. Getting rid of me cleared his conscience. But getting rid of me didn't keep Pa any closer to home. He still left Ma alone with Junior and worked and played in Hollywood. Charlie Chan's Number Four Son. The Chinaman Who Dies. The Yellow Playboy of the Western Range."

"Now don't be bitter. I think you and I have talked about that before," Auntie Orchid buzzes in a voice of honeyed strings I have trusted all my life.

"I'm not bitter. Those were the happiest days of my life. Out in the country with that redheaded old vaudeville acrobat and Aunt Bea, the silent-screen bit player, raising me like a princely being: the 'American of Chinese descent.' Right there by the creek where the coyotes and deer came down to drink at sunset, where the hill people showoff the twitching carcasses of rattlesnakes they've stomped with the broadside of an axe, stretched out on the running boards of their model Ts, standing around a rock and spitting tobacco juice on it as they talk. There was no other 'American of Chinese descent' within miles, within memory of the two-room batten-and-board tarpaper shanty near the shale tailings of the defunct New Penelope Mine. I saw snow there. I saw wild pig. Owls. Eagles. Hawks. Vultures eating the bellies out of dead rabbits. I saw a pig slaughtered, bled, and its sidemeat and hindquarters cut out to be smoked into bacon and ham. I saw coyotes come down the creek and drink with their pups at dusk. I learned to swim in cow-plop and watersnakes."

"Ugh," Aunt Azalea shudders.

"That's a lie, sorry. I didn't learn to swim. I saw hail the size of softballs cover up the wiry skeleton of an old mattress outside. I saw my first lunar eclipse there. I saw a cow fall into a hole, die, get eaten by vultures, rot, decay, and become bones. I had a great childhood there. I'm not bitter. I loved it."

"You sound pretty bitter to me, young man," Aunt Azalea says with her false teeth out of her mouth and lips loose.

"Why? What have I got to be bitter about?"

Big Aunt Willy points her chin at Ma's oldest sister, Big Aunt Poppy. Big Aunt Poppy sighs and picks up the shoebox from the empty seat signifying Hyacinth, my mother, and hands it to me. It's stuffed with old letters. The stamps on the envelopes are all collector's items. They're all addressed to me. The return addresses and postmarks on all the letters are Diamond Springs. I had never received them. Some of them were opened. I'd never opened them. Someone had read some of them. Not me. I had wondered why they never wrote to me.

"Your mother wanted you to have these after she died, but I saw no good coming from it," Big Aunt Willy said. "Now that you are head of the family, I see no harm."

"Ma kept these from me?" I say.

"We all thought it was better you forgot the Conroys."

"Sure, you all chose me to become head of the family."

"Believe it or not, we did. You were always strong, fearless, and too smart for your own good. Beating you never changed your mind. You were like an orphan from the old stories, sent to save us. You never complained, no matter how badly—"

"Yeah, yeah."

"As in the fairy tales, we promised to raise you as our own child," Big Aunt Willy says.

"Aren't you going to read them?" Big Aunt Poppy asks on the edge of a faint.

"After all these years? In front of you? Why?" I ask.

"Now, don't be bitter," Auntie Orchid says.

"I know what they say. How are you? Do you see any hawks where you are? Do you remember the dog named Guess? The postmark on this letter is 1950. I was a ten-year-old kid."

"I said, don't be bitter!" Auntie Orchid repeats.

"You were running away from home," Aunt Azalea says without breaking the rhythm of her knitting.

"I never ran to them because I thought they never wrote me."

"Your mother really loved you. I know she did. She told me she did," Aunt Azalea says. "She always felt you blamed her, you hated her for abandoning you. It's a terrible thing for parents to betray their children. Terrible. She never knew how to talk to you about it."

"I didn't know what parents meant. I had no idea of what a mother and father were supposed to be, the proprietary rights they had over their child. I didn't grow up with that. I grew up with Uncle Jackie and Auntie Bea Conroy, a childless couple from Florida who took care of me in this safe wonderful place in the middle of World War II. I had never even heard of a mother and father. I was somebody, some thing, that had no explanation, and needed none from the first of my memory."

"Now you're going to dare to say that you aren't bitter?" Azalea snaps. "Huh? You sound bitter to me!"

"That's reminiscence, not bitterness."

"What did you think the words *Mother* and *Father* and *Mommy* and *Daddy* were when you heard them on the radio?" Big Aunt Poppy flies on hurt wings. "I mean when you heard the words *Mother* and *Father, Mommy* and *Daddy* on the radio, or when your playmates . . ."

"I didn't have any playmates. Only Mary Susan. And she was an orphan, just my age. Aunt Mercedez took her in. And Mary Susan didn't talk about Mother and Father and Mommy and Daddy. She was like me. No experience with parents."

"But you must have heard the words somewhere," Big Aunt Poppy pleads on the last breath of a dove. Her eyebrows float, and her brown, slightly bulging eyes wet up and go sad Chihuahua on me.

"Of course he heard the words, even out there in the berry bushes and briar patches," Auntie Orchid sings heartily. "Tell her what you thought when you heard those words, *Mommy* and *Daddy*. Tell her!"

"I thought Mommy and Daddy were nicknames for people, like Baldy, Slim, Curly, like that. Nicknames."

Auntie Orchid squeezes the center of her face into a frown and looks as if she's putting a spell on me.

"What're you looking at me like that for?" I ask.

Aunt Poppy sags and speaks, "Your mother had to take care of Longman Jr. to stay in good with her mother, I mean that was her reasoning. You don't have to like it, but you can understand it, can't you, Ulysses?"

"A year and a half after I was born and last seen being carried off to a tarpaper shanty among the shale piles of the old New Penelope Mine, Junior was drafted and off to World War II at the personal invitation of the President of the United States. What's for me to understand? That's just an observation. Not a complaint," I say. "I don't mind being the outcast of the family. You guys didn't either. Hell, I've never been in this house before. I don't know where you people live anymore. Now, I'm the head of the family and you give me a box of letters from dead people? What do you all have against this family, that you'd make me head?"

"You are the oldest male," Big Aunt Willy says.

"Figurehead head of the family, please," Big Aunt Poppy whispers.

"My only complaint is, since everybody was so happy without me, and I was so happy without them, why didn't they do me a favor and forget me, just leave me in the country?"

Longman Kwan: The "Anna May Wong"

I hate this life. I don't taste anything anymore. I have had all the friends I will ever have and they are all dead. I have had all the fun I will ever have and now the memory of the fun and good times I have had are good for nothing. No fun. The drone of nothing gets louder. Why now? I have heard nothing about nothing up to now, and now I hear the drone of a TV tuned to dots growing louder, more insistent in my hearing, deeper, resonant, like a multiengine bomber.

I know that sound. It's the sound the Pratt & Whitney Twin Wasp R dash 1830 dash 43, 14-cylinder, two-row, radial, air-cooled aircraft engine. Four of them. The Consolidated B-24 Liberator. Bathtubs with long thin wings, high on the body. Big-shouldered, hunching ugly high-altitude bombers that are famous for one of the great low-level bombing raids of all time. The four of us, the four sons of Charlie Chan, made a war movie that was only shown in China, but we loved it. It was an airplane movie. We were the all-Chinatown crew of the *Anna May Wong* a B-24 D that flew on the first low-level mission over the oil refineries of Ploesti, Rumania.

There's Keye Luke in a flight suit and leather jacket waving me toward the *Anna May Wong*. Victor Sen Yung with the slightly sad eyes and Benson Fong before he became successful and pitiful. I approach them. The noise of the other bombers warming up their engines makes every bone in my body shudder and chatters my teeth so I have to clench them as I pass under the wing. I am dressed in the black hat with paddle wings and red robe and belt of a prime minister, a magistrate, the kitchen god.

There's the great Kwan, my old opera brother in the same costume. And Wong the handsome. And Lee Hoi Chun the opium smoker, Bruce Lee's father. Yes, to be famous in the opera, then made famous again by his son. Of course. I am the young Kwan among these fine opera masters. We are stranded here in San Francisco to be treated like kings in Chinatown after the Japanese attack Pearl Harbor on December 7, 1941.

This is a *fung serng* ceremony, the initiation of a venue our company has never played before. Each class of actor, the high ministers, the low ministers, the generals, the high ladies, the low ladies, the common man, the common woman, the young warriors, the young girl, the clowns, each performs a compulsory set that shows their classic stuff and tests their skill. The form of the opera initiation duplicates the ceremony of a prime minister presenting his chosen staff to the emperor from the Period of Warring States, when there were a lot of kingdoms and a lot of emperors and they all kept changing.

We climb into our B-24, the *Anna May Wong,* through the belly. I'm delighted our huge costumes move easily through the tight entry into the plane. It's cold inside. The plane is not pressurized. We are to fly toward Corfu, then north, high over the Pindus Mountains, before descending low to attack the refineries and tank farms. The great Kwan, by rights, should take the pilot's seat, but no, they all insist on giving it to me.

Kwan takes the copilot's chair. Wong the handsome is the navigator. Bruce Lee's father is the radio operator. Willy Fung, the flight engineer, stands outside the plane by number three engine. I pull back and forth on the controls. The Great Kwan looks out of his window and tells me which direction the rudder and ailerons are moving as I work the control surfaces on the wings, the rudder, and horizontal stabilizer. All the switches are off. Willy pulls the propellers through—six blades on each engine—to clear any oil or fuel in the combustion chambers. The covers are removed from the pilot heads. Wheel chocks: In place. Bomb doors and Cabin Doors: Open. Fuel tank valves: On. Fuel: 1,200 United States gallons. Mainline and battery switches: On. Generator switches: Off. Auxiliary power unit: On. Electric auxiliary hydraulic pump.

Adjust seat and rudders. I'm taller than the great Kwan.

Parking brake: On. Instrument power switch: On. Navigation and cabin light: On. It's night. I didn't notice that till now. Supercharger: Off. Mixtures: Idle cut off. Automatic pilot: Off. Intercooler shutters: Open. Cowl flaps: Open. Altimeters: Set. All clear of the propellers. Propellers: High RPM. Throttles: One-third open. Ignition switches: On. All engines. Fuel pressure on engine one: Booster pump started. Primer. Starter energizer twelve seconds on engine three. Mesh while holding energizer: On. Engine three starts. Mixture: Automatic lean. Idle at 1,000 RPM. Cowl flaps: One-third open. Then the outboard engine on the port wing. Engine four. Then engine two. Then engine one.

Away chocks. Cabin and bomb doors: Closed. Surface controls, rudders, ailerons, tabs: Checked and set for take off. Mixtures: Auto rich. Fuel pressure with booster pumps: Off. The head temperature reaches 150 Centigrade and we run the engines up to 2,000 RPM. Check switches. Sweep the instruments. High RPM lights: On. Manifold pressure: Twenty inches Hg. Supercharger: Set and locked.

We head into the wind, open the throttles slowly, and then pull out to the stops. Hold brakes until manifold pressure reaches twenty-five inches Hg. Number three run up. Wing flaps: One-fourth. Auxiliary power unit: Off. Generators: On. Landing gear lever: Down. Kickout pressure: 850 pounds. Gyro instruments: Uncaged. Nose clear of crew.

I run the *Anna May Wong* into the wind for the take off. She wants off the ground, I feel it at 130 miles-per-hour ground speed, and pull back on the wheel, help her off, push hard to reach the safe airspeed of 130 miles-per-hour. The engines are all running fine. I push for 150 miles-per-hour and climb after my formation. Wong the handsome, in his cowboy hat, six-gun, and bullwhip! Cantonese opera has never seen anything like this.

Ulysses: Gunga Road

The drive south from Frisco is cloudy and dry. Parris Ranch is being remodeled. The counter is closed. I sit at a table in an adobe room with high ceilings, a skylight and a fountain like three birdbaths stacked on top of each other. I miss the counter and the truckers reading the newspaper. The menu is no fun at all. I don't like the place any more. I buy a New York strip to carry home. The meat, vacuum-sealed in plastic, is cold and seductive. I can't wait to get it home to wash it, wrap it in a white towel like a mummy, put it on the bottom shelf of the fridge, and wait a month for true aged steak. It is something to go home for, for now.

I'm walking across the Spanish California mission-style parking lot when I see a silver B-24 D, a four-engine flying boxcar with a high-shouldered, long thin wing that makes every move it makes pretty to watch. The unpainted fuselage and wing gleam silver. Only the red rims of the engine nacelles, the American insignia, and the nose art show any color. The windshield and nose bubble are glassy shiny black. The plane floats low and flies so close I can hear the engines and see the nose art. A saucy Chinese girl sits on a crescent moon and glances over her shoulder as Milton Caniff might have drawn her in *Terry and the Pirates* in the Sunday funnies. The doughy letters with drop shadows spell out, *Anna May Wong*. It flies over me. I turn and watch it fly away toward L.A. It must be the last B-24 in the world that still flies.

Ulysses: "Night of the Living Third World Dead"

I'm on the phone taking notes on the latest version of the script to *Night of the Living Third World Dead*. Pestilence, the horseman in charge of marketing, is praising the kitchen scene, where a chef boning a leg of lamb slices the face off a zombie. The zombie's face peels off the skull by its own dead weight and dangles off the chin from a bit of putrid flesh. The zombie goes through the movie slipping the face back on over the skull only to have it gradually slip off again and dangle.

"I love it. I can market that, that skull with the face that keeps slipping off and dangling," Pestilence says.

"Yeah, Dangle Face," I say.

"That's it! Dangle Face!" Pestilence yells as the call-waiting signal fluffs in my ear.

"I have another call." We laugh and happy talk, then I answer the other call. It's Auntie Orchid saying she's in Oakland.

Pa is dead. The race with Polly Jade for the safe deposit box I own jointly with Pa is on.

I intended to take China Brother, his wife, Connie, and Aunt Orchid to lunch at a Chinese Vietnamese soup house, or Pho Hoa, down in Oakland's Chinatown. But China Brother has other plans. He takes us all down to Oakland's Jack London Square for abalone steak to listen to him long for a loving father.

He says he went by the hospital with his wife and shouted at Pa till he was hoarse. He finally told the old man off, told him what he really thought of him, he says. Nobody believes him. In a coma or out, Pa is too stupid to get told off. China Brother is not overburdened with smarts either. He's the first son, head of the family. He hated going to visit the tongs where Pa was a big shot, bringing gifts of candy, telling them Pa had died. He hated the talk of white gold, *bok gum*. White is the color of death and mourning.

China Brother never called me. He acted on impulse and visited the tongs with Polly Jade, even though the news was out that she divorced Pa two years ago. Auntie Orchid tells China Brother he gave Polly Jade face. He gave her recognition she did not deserve. He's giving Chinatown the impression he and Polly Jade are joined against me.

"You want a wake for Pa?" China Brother asks me and continues without waiting for me to answer. "I said no wake. Who would come? The old guys are too old to come. I don't want to sit at a wake for him. If you want a wake, you pay for it."

I talk about food. "You? Cook?" Connie says, and stares at me.

"I cook all the time."

"No!"

"Yeah. I just did a leg of lamb. Boned, butterflied, and marinaded in wine, dried apricots, apricot jam, garlic, chili peppers, green onions, Bermuda onion, and chicken stock," I said.

"Apricots?" Connie asks, her surprise undiminished. "Sounds good!"

"Sure!" China Brother barks, "Apricot like papaya! A meat tenderize." He speaks all choked up, tense, and can't eat.

But I eat. I order oysters Rockefeller and share them with Auntie Orchid. I eat. Prosciutto and melon. Hearts of palm salad. Fettucine Alfredo, abalone steak. Fried zucchini. And Auntie Orchid eats a whole cracked Dungeness crab, spaghetti alla carbonara, abalone steak, and deep-fried mushrooms.

"You cook! You! Ulysses!" Connie says, surprised at everything she says, every thought she has. "Apricots and lamb. Yeah, that sounds good. You do know how to cook!" And I am not sure if I have heard this before, had this conversation with just these words before. "You cook Chinese too?" Connie asks, "Or just American?"

"Everything except pastries. I steam catfish in garlic and black beans all the time," I say and describe my oven steaming technique.

"I can't believe it!" Connie says. "You! You know cooking. You really do."

"I make vegetable soup out of tomatoes, carrots, beets, old lettuce, radishes, and celery, garlic, onions, and whatever vegetables look about to turn bad, and ginger cinnamon, star anise and a pinch of nutmeg in water I've used to cook artichokes. And when I do a roast prime rib I get from a supermarket, I marinade the thing for a day or two in red wine. "

"Yeah! That sounds good too! You really know cooking. I can tell from how you talk."

"I can't believe it!" Joe Joe grinds through his choked voice. "I never expect anything like that from you!"

"Go on, tell him about the time your father ate your cooking!" Auntie Orchid says, punching me in the arm. When I say nothing, she continues. "Ah-Ulysses is proud of his oxtail stew. He was experimenting with perking up the five spices powder with a heavy dose of fresh ground cumin. The meat was perfect, just falling off the bone. The soup was thick and hearty. Spicy, but not gassy. Ah-Longman hated it because Ulysses here forgot to peel the potatoes before putting them in."

"I didn't forget. I like the potato skin in the stew."

"And you know what? Your father refused to eat stew with potato skins in it. He was convinced potato skins were filthy masses of germs and should not be eaten."

Joe Joe wants me to go by the florist to pay for my half of the floral piece he's ordered for Pa's funeral in our name. Auntie Orchid convinces him that would be incredibly tacky of him, that he has to front the whole amount to the florist for appearance's sake, and I should write him a check for my half. China Brother glowers angrily at his wife. She nods. He agrees.

We tell China Brother our plan is for Orchid to go up to Polly Jade at the *gah way fon,* the banquet after the funeral to celebrate life, and tell her, not ask her, but tell her, that we will be over to her house at 1:00 P.M. the next day to talk. She's put us off till after the funeral. So we'll hit her right after the funeral.

Joe Joe says he got a good deal on the flowers. It only cost $90 for the piece. A cheap one usually sells for $150. A good one for $250. I tell him I don't care. If he wants to go cheap, he can pay them a little more and tell them to use dead flowers. Or just make the thing out of stuff thrown out of his garden or make it out of plastic flowers. Whatever he's doing with the funeral is okay. It's too late to change things now. He's the first brother. I have to trust him. He says he has let Polly Jade get her Catholic priest to do Pa's funeral service.

"But he's not a Catholic," I say. "You believe in virgin birth, brother? You stupid crybaby piece of shit! If that Catholic priest shows up, I will point my finger at you and walk out."

"You would walk out after I agreed?" China Brother gags out.

"That's a promise!"

"Ulysses! A little respect for your father's memory, stupid!" Auntie Orchid says rapping me on the skull with her ring.

"Okay with me," Joe Joe says. "If that's the way you are. It's no big deal to me."

"Obviously it's no big deal to you, or you wouldn't have fucked it up completely."

"He don't care about me live or die, when he's alive. So why should I treat him nice when he's dead?"

"Why bother making this big little funeral and *gah way fon,* and then fuck it up? You want to show the world what you think of Pa? Let's just get his body, load it up in the back of your Rolls, and dump him in some ditch in the next county," I say. "You could have saved me this trip."

"No, Ulysses!" Connie says, "You can't walk out of your daddy's funeral!"

"He never give me any love!" China Brother barks, beginning another story about Pa being hateful, and I cut him off.

"I've already heard this five or six times, Joe Joe. I don't want to hear it again. I'm not Pa. I wasn't close to Pa. I didn't particularly like him. And he didn't particularly like me. In the last few years we have been friendly only because I go out of my way to avoid fights."

"My father left me to take care of my mother when I was twelve. Then the next time we talk, he won't let me in to sleep on the floor because of you."

"Not me. Your father made Ma give birth to me in a foundling home in Berkeley. I was farmed out to a retired white couple and lived in a tarpaper shanty near an abandoned gold mine for the first six years of my life. So don't expect me to be offended at you pissing on his dead face or whatever you want to do, man. Just do it. I don't want to hear about it. Surprise me."

"No," Connie says, "Are you telling the truth, Ulysses?"

"What?"

"Your mommy and daddy didn't raise you as a baby?"

"No, they didn't."

"Naww! " China Brother yawns through his nose, "You know him. He'll say anything."

"It's true," Auntie Orchid says.

"The difference between you and me, China Brother, is: I never had my father's love, never missed it, and never wanted it. You had it, you miss it, and you want it."

The funeral is on a Tuesday. Scheduled for 2:00 P.M.. Orchid says get there early to see Ah-Joe Joe and be there to receive the family and friends come to pay their last respects. I'm up early and drive Ma's fine, two-tone green-on-green '53 Chevy across the lower deck of the Bay Bridge to Oakland and have lunch at a Chinese-Vietnamese soup place. Out of respect for the dead, the electronic Buddhists of my family, like the Japanese of Chushingura, aren't supposed to eat meat on the days of funerals and death anniversaries. Not even the meat of fish. Nothing animal. I have a big bowl of three kinds of sliced beef. Raw eye of round. Rare flank. Barbecued flank and big jiggly gobs of gelatinous tendon in a broth spiced with cinnamon and nutmeg.

A black man with a Chinese-Vietnamese wife, mother-in-law, sister-in-law, and three children from five months to eight years sits at a front table. He wears a black baseball cap with the initials and numbers of his Marine Corps unit. He wears a black T-shirt that reads *Vietnam Vet* and the dates of his service, his service number, and Marine unit. When he pays up and follows his family out of the restaurant, he salutes me. Am I sitting up erect like the little soldier the retired silent-screen bit player told me to sit like in restaurants? Auntie Bea. There always seems to be a commanding aunt civilizing my life. I wonder if he took me for an officer or merely a fellow vet. From which side did he think I had gone soldiering? I wonder.

I drive up Arroyo Abuello Road to the neighborhood of the dead. The fringe of florists and tombstone cutters. Then the palaces, fantasy medieval temples and ancient monuments where the soft-spoken and untanned keep the ashes and remains. Places where they keep the dead buried underground and stored in air-conditioned marble warehouses above ground. Ma is stored in her all-metal casket at the Little Chapel in the Pines. I scuff and huff up the little flights of marble steps from room to room, decade to decade, of the crematorium mausoleum's development in materials and design. I climb this version of a dream castle from limestone to marble and glazed tile to tinted prestressed concrete, with the sound of spattering and dribbling water, to the room under a skylight where my mother has been entombed alone since her death on the right side of a double crypt marked "Joe-Kwan." She rests on the Kwan side. Pa will fill the hole on the Joe side of the hyphen.

Joe Joe, my China Brother, gags, chokes, clenches his teeth and tightens his tie at the sight of me. He, his wife Connie, and his three grown children—a daughter in her late thirties and two younger sons—are early but are not the first ones at the Little Chapel of the Pines. And here, China Brother is sending Charlie Chan's Honorable Number Four Son, Chinatown playboy of the Pacific Rim and tongman, out of this world without a parade. No marching band on Grant Street on Sunday morning. No long black limousines. No private mortuary motorcycle cops whistling and whirring motor leapfrog, stopping up the streets to keep the caravan of cars out to the cemetery together and moving. Auntie Orchid is here with Uncle Buck. I see them through the door, standing by the open casket. Connie pins a black band around my left arm.

"Are you the one who put Pa's toupee on his forehead?" I steam low into Auntie Orchid's ear. We step down off the platform and away from Pa's casket to say hello and shake hands. Uncle Buck is as youthful and handsome as ever. He dyes his hair, like Auntie

Orchid, but all opera people do, as long as they're still taking to the stage and singing.

Outside I see a couple of reporter-camera teams from the local TV news standing back, mikes to their mouths, cameras aimed at the chapel door. When Polly Jade arrives in a white limo, wearing a white fur coat, she is accompanied by a fat and decaying white man wearing white duck, a Panama straw hat with the brim turned up, and a Charlie Chan moustache. I recognize him. It's Charlie Chan, Anlauf Lorane, the white man who will continue to play Charlie Chan to Pa's Number Four Son on late-night cable TV movies forever. A tall, bald-headed, skinny Chinese guy in glasses who has a nervous kissass smile on his face also arrives in the limo with Polly Jade and her strange boys, my young half-brothers—the only kind I seem to have—the fourth and fifth known sons of my father. All of them are dressed in white suits, white, the Chinese color of death, white, the white of Charlie Chan's white duck. The Charlie Chans wear Charlie Chan Panama straw hats.

The bald-headed Chinese is straight from the funny papers. He's Big Stoop from *Terry and the Pirates*. And the boys . . . One looks like Pa and is shy and sickly. The older boy looks like Polly Jade and gives off something that violently warns me away. It's his good looks and his eyes. Especially his eyes. He has the big black eyes Chinese call phoenix eyes. But they don't shine. They don't warm. They suck up light and swallow the bright out of it. Everything his eyes see feels like shit for being seen by this little creep.

I don't want to get anywhere near him. The small group of news-people move in on Polly Jade and the last white man to play Charlie Chan. He looked near death when I saw him last at the Star River Festival twenty years ago. He looks beyond death now. He's a mummy who's been unwrapped a little early and isn't keeping well. The story's a natural for the weekend news: Charlie Chan comes to bid farewell to Number Four Son with Polly Jade, the widow. The networks and wire services will be sure to run it. What did Number Four Son think of the new Charlie Chan movie scripted by Pandora Toy? What does Charlie Chan think about the part being played by a white man again?

Charlie Chan and Polly Jade go inside the chapel and take over the front pew, in front of the casket. China Brother tells me she has the left side. We have the right. She and he have agreed.

"You agreed?" I say, "You agreed to a Catholic service? You agreed to give her the position of his wife, when she hasn't been his wife for two years? She's not even a member of the family and you agreed?"

Ben Mo and Pandora Toy arrive with Martha, their daughter, grandson Justin, Martha's lover Rudy, and two strangers, one white and one yellow in a white limo that matches the one that just deposited Polly Jade and her odd party. This is why the local TV news is here. They're here at my father's funeral expecting the white man playing the new Charlie Chan and the Hollywood yellow playing the new numbered son to appear at the original Number Four Son's funeral. Two generations of Charlie Chans and sons, the real and fake, and Pandora Toy the million-dollar Chinese-American writer scripting the new movie, all to pay their respects to Chan's departed Number Four Son.

Ben and Pandora and Justin and Martha and Rudy from Portland and all the Charlie Chans and the new numbered son join Polly Jade in the front row.

"Good going, Joe Joe. People will step down from Pa's dead body to give their condolences to Polly Jade, Charlie Chan, Pandora Toy, and strangers. Why did you bother showing up?" I say and pat China Brother on the back. Was it you, Ben? Selling me out to Pandora, a cut of me at a time, a chop now, a steak later—is that how you keep your marriage together? Now you see the only proper sequel to using me in *Fu Manchu Plays Flamenco* is to use me again in *Gee, Pop! Charlie Chan at Number Four Son's Funeral.* Even in the story of your own funeral, Pa, you're the second banana, the comic relief, thanks to your first son. Why didn't you love him, Pa, and save me from putting up with him sniffling and wrestling your funeral into a grotesque personal expression? You should have stayed a mystery, China Brother. A shadow in the alley.

I feel Joe Joe clinging to me, determined to put me in my place and make me apologize to him before he goes inside to face the front row full of strangers. I bend low to his ear and say, "You could have walked away and been a man instead of kissing the ass of a man who despises you and your kids all your life. Now he's dead and what have you got except the same old stories of Pa giving back shit for all your nicey-nicey good son? I bet you called the TV news, too, China Brother."

"Let's not talk about that now," he says.

"When you die, brother, don't bother calling me. And vice versa. Let's say our goodbyes now and be done with each other."

Joe Joe shakes his head and ducks inside the chapel to keep Polly Jade's people from occupying the whole front row. I stay outside. Aloha appears with Imogene, Longman Jr.'s high-strung high-wired first daughter with her artificially augmented boobs.

Imogene tells me Aloha went through college and came out a nutritionist but couldn't stand to see people dying after all her menu planning and avoided patients and taught nutrition awhile. Then she became a Satanist and is now a born-again Christian, carrying a paper shopping bag with string handles full of funda-mentalist tracts to pass out at the funeral.

Aloha doesn't put her bag down to hug me. She keeps hold of it, swings it up with her arms closing around me, and the bag full of pulp born-again Christianity bumps me in the small of my back. "God loves you," she says. Terrific. I'm thrilled.

The tong men, Pa's longtime friends, begin arriving. The last of the first generation of old-time Chinatown big shots. Pa was a big man in the Chinatown orgs. His village association. His family association. The Alliance of Four Families. The Canton City Wooey Goon. The City Wooey Goon's "Young Men's Club," the tong within a tong.

The Young Men's Club is to the City Wooey Goon what the Shriners are to the Masons. Pa was also a past president and advisor to the all-powerful tong of the tongs, the Big Alliance. He was famous in Chinatown as an immigrant who made it in Hollywood, and as a legendary Chinatown snappy dresser, womanizer, and spendthrift. In the tongs these very same rotten qualities made him a skillful and popular arbitrator and soother of trouble between tongs, between brothers, and between Chinatowns.

The old men climb out of their sons' or sons-in-law's cars. Some are helped out. As they pass me, they hand me the white envelope of *bok gum,* white gold, a sign of respect and pledge of brotherly protection, from Pa's brothers of the tong within a tong. These are the old, old men, the ones I have not seen before, the ones who come out only for the funerals of their own kind. One old man in a five-year-old suit asks me who is going to speak for the three big tongs Pa was big in. "I don't know," I say in basic bad-manners Cantonese, "All I know is a Catholic priest is going to speak."

That shocks the old man. He recovers and says, "Funerals are for the children, the family, and the friends. Why is this stranger speaking, and none of your father's friends?"

"Please wait a minute," I say, "I'll get my older brother." I go into the chapel after China Brother, and a few of the old men follow me in. They stand at the back of the chapel with a view of the high vaulted ceilings and woof at him. China Brother whines and yaps. The clashing voices form an off chord that hovers saxing on an endless breath high over the funeral. I ask them to step outside with China Brother. They all step outside. China Brother's wife peeks out of the door and wants us to go back inside and talk. She doesn't want the TV news to see. I say, "No! No! No dickering and niggling bullshit over the old man's dead body. His funeral is enough of a humiliation already. "

Ah-Joe Joe puts his hands in his pockets, shifts his weight from foot to foot, looks down at his toes, and whines and peeves. He insults everyone and is too stupid to see he's embarrassing himself. "No, no one speaks," China Brother says. "It's too complicated. I don't want complications."

The old men are pissed. They got up early to ready themselves for the drive across the Bay. "No matter what you think of your father, you can't humiliate him this way. You can't let a Catholic priest speak when your father wasn't Catholic, and then not let his friends speak. You want to insult your father's friends too? That's not what funerals are for. Think of your funeral and what you're showing your children with this business, Ah-Joe Joe."

They come to a compromise. A friend of Pa's who, like Pa, is big in the big three associations, will speak for all three and that will be that. Fine, I think. It's settled.

Inside Aloha insists on sitting in the front row next to me. Pa looks awful. His toupee is still on his forehead. No one has touched him. The tong men are confused by Polly Jade's presence and will not go up to Pa's casket because they will have to pass her. Still a few brave ones walk up, and breaking all tradition, forced to commit an insult, they do not acknowledge any of Pa's kin. They shake no one's hand, and offer condolences to no one. I'm thinking China Brother has, in his anger and self-pity, not failed to fuck everything up, just everything about Pa's funeral. When he asks me to say a few words about Pa, I refuse. "It's too late. Let the tongman speak and that will be that."

"The tongman is not going to speak," China Brother says. There's no one to make the announcement about the time and place of the *gah way fon,* the banquet after the funeral. He wants me to do it. No. No. No. "Go tell them Jade Village. Four o'clock," Joe Joe growls and gags.

"You write a note and I'll take it back to the Catholic *muk see,*" I say.

"You write a note," China Brother says.

"This is your party, your word, China Brother. You write the note, or no note, period," I say. It takes him ten minutes to control himself enough to write the name and address of his restaurant on the back of the business card that already has the name and address of his restaurant. He adds the time on the note.

On my way down the aisle to the back, I see all my mother's sisters are here. Longman Jr.'s daughters and grandchildren by his first wife and his son and daughter by his second wife are here . . . Uncle Mort is here with his radiant redhead. The priests look like

I'm catching them doing nasty things with each other. I ask them to make the announcement, please. Jade Village. Four o'clock.

Polly Jade is fattened up, bawling. The boys are bored. Polly Jade's white friend, Charlie Chan, and Ben Mo and Pandora are not immune to the mean hostile vibes aimed their way. The tall bald-headed Chink in glasses grins stupidly and catches my eye. You wanna connect with me, fuckhead? How about a crowbar up your ass, sugarlips? He hides behind Polly Jade's bulk.

Aloha opens her Bible and points a verse out to me and reads it out loud. "Idolatry!" she says.

I take out my felt tip and write, "Cool it!" over the verse and close her Bible. The shuffle of the priests' skirts scratches and echoes around the chapel. Aloha sits on her heels by Polly Jade reading the Bible to her. I have had enough.

I stand and turn and see my mother's Big Aunt Willy and her drones, my mother's sisters, the four living reminders of the legendary five beauties. Big Aunt Poppy, her fine black and hennaed hair thin as prairie grass after a fire, puts her glasses on to see me. Her eyes bulge and swell up in the lenses into fish-shaped smears. My brother's children and their children wear clothes as light and bright as paper. They look like lanterns. Imogene pouts and Irma wears no make-up. They're looking at me as if I'm on stage.

And to my right is my father's dream come true. My father's real Hollywood father in the front row. The old Charlie Chan seems to be trying to look down between Aloha's legs as she crouches in front of Polly Jade. And next to them, the new Charlie Chan. Two white men. And the new authors. And the new numbered son. But none of my old friends.

I'm in the center aisle playing chicken with an elderly Catholic priest and his Chinese servant. Everyone seems to be wearing noisy paper clothes. Yes, no one wants to wear what they're wearing here, ever again. In the name of Charlie Chan the Father, Charlie Chan the Son, Charlie Chan the Ghostly Host. I look into the Catholic priest's eyes through his glasses and see frothy whites with two winking dark holes in their centers, like the foam of two cups of cappuccino jiggling around holes made by two quarters.

I walk out. Fuck it.

I go to see Longman Jr., The Hero. He's back in the hospital. The pain is worse. His liver is so much enemy meat eating him out of the picture. He floats on the bed. Virginia is with him. I want to thank her for not being at the funeral but don't.

He smells like death and maggots covered in baby lotion. I'm right about the baby lotion. His skin is as dry as paper matches and hurts. The rest of the smell is Junior. The TV is on above the bed. It's an old black and white. George Stevens' *Gunga Din,* with Cary Grant, Victor McLaughlen, and Douglas Fairbanks Jr. in pith helmets, playing three British soldiers in Colonial India and Sam Jaffe in a turban as Gunga Din, their water boy, who helps the British make war against his people. This is not The Movie About Me. Pa is neither Number Four Son nor The Chinaman Who Dies in this movie. Pa is not in this movie. Or is he? He might be. I don't change the channel.

Virginia sits by the bed. The window lays light over her shoulder and she uses it to knit by. I haven't seen a woman knit in years.

"I wondered how much you would take before you came down here," Virginia says.

The Hero sleeps. I give Virginia the spectacle and dreariness of Pa's funeral. Charlie Chan. Polly Jade. The Jekyll-and-Hyde boys. Pandora Toy and my blood brother Ben Mo. Two white limousines. The news. The rickety old bones of the tongs. China Brother's art of negotiation. Aloha and her Christian shopping bag. The skirts of the Catholic priest sounding like someone chewing corn flakes.

Longman Jr. is somewhere in 1944. How did he get there? Virginia says it's the morphine. He's taken a little at seven this morning, but because his liver's not cleaning his blood the way it should, the morphine stays in his blood and sends him on this tall one. We joke about him becoming hooked. Virginia says Imogene actually doesn't approve of the drugs for fear of Longman Jr. becoming an addict.

We talk a little. Virginia and the kids, Haley and Horatio, found love letters to The Hero written in 1946. From Switzerland. They were written in English, but each by a different hand, and signed by a woman. I seem to be the only one Longman Jr. ever told about his month in Switzerland after the German surrender. Virginia found photos of the woman. Blonde? Brunette? I don't remember. I don't ask Virginia. She figures the woman had English-speaking friends write her letters for her. I don't tell her Longman Jr. had been cherry, that the white woman had taken his virginity and given him his nuts, his first immersion in affectionate drooling flesh.

"What're you doing, huh, Ulysses?" the words pain out of The Hero's withered face. His face is too far gone. It hurts too much for him to wear his glasses. He can't see me. I know he's trying. I can't look at him. Instead I look up at the TV.

It's the night funeral scene at the end of *Gunga Din,* I say. "Pa's favorite movie." What am I doing? The campfires burn. Rudyard Kipling stands by the officer reciting the poem "Gunga Din" over the coffin as Cary Grant and Douglas Fairbanks Jr. and Victor McLaughlen look on, wounded, rescued, heroic. By flickering firelight the officer reads:

> 'E carried me away
> To where a dooli lay,
> An' a bullet come an' drilled the beggar clean,
> 'E put me safe inside,
> An' just before 'e died,
> "I 'ope you liked your drink," sez Gunga Din.
> So I'll meet 'im later on
> At the place where 'e is gone—
> Where it's always double drill and no canteen.
> 'E'll be squattin' on the coals
> Givin' drink to poor damned souls,
> An' I'll get a swig in hell from Gunga Din!
>> Yes, Din! Din! Din!
> You Lazarushian-leather Gunga Din!
>> Though I've belted you and flayed you,
>> By the livin' Gawd that made you,
> You're a better man than I am, Gunga Din!

The pipes and drums squeal and thud "Auld Lang Syne" and march off into the darkness and Sam Jaffe in darky make-up and a full-dress uniform emerges superimposed ghostly over the scene. Not my father in darky make-up. Not my uncle Mort. Not Spencer Tracy. Nothing but the real old movie. The ghost of Gunga Din smartly salutes and breaks into a grin. The End.

"I'm writing zombie movies and novels, Junior. I write the movies for this company of four guys. I write the novels for myself. The first movie I scripted for them, *The Night of the Living Hollywood Dead*, made them lots of money. It made them so much money they bought me a stadium bigscreen TV that covers a whole wall of my place in L.A. and pay all my electric bills for the next ten years. They're all ancients of TV Hollywood producers, harkening back to the days of *Studio One* and *Playhouse 90*. Last week they called me for a script conference on the new zombie movie, and they tell me, Ulysses, we want to open this with a pastel dream sequence. Pastel? You mean colors? You want to crap up the script with descriptions of colors and decor? No, no no, they say, Pastel. You know what we mean. Pastel! Oh, pastel. What is that, some new Hollywood code word? What do you mean *pastel*? You know, Ulysses, they tell me, *Pastel* . . . The birds are singing, the bees are buzzing, the sun is shining, the grass is green. *Pastoral!* I say, *pastoral!* Yeah! the Four Horsemen say, pastel!"

I shake my head. It's too much to expect The Hero to laugh. I don't want to hear him laugh. I laugh. "After all this time and making all this money for them and writing this new zombie movie for them, I realize the English we are speaking to each other is not the same language at all. English is not a common language."

"You going to Cal, Ulysses?" Junior asks me. His breathing sounds like crumpling cellophane. I look at him. He's carved out of a carrot and the carrot's dried up and moldy. If he were meat, he would have been thrown out weeks ago. Where is he now? Nineteen fifty what? I nod.

I say, "Yeah, Junior, I'm going to Cal. It seems to be a good school."

"Go down to the yard office and get a job for the summer, like I told you," he says, answering true to the way it was back then. Junior dozes in and out of who knows when and where. Virginia knits and I watch TV till it's time for me to leave for the *gah way fon,* the banquet after Pa's funeral where China Brother still shakes his head and publicly tries to refuse the white envelopes of *bok gum.* The third-tallest tongman there, in a wool suit the color of Rita Hayworth's hair in *Pal Joey,* shoots me a look of anger and weariness and gently influences China Brother to a table on the other side of the lacquered screen partitioning the room. China Brother gets up from the table speaking too loudly, sounding offensive, petty, and stupid all the way, but accepts the influence. A few soft pats. Heavy sighs. A show of restrained irritation and uncomfortable feet.

"Go with them," Auntie Orchid says. I stand and walk away from our island of seven occupied tables through an orchard of empty tables and white linen tablecloths to the table behind the lacquered screen. I sit down without being asked to across from the tall old tongman and next to China Brother.

"I thought you ask the Catholic *mook see* to make announce where and when is the *gah way fon?*" he says, leaning back and putting me in my place in front of the humiliated tongmen.

"You mean he didn't make the announcement?"

"No, he didn't. What're you say about that?" China Brother asks as if it's my fault.

"It's your problem. You trusted that Catholic priest, not me. I'm a Chinaman, I know Christians never keep their word. To them lying to each other and breaking promises is called faith in God. Ask the Aztec, ask the Mayan, ask the Modoc, ask the . . ."

"Ask me," the tall tongman says, leaning over the table.

China Brother stacks all the bills face up, then flattens them out one by one, and stacks them again. Then he makes separate piles of the twenties, the tens, and the fives. The ones. The checks. There is one $100 bill. Brand new. Flat and crunchy. Two $50 bills. Also new. He adds up the worth of the bills in each pile, makes a note of the total and adds up the totals of all the piles. Seven hundred and seventy-five dollars. The tongman has other envelopes of *bok gum* from the Alliance of Four Families of Stockton. Another check from the Alliance of Four in Sacramento. And another from Los Angeles. The tongman has little handmade booklets of white pages. On each page is a list of names and an amount of *bok gum* given in tribute to Pa's greatness in the tongs. China Brother ignores the offer of the books.

The daylight manager of the Jade Hamlet, a slick young man in a tuxedo and bowtie, comes to the table and hands China Brother a white envelope.

"No, no. Keep it. Give it back! I don't want it!" China Brother says. The tongman watches a moment, embarrassed, then stands and leaves the table. The daylight manager gently forces the envelope on China Brother and turns to go. Ah-Joe Joe stops him. "Bring me the bill. I want to pay up right now. Get this over with. I give the tip, everything. Right now."

"You don't have to," the daylight manager says in polite Cantonese, "Please, don't be this way. There is no hurry about paying." Ah-Joe Joe is the general manager, the big boss of the Jade Hamlet. The daylight manager, more by tone and timing than the words he uses, suggests that it is bad form to be dealing noisily with money and bills at the banquet for the mourners on the day of his father's funeral.

The tall tongman gingers in on his pinching shoes and asks China Brother to start serving the food. He is angry. "Everyone is here. No one else is coming. It is not right to keep them sitting and waiting. Why not start serving now?"

"Not till I pay first," Ah-Joe Joe says. As he waits for the daylight manager to return with the bill, he opens the white envelope of *bok gum* from the restaurant employees, counts it, $100 in bills, and adds the bills to the other piles of bills. Then he makes one more count of the piles, notes the totals, and shoves the addition to me. "You want to count it? See for your self! Go ahead."

"No, you're the first son. What you do is right," I say.

"I want you to count it!"

"Ah-Joe Joe. Don't be this way," the tongman soothes. "Accept things for the gesture of respect to your father they are and don't be this way. No one is giving this *bok gum* to offend you."

China Brother doesn't flip a glance the old man's way and before the old man has all his words out, says to me, "Here, I want you to add it up for yourself. Count the money for yourself. I want everything on the up-what's-up! That's the kind of guy I am. I want everybody to know that about me. I don't want any questions about my honesty!"

"It's not your honesty that's in question," I say.

"You don't count, nobody eats," China Brother says.

I laugh. I have him. "I don't want to touch that money after you've shit on it. I don't care to eat here myself, so I don't care if anybody eats. No matter what. You are the first son. Eat or no eat. You are in charge. It's your word that counts. Not mine," I say. "But Pa's friends don't deserve this. I'll count the money. And you and I never have to speak to each other again. Don't call. Don't write. Don't drop by. Ever."

The tongmen looks down at the floor. I count the money.

China Brother calls a waiter over and has him trot off to fetch back two cases of 35mm movie film. "Pa leave these old movies at my house before they paint his apartment and never took them back. You want 'em? I got no use for them," China Brother says.

"What are they?" I ask and turn the cans around for labels. The cans are labeled "Anna May Wong." I guess they're reels of Anna May Wong's clips and outtakes from her movies. "Yeah, I'll check 'em out," I say. "You got these from Polly Jade, not Pa, right?" I look him in the eye and see I got him. "Tsk tsk tsk. You still haven't learned that you can't bullshit me. Here's my count. It's the same as yours."

He nods toward the waiter. "Give him the keys to your car and he'll load it in your trunk," Joe Joe says. He wants to get rid of these things right now.

I give the waiter directions to my car and the keys. Joe Joe hands him a $10 bill.

"You don't have to do that," the waiter says. Joe Joe waves him off and turns away.

Joe Joe peels off three hundred dollars in $50 bills, lays it on the table in front of the daylight manager, and pats the pile with the palm of his hand. "This is the tip for the cooks, waiters, and captains."

I should have known. Everything we talked about at lunch, his plan to force Polly Jade to open her books and reveal Pa's assets and bank accounts and joint accounts and settle and avoid probate, is so much passed gas. The bills for the funeral and banquet were supposed to be paid out of what Polly Jade hasn't stolen from Pa's estate in the last two years since she divorced him. Ah-Joe Joe had made a big deal about giving the *bok gum* to the Chinese Hospital in Pa's name. Now on the adrenaline high of his self-pity and self-contempt, before an audience of his father's closest friends and family, in one gesture, he pays the bill for the banquet with the *bok gum* and goes back on his word. No donation to the Chinese Hospital. He is greasy with his new-found power. He pushes all the money left over from the bill into a pile and says, "This is for the busboys, dishwashers."

Everything China Brother does continues to be wrong. Everyone puts up with it, humiliated and miserably saddened for their friend. To see their friend's sons treat him so shabbily at his funeral.

After the money is in the daylight manager's hands, China Brother leans back and holds his empty hands over the empty table in a kind of triumph. "So what do you think, huh?" he says, turning to me.

"You did good, brother," I say. "I didn't make a fool of myself in front of Chinatown. I didn't tell all the powers of Chinatown Pa cultivated so lovingly all his life to go fuck themselves. I don't manage a big Chinatown restaurant. I don't have to deal with the wholesalers and suppliers of Chinese foodstuffs who are beholden to the tongs and Chinatown business. You did real good, Joe Joe. You treated them all like shit and now they're going to treat you like shit. Goodbye discounts. Goodbye early delivery. All the Chinese in Chinatown are going to know where you work and who you are. I hope you get the white people coming in here, brother, because Chinese won't eat here anymore for fear they'll be seated at this table where you counted and dealt that money and broke your word and Pa's honor in front of everybody."

Ah-Joe Joe signals the waiters to begin serving the food. The food is good. Roast pig. Melon soup. *Lohawn jai. Gingjo pai gwut.* The poached plain chicken looks white and naked on the platter. The garnish of slivered chives curling and fluttering on the belly of each naked chicken is some cruel macabre parody of feathers. In the old days white boxes were not passed out and the leftovers from a funeral banquet not taken home. Because food costs so much now and this food is good and China Brother is in a hurry, the waiters bring white boxes out with the first course.

Ulysses: Home Terminal

Diego says, "I stayed away from the funeral, man. I knew it had to be awful. And, knowing you, you'd probably have to make some point and walk out, leaving your friends to admire your father's dead body. No thanks. He never gave me the time of day, never cared if I'd eaten yet, and the funeral didn't sound like shit the way you talked about how your China Brother was planning it, so whaddaya say? Whaddaya know? Kingdoms rise and fall. Nations come and go. Life is war. It's a good day to die. Let the good times roll!"

We sit at the kitchen table by the big glass wall with the sliding door opening onto his deck and play guitar, smoke good stuff, and he talks me down from the funeral, the visit with my brother, and the *gah way fon.* He's surprised, then is not surprised, that Ben shows up with his wife Pandora Toy, sits in the front pew with her, sits at her table at the half banquet after the funeral. I'm surprised Ben shows up at Diego's.

He has a job doing a column on the Pacific Rim for *The New York Times*. He can travel anywhere around the Pacific Rim and spin his mind and unreel his words. Anything that he wants to write. For a moment he thought he was moving to New York. Pandora is moving. She thinks it wise to play down Ben being her husband, as he is Asian and likely to stereotype her as an Asian-American writer. So he'll hang on to his hated job teaching Asian American Studies for another two years till he qualifies for early retirement. Ben doesn't understand what I have against Polly Jade. She and Pandora get along famously. She really loved my father. She's really kind of pitiful and sad, Ben says. He smiles.

"Hey, remember me? I'm the kid from China with the total Asian eclipse, the Oriental amnesia. I forgot it once. I can forget it again! Three Kingdoms is just a kid's book, boys. We're not The Brothers of the Peach Garden. We are not the Lowe, the Kwan, the Chang of this Chinese kid's novel. I changed my name, Mo, remember? Wrong book. Wrong movie."

Thump! on the floor above us and the housekeeper's husband shouts for Diego. His wife's in labor, he's sure.

The pregnant housekeeper comes downstairs in the arms of her wiry husband, who begs our pardon and asks for a ride to the Chinese Hospital in Chinatown. All aboard for Chinatown.

We pile into my car, Ma's cherry '53 Chevy. Diego's housekeeper and her husband in the back seat with Ben Mo. Diego with his pubescent daughter, Vanessa, on his lap, and Jason Peach riding shotgun in front and me driving the Iron Moonhunter home.

Can we get to Chinatown before the baby is born? The light on the block signal ahead shows green. GREEN!

I'm young and behind the wheel of a car carrying my ass low to the cold raspy road and up in the oily air of a chortling black SP loco, high over the right of way. I feel the hundreds, the thousands of percussing children tumbling folk songs in the hollows of my bones. My skeleton, bone by bone, hums with speed, singing round the long curve past Port Costa by the water in the dark of the early morning. Long fish twang through the water. I hear my voice through the incessant good-humored gossip of engines. My mother yells when I am made—I feel it. The power brings me out of a bang, and I savor the shudder and growl scattering me across the country, and I fill more and more silence, and grow loud, and grow dense.

The freeway is closed since the '89 earthquake. I cross under the freeway and the broad streets paralleling the waterfront and drive to Chinatown along the streets where the trains used to run. Green! I shout to the hoghead when I see the green light on the block signal ahead.

The hoghead at the throttle looks as if he's made of dollar bills in the light of the dials, and the light of the moon spatters silently in the sea like a butterflied battered shrimp simmering in a great deep fry. To be heard across the cab by the wadded dollarbill, I have to grimace, show my teeth, kick in my lungs, and shout for the stars until I'm dizzy and the darkness closes its lips behind me as I'm sucked deeper into the noise of the engine beating my heart, blowing my lungs. My father farts as he comes on the last lunge that makes me, sends me spinning past the box office, into the darkly gleaming sea of the moviehouse where my mother feels herself sobbing when she goes to bed that night in grandma's house. Back to the movies with my father in my brakeman's gunbarrel night as my mother lies on her back to steam in the debris of movies to which she gives her flesh, Hollywooding the mechanics of an act of passion at the movies. I come into being in the dark of the dark of a backrow balcony fuck at the movies. *Pom! Pom!* the Japanese battering ram thuds through the rain against the mission door in China and echoes inside. *Pom! Pom! Kapom!* shudders her body as the door crashes and here they come, slopping their feet out of the rain into the church where it's dry. *Pom! Pom!* Japanese artillery fires on the missionary compound, in counterpoint to the rain. Pa is a twelve-year-old boy in this movie, standing upright under the cross and an American flag, singing "Amazing Grace" in the sweetest Cantonese ever heard. Damn, Pa can act! A fine stillness follows the shot that drops Pop on the shadow of the cross under the flagpole.

GREEN! I shout to the hoghead as the lit green block signal grins out of the dark. GREEN! the hoghead shouts back, and we stay calm and powerfully still in our seats, crunching a hundred tons around a long curve past the Hercules powder plant at 60 miles-per-hour faster than we can hear the crickets cricketing all around us. But still we hear them. For we are within our speed, like planets. Still in the smell of breakfast being cooked out of the dark houses on the hill. Still in the curl of wash left on the line. Still in the eyes of the couple naked and fleshy and who knows who's the he and who's the she in a milky white flash, under a tree. Adios, amigos.

GREEN! So fast we feel the bones of skeleton of night break against our faces, one at a time GREEN! Our voices are a little richer in our ears, set to grab the sound of quail breaking into thickets from out of our speed.

GREEN! we shout into the liquor of the night every quarter mile, GREEN! past the rabbit eyes of startled lovers, warm bacon, swooning steel, past Richmond toward my mother's old woman passenger riding to her death, carrying things I don't know in her baggage. *Pom! Pom!* The old man has a vicious rhythm. And she groans, opens her genitals to sentimental movies where she and Pa hide themselves away from China, and Cantonese opera, and Chinatown—the languages and gossip and eyes of Chinatown. For fifty cents apiece they are alone together in the watery light of Pa dying in another movie. Man, does he know how to die! And the eyes of Chinatown look up from the all-night TV, watch me slip into town, and watch me leave.